DISCOVER THE WRITER'S LIFE IN NEW YORK CITY.

Master of Fine Arts in Creative Writing

Over more than six decades of steady innovation, The New School has sustained a vital center for creative writing. The tradition continues with our MFA in Creative Writing, offering concentrations in fiction, poetry, nonfiction and writing for children. Study writing and literature with The New School's renowned faculty of writers, critics, editors and publishing professionals.

Faculty 2004-2005

Jeffery Renard Allen, Hilton Als, Susan Cheever, Jonathan Dee, Elaine Equi, David Gates, Vivian Gornick, Fanny Howe, Shelley Jackson, Zia Jaffrey, Hettie Jones, James Lasdun, David Lehman, Suzannah Lessard, David Levithan, Phillip Lopate, Sarah Manguso, Pablo Medina, Honor Moore, Maggie Nelson, Dale Peck, Robert Polito, Francine Prose, Liam Rector, Sapphire, Helen Schulman, Tor Seidler, Dani Shapiro, Prageeta Sharma, Laurie Sheck, Darcey Steinke, Benjamin Taylor, Jackson Taylor, Abigail Thomas, Paul Violi, Sarah Weeks, Susan Wheeler, Stephen Wright.

Visiting Faculty

Ai, Martin Asher, Susan Bell, Frank Bidart, Deborah Brodie, Patricia Carlin, Glen Hartley, Dave Johnson, Rika Lesser, Thomas Mallon, Harry Matthews, Sharon Mesmer, Robert Pinsky, Lloyd Schwartz, Jon Scieszka, Susan Shapiro, Jason Shinder, Ira Silverberg, Tom Sleigh, Frederic Tuten.

**CALL FOR MORE INFORMATION
OR TO REQUEST A CATALOG:
(800) 862-5039 OR
WWW.NSU.NEWSCHOOL.EDU/WRITING**

Director: Robert Polito

New School University
The New School
66 West 12th Street New York NY 10011

THE NEW SCHOOL

COUNTRY LIFE

GRANTA

GRANTA 90, SUMMER 2005
www.granta.com

EDITOR *Ian Jack*
DEPUTY EDITOR *Matt Weiland*
MANAGING EDITOR *Fatema Ahmed*
ASSOCIATE EDITOR *Liz Jobey*
EDITORIAL ASSISTANT *Helen Gordon*

CONTRIBUTING EDITORS *Diana Athill, Sophie Harrison, Gail Lynch,*
Blake Morrison, John Ryle, Sukhdev Sandhu, Lucretia Stewart

FINANCE *Margarette Devlin*
ASSOCIATE PUBLISHER *Sally Lewis*
MARKETING/PLANNING DIRECTOR *Janice Fellegara*
SALES DIRECTOR *Linda Hollick*
TO ADVERTISE CONTACT *Lara Frohlich* (212 293 1646)
PRODUCTION ASSOCIATE *Sarah Wasley*
PUBLICITY *Jenie Hederman*
SUBSCRIPTIONS *Dwayne Jones*
LIST MANAGER *Diane Seltzer*

PUBLISHER *Rea S. Hederman*

GRANTA PUBLICATIONS, 2-3 Hanover Yard, Noel Road, London N1 8BE
Tel 020 7704 9776 Fax 020 7704 0474
e-mail for editorial: editorial@granta.com
Granta is published in the United Kingdom by Granta Publications.
This selection copyright © 2005 Granta Publications.
All editorial queries should be addressed to the London office. We accept no responsibility
for unsolicited manuscripts
GRANTA USA LLC, 1755 Broadway, 5th Floor, New York, NY 10019-3780
Tel (212) 246 1313 Fax (212) 333 5374
Granta is published in the United States by Granta USA LLC and distributed in the United States by
PGW and Granta Direct Sales, 1755 Broadway, 5th Floor, New York, NY 10019-3780.
Granta is indexed in The American Humanities Index
TO SUBSCRIBE call toll-free in the US (800) 829 5093 or 601 354 3850 or e-mail:
grantasub@nybooks.com or fax 601 353 0176
A one-year subscription (four issues) costs $39.95 (US), $51.95 (Canada, includes GST),
$48.70 (Mexico and South America), and $60.45 (rest of the world).
Granta, USPS 000-508, ISSN 0017-3231, is published quarterly in the US by Granta USA LLC,
a Delaware limited liability company. Periodical Rate postage paid at New York, NY, and additional
mailing offices. POSTMASTER: send address changes to Granta, PO Box 23152, Jackson,
MS 39225-3152. US Canada Post Corp. Sales Agreement #40031906.
Printed and bound in Italy by Legoprint on acid-free paper.
Design: Slab Media.
Frontcover illustration: pen-and-ink drawing by Clifford Harper, www.agraphia.uk.com
Back cover photographs: courtesy Daily Herald Archive/NMPFT/SSPL
Acknowledgements are due to the estate of Roald Dahl represented by David Higham Associates, and
Random House, Inc to quote from 'Fantastic Mr Fox' by Roald Dahl.

ISBN 1-929001-20-7

GRANTA

A new page in fiction.

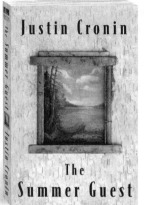
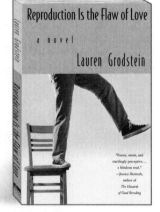
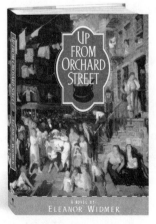

Motley Notes

That this issue is called 'Country Life' owes something to another magazine which carries that title and which every week is pushed through my letterbox at home. *Country Life* is a glossy magazine, rarely fewer than 140 pages, priced £3, published every Thursday. It is, among people who don't read it (and perhaps among certain of us who do), a faintly risible thing. Like magazines called *The Lady* or *The Field* or *Horse & Hound*, it suggests old money and an old social class: landowners, fox-hunters (it was firmly opposed to the ban), people with 'The Hon.' or 'The Earl' before their names who live in castles, moated manors, granges, or at the very least The Old Rectory, and have invitation cards in black italics propped up along their mantelpieces. Is there sneering resentment in that last sentence? I hope not, because it would be hypocritical. I am an avid reader of *Country Life*, though until now I haven't disclosed the fact to many people. It seems an odd thing for me to be, almost traitorous, in the context of my socio-political stratum in British society. I live in London. I have never voted for the Tory party, even after Mrs Thatcher substituted real-estate agents for landowners among her closest followers, or, as somebody (maybe a *Country Life* reader) once said, Jews for Dukes. I don't have the money to buy the houses it so lavishly advertises ('period grandeur with a wonderful outlook…exceptional opportunity to acquire a magnificent country estate…guide price £3,900,000'). I didn't marry the kind of girl whose portraits form the magazine's weekly frontispiece, the 'girls with pearls' as they used to be known. (Very few pearls now, but a lot of gap years: 'Miss Kate Winser, daughter of Mr and Mrs Nigel Winser, of Finstock, Oxfordshire…will spend part of her gap year working with the Masai community at the Il N'gwesi Group Ranch in northern Kenya.') I long ago vowed never to live anywhere where I needed to get into a car and drive two miles to buy something as ordinary as a pint of milk.

So why do I buy it and read it? Many of its articles are interesting. In the issue before me now I can read about birdsong, small English breweries, one of the last remaining traditional wheelwrights, a very splendid Cornish garden, and Old Wardour Castle in Wiltshire, 'one of the most imaginative buildings of the late-medieval period'. It has a well-written editorial column. The typography and design, though recently damaged by 'improvements', are seriffed and clear. Celebrities, unless noble (the Duchess of Devonshire, say), never appear in its pages. Urban, turbulent, televisual, multicultural, web-driven life remains a rumour. In fact, *Country Life* is produced by a publishing conglomerate in an ugly London tower block just south of the Thames, but it seems to come from some other place. That place is 'the country', and I suppose that like several million others I am a symptom or victim of its fanciful hold on the British, and particularly English, imagination.

Save the Vatican City and possibly San Marino, every state in the world has countryside. Even desert nations have it, in the antithetical sense of the spaces that are not towns. Some nations admit to its agricultural necessity rather than enjoy it. In India, for example, the country can (or until very recently could) inspire a general satisfaction among city-dwellers that they didn't have to live there. To go 'up-country' in India meant leaving behind the comforts of town. Poor people lived there down dusty or muddy tracks, without electricity, flush lavatories, safe drinking water. A London gentleman in the early eighteenth century might have felt the same about, say, Wiltshire. He would struggle through the mud on horseback to Old Wardour Castle, asking directions from rude and incomprehensible peasants, and on his arrival cry out with joy at the elements of civilization—a book, a commode—that had been imported from town.

Most of the older industrialized nations, however, now associate the countryside with pleasure: fresh air, animals, grass, trees, and the chance (now remote in Europe) that the urbanite can discover charming old folkways, thick accents, ancient and unchanged pubs. But only in England is the geographical variety on offer lumped together in those two words, 'the country'. In Scotland, people speak of going to the coast or the Highlands. In North America, they might refer to second homes in New England or trips to the Rockies. In London, at least among a certain class, it is just 'the country', as in 'They have a place in the country', 'He's up from the country', 'Do you ever get down to the country?' Derbyshire, Devon, the Isle of Wight: their separate identities are disguised in a simple phrase that packs inside it all kinds of complicated thoughts and feelings which began with the Romantic poets and then soared into the national mythology in the later half of the nineteenth century as England became (along with another small country, Belgium) one of the two most urbanized countries in the world. By 1914, 'the country' was not only pretty and quaint and a refuge and balm to the industrialized soul; it had become the true repository of England's history and character, a sacred place. Many people—many of them clever cosmopolitans—subscribed to this idea. Among writers and apart from the usual ruralist suspects—Hilaire Belloc, G. K. Chesterton, Rudyard Kipling, Rupert Brooke—there is E. M. Forster, D. H. Lawrence. In *Howard's End*, published in 1910, Forster voiced his thoughts through his heroine, Margaret Schlegel, as she visits the eponymous house. 'Here had lived an elder race, to which we look back with disquietude.... In these English farms, if anywhere, one might see life steadily and see it whole.' Even Lawrence, the coalminer's son, was not immune. He wrote in 1915 from Ottoline Morrell's country house that 'Here one feels the real England—this old house, this countryside—so poignantly one is tempted to give in, and to stay there, to lapse back into the peaceful beauty of bygone things, to live in pure recollection, looking at the accomplished past, which is so lovely.' (Adding, just in time, 'But one's soul rebels.')*

The magazine *Country Life* was born into, and of, this ripening anti-urbanism in 1897, when the market in country homes (built mainly for people who made their money elsewhere) was booming, with a corresponding boom in property advertising, which is still how the magazine earns most of its revenue. It has a distinguished history. Its first purpose-built offices were designed by Edwin Lutyens, the last great architect of English country houses (and of New Delhi). An early contributor was Gertrude Jekyll, whose designs changed the look of English gardens and made them...English gardens. It has fought successfully against plans for dams on Dartmoor (1920) and an aerodrome and cafe at Stonehenge (1926). During the Gulf War in 1991, to quote from one of its publicity sheets, a lieutenant colonel in

Ian Jack

the Queen's Royal Irish Hussars wrote to tell the editor that he kept the Country Sports edition beside him in his tank: 'In these last few days before we go into battle, your magazine continues to give us glimpses of the familiar and much-loved world that is so far away at this moment.' It could have been a missive from the Somme; perhaps there is, after all, something eternal in England.

The pieces in this issue of *Granta* do not quite reflect the *Country Life* view of the country, whether in England, Scotland or the United States, but the persistence of it deserves to be noticed and, possibly, cheered. Dreams are not to be carelessly trodden on.

IJ

*These passages are quoted in *English Culture and the Decline of the Industrial Spirit 1850–1980* by Martin J. Wiener, a brilliant and deservedly famous account of English ruralism (and its rotting effects), first published in 1981. Wiener, an American, takes his epigraph from Enoch Powell: 'The life of nations no less than that of men is lived largely in the imagination.'

A clarification
In issue no. 87 of *Granta* we published a piece by Tim Adams called 'Benjamin Pell versus The Rest of the World'. It described the complicated life of Benjamin Pell and in particular his connections with litigation, whether involving others or himself. The aim of the piece was to give a dispassionate account of an unusual character in some extraordinary situations. The journalist Mark Watts, who wrote a story for the *Sunday Express* about Benjamin Pell which led to litigation and therefore played a significant part in Tim Adams's piece, considered that the article contained a false allegation that he took part in a conspiracy to pervert the course of justice. Benjamin Pell made that allegation in an application to the Court of Appeal which was rejected. Both *Granta* as publisher and Tim Adams as author are happy to recognize Mark Watts's right of reply and make it clear that neither of us intended to make that allegation.

GRANTA

RETURN TO AKENFIELD
Craig Taylor

ILLUSTRATIONS BY CLIFFORD HARPER

Ronald Blythe, April 2005

R onald Blythe's *Akenfield*, published in 1969, is a rich and perceptive portrait of life in an English village, told in the voices of the farmers and villagers themselves. Blythe, who had published fiction and a work of social history and had edited editions of Austen, Hardy and Hazlitt for the Penguin Classics series, spent the winter of 1966–7 in what he called 'a kind of natural conversation with three generations' of his Suffolk neighbours, teasing out their thoughts on 'farming, education, welfare, class, religion and indeed life and death'. The best-selling book that resulted captured their lives and the nature of rural life in England at a time of great change. *Akenfield* has remained in print ever since, been translated into more than twenty languages, and inspired a film by another Suffolk man, Sir Peter Hall. 'My only real credentials,' Blythe wrote later, 'was that I was native to its situation in nearly every way and had only to listen to hear my own world talking.'

The world that did the talking was vivid in the detail it accorded everyday tasks and poignant in its evocation of a disappearing past. The farm worker remembered the horrors and adventure of Gallipoli before returning to life on the farm; the blacksmith described forging his own nails; the thatcher recounted his pleasure in the look of a finished roof, where 'the reeds shine silver and grey, and the deep eaves are cut razor sharp'.

At a time when farmers were becoming more like 'agricultural technicians', the farm workers in *Akenfield* described their connection to the old clay of Suffolk's soil—how they coaxed it, marked it, ploughed it, cursed it and occasionally questioned its worth altogether—and revealed stores of knowledge that technological progress was beginning to erase. 'Science is a footnote to what the countryman really believes,' Blythe wrote. 'And what he knows is often incommunicable.'

But *Akenfield* did not bow to sentimental ideas of the countryside as idyll. Blythe's villagers spoke, too, of the brutality of country life, and of their hopes to escape the village. Their lives were a complex mix of wide-open spaces and limited opportunities. As Blythe later remarked: 'I think my view of human life is how brief and curious most people's lives are. Yet when you come to talk to them you realize how strong they are and how unbelievably rich their lives are; also subtle and various.'

Craig Taylor

I grew up in western Canada, thousands of miles from Suffolk, but like so many readers I was taken by the vividness of Blythe's book and the way it prised open this far-off world, a place with its own songs, its own traditions of planting and harvest, and even its own breed of horse. Last year, living in London and rereading *Akenfield*, I wondered what the lives of those who lived and worked in Akenfield now were like, and how much had changed—or remained the same—in the generation since the book was published. Around harvest time, I took two trains and a taxi to the two neighbouring Suffolk villages Blythe had renamed Akenfield. I rented a room in Blythe's old house, which is now a bed and breakfast with a stack of board games in the sitting room and a sturdy three-speed bike in the shed. I cycled around, often turning off my headlight at night when the fields were bright with moonlight.

Akenfield now is in many ways still as Blythe described it.

The village lies folded away in one of the shallow valleys which dip into the East Anglian coastal plain. It is not a particularly striking place and says little at first meeting. [It] is approached by a spidery lane running off from the 'bit of straight', as they call it, meaning a handsome stretch of Roman road, apparently going nowhere... It is the kind of road which hurries one past a situation. Centuries of traffic must have passed within yards of Akenfield without noticing it.

But some changes were obvious. There has been a noticeable increase in the population: according to Blythe's book, after a steady decline through the middle of the twentieth century, there were 298 people living in Akenfield in 1961; the 2001 census lists 358. The two shops and the post office mentioned in *Akenfield* are gone, converted to private houses, and the vicarage sits empty behind disused tennis courts. A street built in 1976 to house British Telecom workers at their new research centre in Martlesham wouldn't look out of place in any London commuter town. On the back of the cutlery in the pub's bright dining room is that telltale sign of contemporary life: IKEA. And just a few days before I arrived, the village was wired for broadband Internet access.

Other changes became apparent as I sought out people who had appeared in *Akenfield*. All of the villagers who worked in the old professions—the wheelwright, the saddler, the blacksmith—are dead, and most of their professions have gone with them. Others have moved on: the assistant teacher became the head teacher and retired to a nearby town, the farm student became a farmer elsewhere. In their places now are commuters and entrepreneurs and retirees from other parts of the country. The family names in the local graveyard are no longer the surnames of the people living in the houses.

The broad Suffolk accent caught in *Akenfield* is more muted, too. The language of the 'old boys' was full of mischievous *o*'s that sneak into words normally without them. But the families moving into the village often speak in the 'Estuarine' accent (the estuary being the Thames) that has spread throughout southern England, or in what was once called BBC English. The head teacher told me she was a little worried when she heard her young son say the word *compoo-ah*.

Akenfield appeared at a time of enormous changes in British agriculture. The hum of the large combines in the fields was still new to some; less labour was needed to pull in the crops, making farm jobs more contingent and less secure. The power relationship between farmer and farm worker was in flux, as increasingly they were the only two people working in the field. All of these changes have continued. Farming now is a story of amalgamation, of increasing specialization, of slow decline and tenacity in the face of supermarket rationalization, foreign competition and government regulation.

B lythe now lives an hour away from Akenfield, near Colchester, in a small cottage that once belonged to the painter John Nash. The people of his old village have not forgotten him. A hardcover copy of *Akenfield* sits on the sidetable at the bed and breakfast and the building company in the village is now named after it. Over several months I interviewed him and about forty of Akenfield's current residents. Some of what they had to say appears in the pages that follow.

Once when I was speaking to Blythe in front of his fireplace, he paused and looked out the window. 'Imagine what the farmers who lived here would think of this,' he said. 'Us doing nothing but talk all afternoon.'

Malcolm Peck, orchard foreman, 58

He is in his sitting room, before a crackling fire, reading short humorous stories printed by the Farmer's Press. *There is a selection of fresh apples in the basket by his easy chair. He is soft-spoken but belongs to the local Amateur Dramatics Society, and over the years he has brought to life some major roles at the village hall, including* Jack *in* Jack and the Beanstalk.

I was born in 1947, just up the road. Before you get to the farm there's two cottages on the left-hand side; I was born in the one on the left. When I got married I moved down the road. I'm still here.

My father lost his dad quite early, so he had to work to keep money coming in for his mother and sister. He started on the farm when he was fifteen and spent all his life there. It must have been about 1980 when I took over as foreman from him. He retired and I just slotted in. The first day weren't as bad as I thought it was going to be, as they were all great men what worked there. There was eighteen men working on the farm full-time. Now there's three. There's hardly anybody there these days.

I didn't have much to do with the agricultural side, the arable side of it, which is now all done under contract anyway. I was just foreman over the fruit. There used to be 140 acres of apples and pears. Now, I reckon we've got twenty-five acres of them: about fifteen acres of Coxes, six or seven acres of Bramleys, some James Grieves and about five acres of Conference pears. That's all the apples and pears we've got left now. We've also got five acres of plums, about a hundred acres of blackcurrants and the rest are made up of sugar beets, sweetcorn, that sort of thing.

All our Bramleys go for what we call peeling. They're peeled and put into Mr Kipling pies and things like that. For the peeling machine you have to have an apple between seventy millimetres up to one hundred millimetres; anything over that is too big. The peeling machine won't take it, so you just can't sell the big apples. This year we've had wet weather and the apples were just exploding. Big, beautiful apples. All those will be thrown away. We've still got about a dozen bins in there of oversize. When the ladies pick them off the tree they sort them in the boxes. That's how they're graded. The small ones that are sent away go in one box and the big ones go in another box. Sometimes we'll sell the oversize, sometimes we won't. You work all year pruning the trees, spraying the trees and then you just see them all wasted.

For the last few years, we've had some organic apples. You don't spray those trees for three years before you can sell them as organic but you still spray them with a sulphur. People think organic stuff is not sprayed at all, but it is. The sulphur's supposed to keep all the bugs away but it don't. The results are terrible, the trees are dying. You just have to sell it for juice.

All the apples the supermarkets want now are Coxes and Bramleys. We used to have Worcesters and they were lovely and sweet, a real tasting apple. It was a lot redder than those. It was red all round. We used to have George Caves, Scarlet Pimpernels, Laxton's, but we haven't got any more. The Coxes have size restrictions, too. We don't pick Coxes over eighty millimetres to sell in the supermarkets. You don't see apples like that in the supermarket because they don't sell them. I suppose they think a child wouldn't eat a big apple, would they? Well, we had one between us last night, me and the wife. It was lovely.

The supermarkets don't sell them small and they don't sell them big. The apples have to be a perfect size and they have to be a perfect colour, too. For a Cox it has to have about twenty-five per cent flush colour. Anything greener is not picked. They need the colour and they need the proper size to sell in a supermarket, or so they say. If they see it's got a mark it will have to go on the floor. But look at this big Cox. That's a lovely apple, isn't it?

Years ago, they used to pick everything. The orchard was picked clean, and they used to pick the ones up off the floor; those were used for cider. But no one wants them now.

I think in years to come the English apple will be gone. So far this year we've cut down five acres of them, and we're cutting another eight down, so we'll have cut down over ten again this year.

There was a lady walking through the orchard the other day. There's one or two public footpaths that go through and this lady walks every day right by the fruit shed. 'I love this walk with all these trees this time of the year,' she said to me. 'They begin to change colour. What are you doing cutting them down?' She said she didn't want the landscape to change. I told her that I'm sorry to see it go as much as her. It's just that it's my livelihood, and I've got another eight years to go until retirement.

We get rid of the orchard tree by tree. We cut the apple tree down with a power saw and dig it out with a digger. We save the wood because the farmer's got wood burners at home, so he burns it on the fire. We push all the other stuff in a big heap and burn it, just plough it up and there you are. We had some Worcesters up to this year but we just cut those down. I've got some Worcester wood stacked in my garden. I burn the trees at home as well. That's what's on the fire right now. We get two warms out of it, you see. We get a nice warm as we're cutting it down and we get a warm as it burns.

The ones we've cut down this year are trees that were put in in 1956, almost the oldest. For a long time, a man named Bernard Catchpole worked here with my father, and he kept all the records. He used to put everything down in his diary. My dad and Bernard were here the other day, and I asked my dad when some of them were planted. He said, 'That was the year Jack Kindred started but I can't remember what year that was. I'll ask Bernard.' So Bernard got his little book out—1956, right there on the page.

My dad loves his apples. He comes over and picks his apples even now. He doesn't like to see them left on the trees because, you see, in his time we didn't used to leave them on the trees. He lives in sheltered accommodation nearby, looks after himself during the week pretty well. He's learned to cook. He comes in his car to get his apples. He says to me the other day, 'I was thinking about coming over and getting me some more Bramleys.' I said, 'Well, I'll get you some if you like, Dad, and I'll bring them down when I see you.' 'No, no, no, I love coming,' he says, 'I'll come and get them.' He's eighty-nine, it does him good to be out with the trees. He wears his old cap. Not his overalls but his old coat, and he still knows how to pick an apple properly. The other week, he was making a list of all the apples and plums he knew. I think he's got over thirty different sort of apples he could think of.

When we take down the apple trees we'll replace them with blackcurrant bushes. It looks...different. Bushes are different from trees. There's a hundred acres of blackcurrants and they're all Scottish varieties. They begin with a Ben—Ben Lomond, Ben Hope, Ben Avon, Ben Alder. The Ben Lomond come first and then you move on to the Ben Hope and Ben Alder are the later ones, so they don't all come at once.

They used to have women come and pick the blackcurrants, pick them by hand. Then they started with the machine. We would cut all the bushes down and feed them through the machine. They would crop every other year, you see, so the blackcurrant bushes would grow up one year and we'd cut them down the next. Now we've got these straddling machines, they straddle over the bushes and have little fingers that vibrate and shake the bushes and the blackcurrants fall down on to conveyor belts. The fingers are fibreglass spindle things, so they just sort of go round like that, shaking. It's amazing, really. The blackcurrants go to the back and fall into the bins and the bins fill up. That's all for juice, you see, for Ribena. They say years ago, when they first brought these machines out down in Kent, the gypsies what used to work down there sabotaged the machines at night because they were doing them out of work.

The machines cost £40–50,000. The new one this year has gone without problems but it needs to be maintained fairly regular before the season starts. Three weeks at the most they'll go during the season. You'll spend all that money for three weeks' work. When we're blackcurranting we work to about nine o'clock at night, weekends, just to get it in. You have to with blackcurrants because they get ripe so quick. We'll start at half seven and we'll work through till nine at night. We don't work Saturdays because the factory where they go is not open on a Sunday. We take a break from 12 to 12.30, and a quarter of an hour at five o'clock time.

If you look under the bushes a lot of blackcurrants lay on the floor, but we just don't worry about them. It takes so long to pick them by hand, it's much cheaper to waste them. There's just so much that goes on the floor these days. I guess it would be frustrating if you wanted to buy a pound of blackcurrants. You see them laying there on the floor, you'd think, why can't I go pick them up?

Chris Green, dairy farmer, 41

He is wearing jeans and a dark blue corduroy shirt. He has a few lines on his face, in places that suggest laughter rather than worry. As he speaks, a plate of spaghetti cools in front of him.

I left school in Akenfield in 1980, something like that. I didn't excel, not really. I was quite a stupid pupil, I guess, except for physics. I was top in physics but I dropped it at fourteen because the mix of subjects meant I had to do German and I didn't want to do that. So I dropped it to do cookery, which wasn't like proper cooking—it was just 'go-there-for-half-an-hour-and-shut-up' kind of cooking. So I decided to jack in the only subject I was any good at because it didn't suit the way I wanted to live. Nowadays, parents wouldn't let a child do that. My parents didn't let me do everything I wanted, but they certainly let me make my own decisions. If you wanted to make a fool of yourself, well, it's your life, idiot.

I went to college at Portsmouth Polytechnic. I attended a few lectures, played a lot of cards. I get up for work at about half four now and don't bat an eyelid—but back in those heady days nine o'clock was quite a stretch. I honestly don't know what I did. I only stayed a year before coming back to Akenfield.

Farming was not very high on my list back then. Not very high at all. I sort of fell into a job at my father's dairy farm. They didn't really need me when I came back, there was another bloke working. But he died when he was still young, thirty or thirty-one. Maybe if he hadn't of died it might have been different. He just had a heart attack. A dramatic stop, and after that I was required. I still work with my father now.

The way our parlour works is, we have five cows come in either side. You milk one side and while they're being milked by the machines you clean the next five, and as one finishes, you substitute another. Once this side is all done, they go out a gate and the next five come in. And it just goes from one side to the other, really. It's called a herringbone parlour, one oblong-shaped building with cows on either side. It's a relatively old system, we've had the parlour since the Seventies, but it works well. The mainframe is probably the only original bit left. I expect every bit has been changed, every little piece.

Most farms were set up around families, but that's gone. My grandad hardly milked a cow in his life. Instead, he was the one who bought and sold cattle all the time. With that money he bought this farm and my dad ran the cows. My dad now buys and sells cattle and I look after the cows with my uncle. We've managed to survive. We have a great... I mean, we have a good life. But you couldn't financially start a farm up now and make a profit out of it. The land costs too much and the houses cost too much and the returns, the returns are just about good enough to warrant doing it but not to leap into it. The only kind of people buying land now are people coming from other businesses, just rolling money over or wanting to do something else if they're rich enough.

To set up even a dairy farm of our size—we've got about 140 cows—you'd need £1,500,000. Land is £2,500 an acre, and you'd need 200 acres. That's half a million at least to buy the land, and then you got to buy the animals. If you wanted just a hundred cows that would be £500 each, so there's another £50,000. Then all the equipment. I suppose you could buy a dairy farm with the facilities but you'd obviously have to pay for those as part of the deal.

A lot of the farms around here are gone because they've all amalgamated. Most of the land in this area is farmed by about four or five businesses now. Now, if you're in arable—we're dairy—but if you're in arable, each man is supposed to work 500 acres on his own. Obviously not with a spade and a fork; the equipment's improved so much. In 1974, 500 acres would have been a big farm.

It's all about insurance now. When I was a child, no one was concerned about getting hurt, there was always someone riding a motorbike across a field. Now the school has closed the adventure playground because—I don't know, the ground's too hard, or something. It's the insurance. Everyone's got to second-guess what could go wrong. It's the same with the farm. For our dairy contract we have to have contingency plans for almost any eventuality. I remember one of the questions I got asked by the guy who came around was, 'What happens in a fire?'

'Well, we call the fire brigade,' I said. 'What do you expect?'

He said, 'Where's your appointed assembly point? Where do you assemble if there is a fire?'

'Well, we assemble where the fire is and we have a look at it. I don't know.'

He said, 'You do need an official assembly point.'

'It's around this table,' I told him.

He said, 'That's okay.'

That was his box ticked. For us to have a contract with him we had to have a flood plan, hurricane plan, all these stupid things. 'If all your buildings blew down where would you house your cows?' Good question! Assuming my own house has blown down, I've got larger priorities than the bleeding cows! I'd just let them out in the field. But they'll say, 'That's not right, they haven't got shelter.' I just think, God, give us a break. Eventually you get to some sort of compromise. I think we are going to erect buildings out of Heston square bales. That's the contingency plan if all the buildings get blown down. I have no idea what will really happen, but that's what's written on our dairy contract.

I know a lot of people moan about subsidies, and quite rightly too. It's ridiculous that we get paid money for just having fields. But we get quite good subsidies because we get such bad prices. Our milk is sold, as of this month, at about eighteen and a half pence per litre, and that, at best, is around about the cost of production. If you count all your costs you're lucky to produce milk at 18p. To keep in business you need subsidies.

There's a new subsidy coming in from a more environmental point of view. We're going to get 60p for every metre of hedge and ditch we've got. Quite honestly, that's ridiculous. You read it and think, blimey, that's quite good because we've got a lot of hedges and ditches. But that's beside the point. You feel almost obliged to meet all the regulations because there is so much money coming. It's daft but we have to have it, because ultimately the likes of Wal-Mart and Tesco's are not worried at all about us. They want the supply and that's all they care about. We sell to a Footsie 250 company, quite large, and even they can't go to Tesco and Wal-Mart and drive a bargain. They still have to take the price and as a consequence the guy at the bottom of the chain, which is us, eventually takes the hit. And because we take the hit we have to take the subsidy, which comes off the taxpayer.

Food is relatively cheap and people don't appreciate that. If you didn't have the supermarket stitching us up in the first place it would all work the other way around: people would have to pay less tax because they wouldn't have to subsidize us. But that's how it is. As a result, I don't think farmers are particularly popular. I can understand it, though. If I had a tough job, you know, working in a call centre and getting paid £12–15,000 a year and I was aware how much subsidy was going to agriculture—and it's enormous, the actual numbers are phenomenal—I would resent it. I would just see the number and think it's going straight into someone's pocket as profit. That isn't the case, but I would feel kind of resentful if I was, you know, not having a great time answering phones.

Most of the farmers I know live in nice houses and we've all got bleedin' big gardens. Certainly more than fifty per cent live, if not on big incomes, then in houses that are better than the average. I couldn't afford to buy this house on what I earn. In the real world, on what we actually make, you couldn't have this house. That's why we're the only farmers left in a house like this. Most sell up because the money's too good.

People who move out to the country start to realize that farmers do farm. They find out it is a kind of business. Then they throw it back in your face and say, it's not a business because you get subsidized, you know. I accept we get subsidized, but so does nearly every other business in a roundabout way. The nuclear power industry is subsidized, all the transport systems are subsidized. Anybody who works for the government has a subsidized pension. But we're the ones who get the most obvious subsidies.

If you've got two products at the same price, people will tend to buy local ahead of foreign. But the problem is, most people buy on price. I buy as much British stuff as I can. I like to buy as much British machinery as I can but there are some things we can't get here. Having said that, we've got a Daihatsu four-track, four-wheel drive because it's quite a lot cheaper than a Land-Rover Discovery. It's quite British, isn't it? I mean if you wanted a four-wheel drive to drive around Mayfair you wouldn't buy a Daihatsu. But if you wanted something to pull a trailer—well, there's nothing wrong with Discoveries but on price, you know, as a business option, in our opinion, Daihatsu's a better option. The guys in Korea, they're doing a good job on that one.

I don't know if there is a great future for agriculture in England. I hope there is, because it's a nice life. But we're never going to be able to compete with the Ukraine and Poland. Well, until Poland gets richer. If you were going to put agriculture in any particular part of the world, you wouldn't put it in England.

Farming is nice because it's simple. It's too simple for some people; a lot of people like things to be a bit more complicated. But I like it. We've got cows: you feed them and they give milk. Once a year they have a baby calf. And that, for all the technical jargon you read in the press, is about as far as it goes. It's not as boring as that sounds. I wouldn't have ever believed I would end up doing it. When you actually analyse it, it's like, why on earth would anyone do it? But tonight, for instance, we've got two cows in the shed which will probably calve. I like calving cows, to see them flap their ears and stagger up. I'm not saying you stay out there every night to watch them do this, but just occasionally, if the moment is right, you see these things that are born! In fifteen minutes' time they try to get up. It is remarkable and it doesn't stop being remarkable, you know. A lot of the time you're too busy to take notice of it, but if you have got the time to sit back and see this thing just sort of laying there get up and walk within the hour—it is a miracle. It's more of a miracle than a lot of the miracles of technology we have. They're wet and covered in afterbirth, but their mothers lick them clean. They look weak and vulnerable, they look like Bambi, they're all legs. But you don't as a rule take any notice of it, because it's just work.

I think these are the best days of my life. I'm in my prime, like Miss Jean Brodie. I know every...well, not every blade of grass, but I know the land very well. It's just dirt, but it's what I see every day. This is one of the great privileges of doing what farmers do. You've got a hell of a lot more of the planet than most people.

Julie Taplin, mother, 36

In her home, a converted cottage, her four-year-old daughter is doing arts and crafts in the living room while her two-year-old son smiles and drools. Her husband Rick brings a few biscuits. On the road outside, lorries rumble past every couple of minutes.

Neither Rick or I are rural people by nature but when we saw this property everything just, you know...fitted. We could get to work in the middle of Ipswich in twenty minutes but we were also near to Rick's parents, who live in a village. We needed to find a house with off-road parking. We needed space because Rick rebuilds motorbikes.

I used to imagine living here and remember thinking, goodness me, we really will be in the middle of nowhere. I imagined there would be no street lights. I imagined this darkness, complete dark, so that you can see the sky. I was a little bit scared thinking about it. Instead we get the glow from the warehouse. There's a hum from over there.

Our place had been redeveloped from a farmer's cottages already. It was still old fashionedy but completely done up. It had a bit of character, coziness. We were a few years away from having kids but there was enough space for the beginnings of a family. We knew there was potential.

Here you always have to travel in the car. Ideally, we would like to be living near a pub and have places we could walk to and meet up with people, more of a community feel. I would have imagined there would be more of that in the countryside: walking around the village, bumping into people you know, and knowing one another in a supportive way. That would be in the back of my mind as to what it should be like to live in a village. But we don't actually have that here.

Some of the local characters can be quite reserved. It is quite hard to get to know some. They're not being rude in any way, just careful. That said, we know all the people and I know I could ask anyone for help if I needed it. But it's not easy to meet up, it's not a natural meeting place. We don't walk anywhere so we don't bump into anybody. I hadn't thought that through at the time of moving here. There are people in the village you always wave to and who you see at the annual fête. But because you don't naturally bump into people it's hard to build a proper relationship with them. We've got this fast road, this dangerous road, with big lorries going through what is really just a little hamlet.

As a young mother, you need a little bit of time away from the children. Every week I'd like to have two hours without them, just to go into Woodbridge without them or even into Ipswich would be nice. Just to wander around and browse. I don't do any browsing any more. Catalogue shopping and Internet shopping are a big thing now. We use Tesco Direct every few weeks. We get everything from them, all the vegetables and meat and groceries and the dried foods as well. The nappies and stuff. I don't get newspapers from them.

Every two or three weeks I'll do a big order and then I'll pop to Wickham Market to get the bits. I thought when we set it up that I'd be going to all the local farm shops and getting the lovely fresh food and then just getting all the toilet rolls and cereals from Tesco's. That was the original plan. But it's just worked out this way. It's easier; if these two are asleep I can't leave them in the car and go shopping. I have to wake them up to go into the shops and pay to park the car.

I do hate it. I hate Tesco's having a monopoly. I always say I'm determined, once our son Jamie's going to nursery school and I have that freedom, to go via a farm shop on the way home. There's one not too far that sells fruit and vegetables, cheese, home-made cakes, meat. Farm produce. I'd like to... But again it always involves journeys by car.

It seems strange saying this when you live in the countryside, but if I could easily access farm shop produce, I would. It does come down to ease. We get our bread on Thursday from the little shop attached to the garage in Akenfield. That was the beginning of us trying to buy local things. And then it stopped. I do want to support the local farmers. I think it's just because Rick and I have just come out of surviving Jamie's early years. I never knew it was so hard. You have all these ideas of being greener and more environmentally aware and it all goes to pot for a couple years. But the aim is definitely to work back.

Tesco's makes it so easy. You just go through the list and tick off what you want. Once you've set up the system you have your favourites in and you can click on how many of everything you want. You can add on extra items, or tidy up your list and get rid of baby items you don't need any more. It's great.

Anything else means using a car. It really annoys me when I hear the government talking about car owners as if we are really naughty. The thing is, we have to rely on a car here. There are no other choices. Everything has been taken away. There aren't local shops. They haven't been taken away by the government but it's the government that has enabled the big superstores to develop, isn't it? They've encouraged it. So therefore there aren't the options. We will always have to travel by car. There's got to be changes but it shouldn't really be our fault, it's not because we've done something wrong that we have this. We just have to live with the situation as it is now, really.

In the meantime, you have to be so organized. Get loads of something and always have spares. Two packs of Weetabix as opposed to one. When one's finishing I can move straight into the next one.

Chris Knock, National Farmers' Union representative, 48

He is a pig farmer by trade, and used to run a company that spit-roasted hogs at social events. He has a thick thatch of hair and a confident way of speaking that comes from putting forward farmers' arguments for years.

It's a culture, farming. Farmers tend to have grown up in farmers' families and that's why they're farming. If you're cruel you say they're there by accident of birth. If you're kind you say it's a really enjoyable lifestyle growing up on a farm. The reality is that when that character looks at what he's good at, there might be other things he can do (or she can do—a lot of ladies in farming, don't forget the ladies); but if you enjoy what you grow up with, you're very reluctant to let go of it.

The average age of a farmer in the UK is sixty. The average age of a livestock farmer is sixty-eight. So structural change is going to happen very soon, purely because of the age of the farming population. Out of the 50,000 national workforce about a tenth is in this eastern region. We've added it up. There are 8,000 active farming businesses in the region. They don't own the land, they're actually doing work on other people's farms. There are about 15,000 people holding land in the region. On average you've got one farmer who's looking after somebody else's patch of ground. Now, as those older farmers go on and retire or move on to semi-retirement, they're just going to keep asking their neighbours to run that patch of ground for them. So you're going to see more and more opportunity for someone who dearly wants to farm. He's going to be offered and he's going to have opportunities to take on more land, so the people who psychologically can't do anything else, the ones who can't think of anything else other than farming, they'll be able to farm bigger acreages and expand.

The limit only comes with the size of the machinery and getting the machinery into the fields and in between fields. You get a machine more than four metres wide and it would be hard to move down Suffolk lanes. Right now we're starting to see the limit in those big six-row sugar beet harvesters. These are big, big combines. A couple of years ago I was going down one of the small lanes near home. I have a neighbour who farms 2,000 acres. He's got a combine that he was moving around to where he was going to start cutting. He came up the road with these huge flotation tyres. They were on the verge, so there was actually nothing of the combine touching the tarmac of the road. The thing was so wide he was just running on the two verges. There were quite steep banks either side; he was way up there. I could have sat my car in the middle of the road and he would have driven right over the top of me. They are enormous machines but they can't keep getting larger in this country, purely for the physical aspect of moving them between fields.

What's most frustrating about being a farmer is that you have to stick to a set of rules, but then the public turn round and blame farmers for sticking to them! In the Sixties and Seventies, the government policy was to take out hedges and increase the size of fields. So farmers went and did that. Ten years later, everyone asked why they did it. All those nice hedges for wildlife and conservation and so forth. Well, it was done because after the war this country was convinced it had to increase the efficiency of farming, so it could feed itself. The Agriculture Act of 1947 said we will increase our self-sufficiency in food and this is how we're going to do it: we'll take some hedges out and we'll drain the land so it grows more and you can use bigger machines on it. That worked, there's no doubt about it. By the late Seventies we were as self-sufficient as we possibly could be. We were growing seventy-five per cent of the stuff in the shops.

Now, because of the environmental agenda, the self-sufficiency level has dropped back to sixty-five per cent. Food can be produced cheaper elsewhere in the world. Eastern Europe, South America, Australia can produce cheaper grub. There's a lower cost of production and it's being shipped in because the cost of transport is relatively low.

For older farmers it was a huge change for them to be suddenly asked to produce less, to grass things down. The countryside is for wildlife conservation, they were told, the whole farming operation should become less intensive. Whereas for fifty years they'd been told to become more intensive, to grow more. Now we're saying no, we don't want that any more, and half of that is because we're now an affluent country. We can afford to not grow wall-to-wall wheat. We can afford to take a more benign attitude to where our food comes from. If it's cheaper to bring pork in from Hungary, we'll bring it in from Hungary rather than have our own pig farms. And that argument runs until for some reason we can't ship it in. If the Channel Tunnel gets blocked or the transport costs go sky-high then this country will start to look pretty silly, because we've ignored food security. I think every nation should be able to produce half and preferably two thirds of what it needs.

I don't think we should go back to growing everything ourselves, but we shouldn't dumb our agriculture down so we're only producing, say, ten or twenty per cent of what we need, and we have all these pretty flower meadows people can walk in, and everyone says, 'Oh isn't the countryside beautiful, isn't it wonderful?' Farmers just become park keepers. It's like pressing a self-destruct button, isn't it?

European workers started arriving here quite recently, about five years ago. As soon as they worked out the timetable of the accession countries to come into the EU, the tap was turned on. It's relatively straightforward for them to move over here and earn big money, as far as they are concerned.

They have a very strong work ethic, so they've been a joy to employ. It's the professionals and middle class from the ten accession countries who have come over here so far. Farmers will tell you it's accountants, doctors, dentists that they're employing. The prime reason for them coming over is that they want to build their house. In six months a couple can come to this country, work like stink and earn enough to go back and build themselves a house. If you're a young professional couple, you've just got qualified, you say to yourself we'll take six months out before we're locked in to a job and we've got kids and so forth. We're going to trot off to the UK and do a menial, manual job— but we're doing it for a real reason. So they're intelligent, they've normally got a good grasp of English and they've been great to employ.

Anybody who wants to work on a farm only has to make a dozen phone calls and they've got themselves a job. Organic farmers who need a manual labour force to do some hand-weeding couldn't get English people to do the job. You've got these people still in their twenties or thirties who think that manual labour is too hard, too difficult. They've been sold this office job. They sit in front of the computer and don't have to work too hard to get their money. You put them in a field and say, 'Right, here's twenty acres of carrots— pull all these weeds out of it.' They think, 'Bloody hell, I don't like that idea!' They tend to turn up for a day and then you don't see them again. Whereas the people from Eastern Europe haven't been sold that cushier lifestyle, so they're quite prepared to get down on their hands and knees and weed a whole field.

Przemek Kowalski, farm worker, 27

His voice is warm and not heavily accented. He is passionate on the subject of agriculture and even more passionate when it comes to Polish agriculture. He is rushed; his flight back to Poland leaves from Gatwick later in the day.

Kowalski is like Smith in your country, it's a very common name. There are many of us. I come from the southern part of Poland. I grew up in a small town of about 10,000 people called Tarnawa, which is about one hour from Kraków. My grandfather had a small farm, nothing like what you'd get here. My mother worked in a milk processing plant and my father worked part-time on the farm and in transport the rest of the time.

Craig Taylor

The first time I came over here to work was 1998. I was studying agriculture and economics in Poland. It was my second year and I had done a placement for economics, now I was to work in agriculture for a while. I was brought over by an organization called Concordia, which brings students to the farms, and I started in May at a farm that had strawberries and apples. After two weeks of picking fruit I was given more jobs to do. My driving skills and supervisor skills were put to use. After one month I was driving the minibus and the forklift. It was a medium-sized farm. There was all kinds of work: irrigation and organizing the workers. We came from all over. There were people from Poland, Bulgaria, the Ukraine, Belarus, Macedonia and even Hungary.

Most of the Polish people who have not been abroad before come by coach so they can see the other countries on the way. They've never seen Germany before, or Belgium. From Poznan in the west the coach ride takes seventeen hours. From the eastern side of the country it could take twenty-four or twenty-six hours. I think for people coming for the first time, it can be lonely. I was going alone the first time, but most people go with someone else. It wasn't so easy the first time, but my motivation was high.

The motivation to work is different for people who come from Poland. There are not many possibilities to get money for university there. People who are coming over are from smaller towns, small villages. First of all they have this great motivation to get to the cities to study. But since their families are not able to help them, they have a great motivation to find something, anything, to pay for the university. It is hard work, but what are the options? Here people take out loans. Taking out a loan in Poland is...let's just say it's not easy. Everyone is worried where the money will come from.

So they come for the money, the experience, to improve their English. When you are picking fruit on the farms there are not always opportunities to speak English, but at some point you have to speak to the farmer. You can listen to the radio at night, go into town, make contact with the language of this country.

At night, most of us would sit around discussing things, drinking beer. Some nights we would go with the farmer to the pub. We would make plans to go to London. During my second time here, when the soft fruit finished and before the apples started we rented a car, four of us, and drove to Snowdonia, to the Lake District, to Edinburgh. It was lovely, such lovely places. But this country: it's so expensive!

I remember first coming to England and being impressed by the solutions. Because even eight years after changing the system in Poland we did not have solutions like they did here. And everywhere—in the library, in the shop—people who were working in the service sector were nice. They were so open, they would speak with you. Our system: impossible. You have to ask so many times for someone to do the easiest thing, and they'll probably get upset first.

I was so impressed by the irrigation systems and all these fertilizers. Only the best farms had these systems in Poland. But the strawberries have a different taste—fresh and full of water. Polish strawberries weren't so big; they weren't so good-looking like the ones here, but in Poland the strawberries had more taste. Here, I was impressed at how fast they went from the field to the supermarket.

The work is difficult and the money is not so good. People here would rather get others to do the work. I think it is much more easy for a person in this country to find the work he wants to do. And the work they want to do is in an office, or in a bank.

When Poland was Communist, there were many people who wanted to come to this country and just stay, just to get away from Poland. Now, we come to this country, we get experience from the farms, we earn some money, and we go back to Poland. Polish people want to apply what they've learned here to Poland.

Patrick Bishopp, entrepreneur, 32

He is dressed in a smart-casual shirt and trousers. The inside of his house includes an original mullion window, as well as some exposed beams which have held the house up for centuries. He is sitting in the bright, renovated kitchen.

I moved to Suffolk when I was eleven, from the Midlands. Went to university, spent six years in London, met my wife Sarah, had my first child and knew straight away when we had that child that I would leave London. I think Suffolk's one of those counties people tend to come back to. It's just a really... It's a bit of a community. And there are the pluses—it's an hour from London, we're by the coast, it's very beautiful. It's a very friendly place. Even though I only came here when I was eleven, Suffolk is the place I'm from.

When I was in London it was a great time to be in the Internet, and I've been in the Internet ever since. Now this is my first time out of it and I'm actually really glad to be out of it. When we came here we looked at setting up an Internet advertising site for small businesses in Suffolk who couldn't afford a big fancy website. My aim was to bring all these companies together, charge them £1,000 a year. They would get a little website and they would advertise my own website as a sort of directory of local Suffolk companies. It became obvious after four or five months of researching that Suffolk just wasn't ready. The Internet was at the stage where everyone was wary and wasn't really seeing where it was going or how it worked. They weren't willing to stick £1,000 of their marketing budget in.

After six months my wife and I decided we weren't willing to invest any more of our time and money into it. It wasn't a small amount, so we hedged our bets and said, fine, it's not something we're going to follow up. It will be on the back burner. We could always get all the files out and start it up again. It got to the stage where there were five people working there, so it was a proper business—but we never launched it.

That left us in a situation where I thought, what do I do next? Do I retrain? However lovely Suffolk is, the biggest flaw about Suffolk is jobs. There's just hardly any well-paid jobs in Suffolk. It's at the end of the road. You only come to Suffolk because you're going there. I was really struggling. I joined lots of recruitment companies. Not one phone call. I could have been overqualified. I've always worked for small companies. My roles have always been, you know, making sales. I started off in brushes and razors, and then moved into the Internet, so I've got a varied CV. But I think a lot of companies just didn't think out of the box. It got me thinking: are we just living a dream in being here? It's lovely, but in reality we have to support a family. I thought, am I just looking in the wrong place?

We did it the wrong way round. We should have found a career before moving instead of just moving and thinking, right, we're here now, what next? If we did the whole thing again it would be a career move, a job move, not a lifestyle move. But we wanted to make this our family home. It used to be a classic farm but over the years it's turned, as most farmhouses have, into an unclassic farm. We plan to be here for the rest of our lives.

When we moved here, we'd meet people and they'd say, oh, you're the Internet guy from London. They knew everything about me already, which is very much village life. I think we have been accepted, but we've only met a very small part of the village, even as a small community. I think it'll change over time. We've only been here two and a half years.

I think people are very intrigued by us. We are a young couple, I worked in the Internet. I'm seen walking my dog during the day when most men are out at work, so I get a lot of comments like, 'Is it your day off? Working from home today?' A lot of people trying to get an answer without asking direct questions like, 'What are you doing walking your dog during the day? Why aren't you earning money?' But I'm not an Internet millionaire.

One of the saddest things about this village—and I think it really stops the village from being as close as it could be—is that we don't have a good village pub. When I was sixteen, seventeen, eighteen, my parents used to eat in the local pub here two or three times a week. It was a lovely village pub with a really good landlord, who did really good food. It looked like a country pub, felt like a country pub. It was popular. He left, hasn't been the same since. Now, they've gone for a wine-bar look, which to me looks like an IKEA look. It hasn't got a village atmosphere, that's the problem. It's just not a lovely village pub you feel you can go in and sit down and have a few drinks and chat to the locals. If Akenfield had that kind of pub it would be a much better village, and a much closer village as well.

And it's no cheaper living out here than it is living in London. That's a myth. It is, I'm sorry. I'll dispute the food is slightly cheaper. Tesco anywhere is going to be the same price. Local food is probably the same. Pub food: Suffolk for some reason has become a real gourmet pub place. You're very hard pressed now to find really good pub grub that isn't London prices. What you're saving on other things you'll spend on petrol. We've got two cars and we probably do a tank a car each week. That's eighty quid a week!

After my last idea failed, I started thinking, what do I really want to do? What's my passion? It's food. I love cooking. I love sourcing food and buying food. I'm a real foodie. Sarah was saying I should do something with food, and I came across the idea that it's really hard to source local produce.

I'm a real Tesco-ite. If we need to do a shop we go to Tesco's because it's on the way to our son Angus's school, it's on the way to everything. If you ever try to go shopping with two children, you can't pull up to a small farm shop and drag the children out and to another place.

I looked at the whole local produce thing. My initial idea was to sell local produce to pubs, restaurants and shops wholesale and get them to start buying locally-sourced produce instead of going to the big wholesalers and just buying the cheapest stuff they could find. While I was researching I spoke to a couple of suppliers and they asked, 'Why don't you sell it directly to the consumer?' So I looked into that angle. To have a localized Tesco Direct.

Let's say you wanted to buy some local sausages, some local bacon, local fruit and veg, a couple of pork pies, and some chutneys. At the moment to buy locally you'd probably have to go to three or four different places. What I'm offering is really good local food: come to me and instead of having to drive to all these places to pick it up, I'll come to you. If I can bring that convenience and a similar service but have local produce, then there's no reason why people won't buy it. They'll still have to go to the shops. I won't be selling loo rolls or washing-up liquid.

This isn't an Internet company. I'm just using the Internet as a tool for ordering. So people will be able to order by telephone, they can email me, fax me, stick a stamp on an envelope. It's right across the board, because I think it's all about choice. Some people like to use the Internet, some people like to pick up the phone. My dad, for example, he just wants to send a fax over.

I don't have a van yet. I will. I've got to source a good second-hand van. Locally. But in ten years' time I'd like to think there will be about twenty vans, every day doing every part of East Anglia—picking up and dropping off food. Eventually maybe other counties would have a look at it. The worst outcome is that no one orders from it. But I'm going to stick with it. Even if it means doing night shifts at Tesco's to make it work.

Jonathan Pirkis, farmer, 59

His father owned a livestock farm in Akenfield which Jonathan now runs. He has the reddened skin of a man who has spent his life outside. It is just after lunch and he is clearing the remains of fresh vegetables from the table.

School didn't do anything for me. My parents had a friend whose son had gone to a sea training school—the HMS *Worcester* on the Thames—and it seemed like a good idea. We'd been brought up with visits to navy ships. They'd come in to Harwich and father would take us down to see them, so I think the idea of going into the merchant navy appealed because it had this feel of commerce and this great idea of carrying things from A to B, from where it was to places of shortage. I spent three years at the HMS *Worcester* and came out as a cadet on a merchant ship. For about ten years we did runs to Barbados, Trinidad, Guyana, Venezuela, Colombia, and all around the southern United States. We'd come back having unloaded in the Grenadines, then load up with sugar in British Honduras [now Belize]. This was 1965 through to 1976, so I saw a changing world.

Life on the sea was exciting, and the worse the ship, the happier the crew. We sailed on a ship with a triple expansion engine and a little turbine stuck on the end to get the last few pounds of steam out. It was hot; the steam made it hotter. There was no air conditioning but the atmosphere was wonderful, probably due to the amount of beer. The modern bulk carrier has air conditioning, so you don't tend to sit outside. You sit in the cabin and read a book. On these journeys we would sit under an awning with the smell of a barbecue coming from down on the afterdeck. It was a great feeling of mateyness.

The ships were usually filled with Liverpool lads or Scottish lads. They were fairly townie orientated. I think they thought I was a bit of an outsider because I didn't have a Liverpool accent. But they were great mates. We used to go to shore together and played lots of cards. They were into their football and I don't think they really had much interest in Suffolk. I'd get nicknamed Captain Birds Eye because of the peas, they'd seen that on the telly. I suppose at that age I was going out away from Suffolk and I was tending to forget it. There was this great feeling of going out and seeing places that were there to be seen.

Then, when I was nearly thirty, I'd had enough of it. I think it was the animals I thought of most. The dogs and cats. I remember books like *Watership Down* which was very English, and even Jane Austen. I remember having a vivid dream. The ship was working twenty-four hours a day in Kenya, so we would work twelve on and twelve off. I did the nights and then went ashore to a rather mosquito-ey hotel and tried to get some sleep, though in that sort of heat it was hard. I don't know what it was, but I had the most vivid, colourful dreams I've ever had of Suffolk, of the countryside. It was all in great contrast to the heat and the sea and the beach in Kenya. The dream consisted of these wonderful lush green fields and hedgerows, a typical English, Suffolk spring. So in the subconscious I was obviously feeling a longing for it. I suppose it's always a natural tendency to remember the best parts of things. Hence the spring— I didn't dream of the bleak winter, snow and black hedges. Now that I'm here I tend to read books about the sea.

Of all the places I went to, I never saw anything like Suffolk. To go up Highgate Lane on a slightly murky evening and see those mauves and greens and the colours of the trees and the way they follow the ditchlines and hedgelines—it's just unbelievably beautiful to me. I didn't see anything approaching it on my travels because in most of the countries I've been to the landscapes are so much bigger. You don't have the subtlety of variations, all these variations over a small distance. I remember a neighbouring farmer who took a train across the United States. He said it just doesn't change for hour after hour after hour and then the next day it doesn't change either. Whereas here you go ten miles up the road and you're in something completely different. Even the land on the other side of the A12, because it's light soil, is different and quite markedly so.

The A12 seems to be the demarcation line. I suppose because it's near the River Deben. It's more salty and sandy and flatter, whereas up here it's heavy clay soil, more difficult to work and rather horrible when it gets wet. We tend to grow things like wheat, oilseed rape and peas, whereas on the lighter soil they're much more diverse. They can grow veg crops and I suppose the latest thing is this grass for turf, great swathes of green, very flat grassland, which you could never do on this soil. You could never get it up.

You spend so much time with the land you get to know it very well. You get to know your machines. I suppose nowadays this idea of changing machinery puts an end to that, but I can get quite fond of pieces of equipment I've used. My favourite would have to be the drill, and drilling time. Autumn time is my favourite part of the year because the colours are so diverse. The variations, the subtleties. It's a time of great promise. You're forward looking, putting these seeds in the ground in the hope things are going to go forward and it will be productive, whereas harvest is the day of reckoning. It's either there or not.

What's driven me for the last twenty years is seeing starvation in Africa and Honduras and other places I stopped. It puts food in a different context. The idea of the supermarket with shelves stuffed with food, and obesity being a big problem, you know, it does affect me. I still feel food production is important because no one knows what is around the corner.

Local food production rather than global production is a very important idea because of fuel shortages, strikes, conflict. Also, you can monitor what goes into it and how it's done and all that sort of thing, whereas if it's produced in South America we don't know what's gone into it.

On this farm we tend to grow things like milling wheat for bread. We have a contract with a company up in Manchester for this special variety called Arrowwood, and that gets taken right up there because they want this particular variety and they'll pay for it. We grow the peas for Unilever, Birds Eye. They're quite a good profitable crop most years, not always. We tend to go for slightly upmarket things we can grow on this soil, and if I can get that harvest in time we get a better price for it because the weather hasn't got at it.

The great difference between Akenfield a generation ago and now is that even on a small farm then you had three or four men; now there's only one. I can give him jobs like painting fuel tanks, but he's not going to want to be here in the winter with very little to do when it's all a bit cold. If you've got a very young chap you really have to be there with him, but I can't do that because I've got paper and meetings. You have to keep them interested. It would be great if we had something like turkeys or Christmas trees or some other small crop, but there's enough people doing that as it is. I've thought of things for the winter months but nothing new. On a small scale I had visions of growing really hot peppers but there just isn't the market for them. People like the conventional peppers; they don't really go for the hot. Even our taste is a little bit staid in Suffolk.

In the future, there is a possibility that the big farmers will have labour problems, they'll have machinery problems, they'll have logistics problems and if it gets much tighter they just won't do it and farms will be split up and small people may come back in again. It's a possibility. Large-scale farming has never worked over here because we've got small fields and high population. And it doesn't seem to me the large-scale farmers are making big profits. They never look very happy to me.

But I think the biggest thing against English farming carrying on in any great way will be just human interest. The average school kid isn't really interested. They don't want to be on their own, they don't want to be in the mud and wet. I'd be happy if my own son was interested. But I think I'd rather he went away and did something else first. When I see young people going straight into the farming business, by the time they're forty they're wondering whether they did the right thing. Whereas coming into it a bit late, like I have, and seeing what the alternatives are, it keeps you going through the downsides.

If I were really trying to be optimistic, I would just hope that some kids will see through all the glamour and the IT and the form-filling and the computer screens and want something real. That's my big optimistic hope: that consumerism will seem so shallow that they'll want to get back to reality and get into producing something that we can touch and that we all need.

Rev. Betty Mockford, priest, 60

She has short grey hair and wears a long shirt and a fleece vest. She had a life in classrooms before the calling and deals confidently with the secular world.

I started here on Shrove Tuesday in 2001. It was just at the time when the foot-and-mouth crisis began, so I was thrown right into it. A local woman came up to me at the service where I was licensed and said, 'I think it would be a good idea to pray for the farmers.' I was very grateful for the tip because it certainly wasn't built into the service. We prayed for them. And almost immediately we closed two of the churches. One which was right next to a cattle farm and another which was actually on farm land. We had to.

I am responsible for six villages, five churches. One of the churches in Akenfield was closed in the Seventies. It is not an old building compared to the others, which are medieval in origin; it is, I think, a Victorian church. It was in a very bad state of disrepair and the decision was made to close it, which must have caused a lot of heartbreak at the time. Various artefacts from the church were supposed to go to other churches in this area. Some of the pews, for instance, and some communion silver as well. The organ was supposed to go to Monewden, but there was a lot of vandalism in the church when it was left empty. I think the roof was in bad repair, so the organ never went to Monewden.

We don't have any plans at the moment to close any of the other churches as places of worship. There are some churches in the diocese that probably have three services a year on special occasions to keep the building alive. It's very difficult to know when to close a church. I suppose there should be a level where the congregation is so small, but then some of our congregations are already small.

Sometimes there will be five or six of us at the 8.30 communion, sometimes we get as many as twelve. I don't mind if I'm just looking out at two or three people. I never mind. For two reasons. Jesus told us that when two or three are gathered in his name, he is there in their midst. And then there's that wonderful sentence in the Book of Common Prayer, in the Eucharistic prayer, which reminds us we are joining the worship of heaven. Therefore we are with angels and archangels and all the company of heaven. So we are part of a much, much larger congregation, even though there might only be a handful of us out there in the pews. Churches have their peaks and troughs and it may be that two or three people keep that church alive now, but in two years' time, three years, five years, ten years there might be a completely different pattern in the population and you might find that numbers will rise.

The nature of the populations in these villages is changing. The Sixties was a crucial time when agriculture changed and the kind of people who lived in your villages changed. I looked through the baptism registers, the old ones that went back to the nineteenth century, and they showed that up until the Sixties the father's occupation, almost without exception, was farm worker. You might have had the postman, or the woodsman, but ninety-five per cent were farm workers. Suddenly you get the change. You get British Telecom building its research station at Martlesham, which is between here and Ipswich. You get people moving in to take up jobs and looking for accommodation in the villages round about. People with an income move in so they can buy a couple of cottages and make them into one big house. It's the influx of professional people. You still have the residue of the agricultural population, particularly in Hoo, but you do get this change. In some of the villages, like

Dallinghoo, there are a lot of young families. There is the potential there of drawing in a new congregation. Not to a service like Book of Common Prayer, or early morning communion, because that's not what they're familiar with. They may not be familiar with any church service. So I try to get them to something which is family-oriented.

Church life and village life overlap much more in a village than in a town. Living in a village doesn't necessarily make people church attenders but it might draw them in to supporting the church in other ways. There are a lot of villagers who will arrange flowers, who do the cleaning. They'll go to fundraising events and even organize fundraising events for the church. Because that's part of village life. But they might not necessarily come to church services, or they might come only when it's harvest or Christmas.

So for me, I have to make as much as I can with the services that draw in larger numbers. Mothering Sunday, for instance, is still very popular. In some urban areas it doesn't make sense any more, where you've got broken families. My husband's eldest son is a vicar in Stoke-on-Trent, which is one of the most deprived areas in Britain today. It's more difficult having a Mothering Sunday service in the traditional way in a place like that. But in the villages you can still build on the tradition. Mothering Sunday and Harvest Sunday: if I do these services well, make them attractive and make people feel welcome, there will be the possibility of their coming again. You will find families bringing babies for baptism much more in the villages than you find in the town.

When I started here I was doing four services on a Sunday. The pattern I inherited was half past eight, half past nine, eleven o'clock, six-thirty. That meant I had no time to talk to people after the morning services.

I'd get up at half past six. I'd just have time for breakfast. Usually I'd try to listen to the eight o'clock headlines before I left home. During my first year of being a curate at St Augustine's in Ipswich, Princess Diana died. I arrived for communion and the vicar said to me, 'Have you heard the news this morning?' I said no, and neither had most of the congregation. He had the job of breaking the news to them. So I never do a morning service now without having listened at seven or eight o'clock to the headlines.

I would get to the church at a quarter past eight. I don't have my own parking space but it isn't as though we've got great crowds fighting for space. After the service, no time to talk; I'd have to be somewhere else by half past nine. So I'd shake hands, jump in the car, drive like the clappers. Usually I'd still keep my cassock-alb on. I could time the journeys to the minute, so straight in, start the service at half past nine. I gave the wardens instructions: if I am ever late for a service, give me five minutes; if I'm still not there announce the first hymn, and you can take the first part of the service on your own.

They could actually take it up to the reading of the Gospel, if necessary. If they used the 'we' and 'us' form of the absolution. Now, it never quite got to that, but I did sometimes arrive once the confession had started, or quite often I was processing up while they were singing the first hymn, rushing in. I would take a second to see how I looked, then off up the aisle. That service would end at half past ten, which would give me a few minutes before I needed to be in Akenfield by eleven o'clock.

It was all so fast. I would have to leave conversations halfway through, and they would just see this white figure in a cassock-alb rushing past. It was absolute nonsense. The church wardens could see the pastoral implications of changing the pattern of services so I could at least talk to people, some of whom I would not see for another month because that was their monthly service. The ten or fifteen minutes after a service is very important sometimes, especially with an elderly congregation.

I suppose there's still something of the old kind of faith around. It's different where you've got people who've lived elsewhere and have had experiences of other churches. But probably the traditional belief in a place like Akenfield is very similar to how it was years ago. It's a belief in God rather than in Jesus and the Holy Spirit. Maybe that's because it's rural and you get the sense of the creator God. So it's not a very trinitarian faith in some cases. And also because there are some people who have only ever worshipped in their own church here or in another church in the benefice. They aren't aware that there are other ways of doing things. I would like to broaden their experience and help them to see that what happens here isn't the only thing that has to happen. The question of music always comes up. People dislike what they consider to be 'happy clappy' music. That's the actual phrase. I'd just like to help people to see that maybe there are one or two modern worship songs which are as good as, if not better than, some of the old-fashioned hymns we sing. I often get accused of choosing hymns that people don't know and I cannot believe they don't know them, but that's because my experience is much broader.

I think it may be a very rural thing. I've only got my experience to go on, but certainly in the town, if anything, it was a much more Jesus-based faith, because both churches I was associated with were much more evangelical and preached putting faith in Jesus quite regularly. The difference is being aware that Jesus is God. I think if you were to ask some people here they wouldn't think that he was. They would think of him as a good teacher, a miracle worker, but not God incarnate. The Holy Spirit doesn't always get that much of a look-in either because that can be a difficult intellectual concept, unless you've been taught it. So much safer to stick with God. We know about God: God the creator, God the one who provides the good earth and the rain and the sunshine.

Bernard Catchpole, former orchard worker, 75

He recently moved to a bungalow a few miles away from Akenfield. We sit in the front room as the light fades. Soon only the glow from the artificial fireplace illuminates the photos on the walls: pictures of him holding ripe apples, an aerial shot of the house in Akenfield where he spent most of his life.

I was born in Ivy Cottage, Akenfield, in 1930. The name Catchpole is a very old Suffolk name. There are a few Catchpoles in the graveyard here, including my mum and dad. My grandfather worked on the farm for fifty years, my father worked on the farm for fifty years and I worked on there for fifty years, so there has been a continuation for a long while back. My grandfather helped build some of the older fruit sheds on the farm. They've stood.

At sixteen I went to my first testing with my grandfather to see how to grade colour and size. By the time I was seventeen the farmer said, 'You can be in charge of your fruit.' I took care of the fruit until the time I retired. I always felt that if you were interested in a job, then job satisfaction meant a lot. I had opportunities to go to other farms as manager or foreman; I turned them down because I was happy where I was and didn't want all the hassle. I had responsibility, which I enjoyed, and I was with nature. I'm a proper nature man and like seeing things grow up.

There used to be social evenings in villages like Akenfield. Now the most people get together is when we have the flower show, which has kept on. It must have been going well over fifty years now. There used to always be the church fête, a big occasion in June. Well now, they haven't got a vicar in the village. The lady vicar they've got now has to see over five different churches and there hasn't been a fête for four, five years now. Them occasions have disappeared, sadly. They were occasions when the village people mingled together. In the summertime in the orchard where I worked you'd get a gang of about a dozen, fifteen women. They were all together and there was a sort of community spirit. Now the machines have come on and where we used to have one hundred people picking the blackcurrants, now two machines do the lot. Gooseberries are gone, too. The children used to come along and pick no end of gooseberries.

We used to have the old Suffolk horses. We used to have herds of cows, pigs. They're all gone now. On the way to Akenfield now there's a pig farm there, but they're all shut up in the buildings. You can go right by in the car and nobody would even know it's a pig farm there.

And the way people look has changed. Workers' hands have changed no end. The old boys—we used to call them that when we went on the farm—their hands were big, rough, hoary hands, horny hands. They'd be using them in the harvest time with the pitchfork, grappling the stave of a fork about an inch and a quarter diameter. During the wintertime they'd be having a digging fork and they done a lot of hedging and cleaned the ditches out. I know they had gloves on but their hands were great, big, wide hands with tough old skin. I mean, my hands are workers' hands. I even lost a finger when I was working on the soil bench. Their hands now are completely different.

The clothes are so much different, too. When I first went to work I was pleased as anything to have a pair of boots like the old boys had. They were great big boots and they were all studs and hobs, as we used to call them, all along there. You know, all metal. Gracious me, nowadays you wouldn't be able to lift them off the floor, hardly. Then they'd have buskings to keep the dirt and that out. Wellies weren't very much used in them days. That was always the thing—have a good old pair of them hobnailed boots and have these old buskings around here to keep you dry, keep your mud from your trousers. In the wintertime you'd be digging in the ditch and the water would be running away and you'd get splashed all up with water and mud.

Even when I started working the machines it affected my hands. When you got on the back of the machine the blackcurrants were constantly coming at you all the while, you see. You had a tray that held twenty-eight pound, as they come through you had to keep them moving. Your hands were in blackcurrant juice nearly all the time and blackcurrants are not the pleasantest thing; the juice is rather sticky and sweet. Thankfully I wasn't a smoker but if someone wanted a fag they'd roll it and get blackcurrant juice all over the cigarette. Even if you wanted a sweet, you'd get juice all over. We'd just have an ordinary bucket with water because we were in the open field, a thirty-acre field, and you'd have an old piece of rag there and wash your hands as best you could and get your tea. Now, thankfully, the blackcurrant machines have got these boxes on the back where the currants just go. Somebody's still got to stand there; if a leaf or two go in, you pick them out.

The blackcurrants was the worst time on the farm because we used to start at seven in the morning and we kept at it till half past eight at night. You was out there on the back of the machine. You had the heat of the machine, the heat of the day, the drum of the machine, the dust coming off the bushes. That was terrible working that was. That went on for three weeks and that was the three weeks I detested most on the farm. That was about the only three weeks on the farm when I was tied down to a machine because the rest of the while I was nearly my own boss. I would do my own fertilizing and take care of the women. But when it got to a machine I was tied to that from half past seven to half past eight, that wasn't me at all.

Machinery has advanced tremendously well. I said they'd never get a machine to do the blackcurrants. They were so soft they'd squash when we used to pick 'em. We had the first machine come there and that made a terrible job of it. I said, 'There, what did I say?' Next year the machines were a little bit better. Now, they've got a machine that do it better than the women. I was proved wrong after all my years' experience on the farm. The machines do a better job than what the handpickers do.

When I was on the farm, for forty years they were all just open tractors. You sit there in all the elements. We used to have a sack or a rug over our knees to keep warm, to keep the wind out as you were going along. Now they got the cabs there, power steering, you can sit in there and steer away. You got a radio in there. I'm pleased for the boys what are out there now, but they can sit in there like it was an armchair. The seats are sprung, whereby we used to have a solid little thing with your bones shaking about all day long.

They're finding by sitting there all day long that their fitness is nowhere like ours was. Some of them are suffering healthwise a bit because of the lack of mobility. There's problems with high blood pressure and cholesterol because their life is sitting there on the tractor all day. Some will put on a lot of weight, and have to go on a diet. Although it's a lot more concentrated mentally, physically it's not. It's just sort of sitting. They're not couch potatoes, don't get me wrong. But you're sitting in a comfy cab, you've got air conditioning and the radio on and all you've got to do more or less is steer and concentrate on your steering. Hence your body is not moving. With people like us whatever job you were doing you were in your tractor, off your tractor, manual work and all things like that, that's some of the reason I'm as fit as what I am. I had a lot of physical work all the while.

I like the view from the Ipswich road, the A1078. Around you are the hawthorns, and the sloes and blackberries. You'd think, oh, that's beautiful. If you stand up there you can see in the distance the church and the vicarage and then look right across the valley to the fruit trees, which are all dead in line. Then you can see a white cottage up there.

That's where I used to live. I've still got a good heart for Akenfield, where I've been living all my life. I ain't got no regrets in moving, I'm quite happy here. But as I come by that way I look across there and the memories are coming back, I think, right, I spent my life going to the village school. I was brought up there. I went there when I was about three and a half to start school, playing about. And then my life was centred around the village. I can see the field where I worked. And I must say there's pride in all them trees because they're always planted on a square. Whichever way you looked there were rows. We used to plant them eighteen feet squared and if you looked this way, that way, corner ways, they all come in dead straight.

My wife say they could come in here and take the clock and I wouldn't notice it was gone. But if they took a flower out of the garden, I'd miss it. Give me a television set or a Hoover and I know nothing about it at all. But give me a rake and a fork and I'm an expert.

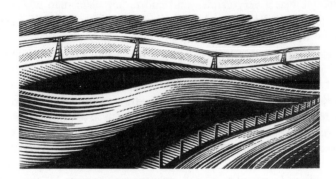

Ronald Blythe, writer, 83

He has well-combed white hair, a small, curving smile and a patient voice. He lives alone in a low-beamed, seventeenth-century cottage, with an untuned grand piano in the sitting room and woodcuts and paintings of the Suffolk landscape on the walls. When we walk around the perimeters of local fields, he occasionally jumps a ditch as we talk.

I was born in Acton in 1922. It's a typical Suffolk village between Lavenham and Sudbury, in west Suffolk. My parents and grandparents lived there, but we moved away when I was small. Well, only about two miles away. That first house had a thatched roof and pond and pigsty; it was an ancient East Anglian house made of beams and thatch. It burned down after the last war, so I used to see this great chimney standing up in the garden when I passed on my way to Bury St Edmunds. Now it's just got three modern bungalows on the site.

I'm the eldest of six. I've got two sisters and three brothers. A big family, and all the brothers and sisters are still alive. We were country children. We walked and bicycled everywhere and knew the whole place for miles around. It was during the time of the great agricultural depression, which started in the late nineteenth century and then bucked up because of the First World War, when agriculture was subsidized. Then the subsidies were taken off, so we were brought up in a kind of beautiful, ruinous landscape of great rural poverty. But we didn't know it, because the fields were full of wildflowers.

My father was at Gallipoli, a young man off a Suffolk farm in his teens. He was a very gentle, kind and rather silent man who loved animals, especially horses. At that time, Suffolk Punches—the biggest horses in Europe—pulled the ploughs. My father was a great horseman. I've got snapshots somewhere of him in the Middle East during the First World War, on a horse near the Pyramids. He was what was called a dispatch rider: he'd take messages on the horse. Farm workers weren't called up until 1917—they were meant to grow as much food as they could—but my father went in 1914. He was glad to go, it was such a romantic thing. Country boys like him had never been abroad, and they all thought that it was wonderful to get off the land in those days. He went on a great liner called the *Aquitania* to Gallipoli, and was not hurt at all, right through the war. He came back and worked on a farm as a stockman, looking after all the animals.

My mother came from London and was well read, a different kind of person altogether. She loved the country. She didn't like London; she repudiated it, really. One of the things I remember most from my childhood is going for walks with her and telling her lies about the distance. 'No, it's only a little ways further,' I would tell her. And we'd walk and walk.

I was a great watcher and listener, an explorer. I loved history and looking at old churches. I was very much a country boy of that period, the kind that hardly exists now. One of the things I think is sad these days is this business where people think children are going to be molested all the time. They're all cooped up with their computers. But when we were children we were outside. You couldn't go anywhere without seeing boys in the summertime in the river or walking or playing football or just wandering about on their bikes. The countryside was full of children, it seemed. It was the last scrap, I suppose, of that old life.

In every country there are indigenous writers who are made by landscape. The great ones, of course, are Thomas Hardy and John Clare and to a degree Wordsworth, but in every country there are people who haven't gone far and have drawn everything they know and understand from quite a small place. I think that might have happened to me, but without my knowing it. My knowledge was extended by reading widely and in other languages, that made a lot of difference, but on the whole I think that I was made by this place.

My two or three greatest friends were botanists, including John Nash, the painter. I learned from them about plants and ecology and the climate. Later I discovered all sorts of things about architecture; East Anglia is full of the most wonderful buildings from the Middle Ages. I suppose I lived very much in the world into which I was born, but with a wider culture.

I was really brought up by artists. They all lived in the middle of nowhere and painted. First there was Sir Cedric Morris. He and his friend Arthur Lett-Haines had come to Suffolk in the mid 1930s and set up the East Anglian School of Painting and Drawing at Hadley. He taught Lucian Freud. I used to go there and it was like a little bit of France in the middle of Suffolk, because the house was painted blue and it always smelled of garlic and wine. All sorts of people were taught how to paint there, in the old-fashioned way without classes and exams.

I was working as a reference librarian at Colchester when I met Christine Nash. She was a charming woman who had married John Nash, who had been an official war artist and had come to live on the Suffolk-Essex borders. In the midst of all these painters, Christine knew perfectly well I should be a writer, and told me so. Somehow she got me out of this job at the library, to my mother's anxiety, and she found me this little house on the Suffolk coast. Later that year I was introduced to Benjamin Britten and he gave me a job of writing and editing the programme book for the Aldeburgh Festival, all sorts of

Craig Taylor

little literary things. I stayed there two years and wrote my first book, a novel set by the sea. And then I went off and to my own amazement found myself a little house by myself, near the village I called Akenfield. It was the first time I had ever done anything sensible, really. I moved in there in 1960—I was in my late thirties, thirty-seven I think. I stayed there for about twenty years. I wrote a lot of books there.

One day in the mid-Sixties, Viking Penguin and Pantheon Books of New York contacted me. Village life was changing all over the world, they said, and they wanted to do a series of books about it. They would send a Russian writer to the French countryside or a French writer to Russia, that sort of thing. Mostly the books were to be written by sociologists. When they came to me and said that I should do one about Britain, I told them I was not a sociologist remotely, nor had I heard of the term oral history at the time. Besides, I'd seen outside the window of this house all my life. What was interesting about it? But I agreed to do it. I thought to do something unusual.

I did vaguely think about doing it in Wales, where I had some friends, because it was so different and stimulating. But I couldn't get started. I was editing Hazlitt at the time for Penguin and I quite liked this bookish thing, working in libraries and being scholarly. They said, 'Have you started this book yet?' So I went for a walk around Akenfield. It was an awful February day. The ditches were full of churning water coming through the field drains. These were partly the medieval ditches of the village. When I looked down I could see what people had seen for centuries. That is, a limited place of seasonal toil. I went to speak to the village nurse. Although I knew her very well, I soon realized I didn't know her at all. When she started speaking about her own life, another person emerged. When I got home, I was astonished, shaken really, by knowing what I now knew about her. When I wrote it down, that other person emerged: she worked in what was really an army hut, she'd got a club foot (which I never put in the book because I thought it would upset her), she delivered all the children and laid out all the dead and patched people up with basically nothing more than vaseline and strips of sheets. It was a terrible time she was in, full of hardship.

From there, I just shaped the book. I would ask somebody to talk to me about keeping pigs and then suddenly he would tell you something astonishing about himself or be so open about his emotional life that I was astounded. Often I hardly asked any questions at all, I just listened.

I did it all on my bike, I cycled around on a Raleigh which I've still got. These were people whose lives covered the 1880s to the 1960s, and they talked about bell-ringing and ploughing and the church and the village school. I was quite a shy person, but I knew who people were, so I made a pattern of the class structure and of the craftsmen and of all kinds.

Writing about my own part of the world was challenging because it was so minimal. Akenfield could be anywhere. It's not spectacular, it's just an ordinary farming community with much the same history as hundreds of villages in this part of the world. They started out as Saxon communities with one or two fields, usually with moorland or woodland all around them, and they just spread out over the centuries. They have medieval churches and sometimes a Baptist chapel, and the pub of course.

So the book was meant to be about not a special village, but any village. At the time we had no idea these professions wouldn't last forever. There used to be a joke when we were at school: 'Forward men of the Middle Ages!' But then there was a sense of things changing. The book was just a pattern of the world into which I was born.

I shouldn't think there's half a dozen people in this village of nearly 400 now who work on the land. When I wrote *Akenfield*, I suppose I was seeing the last of all the ordinary farm work being done. So without meaning to it's become a period piece of village life before the commuters and the telly and the new farming methods all arrived. I wasn't interested in quaintness or crafts, picturesque things necessarily. It's slightly a hard book, not sentimental. There's not a lot to envy in the old days. People were extremely poor. Their houses were uncomfortable and damp. Children left school very early. In that village in that time it was very hard to get away, do anything, or be yourself, and people worked and worked and worked until they died. Between the wars they were getting twenty-seven and six a week and could be given the sack any minute and worked sixty to seventy hours a week on the land and often got one day's holiday a year, Christmas Day.

But something has been lost. People took immense pride in their crafts, laying hedges, ploughing itself. Now a young chap comes with a plough with I don't know how many shares—twelve on either side?—and he goes up and down for a couple of days, and a vast field that would have taken a month to do is done. In autumn he comes along again and cuts it all, all by himself. There's a great loss, too, of the old festivity which you see in Hardy, of going into the harvest field when everybody had to help to get it in. It was hard work but people would be sitting in the hedges eating meals and children played and dogs ran about after rabbits. People used to shout when I was a boy, 'They're cutting at Cardy's! They're cutting at Smith's!' We went over on our bikes. There were ever so many people in the field and they went round and round until the last little disc of corn when all the hares and rabbits ran out and were killed with sticks and dogs and taken home to be eaten.

Harvest has taken on a different meaning. For generations it was the height of the year. It was symbolic to the most astonishing degree in August and September to cut the fields and put it in barns. There's very little sense of that agricultural celebration in the village any more. There's celebration of Christmas, which has become...I don't know, a celebration of buying? But the celebration of harvest is lost, as is the May time, which was such an important part of country life, when the warm weather came and there was a little break between the hard work of sowing in the spring and the hay harvest. People cut the grass, but you can hardly call it a hay harvest like it used to be.

People don't look at the fields now. It's a very beautiful place but you hardly ever see anyone walking or looking at anything. Nor do they know much about what's growing. Some people now live in the middle of a village but seem to take no part in it. They're living urban lives in the countryside—not just here, but all over the place. Because after all is said and done, the same television programmes, same newscasters, same everything are seen by everyone in Britain, every night, from the Orkneys to Cornwall. Most people live in identical places with fitted carpets and all the latest gadgets. It is the normality of the new comfort.

I think there's also a sense of loss in villages like this one that isn't articulated. To some, it's a good loss, good riddance. Others don't know how to frame it in words. I take their funerals sometimes. I took the funeral of the mother of one of the bell ringers not too long ago and nearly the whole village came out. Not any of the 'new people', as they call them. The remnants of all the people who have been here forever. And for a little while in the service with the hymns and what I read to them, they are all as they were long ago. Yet I know perfectly well they're going to drive to Ipswich tomorrow; they'll have the telly on in the evening. Of course they will. But for that time it is very moving.

We're seeing the last of the people who were domestic servants and farm workers. The squire who died a few weeks ago, an old Etonian and a dear sweet man, was an old friend of mine. He didn't belong to this time at all. He belonged to a long, long time ago. He was seventy-eight. When this last generation is gone there will be a break from people who have had any experience with this life. It will be missed. Some of it will be missed: the part that cannot be put into words. □

THE CASE OF THE FEMALE ORGASM
Bias in the Science of Evolution
ELISABETH A. LLOYD

"Lloyd's book isn't just a "must-read," it's a must-own, must-cite, and must-assign-to-one's-students." —Rachel Maines, author of *The Technology of Orgasm*

"This will make great bedside reading. What, after all, is sexier than a well-constructed argument? Lloyd provides a measured and scholarly evaluation of adaptive and non-adaptive explanations for human female orgasm…and she does it without jargon or acrimony."
—Marlene Zuk,
University of California at Riverside
New in cloth

POPULAR FRONT PARIS AND THE POETICS OF CULTURE
DUDLEY ANDREW & STEVEN UNGAR

"Ambitious and original. This is an interdisciplinary study of culture in 1930s France, especially at the time of the Popular Front. Through the study of film, literature, and other media (such as journals, both learned and popular, photography and radio), the authors define and study a 'poetics of culture', a culture which they see primarily characterized by the move from culture to politics under the pressure of national and international developments."
—Ginette Vincendeau, author of
Jean-Pierre Melville: An American in Paris
New in cloth

GRANTA

THE SEVENTH EVENT
Richard Powers

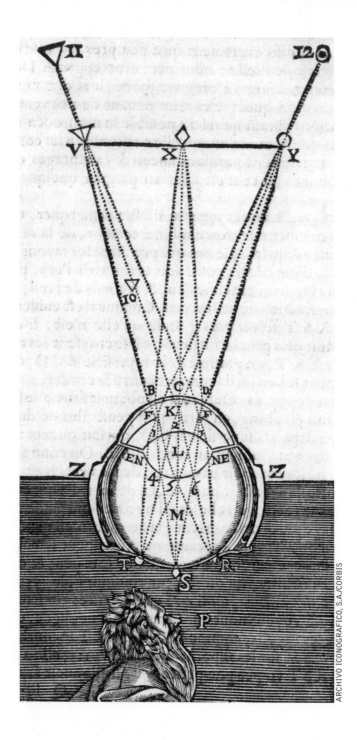

Six

The world shall perish not for lack of wonders, but for lack of wonder.—Haldane

When Mia Erdmann passed away last May, ecocriticism lost a singular voice and all of us who were changed and then changed again by her two books lost the chance to see where she might push the field next. She published her first book, *Hitched to Everything: Literature and the Unseen World*, in 1989 at the age of thirty-two. I can still recall my first exposure to those accusing opening words:

> To our embarrassment, we critics have belatedly begun to see a basic lack in how we talk about literature, and a corresponding lack in how a good deal of literature talks about the world...

Scholars often cite Erdmann's book as the sharpest cry in the call to arms that took shape at the end of the 1980s. Her words gave the growing ecocrit movement its most succinct voice. Literary analysis, she insisted, rightly explores the links between written worlds and the worlds they represent. But it wrongly stops, when making those links, at the gauge of the human. Reading her, I still feel her combined amazement and repugnance at the belated discovery. Personal relationships, family, society, even global economics and politics: Erdmann saw these as nothing more than tiny local nodes in a network so large it should have made the human vanish in embarrassment. And yet the human insisted that all of life hung upon humanity. Appalled by our hopeless parochialism, Erdmann revived Jonathan Swift's deadly mockery: 'I have heard of a man who had a mind to sell his house, and therefore carried a piece of brick in his pocket, which he shewed as a pattern to encourage purchasers.' As Erdmann saw it, literary creation and interpretation had increasingly lost itself at the scale of the brick, while wandering about in a house so large that few had yet stepped back far enough from it to do anything like a real architectural sketch. We could not see how big things really are. We were like those first-time concert goers who applaud after the orchestra stops tuning, thinking it the symphony.

Her book had its famous defenders and detractors. As for me, after reading her, I never wrote the same way again. In an act of private homage, I stole and recycled her Swift quote in my third

Richard Powers

novel, a story of molecular biology and ecology which appeared two years after Erdmann's landmark book. My every subsequent attempt at fiction scrambled to rise to her challenge to describe the wider net beyond humanity's few square knots. Anything less now seemed like failure. As Erdmann put it in that same remarkable first polemic in *Hitched to Everything*:

> Living things, faced with the pressure of changing habitat, must adapt or move. The only third choice is death. If the literary mode wants to survive the catastrophic climate change we ourselves have engineered, it must now do the same.

Erdmann scared me out of the fiction of the self. But I feel a little fraudulent ignoring that self, a little fictitious calling her Erdmann like the rest of her public admirers. For in real life I never called her anything but Mimi. The author of two of the most provocative ecocritical works of the last fifteen years was, to me, the girl in my junior high class in International School Bangkok, who, thirty years ago, at the height of the Vietnam war, performed a bizarre talent show send-up of 'Getting to Know You', singing it just like one of Deborah Kerr's happy charges, while dressed in what everyone but the teachers and administrators recognized as Vietcong garb.

We were not exactly friends, in school. It wouldn't have been possible, at fourteen, for a six-foot-four-inch son of an American school principal to be friends with a four-foot-and-a-fraction daughter of a Canadian petrochemical company executive. But we did sniff each other out, two precocious and doubtlessly obnoxious kids, conscious, a little before most, that they might make a little noise in the world, if they chose. She was far more sophisticated and worldly than I was. But I was a quick study and not above stealing from her stance at a distance. I don't recall her showing any particular interest in nature or life science in school, although I do remember our freshman biology teacher, Khun Porani, declaring Mimi's frog pithing and dissection 'an aesthetic masterpiece'. When I reminded Mimi of this, in her hospital room last spring, four weeks before the end, she claimed I'd made up the whole story. 'Remember what Kundera says,' she warned. 'Memory is not the opposite of forgetting; it is a kind of forgetting. Or something to that effect.'

I left Bangkok in 1973 at the age of sixteen. By a coincidence that seemed stranger to me then than it does now, Mimi and I met again two years later, as freshmen at the University of Illinois, one of those massive educational factories whose strengths in the sciences made it a logical place for me to study physics and for her to study bioengineering. I was stunned to see her again, on the other side of the globe. The unlikelihood didn't seem to surprise her at all. I asked her how she had settled on her major, a choice I found bewildering. She replied, 'Are you kidding me? My entire life, I've dreamed about making a living thing.'

We took freshman chemistry together, along with a couple thousand other students. We arranged to be placed in the same lab section. We became lab partners, if awkward ones. I remember our being assigned to determine the molecular weight of one particular unknown sample. We had a long flow chart of measurements and assays to perform. Mimi just laughed. 'Forget that noise. Look at it. Feel it. Smell it. It's mashed up mothballs. Naphthalene. We know the molecular weight of naphthalene. Save ourselves some work.' Science, she declared, had to know when and how to cheat if it hoped to accomplish anything.

It disconcerted me, being thrown back together on the other side of the world, the long descent from Bangkok, Thailand to Nowhere, Illinois. I took the coincidence to be fate, a kind of obligation. I think we were briefly involved, or something that passed for involvement. Mimi teased me relentlessly about the episode later in life. She even told an interviewer that the young novelist-to-be helped her to come to terms with her own preference for women.

Near the end of our undergraduate days, I drifted into literature and Mimi sank deeper into bioengineering. Mostly out of embarrassment, we lost track of each other. By the time I left school, I had no idea where she was headed or what she planned to do. I took off for Boston without hunting her down to say goodbye. Memory is a form of forgetting, not its opposite.

Five

Every luxury must be paid for, and everything is a luxury, starting with the world.—Pavese

I was living in the Netherlands and had written two novels by the time I came across the name Mia Erdmann again, almost ten years later. When a fellow writer mentioned the critical study *Hitched to Everything*, and its call for a literature that tried to recover the obscene majority of existence typically brushed aside by the novel of character revelation, I couldn't believe that my old schoolfriend and this book's author might be one and the same person. But the name was unusual enough that it couldn't be anyone else. I hunted down a copy. An academic book, it carried no author photograph. The author's note identified her as an assistant professor of literary studies at the University of California, Santa Cruz.

The change in life paths boggled me. But from the book's first sentence, the prose style bore the stamp of that unmistakable mind. The writing was big and bold, remarkably limber, and not above saving itself some work. Criticism, she claimed, had treated American literature's centuries-long obsession with wildness—from early shock and awe to late jaded contempt—as simple extensions of the themes of self-fashioning, self-reliance, and self-transformation. It was time, Mia said, to put away such childish things. She demonstrated, in damning shorthand, how all of the then leading schools of literary criticism—Marxism, Deconstruction, even the emerging Post-Colonial studies—were, to some extent, self-exempting, performing much the same kind of cultural work that they themselves were intent on exposing. For even as cultural studies exposed hidden social agendas, it participated in crimes against the non-human worse than anything humanity had ever committed against itself. And fiction, for its part, had for two centuries wallowed in a bottomless vanity that promoted the individual self to be the measure of all things: 'We have let our shot at awareness be bought off with a bauble,' this Mia Erdmann put it.

> An infant is the soul of absolute narcissism, identifying only with
> itself. Growth should be the steady breaking down and
> enlargement of its identity. But judging by our literature, the true
> scale of the world may be too terrifying for even the largest acts of
> identification to grasp.

The prose, as many have commented, alternated between diatribe and epic poem. It bore no relationship to the kind of prose required for academic advancement. Nor did the author bother much with close arguments. *It's naphthalene, damn it. We know the molecular weight of naphthalene.* But I knew, within five pages, that this book would stand the conversation on its ear. My old friend would make a name for herself. And it seemed I had always known this, as far back as junior high. The author had the force of moral certainty behind her, of incontestable urgency. And after my stabs of jealousy over the sheer force of her words, all I could feel in them was the pleasure of recovery.

Some have aligned Erdmann's prose and her position in this first book with the more lyrical voices of ecofeminism. Cheryll Glotfelty, in her review in *Interdisciplinary Studies in Literature and Environment,* calls Erdmann 'a diabolical Annie Dillard'. These comparisons slight what is most distinctive in Mimi's writing. A great deal of ecstatic, first-wave ecological criticism concerns itself with almost mystical communion with other living things. Such a possibility, in Erdmann, is at best problematic and at worst impossible. Even when her descriptions work the hardest to invoke something close to awe at the living world, her gaze is unflinching, less Protestant hymn than house music rave. 'Life,' she declares,

is botched self-replication. It stems from a single command: copy this, again and again and again. Crucially, that copying is not wholly accurate. Otherwise, we would have stopped at pretty crystals. Think of mitosis as trillions of slightly near-sighted, plagiarizing students—speculation on the loose. The crazed self-copier, DNA, is runaway and indifferent, erecting endless botched, diverging organisms as delivery systems. Each one of its current twelve and a half million species serves as a postulate about its environment. Most of them are viral or opportunistic. All are shaped for exploitation, dependent on the whole...We large animals are hopelessly macroscopicentric. In fact, any life form bigger than a thimble is a fluky, precarious, exceptional, composite kludge job. There are more cells in a baby's finger than people in the world, and each of these cells is itself an ecosystem, already a colony of assimilated slave species. A single Amazon tree top harbours three dozen species of ant. What does it mean to be alive? The real, bedrock deal is vegetative, fungal, invisible: superbugs, extremophiles, bacteria that thrive on acid and salt, that never see the sun, that live in suspended animation 320 degrees below zero Fahrenheit, or mass in a spoon of soil in concentrations beyond anyone's ability to number. What would a literature that knew all this look like?

But for all her attempts to terrify the reader with the violent profligacy of nature, Erdmann's world is exhilarating once your eyes attenuate to it. The book's conclusion still holds, in my mind, even after her youthful field's many revisions and revolutions:

If we could stop using nature as a metaphor for reflecting the human condition, we might begin to see how the human condition reflects some small fraction of nature's relentless urge to speculate.

I wrote to the author, care of UC Santa Cruz. This was still back in the age of letters, when you had to put the recipient's name at the top of the message and yours at the bottom. I told her how shamed and rearranged I had been by wrestling with her book. And I asked her all the predictable and necessary questions about how her life had gone in the intervening decade. What had happened to her after leaving Illinois? How did she end up in California? Was she with someone? Was she happy?

Her reply answered none of my personal questions. None of her letters ever did. She found personal details fulsome, indulgent and boring. The only one of my biographical questions she thought even vaguely worth addressing was how she had gotten from a bachelor's degree in bioengineering to a PhD in American literature. 'I got impatient. I wanted to make a living thing from scratch. Those guys weren't quite as far along as they were promising. So I took a short cut.' I asked why, in that case, she hadn't become a fiction writer. She replied, 'You had too big of a head start.'

I hadn't realized we were competing. But then, I'd never taken as hard a look at life as Mimi had. In *Hitched to Everything*, the living world was not some stable, benign equilibrium that humans needed to rejoin after a long self-exemption. In Mimi's view of nature, the two slowest-growing neighbouring sequoias were locked in a freeze-frame battle of life and death, stretching out over centuries.

Four

In the long run, we are all dead.—Keynes

Even in the bloom of youth, she had been spindly and blotchy, one of the homeliest people I've ever met. She took great pride in this. She claimed selective advantage in being able to startle other creatures. I've mentioned that Mimi was short. She topped out at about four feet four. She was forever making a point of this, in her writing and in person. 'Small creatures tend to be scavengers,' she wrote, in the acknowledgements of her second book.

> The world looks different in the undergrowth than it does in the canopy. Small creatures hate to be beholden to large ones, but all of my friends, alas, seem to be giants. I have stolen from each of them.

She claimed to have 'stolen' the title of her second book, *The Monte Carlo Game*, from a citation in my third. But how that counts as theft from me, when I had stolen it already from Jacques Monod, only a mind as scrupulously property aware as Mimi's could say. The full quote from Monod reads: 'The universe was not pregnant with life, nor the biosphere with man. Our number came up in the Monte Carlo game.'

I don't intend to rehash the controversy surrounding Erdmann's second book, controversy already too familiar to be useful again. Seven years had passed since Mimi's first study. She was not yet forty. The environmental movement had embraced her early work, to the point of suffocating it, and she was fleeing that embrace, even as she fled literature for a less compromised life science. Poetry made nothing happen, and to save herself from her admirers, she had to repudiate what she now thought of as the more sentimental aspects of her own first position. I knew before it existed that the second book would raise havoc. She wrote me often during its composition, sometimes with indiscreet, even brutal put-downs of what she called the 'owl worshippers':

> They think that advocating on behalf of some gigantic, fluffy species exonerates them. If they knew for one instant the pressure their own mere existence puts on the rest of the cracking web, they would take their own lives.

Her writing in the book is only a shade more judicious. The central idea of *The Monte Carlo Game* grows out of the conclusion of her first book, but turns far darker. We invented nature. Everything that we mean by invoking the word *natural* must be understood as merely a social symbol with a long and changing history. She writes:

> When our stories yearn for a vanished world, green and pleasant, they do so out of sheer terror, however suppressed, at the real look of the energy bazaar that truly surrounds and encloses us.

And elsewhere, she clarifies:

> Any writer who invokes the environment or the non-human living world as a transcendental moral category does so out of very human motives... Any system that separates the natural from the human is already thinking anti-ecologically.

The book came out at the worst possible moment, just before the election of a Congress that proved to be the most anti-environmental and pro-business legislative body in history. Decades of hard-fought endangered species and environmental protection legislation were being destroyed overnight. The environmentalists were on the run, and they were quick to identify Mia Erdmann as a traitor to the cause. She defended herself in print, in a series of articles perhaps too subtle and combative.

> Nature is not our zoo. We must get away from golly-green wide-eyed wonder. Wonder is too easy a dodge, a massive distraction from the more prosaic question of just what toxins we are sending downstream.

Maybe her critics are right, and Mimi suffered from a fatal perverse contrarianism. But that quality made her a useful writer. 'Life will survive all our theories of ecology,' she wrote in the May issue of *Harper's* in 1995. 'We cannot damage it. We will press it to the wall, and in its own time, it will come roaring back in spectacular speciation, like a forest after a fire.' That article made her scores of enemies for life. But it also forced many to think about just what they meant by ecological thinking. With the passage of years, *The Monte Carlo Game* has been attacked and defended in as many ways as readers have needs. Ultimately, most ecocritics have conceded that Erdmann was once again early in cautioning against mistaking the interdependence of all living things for a sentimental, universal affirmation.

> Nature has no philosophy. It makes no judgements and writes no books. Only we do that. We cannot look to nature for a moral foundation, for nature will try everything at least once, not least of all perpetual cheating and exploitation. The web of life does not mourn extinction. It *uses* extinction.

Her short pieces increasingly suggested that being green was not about saving the spotted owl but about saving *Homo sapiens*. She grew fond of quoting John Maynard Keynes's 1930 article, 'Economic Possibilities for Our Grandchildren': 'With psalms and sweet music the heavens'll be ringing,/But I shall have nothing to do with the singing.'

Mimi and I didn't write each other often, and with the advent of email, we wrote even less. Something in the new medium felt too close for comfort. We two liked each other better in the abstract, at the level of ornate sentences, than we did up close, at the scale of gritty punctuation. When we did write, we argued a lot, challenged each other, and basically indulged various crackpot ideas about literature's relationship to ecology that were not yet ready for the free market.

I wasn't sure I understood the direction that her thinking was taking her. Sometimes she sounded almost Spencerian, like some horrific sterile hybrid of E. O. Wilson and Richard Dawkins, or like a molecular-biological Ayn Rand, with the indomitable Human Will replaced by nucleotides, a story where everything that life cobbles up or stumbles upon is Right. I tried drawing her out, citing the most predatory of her critics and asking her what kind of retaliation she was working on.

She claimed that she had graduated from retaliation, that she was now exploring the possibilities of commensalism, or even mutualism. I asked if that meant she might be working on a book on symbiosis— say, about literature and networked cooperation. 'I'm not working on anything,' she wrote. 'I'm just listening.'

Three

We are remodelling the Alhambra with a steam-shovel, and we are proud of our yardage.—Leopold

Over the next few years, she wrote almost nothing about literature. When her name appeared anywhere, it was on nothing longer than reviews, thorny struggles with books on the ecology movement that themselves had no patience for narrative fiction. Her earlier attempts to understand the American Eden and the American Frontier—her great acts of synthesis running from Jonathan Edwards to Jonathan Franzen—died away, replaced by terse social critiques and brute science. In these pieces, she moves away from the theoretical high ground of *The Monte Carlo Game* towards a simpler, statistical desperation. The evidence pops up in quotes scattered here and there through subtler arguments:

> The six hottest years in recorded history have occurred since
> 1991... The fossil-based phase of civilization is ending. The race
> has perhaps fifteen years to prepare for what happens next.
> Already, we consume twenty per cent more natural resources than
> the earth can produce, and the figure is rising steeply... Humans
> are quick at all things, and we are driving the seventh mass
> extinction three orders of magnitude faster than the natural
> background extinction rate. If present trends continue, one half of
> all species of life on earth will be gone in one hundred years...

I learned of Mimi's illness from the Literature and Life Science LISTSERV. How anyone on the LISTSERV found out, I don't know. She'd been ill for over a year without a mention anywhere. Contrary to popular knowledge, she did not have ALS, but a related motor neuron disease called Sandon's disease. Like ALS, Sandon's is a rapidly progressing degenerative neurological disease that attacks the nerve cells responsible for controlling voluntary muscles. Like ALS, it is invariably fatal, usually running its course in three to five years. The National Institute of Health fact sheet says: 'The cause(s) of most MNDs are not known, but environmental, toxic, viral, or genetic factors may be implicated.'

I called her the afternoon I found out. Mimi was furious. 'You go twenty years without telephoning, only to call because I have some disease?' She accused me of ambulance chasing. 'What is it about people? What's so damn exciting about talking to a sick person?' After a while, she calmed down, fascinated by how different my voice sounded, after all that time. 'Are you sure it's really you?' As proof, I reminded her of the International School Bangkok talent show, her chirpy rendition of 'Getting to Know You', delivered in black Vietcong pyjamas.

'Sadistic *and* fictitious,' she declared. 'It must be you.'

Before too long we were talking again, as if we had just come out of freshmen chemistry lab. She was remarkably animated. 'I wanted to ask your opinion on something. A question I've been turning over a lot, lately. Why is it that ecosystems produce rich networks, while markets—including literary markets—tend to produce monocultures?' I had no answer, but she talked to me anyway. Over the next several months, as she lost control of her fingers, we used the phone more often. She went into a nursing home. 'It's like time travel,' she told me. 'Jumping into your own future. How often do you get to gaze upon your eighties, while you're still in your forties? Useful, really. Senescence is wasted on the old.'

She got so she couldn't handle a phone, and she refused to wear a hands-free headset on principle. I went on writing her letters, but I don't know what she made of them.

Two

We are not unified.—Rilke

I used a book tour with readings in San Francisco and Berkeley as an excuse to visit her. I don't know what I was expecting, but I failed to hide my shock when I walked into her nursing-home room. Something like a capuchin monkey was sitting up in the private bed, just waiting for the organ grinder to strike up a tune. For her part, Mimi didn't seem to recognize me at all. It took me a moment to realize that she was suffering from the Sandon's 'mask'—the inability to move her facial muscles in anything like an expression.

Bizarre pitched sounds came out of her, and it took me two phrases to recognize the song: *Getting to know you. Getting to know all about you.*

I sat down at her bedside. Flustered, I said the only thing I could think of. 'How are you going?'

'Going,' she responded, in a thick, deliberate voice. 'A fair amount of dread on this end. I keep telling myself that it's just the serotonin levels, but my Self keeps insisting, "No, girlie, it's dread."' She didn't want to talk about her illness. 'Tedious,' she dismissed. 'It's not in the chest walls yet. Lungs and oesophagus still work. That's all that matters.'

I spent the day with her. An eternity; an eye-blink. She wanted to talk, about anything in the world, so long as it wasn't about anything concrete. 'It's all we're good for anyway, isn't it?' she claimed. 'Trading abstractions. Talk and more talk.' She spent most of the afternoon taking issue with everyone. Peter Ward's belief that humans were immune to extinction struck her as quaint and beside the point. 'Do you know that ninety-nine per cent of every species that ever existed is extinct?'

I said that seemed almost hopeful.

'Annihilates every possible position,' Mimi said.

To David Abram's assertion that political and economic institutions not aligned with earthly realities are not likely to last, she countered, 'What do you suppose he means by "last"? That's the final question, isn't it? What should we care for? On what time frame? Who's "us"? How much, *at last*, can we hope to connect with?'

Her voice was faint and uninflected. I couldn't always understand or follow her. But then, that was nothing new. She was out ahead of me again, ahead of everyone, lying frozen in her bed, looking out on a future of superbugs and extremophiles, bacteria that wouldn't even be starting over again, after big life was gone, but just continuing.

'I'm struggling with consciousness,' she said, then laughed at the slippage, the treachery of words. 'Well, not with *consciousness*, but with the idea of it. I just don't see the survival value. It seems to me revenue-negative. As far as I can see, what Einstein called the 'optical delusion of consciousness' is exactly what has pulled this whole game apart. Slows you down and leaves you permanently exiled. The so-called integrated self is exactly the thing that made us torch the place. If only we could grok what the neuroscientists are telling us.' She banged her skull hard against the hospital bed headboard. 'A billion years of inherited apparatus, all those earlier species, still inside, still up there. A whole reef of neural modules, all updating each other, changed by everything we look at, and little bits of self scraping off on everything we brush up against. And we want to simplify all *this* into character? Personality? Self-realization?'

She let me feed her, and she laughed at how pathetic I was. 'Not much practice at this, huh?' After lunch, she said, 'Want to go for a walk?' I practically had my coat on before I remembered. She laughed at me again, although not without sympathy. 'I mean the other kind of walk.'

'You know what I want to write? A book made up entirely of quotes. Or, you know: quotes inexactly copied.'

'Botched replication?' I suggested.

'Yeah, what *you* said. Actually, I *am* writing something. Have been, for a few months now.' She saw my reflex glance at her stiff body. 'In my head, dimwit.'

I offered to find her someone to take dictation, but she didn't seem to hear.

'The hardest part is getting away from *wonder*, damn it. Not easy, in my present condition. At the same time, I hate the idea of being thrown back on activism. It seems so belated and lame, at the end of the day. But if I could get just one more volume out? I think it would have to be down and dirty Environmental Justice Movement stuff. No literature; just law. Who should get sued for poisoning whom. No theory, no threatened biosphere, no microbes; just the downwind people versus the upwind people. It would do nothing to slow the real catastrophe, of course. But we'd be able to disappear with a clean conscience about something.'

I asked her why not keep to the bigger story, if it's about to erase all others. She sighed, a little disgusted. 'Because humans can't follow a bigger story. They don't want to read anything larger than autobiography. At least Environmental Justice squeezes the story down into a shape some people might recognize. I know, I know: it's tedious and formulaic. Hardly art.'

All art was a formula, I said. I told her I was sure she could make justice interesting. She studied me, gauging whether I was ready for the truth. We were thirteen, all over again. 'I'm not sure you know what *interesting* is. That's the problem with you, as a novelist. Man, you are sitting with your ass in the tropical rainforest of professions. Everything there is, and look at everything that you haven't done with it. You should be writing deranged stuff, completely decoupled stuff. Anti-human. Non-bipedal. Fiction that could save us all from rationality. Fiction that knows what *real life* looks like. Yours is the one line of work where a person gets to create species from scratch. *Make it up, damn it.* Anything! Want to know the best thing you ever wrote? That ghost story, in book five.'

I knew at once which ghost story she meant. Two men, lying in an old hospital, a heart patient and a quadriplegic. The heart patient, through seniority, has the bed by the window, while the quadriplegic lies out of the line of sight. But the heart patient entertains the quadriplegic all day long with tales of life outside the window. Incredible stuff, a constant circus of activity. Tendrils, trees, and vines in full flower. The teardrop pendant mosques of oriole nests. Gravity-defying webbed mammals. Colonies of June bugs so thick they flowed like lava. Mass migrations blacking out the sky. The quadriplegic grows so envious of the view that, one night, when the heart patient suffers an attack and reaches for the medicine on the bedside table between them, the quadriplegic, through an impossible effort of will, rises up and knocks the vial to the floor. When they remove the dead heart patient the next day and promote the quadriplegic to the window bed, he can barely contain his excitement as he turns to see the view for himself for the first time. But when he sees the window, the view that greets him there is a solid, grey wall.

'I love that one,' she said. 'Now *that's* literature.'

'But that one wasn't mine,' I objected. 'I got it from some 1930s story omnibus that belonged to my father.'

'Would you listen to this guy? He wants it to be made up, *and* original! Of course it wasn't yours. A botched quote, stolen since Gilgamesh. That's what makes it great.'

She insisted on watching the evening news. I'm not sure what was still in it for her, but she made me turn on the set, high on the opposite wall. We stopped talking and watched the night's instalment—insurgency and occupation, suicide bombers and nuclear material proliferating through the spot black market. I couldn't tell what the images were doing to her. All I could see was the Sandon's mask.

Pictures came on, from Mars. The two rovers, Spirit and Opportunity. Surreal landscapes, red and spectacular and void. A sound came from her bed: more words. 'Maybe that's why life needed consciousness. To make it to Mars and see how the place was covered in water once. Now just pretty rock.'

It was getting late. I fed her again, dinner. Then I had to go. I didn't know how to say goodbye. 'See you in the lab?'

She looked at me with that stiff face. 'Make me up?' she begged. 'Some demented story? One where I get to make *something* come alive?'

I promised her I would.

One

When we try to pick out anything by itself, we find it hitched to everything else in the Universe.—Muir

When the Sandon's disease reached Mia Erdmann's chest wall, she went on a respirator. And when she'd had all the thoughts she cared to have, she went off.

Awareness—narrative imagination—is just the latest reckless experiment set loose by faulty transcription. Who knows what survival benefits it has? Natural selection may snuff it out tomorrow. The flaw of narrative imagination, in its current form, is that we can only feel the big in terms of the little. We have written the end of our current story, but we cannot read it yet. I cannot begin to grasp the end of big animals, or even the mere extinction of humans. But I could make up Mia Erdmann, and almost grasp her end.

Her estate executors sent me two pages. I don't know when she composed them. She must have dictated them to someone. The first page read: 'The new book: or six things I think I think.' It consisted of a simple list.

1. Muir: When we try to pick out anything by itself, we find it hitched to everything else in the Universe.
2. Rilke: We are not unified.
3. Leopold: We are remodelling the Alhambra with a steam-shovel, and we are proud of our yardage.
4. Keynes: In the long run, we are all dead.
5. Pavese: Every luxury must be paid for, and everything is a luxury, starting with the world.
6. Haldane: The world shall perish not for lack of wonders, but for lack of wonder.

The second page was a letter, with no signature. It read:

Hey, Powers. I have a new story for you. Okay, it's not new. Just a
little botched self-replication, variation on a theme. Thanks for
taking me out for a spin. Don't say I never paid you back. Ready?
There are *three* people in the room: the heart patient, the
quadriplegic, and a stroke victim. And when the quadriplegic gets
promoted to the window bed, and turns to see that solid grey wall,
and the truth of what he's done crushes him, he stops, composes
himself, swallows his murder, and tells the stroke victim: 'You won't
believe what's out there. You simply won't believe what I can see.'

□

GRANTA

WAITING FOR SALMON
Barry Lopez

Barry Lopez

By a stroke of good luck I inhabit a remarkable place, a wooded bench above the upper McKenzie, a whitewater river in western Oregon. It is country for which gentrification is still a long way off. On the other side of the river, the mountains carry old-growth forest steeply up to the sky—it is untenanted land that has never been farmed, logged, mined or homesteaded. Black bear, Roosevelt elk, black-tailed deer and coyote are common in the woods. Occasionally, out walking, I see a mountain lion or bobcat.

Some years ago, I began paying closer attention to the arrival of salmon in front of my house. They spawn here each year on gravel bars along this stretch of the river, a hundred crow-fly miles from the Pacific Ocean. These particular, big, anadromous, determined animals are called chinook salmon (*Oncorhynchus tshawytscha*), the species name an approximation of the word used by Koryak people, the traditional occupants of Kamchatka in eastern Siberia. The fish are more properly called spring chinook, or springers, because they cross the bar at the mouth of the Columbia River in the spring, months before they arrive on these spawning grounds, their natal waters. The adjective distinguishes them from other stocks of the same species that cross the bar in the summer or fall (and that do not, as it happens, migrate to the upper McKenzie). Chinook are also called king salmon, or kings, because of the five species of North American salmon, they're the largest. People also know them as tyee salmon, a word adapted from one used by the Nootka, an Indian people on nearby Vancouver Island, to mean 'older brother'.

Chinook salmon commonly exceed twenty-seven inches and fifteen pounds on the McKenzie, and might approach forty-five inches and forty pounds in other watersheds. Their flesh is Saturn red. An oil painter, one a stickler for this sort of detail, might mix scarlet vermilion with cadmium orange and a little white to get the right colour.

All salmon, but especially the chinook, shaped the spiritual belief and practice, the mythology and art of dozens of native tribes that matured in the Pacific Northwest during the Holocene epoch—the Kwakiutl, Tlingit and Chinook among them. The fish's cultural sway over the past 10,000 years, from eastern Russia to central California, is beyond my ability either to grasp or to appreciate. I have to guess it's fully known to no one. But the breadth of the chinook salmon's impact on human societies, its late-twentieth-century rise to prominence as an icon among non-Indian people in the Pacific Northwest, the infinite complexity of its biology and ecology: all of these combine to compel feelings of reverence, for some, when eating it.

In front of my house, the McKenzie is about 350 feet across and four feet deep, shallowing to cobble flats near the banks, and limpid enough to reveal a stony bottom on the south side to someone standing on the north bank. When female chinook arrive on gravel bars here, they roll on to their sides and begin excavating pits with rapid, vigorous, whole-body undulations. In building these 'redds', the females use the river's strong current to carry away the previous year's accumulation of silt and the organic debris they churn up. A clean and unimpeded flow of water through the now banked and porous gravel ensures that the fertilized roe will be well oxygenated. A micro current, generated by the half-bowl shape of the nest, pins the eggs gently within the pit, and allows the blue-grey cloud of milt bursting from a male salmon to descend and penetrate the eggs before it diffuses in the quick current.

The adults die a couple of weeks after they spawn in mid-September. Their bodies, which have brought the ocean's food web inland hundreds of river miles, are scavenged by bears, foxes, coyotes, otters, eagles, mink and other carnivorous members of the salmon's community. Where the stranded fish rot untouched in the sun, they enrich the soil banks of the river, a related community of trees, orchids, wild-berry vines and bushes, tubers and other plant life that depends on them. Finally, the adult carcasses provide nutrients to the food their own fry will feed on when they hatch.

Over the decades I've lived here and watched these fish spawn, I've witnessed three major changes in the woods around me. The populations of some species of birds—Swainson's Thrush and MacGillivray's Warbler, for example—have dwindled and the range and intensity of birdsong have declined. The probable cause is the elimination of these species' homes in the neotropics, where they overwinter. Fewer now survive to return north.

A second change, more obvious to those for whom news of the loss of birds brings only a philosophical shrug, is that our winters are milder. Thirty years ago, winters here were marked by four or five snowstorms, a couple of which might have made the forty-mile drive to town too risky to chance. I can't recall the last time we had a snowfall that accumulated, that amounted to more than a snow shower, or the last time the temperature dipped into the teens Fahrenheit. The probable cause—a recurrent and natural event likely accelerated this time by the hand of man—is global warming, a phenomenon now so widely reported and documented it makes America's official stance of equivocation look deliberately, cabalistically ignorant. How global warming will affect the fate of chinook salmon, and all that's tied to them, is one of the many Gordian knots in natural history blithely dismissed by Americans still trying to pull Charles Darwin's pants down. Meanwhile the problems—the wholly unanticipated secondary effects of mega-engineering projects, for example—continue to arrive like horsemen on the dawn horizon.

The third change has been confounding—a seeming reversal of the popular assertion, tedious to some, that the natural world is falling apart. Here's what, confoundingly, happened: after years of decline, the number of salmon spawning on the McKenzie suddenly went up. The year I moved here, 1970, I counted sixteen adult chinook salmon on the gravel flats in September. During the thirty-two years following, that number fell, slowly but steadily. In 2002 only three turned up. Then, in September 2003, thirteen appeared. That fall, scientists later told me, four times as many spring chinook arrived on the upper McKenzie as had come—on average—in any of the previous fifteen years. Since the mid-Eighties the total number of returning natives (so called to set them apart from hatchery fish) had hovered at around 1,000. In 2003, 5,784 reached the upper river. A further speculation, at the time, was that these elevated numbers of returning salmon might be just as high in 2004 (they nearly were—4,789 came in) and that they might well be again in 2005.

Biologists at the Oregon Department of Fish and Wildlife, and other concerned historians of the natives' fate, speculated that increased upwelling in the eastern Pacific Ocean (the North American side) caused a sudden improvement in feeding conditions at sea, which accounted for an increase in the rate of survival for three, four, and five-year-old springers. A greater-than-usual number, then, would have survived the familiar gauntlet—hundreds of miles of commercial fishing, toxic spills, dams, gravel-mining operations—to swim up the river and spawn.

Fisheries' biologists, staring at these numbers, have at least two important questions still to address. With feeding conditions at sea suddenly improved, would freshwater conditions show a similar improvement? And, how many smolts born of these larger adult populations would return to spawn?

The sudden recovery of 2003 and 2004 is statistically striking, but it's finally insignificant as a sign of overall health in the ecosystem of which the fish is a part. Biologists did not see 'improvement' in 2003 and 2004. They saw an anomaly, a not-quite-comprehensible 'perturbation'.

I phoned my younger brother in coastal Maine when I learned of the high count of returning salmon in 2003. He told me it had been another bumper year, there, for lobster; but the explanation for Maine's recent record harvests, he told me, was nothing good. Biologists, I learned, attribute them to 'dysfunction' in the near-shore ecosystem. A partial explanation they offer is that stocks of wild fish that feed regularly on lobster larvae, such as coastal cod and rock bass, have declined sharply. In other words, there are more lobster because the predatory fish population has collapsed.

This more complex story—in which global warming again is suspected of playing a definite but unspecified role—has a depth that fits it poorly to television news, with its penchant for summary accounts. Such natural events—when they're reported—are normally rounded up into breezy, upbeat bulletins, suggesting, in this instance, the irrepressible economic strength of the lobster industry. The good times, many people in Maine are encouraged to believe, have returned. Difficult times are too hard to explain.

Maine's huge lobster harvests are an unstable process, one without an end point. We can't 'fix' the 'lobster problem'; it has no solution. And, knowing that its components—warming water, biochemical fluctuations—have some bearing on the biology and ecology of *Homo sapiens*, it is hard to characterize the accompanying news reports as anything but irresponsible. News reporting is a commercial endeavour, and it has no budget for deliberation. It is economically untenable for mainstream news to be too deeply reflective.

To get some better sense of what's behind Maine's huge lobster harvests you have to search out, to take an example, *Ecosystems*, a technical journal, specifically the issue that went online on April 27, 2004 and read 'Accelerating Trophic-level Dysfunction in Kelp Forest Ecosystems of the Western North Atlantic'. This is news of a different sort. It is deeply researched and carefully wrought, it makes references to supporting and dissenting opinion, and it shows some elegance in its logic and conclusions.

Politicians, the men and women who decide domestic and foreign policy where lobster harvesting is concerned, do not read *Ecosystems*. And television news is the common ground politicians share with their constituents. Scientists, like the ones writing for *Ecosystems*, are treated on television (and by many politicians) with a measure of amusement. Offering their vetted reports on dysfunctional ecosystems and global warming, scientists tend to claim, justifiably, an expertise superior to that of politicians and newscasters. The politicians, for their part, bring out their own experts, especially to refute any report that threatens any section of the vaunted economy. These individuals might have no scientific training at all, but they possess credentials (or motives) of some other sort—a talk-show celebrity, a clergyman, say—which serve convincingly to contradict the expertise of the scientist in the eyes of those who have yet to turn the programme off.

This warfare between experts—which began in earnest in America with the simultaneous emergence of computer modelling and a general awareness of the economic threat posed by environmental problems—is as much a menace to human survival now as the natural catastrophes that ignite the arguments. Traditionally, the focus of expertise in the face of catastrophe is solution. It may be, however, that within the grand cycles of the planet earth, its warming and cooling periods and magnetic-field reversals, within the disjointed sequence of its hyper-millennial events, such as the bolide impact near the Yucatán Peninsula 65 million years ago which helped wipe out seventy-five per cent of Cretaceous life—it may be that, on the rough seas of these long-term events, there are no solutions. A lifeboat, instead, may be required.

Expertise with no measure of humility is of no use to us. No one knows why there are suddenly more salmon in front of my house, but their coming and going is more than incidental scenery. It's a sentence in a story about human fate.

During several years of exposure to different societies of traditional people—remnant Ainu on Hokkaido, Iñupiaq Eskimo in Alaska, Pitjantjatjara Aborigines in the Northern Territory—I've encountered individual men and women who possessed what seemed to be a staggering expertise in natural history: a knowledge of the ecology of fire and the signs of coming weather; an ability to predict when a particular creature might be found at a particular place; an understanding of the links between plants, insects, humidity and temperature; an ability to decipher the very recent past, revealed, for example, in faint scribes on the surfaces of snow and sand.

What I learned from this welter of examples were two things. First, to endure as a people you have to pay attention. Second, no individual exclusively possesses this expertise. It's the community's collective creation. The long-term stability of the community depends on the regular and uncalculated sharing of empirical information by close observers. The individuals most impressive in their local knowledge to an outsider (like me) are often merely the most adept practitioners of community knowledge. The response among such people to changing or dire conditions is not to call on experts, as that term is commonly used in the cultural West, but to gather the best minds, those that not only observe but listen, that see something else at stake in life besides a professional reputation.

If you were to visit my home in September, I'd be happy to introduce you to the fish. We'd walk down a few hundred feet from my grey, storey-and-a-half house in the trees to stand on the north bank of the McKenzie. Depending on the angle of the sun, we might see the fish spawning a foot or so beneath the surface of the water as clearly as if we were watching them through glass. I'd only ask you to stay back a little so as not to make them anxious, and after a few minutes to be on our way.

If you would ask me about chinook spawning throughout the watershed here, I'd have to send you to a few neighbours, to the more credible scientific papers and books, to ichthyologists and bioregionalists. Beyond the bounds of my own few acres, I don't really know.

I don't talk about the salmon much with my neighbours. We often consider, instead, the beauty of the river, its wild and lambent surface, or the many osprey that fly over it in summer, hunting for trout. To speak of salmon might lead to contention. Logging, and the road building that goes with it, which fills feeder streams with silt and which historically has been no friend to salmon, has long been the linchpin of our local economy. I don't want the breech an argument could bring.

Of all the tenets of fundamentalism that have recently emerged in American politics and that are embarrassing to cite—foreign policy decisions congruent with the urgings of Revelation, a contempt for empirical science—the one that seems most starkly dangerous to me is fundamentalism's contentious stance with regard to biological imperatives. No matter which political affiliation you choose, no matter whether you own three houses or must work three jobs, no matter your religion or your national allegiance, you must eventually come to grips with the implications of your own biology—your need for water, unadulterated nutrition and protection from solar radiation. In Darfur, while many in the West laboriously pondered the political consequences of using the word 'genocide', a storm of male violence raged over control of water and grazing land. The patrons of this war over natural resources were not distracted by this legal argument. Food and water were on their minds.

A purely biological view of humanity—sans politics, sans religion—is something we are not accustomed to. We tend to think of humanity as exempt from nature, by virtue of its technologies, its impressive eschatologies. To practise our beliefs, however, we must be free to act—a freedom already compromised by our aversion to questions about our biological fate. Scientists—considered Cassandras here again—would inform us that we are an organism no more free of nature than we are free of the consequences of a cultural design we have tried to impose on nature.

To speak of large-scale changes in the natural world that might be traced to human activity is anathema to people still furious with Darwin for suggesting that 'nature' included man.

Imagine a disinterested primate mammalogist or a psychiatric pathologist dispassionately regarding a random, urban population of *Homo sapiens* in North America. He or she would be justified in writing this diagnosis: *increasingly dependent on prescription drugs to elevate or suppress its emotions; living in intense, intersecting fields of electromagnetic energy; drawing its water from aquifers laced with manufactured chemical wastes, including hormones and antibiotics, whose synergistic toxicity is unknown and ignored.* He or she would note that the diseases making inroads in this population include dementia (including attention deficit disorder and Alzheimer's), asthma, hypertension, depression, distraction disorders and various types of cancer. He or she would point out that while the primary cause of such diseases was genetic predisposition, it was likely that they were also culturally driven or stress-related to some appreciable degree. Traditional explanations alone, he or she would be compelled to note, ignore industry and government actions and overlook the unwitting human disturbance of a viral ecology that has recently produced HIV, Ebola, Lassa, Marburg and other problems.

The world, we too often forget, has no investment or interest in the triumph of *Homo sapiens*, a conclusion that Christian fundamentalists, with their Albigensian hatred of the earth, want stricken from the record of human thought.

In a mature nation, where terrorists might be understood as part of a worldwide awakening to the spectre of finite resources, and to the strategic and tactical planning required to secure ownership to freshwater, petroleum and grain fields, it would be possible in political discussion to raise the subject of the fate of *Homo sapiens*. But in no country does this seem possible. As for America, mainstream politics is uninformed by, even hostile to, biology. Further, a major segment of the American electorate apparently believes that any concern about where water and food will come from is a superstitious hold-over from 'an era of primitive people'. Man's destiny, his true home they assert, is in a heaven, alongside their one-and-only God who gave humans the earth to use for whatever it might provide in the way of comfort and material wealth, and for however it might serve their plan to convert all benighted peoples to a belief in Him. That done, the earth would be abandoned. A rapturous departure, an empty warehouse.

I'm glad the salmon have returned in force this year. Their indefatigable determination always lifts me. Last year, I took my infant grandson for the first time to watch them spawn in front of the house. We walked down through the woods to the edge of the river with his grandmother and mother. He sat speechless and intent on my lap while I told him what I knew—to him, my talk must have been only a kind of desultory birdsong. I took him again this year to the same spot, again with his grandmother and mother. We watched the female fish, some the length of my leg and nearly the girth, churn up gravel and shape their nests, while the males streaked furiously across the flats toward other males, warning them away, their dorsal and caudal fins slitting the surface of the water.

I want to bring him here every year. I'm reaching out in an indecipherable language, I know, but last fall I explained the idea of 'dedication' to him anyway, that even though many of the fish are wounded, missing chunks of pale flesh along their spines and missing membrane from their abraded tails, even though their heads are cratered with spots of decay, the chinooks are laying and fertilizing the eggs.

The boy, a few days shy of fifteen months, lay still as a nesting bird in the crook of my arm. We watched the fish, our faces dappled by sunlight glinting on the river. The limbs of maple, ash, and cottonwood stirred in a half breeze. Then my grandson reached for the portable phone in my shirt pocket, placed there so I'd be sure not to miss a call from his father. He held it without looking at it, and then flung it into the river. ☐

GRANTA

AIRDS MOSS

Kathleen Jamie

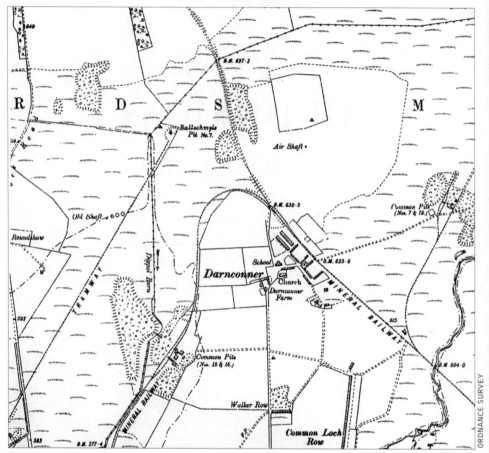

Darnconner as a pit village, from the Ordnance Survey of 1897

If you were minded to visit Airds Moss—and I wouldn't discourage it because anywhere else and it would be in a tourist guide, and it's interesting, if you've a taste for ambivalent places—you could turn off the lorry-laden A70 a few miles west of Powharnal opencast mine, and follow the B-road which links the farms on the moor's edge.

Lowland Scotland, and especially the western part of it, is not a place usually associated with unpeopled landscapes. We have the Highlands for that, and the Lowlands are often considered an unfortunate place you must drive through to reach the wild remotes. But Airds Moss is pretty much undisturbed. It's what is called 'low-altitude blanket bog', and it plateaus off at 600 feet to form a triangle between the diverging valleys of two westward-flowing rivers, the Bellow Water and the young river Ayr, from which it takes its name. It has seen human escapades, of course—a memorial at the moss's eastern edge marks a seventeenth-century Covenanters' skirmish, and there's a twentieth-century forestry plantation. Between these two interruptions, however, there was coal.

Airds Moss sits at the edge of the east Ayrshire coalfield. When coal and ironstone were discovered here, and the first pits sunk in the 1850s, the population began quickly to grow. Railways were built, whole villages grew at the moss's western fringe, generations lived and died. The coal lasted for a long century, and its villages too, but you have to look hard for them now.

I went there on a clear day in early March, leaving the A70 and crossing the Bellow Water, which means descending into a gloomy ravine and passing under a three-arched stone bridge. The bridge is just a crumbling relic now; the railway it carried is long gone. A hundred years ago it would have borne ironstone and coal to the town of Lugar, where the blast furnaces were.

After the river was crossed, the road climbed on to the wide expanse of open moor, which to me was so surprising that I pulled into the first passing place and got out of the car. I hadn't expected anything so rural—rural, but not unfrequented. My lay-by wasn't too bad, there was only a shattered windscreen still contained in its rim, but down the road other lay-bys were strewn with busted tellies and beer cans and bin bags disgorging rags.

I strolled down the road for a while, letting the silence settle in my ears. Overhead flew a party of peewits, so that was a bonus. A hundred yards over the moor stood a brick-built shed with an arched roof which made me think of a temple, rather than a leftover from another dismantled railway. But something about it, and the arched bridge I'd passed beneath, was arousing in me an old memory. Yes, I thought, of course, I have been here before. When I was wee, in a Ford Anglia, with my dad. Two or three times a year we'd come to Ayr, my parents' native place, to visit grannies. We'd travel across the moors by the same A70, down through Muirkirk and Lugar and Cumnock to arrive at the coast, there to be exclaimed over and served high teas. But my dad would always contrive to escape, to take an afternoon away 'on the skite', as my mother called it, which for him meant exploring railways. He'd leave the family and take himself into the countryside, stick his hands in his trouser pockets and saunter along railway tracks to see what locomotives were lying in what sheds and sidings. Sometimes, if I pleaded, he'd take me along too. We must have come up here in pursuit of colliery engines, steamy and black as the Earl of Hell's waistcoat, but that was nearly forty years ago. Now, the mines and their railways are no more.

The reason I stopped was, Airds Moss looked like forever. A wide, silent forever of pale, winter-brown moor. I hadn't expected that. There was no wind to worry the moor grass which, apart from the patch of commercial forestry, visible as a green square in the middle distance, lay as it must have done for 10,000 years. Aside from the old railways and the bings, I mean.

I spread the Ordnance Survey map on the bonnet. It showed plenty of bings hereabouts, little pocks with jagged teeth, but it called them by the more polite English word *tip*. *Bing* is a peculiarly Scots word. From the lay-by here, I could count four eruptions out on the moor, marking where coal and ironstone pits had been. They were dark heaps slowly being colonized by grass and scrubby hawthorn, and each was served by a track from the road but the tracks had been blocked with huge boulders and the track-ends were full of dumped rubbish. But at the foot of one range of bings was a small shining loch. A nameless loch, according to the map, so maybe it wasn't very old, but it was holding a fair number of birds. I got out the binoculars and was leaning against the car looking at a party of whooper swans when, to my surprise, a male hen-harrier glided into view. He was hunting low over the marsh and I followed him until, with a single wing-beat, he vanished behind the bings. Now that was a turn-up for the books. Hen harriers and busted tellies; a liminal place, the edge of the moor.

My great-great-grandmother on my mother's side was a girl called Maggie Rowan and I have a soft spot for her, based on nothing but her sylvan name, though I bet she was a tough cookie. She first turns up in 1881 as a sixteen-year-old mill-girl in nearby Catrine, one of the eight children of a labourer. In 1890 she married a local coal miner, James Stirling, himself a miner's son, and promptly produced John, my great-grandfather.

Though they did their courting hereabouts, on the edge of Airds Moss, both Maggie and Jim were Irish—we were all migrants once— brought over as children when their parents joined the droves of Irish workers piling into Scotland. They were sinking pits quickly then, populations were growing fast, but still more labour was needed and in 1870 the mine owners, Bairds & Co, advertised in the Irish papers. Some migrants were Catholic and famine-driven, some were Protestants with ancestral links to Ayrshire, and over they sailed, bringing their families and sectarianism with them.

My mother is ambivalent about her forebears, and certainly doesn't volunteer much. In her view the past is probably best forgotten, and ours is not the kind of family that tells, or even reads, stories. A Presbyterian distrust of the idle fancy, I suppose. My father has never, to my knowledge, been to a theatre or even read a novel. My mother reads thrillers but is not much interested in the shapings and workings of fiction. The last time the subject of her family came up, she just said, 'Ach, they were all miners,' and reached again for the TV remote. Her tone, as ever, was poised exactly between contempt and pride.

But I had names, and Ordnance Survey maps which give less detail with every new edition, and copied from Dale Love's informative *History of Auchinleck* a 1900 sketch map which showed this area as a populous warren of miners' rows—their mean little terraced houses—and railways, pitheads, stables and schools. The present maps show no more now than a square mile of moor edge with a few stalwart farms. When I told my dad I was thinking of going off on the skite to see what I could find of the old mining places, he warned me there might be nothing at all. He hasn't been up this way himself for a long time, there being no railways now, but I wanted to come anyway, because there's no such thing as 'nothing'. (He meant opencast mining. 'Nothing' as in 'blown to smithereens'.)

So the hen harrier and the quiet moor had left me feeling wrong-footed. Having read census returns and local history, my head was full of miners' rows and dark mines and Victorian squalor, and on the way I'd passed with trepidation the big opencast mines round Muirkirk, so I hadn't imagined sunlit moors and distant hills, the warmth in the spring sun. I drove on. Half a mile further, a farmer was leaning over a gate contemplating some sheep. The animals' field had been cleaved by a narrow, steep-sided cutting, as though a massive axe had fallen there. It could almost have been Neolithic, an ancient and mysterious earthworks. Then the road took a sudden dog-leg round a farm, and this was one of my way-signs, a jumping-off point, if possible, for the hike I wanted to make up on to the Moss.

The mining settlement to which Maggie Rowan had come as a bride was called Darnconner, and it appeared on the most recent map as a farm, the farthermost from the road, well up on to the moor. There were two or three possible approaches shown, but the map was ten years old, and as I turned the corner I was still steeling myself for an industrial-apocalyptic vision.

And there it was, to an extent. At the roadside, wide metal gates were lying open, and the remains of a sign which had once read danger no entry hung on a pole. Beyond the gates a rutted track led into an arena of rubble and rain-flooded craters, and heaps, like sand dunes, of some sort of mineral which was a curious duck-egg green, certainly not coal. (Later I was told it was fireclay.) Beyond this site, a couple of fields' length away, any access on to the moor was blocked by a long dark rampart of spoil, maybe thirty foot high, steep as the curtain wall of a medieval castle. I pulled into the site access and walked a few yards through the gates. It was orderly enough; bulldozed avenues, organized heaps of green stuff, old mangled cars stored in a pile of their own. The whole site was fenced off from the surrounding farmland by wire, nothing that couldn't be climbed, but it was hardly inviting and I didn't fancy floundering through the mud-filled ruts. Anyway, in the direction of Darnconner, like a monstrous mouldy loaf, rose the daddy of the old coal bings.

I scanned the site with binoculars, but it was eerily quiet. No rumbling diggers or men in hard hats—or so it seemed, but right on cue a yellow Caterpillar digger chuntered into view with its bucket raised. Back and forth it went, back and forth. I couldn't fathom what it was doing, and didn't like to watch, because at the gates a yellow sign, itself with an aggressive picture of binoculars, informed me that I, too, was being watched, and so the whole thing began to feel sinister, what with the moor, the stranger's car in the lay-by, the trash in the ditch, the lumbering machine. It might be the gateway to my ancestral homeland, but I didn't fancy it, and retreated to the car for another look at the maps, and plan B.

Pretty sure now that Darnconner hadn't been obliterated, merely obscured by bings, I drove a couple more miles on the narrow road, making a series of right turns to follow the moor's edge as it curved north-west. Then, just before the road entered a forbidding pine plantation, a more promising farm track set off on to the moor. I left the car, determined this time to walk regardless of obstructions and my own unease. It wasn't my patch, and the trash in the ditches felt like the territorial markers of a foreign tribe. Frankly, there was something not quite right about this landscape. Indians behind the bluff, that sort of feeling. But my papers were in order. Like a guarantee of safe passage or letters of introduction, I'd shoved into my pocket the family history I'd written out, the three generations of miners and miners' wives, and all their many children. I took that, the old sketch map and a camera and set off along a pitted track. It passed a couple of houses, but no one was about. Green and wavy like a distant sea, the fireclay site was half a mile ahead, sheep grazed the rough grass at the foot of more bings, a pair of thrushes hopped about on the railbed that ran from them. The sun shone, and somewhere nearby a curlew uttered its lovely, evocative call, and I began to relax.

But just for a minute. All at once, over the moor came an eldritch sound: *I'm forever blowing bubbles*, as though played on a vast heavenly xylophone. I stopped, looked around, but the sheep were grazing heedlessly, the thrushes hopped, the moor and the bings were as before. *Pretty bubbles in the air. I'm forever blowing bubbles...* Then it stopped. I heard it twice more that day, drifting over the countryside.

The track was potholed, but the holes had been repaired so it must have been in use; and it was muddy ('glaur' is the local word for this clinging mud). Where it met the fireclay site, access to the site was blocked by a large boulder and the track did an abrupt left turn and continued slightly uphill, flanked by bings and the fireclay dump on one side, and on the other by a long, ominous embankment. However, I could see buildings at the top of the track and they appeared almost dreamlike. It was hardly Manderley, but it was unsettling to approach an old house through an unnatural landscape of ramparts and bings. And it was the long embankment to my left, screening something from the track, where the strange atmosphere was coming from, where things were not quite right. I squeezed through the fence, climbed the bank and there was what my father had warned me of. All the land between this farm and the next had been gouged out. Opencast. A dirty great hole. But there were no machines, no workings, no noise. It too had been abandoned and was flooded with sullen green water which looked almost ashamed of itself, as if it couldn't help but gather there. It was like a loch, there were even a few ducks. The banks on the far side fell and rose, almost as nature intended, but they were old bings. 'Ye banks and braes,' I thought, 'how can ye bloom sae fresh and fair?' But 'I'm Forever Blowing Bubbles' had installed itself in my head instead.

The farm looked like a proper farm, a single-storey L shape with a steading and a tractor parked there. It was older than any of this intrusion, so had once enjoyed the sun and a southward view, but the big bing had put paid to that. In its yard two white geese came about me, hissing, and an elderly dog shambled up and began licking my hand. A light was on within the farmhouse; a car was parked outside. The farm was not without neighbours; behind fancy railings were two tidy red sandstone houses with decorative ridge tiles, out of place among the farm and bings, more like middle-class townhouses than the homes of miners or farmhands.

The geese kept a wary eye, the dog licked my hand. So far as I could see, the track continued through the farmyard, turned right beyond some stored caravans, and ended out on the open moor. It was out there, according to the old map, that the considerable Darnconner settlement had been, where all the folks rolled into my pocket had lived out their lives.

To read the census returns of 1881, 1891, and 1901 is to read, obviously, lists of names. Miners had big families and, like a dim torch shone into the gloomy interiors, the census illuminates for a moment the faces inside the cramped houses. I suppose the census enumerator must have walked this very track, knocking on door after vanished door and entering with a patient hand the names of all those people he found. In 1891, at No. 41 Darnconner were James and Agnes, my great-great-great-grandparents, with three grown-up children, and a grandson, too. Three generations in a room and kitchen, not to mention the lodger. Maybe they took in the lodger when their son Jim had married Maggie and established his own house a couple of doors along. Their names are noted in the same handwriting, along with their baby son's. Another baby was born a couple of years later but she died. By 1901, however, when the census man again came knocking, they'd filled the house with five children more. In the census, the adult men are 'coal miner', 'pitheadman', 'general labourer'; the women are 'miner's wife'. The census man had to note how many windows each dwelling had, and for every household he has drawn a single pen line—one.

My own knock was answered by a heavy-faced man in green farmer's overalls. He spoke a robust Ayrshire Scots, and though he was quite elderly, he retained some of his youthful stature. Aye, he said, this was the right place, and aye, he recognized the family name, there had been folk of that name here until the end, that is, until after the Second World War, when the last pits had closed and the opencast came. The old man had been born here, so he'd seen a lot of change. Twenty-six pits there had been up here, at one time or another. As one was worked out, another would be sunk, it was like that.

The old farmer offered to show me where the rows had been, so he took a stick and came out into the yard and, with the old dog following and the geese at a watchful distance, we walked together round the back of the farm, pausing to look at the two sandstone townhouses, both with mature trees growing around them. One he said had been the manse, though the church is long demolished, and the other had been the schoolteacher's house. There were a number of caravans parked up around the steading, a whole row of them covered in tarpaulins and backed against a brick wall under some sycamore trees. Maybe storing caravans for winter was a way for the farmer to make a few bob. I mean, folk would hardly come here for their holidays.

I say that, but as soon as we were behind the farm where neither the fireclay nor the opencast site could be seen, I felt the same astonishment at the sight of the open moor of dun-coloured grasses and moss, warming into spring under a huge blue sky. It looked as though we would walk out on to the moor, but at the gate the farmer stopped and with his stick, pointed to two shrubs growing side by side a short distance out on the Moss.

'See thon twa trees?' he said.

I nodded.

'That's whaur the raws were.'

'That's it?' I said.

'That's it. And see thon brick wa?'—This time he turned to point behind us, he meant the wall the caravans were parked against.

'Well, that's a' that's left o' them.'

'Do you mind if I have a look?'

'Not at a'. There's been a few folk, ower the years, come out to see the place.'

By 1913 the miners were growing militant. In that year two union men, Thomas McKerrell and James Brown, made a tour of all the miners' settlements in Ayrshire and compiled a trenchant and sardonic report on the housing conditions they found. They went to nearly sixty places but, being stuck up on the wet moor, Darnconner was among the worst. My great-great-grandparents, Maggie and Jim, their children, Jim's mother and siblings and cousins were among the tenants the union men found here, nigh on 400 of them, living among 'stinking refuse strewn about' and the 'glaur' that, because of the want of pavements, lay inches deep at the doors. Keeping clean amid glaur and ash and coal-dust would have been the womens' bane, but the mine owners had provided 'not a single washhouse for all these residents'. They had boilers for washing, but 'whoever erected them forgot to build a house over them, and the women have to do their washing in the open air'. As for latrines, that was a joke. A mere eleven closets had been provided and 'none had a door, so owing to the want of privacy they cannot be used by females or grown up persons. The floors of the closets are littered with human excrement.'

As the farmer and the old dog made their way back to their house, I stood between two caravans looking at the brick wall that had been the back wall of a row of houses, each not much bigger then the caravans stalled here now. 'The coal houses are so dilapidated several tenants keep their coals beneath their beds.' You have to wonder, with yourself and your husband, your five or six children, and coal beneath the bed, where in God's name do you put the lodger?

The sunshine had enticed gnats from their hiding places and they danced in throngs above the tussocks of moor grass. I jumped clump to clump, trying to avoid the mossy hollows, across the place where most of the miners' rows had been, till I reached an old railbed which, being made of clinker and raised a little, was drier underfoot than the surrounding moor, and I walked along it a way. A spur off the railbed led to the inevitable bing, which supported enough scant grass to allow a couple of sheep to graze and they went bounding off as I climbed on to its summit. My foot slipped and released a few flakes of coal slag, so I put them in my pocket, with a notion to take them home to my mother. The little elevation, twenty-five feet or so, afforded a view of the whole hushed and windless moor and its plantations. Impossible to imagine that folk didn't come out here for a walk on a summer's evening. I was trying to imagine the arrival of the union men, perhaps by train, and how news of their visit would have spread. They might have met Maggie Rowan, mill-girl turned miner's wife, leaning against her door-jamb in a pinny and telling them just what she thought of the excrement and glaur she struggled against. She was forty-seven then, but I doubt she was able to speak because she was already ill, and died just three weeks after. Her husband managed on for a few more years until his miner's lungs got the better of him, and he died here too.

Airds Moss tilted away east and south, to where the Bellow Burn ran, and a mute parade of lorries travelled the distant A70. I could see Powharnal Opencast as long black terraces cut at the hill's foot. My dad says they're thinking of reopening one of the disused railways to serve it. That's how it's done now, opencast. The old pits here were just that, pits sunk 180 feet down into the ground. When one was exhausted, it would be abandoned, another would be sunk a quarter mile away. Above the opencast mine the land rose solemnly into distant, rounded hills, pale after the winter, some still with snow on their north-facing slopes. Up on the hilltops, turning slowly and with no hint of irony, were wind turbines.

The union men had recommended only one thing: a closure order. I don't suppose they had bulldozers in 1913, but that's what they meant. Away with the mean, damp, cramped houses and the ashpits and middens and doorless, unprivate privies. Away with the disease, excrement and glaur. Decent workers' houses provided at fair rent by the council, not the mine owners, that's what they were agitating for.

I doubt they would believe the place a century on; I was having trouble believing it myself. The mines themselves away, and the miners too, leaving no trace bar the grassed-over bings and old railbeds. Where the 'horrible place of Darnconner' had been, with its hundreds of homes, I could see, if I squinted, tiny filaments of cobweb wafting from the moor grass. Where there had been pitheads, clanking trains, and all those reeking chimneys, there was nothing but a sweep of obliviating moor, and a twittering lark. Just two small bare trees marked the place. Hazels, I think, not rowans.

During the First World War my great-grandfather John Stirling bade farewell to his recently widowed father and his grandmother and sisters and headed off with the Royal Artillery. He was twenty-five and already a widower himself. He left spoil-heaps, trenches and glaur, so if he actually got to the front perhaps it wasn't as alien to him as it was to lads from parishes of ploughing matches and harvest home. John had a better war than many; he returned intact and with a new wife and a child, my grandmother. If he brought them up here on to the moors, to the filthy rows, it was only for a short while. These mines were in decline anyway. Belatedly, after the next war, the union men had their wish, the miners' rows were cleared, and the last tenants rehoused in new council schemes in Auchinleck. Then the Coal Board dispensed with the niceties of sending men below ground in cages, and stripped the earth back, dumped the clay aside, gouged out the coal, and left the hole behind.

I scrambled down off the bing and followed the railbed just a bit farther and discovered that the land on the north-west of the moor is being restored. The slow remedial work of nature, a thread of moss here, a crumb of windblown earth there, is being hastened by human intervention. The old railbeds had become paths, new gates were installed, friendly signs announced a forest, which was a tad

NO POSTAGE
NECESSARY
IF MAILED
IN THE
UNITED STATES

BUSINESS REPLY MAIL
FIRST-CLASS MAIL   PERMIT NO. 115   JACKSON, MS

POSTAGE WILL BE PAID BY ADDRESSEE

GRANTA
P O BOX 23152
JACKSON MS 39225-9814

NO POSTAGE
NECESSARY
IF MAILED
IN THE
UNITED STATES

BUSINESS REPLY MAIL
FIRST-CLASS MAIL   PERMIT NO. 115   JACKSON, MS

POSTAGE WILL BE PAID BY ADDRESSEE

GRANTA
P O BOX 23152
JACKSON MS 39225-9814

premature but around yet more old bings many trees had indeed been planted, protected by plastic tubes. The tubes stuck up from the earth as if venting something below ground. There must be tunnels down there still, 180 feet down in the utter dark. The same tree-planting treatment is proposed, if I understood the farmer right, for the fireclay site—to spread a depth of sewage sludge over it and so bring the soil's fertility up, then plant willows—the unlovely term is 'biomass'—which can in turn be cropped as fuel for power stations. Some query the wisdom of using sewage sludge, for fears of pollution and run-off. When the Union men described Darnconner as 'a sea of human excrement', they spoke truer than they knew.

John went to work at Garallan pit, near Cumnock, where his wife Isabel bore another six children. My mother remembers her grandfather coming home and setting his carbide lamp on the mantelpiece. Over six foot, tall for a miner. He died, too breathless to walk, not long before I was born.

The farmer was waiting for me in the yard, but I didn't know what to say, I couldn't decide if it was an appalling place to live or not too bad, considering.

I hazarded, 'Some place to live—funny to think of all those folk here...' but he made a non-committal sort of sound.

'When you read about the housing...' I said.

'Aye, the housing... But mind you, when the last were sent down to Auchinleck, some of the auld anes didnae want to go. And there's been a few have wanted their ashes scattered here, whaur the auld raws were.'

I was thinking, as I walked back down to the car, that if I had a gift for the reconstructed landscapes of fiction I could write an epic novel with an embossed cover, a saga-of-three-generations of miners, migration, poverty, sectarianism, moors and marriage, glaur and war, militancy and the black lung. I could call it *The Cry of the Curlew*. Or maybe *Blowing Bubbles*, because when I reached the car that weird dislocated tune was wafting through the air again. It must have been an ice-cream van touring the housing schemes of Auchinleck. But I couldn't write that stuff. It's too sure of itself. Too...unequivocal.

A child's scooter was lying on the roadside verge but it was hard to tell if it was waiting for the school bus to deliver its owner home, or whether it, too, had just been dumped. I suppose you can understand it, in a way, why folk go to all the effort to cart their knackered sofas and tellies away up here—some old memory of the moor as the place of tips, abandoned workings, closure orders and all that's best forgot. My mother's attitude. I'd taken a few photographs of Darnconner to show her, because I knew she'd be interested despite herself. I'm a poor photographer, though, and the photos won't show much of her forebears' short lives and toil; just a farmhouse and some bings, and a stretch of empty moor. □

GRANTA

FANTASTIC MR FOX
Tim Adams

On November 19, 2004 the British government passed its Hunting Act into law. The Act criminalized anyone who hunted a fox (or a deer or a mink) with a pack of dogs. A pack of dogs was defined as any number of dogs greater than two. Two hounds could still be used to 'flush out' a fox (or a deer or a mink) providing that it was a menace to the 'livestock, game and wild birds, crops, growing timber, fisheries or the biological diversity of an area'. The fox (or deer or mink) would then have to be shot as soon as was reasonably possible. Other mammals, notably rats, were not accorded this protection, and any animal could still be hunted using a falcon. A proposal to offer a free vote on hunting had formed part of the Labour Party's manifesto in 1997, but the debates that preceded the drafting of the Act, had, over the course of the ensuing seven years, taken up 275 hours, or well over a month, of Parliamentary time. To gain its acceptance, the government had been forced to employ the rarely used Parliament Act to defeat the opposition of the House of Lords.

1. The hunters and the hunted

On Saturday February 19, 2005, a day after the Hunting Act came into force, I was standing beside a man named Aubrey Thomas looking over a wall at some of the 14,000 acres of land that form the Englefield estate in Berkshire, fifty miles west of London. Aubrey Thomas had been waiting thirty-two years to be here this particular misty morning. While he had been waiting he had been arrested more than a hundred times, he had been shot at, run over, beaten up, chased through a forest by a man with a chainsaw, and, once, thrown off a bridge at Dartmouth in Devon. He used to wonder how he would feel on the first day of a legal ban against hunting foxes with dogs. Sometimes he had imagined himself sitting on a hedge somewhere, swigging champagne, toasting frustrated crimson-faced huntsmen, but now this morning had come around, he did not feel any of that, really. Instead he was doing what he had done just about every hunting season Saturday for the whole of his adult life. He was chasing men, who were chasing foxhounds, who were, maybe, chasing foxes.

Can you run? Aubrey asked me, looking me up and down somewhat doubtfully.

I thought so. Though certainly it was dependent on how far.

Sometimes we do about fifteen miles, he suggested, brightly. Often around ten. He kept in shape, he explained, running marathons. They took him three hours. But a marathon was nothing really to chasing a mounted fox-hunt on foot all day, because it was often over ploughed fields and through hedges, among big horses, your feet clogged in mud, starting and stopping, sprinting and jogging.

I looked out across the open country all around us, the weak sun casting oblongs of light over distant copses, and briefly regretted my lapsed membership at the gym. Right, I said.

Aubrey is a tall man, shaven-headed with small pointed features, shoulders bunched forward as if for confrontation, long-limbed. Unlike most hunt saboteurs, who wore combat clothes and camouflage and balaclavas, he was wearing a sweatshirt and loose canvas trousers and running shoes. He set off at a loping jog across the rough field, without another soul in sight, on a hunch that the hounds were not far away. And I ran after him, stumbling in big boots on the pitted ground, asking breathless questions. I wanted to know what might become of the saboteurs now they had nothing, theoretically, to sabotage. Aubrey, who had done this longer than anyone, was best placed to tell me. All I had to do was keep up.

This chase started for him when he was seventeen years old, he explained, and only today did it look like stopping. In common with most of the saboteurs I had spoken to, Aubrey went out the first time for a laugh. A friend of his had an idea that it might be fun to go and disrupt a hunt, but the friend could not drive. Aubrey had just got his licence. They were the only two protestors that day and the hunt, in Surrey, was one of the most formidable in the country. On the journey down, a fox had run in front of Aubrey's car, which he thought at the time was odd, and which he has since come to think of as fate. They ran all day, and eventually they caught up with the men who had caught up with the hounds who had caught up with a fox that had disappeared into a drainage ditch at the side of the main A23.

Aubrey and his friend stood by while the terrier-men, the farmhands and village men with dogs who accompanied the hunt, dug down for an hour to trap the fox. All the time the men were digging, and sending in their dogs to engage with the fox underground, Aubrey was suggesting to them that they did not have to do this, that they should stop, that this wasn't any fun for anyone. Eventually, the terrier-men got to the fox and caught it in a net. 'We then watched,' Aubrey said, 'as one of them killed it with a garden fork. It did not die straight away, of course. It wriggled on the fork like a worm. I looked at this bloke, and said: "You have made a big mistake there. I will make it my business to make sure you never do that again."'

Every Saturday during the hunting seasons for the next three years, Aubrey went down to Surrey, often alone, and did everything he could think of to save foxes. He signed himself up to work part-time as a whipper-in, a dog-handler at a local beagle pack, so he could learn to control hounds with a hunting horn. He can remember well the thrill of bringing the pack of hounds for the first time away from the huntsmen and across the field towards him, a skinhead Pied Piper, with mounted hunters and terrier-men on quad bikes and hangers-on in Range Rovers in distant, outraged, comical pursuit. Once, with a basset-hound pack, he ran alone with the dogs for sixteen miles, over the hills and far away, stopping only when it was dark, when he got a friend to tell the huntsman where his hounds were so he could collect them in his van.

Aubrey widened his territory from Surrey to include most of the hunts in the south of England, from Kent to the West Country, and helped to put together a tactical manual—of laying false scents, of horn blowing and havoc—for other saboteur groups. He made forays into the devout hunting country of Wales and the north of England—the places, he says, where you went in a car and thought you would come back in a coffin. He went alone to the Lake District, where the legendary John Peel, huntsman of Helvellyn and Blencathra in the first half of the nineteenth century, had exemplified the dedication of the Cumbrian packs, remembered in the lines of the ballad 'D'ye ken John Peel'. On arrival, he was held over a mountainside with a sheer 300-foot-drop, as it was suggested to him that he should not bother coming up again.

The more often he went out, the more his strategies evolved. Aubrey got a pilot's licence and, on occasion, took a plane and followed hunts from the air, radioing down to his fellow saboteurs the exact location of hunters and hounds and fox. Mostly though, he relied on a mixture of instinct and absolute stubbornness. And, as I was beginning to understand, stamina.

I had met up with Aubrey that morning, along with the rest of the dozen or so saboteurs, at a business park, just off the motorway near Reading, in Berkshire. Like the hunts they follow, the saboteurs had, over the years, developed their own rituals. They had grown up with all this, and they arrived in ones and twos from different parts of the county, and exchanged stories about nights before and the day ahead, and got changed out of the back of cars.

They made a curious group. Pulling on their paramilitary jackets were a couple of care workers and university students, a lecturer and a doctor. There were nearly as many women as men, in a range of ages from twenty to seventy. The eldest, Jerry Esterly, a deep-voiced jovial man, with a bald head and a white moustache, had flown in from Seattle, where he worked as a private detective, preparing defence mitigation for people on death row.

'I see it as part of the same thing,' he explained to me, 'valuing life, and the right of any individual being to live out his life as well as the universe deems he can do.' I nodded. Jerry had been coming over here for years to secure the fulfilled existence of foxes and had been held for breaches of the peace in British jails in places that he had never heard of. He would not have missed this 'last go round' for anything.

When they had their clothes sorted, all the saboteurs piled into a couple of four-wheel drives, one of them a camouflaged Land-Rover. For this, the first day of the rest of their lives—when they had, theoretically, stopped being vilified 'antis' and started being respectable 'monitors', collecting evidence of illegal fox hunting—Aubrey had chosen their hunts carefully. They would look in at the beagle pack at Sandhurst, the military academy, but first of all he wanted to see what was happening at the Vale of Aylesbury with Garth and South Berks Hunt, one of their regulars. Aubrey had dropped off the main group of saboteurs at the back of the Englefield estate, given by Queen Elizabeth I to her favourite Lord Walsingham for his support in persecuting Catholics in 1589, and now owned by his descendant Richard Benyon, who was standing as a Conservative candidate in the forthcoming election. Aubrey watched as the saboteurs wandered into the woods not far from Benyon's vast manor house in single file, as if on a school trip, and then drove around the estate trying to work out which way the hunt was headed.

When he was not trying to save foxes, Aubrey ran two businesses: a vegan chocolate factory, which supplied major supermarkets, and an international freight company. The latter, he explained, was problematic because he tried to run it ethically: he wouldn't deal with America, for a start, 'because of Guantánamo Bay'.

Aubrey would interrupt his talk from time to time to pull over into a lay-by or a farm track and set off at a run across the fields, with me in pursuit. What he noticed most of all was the quiet. On a proper hunting day there would be the cry of the hounds. But today all you could hear was birdsong and the distant hum of cars. From time to time we ran into hunt supporters, and terrier-men—the traditional enemy. 'Having a good day?' Aubrey enquired. And then, to me: 'He and I have battered each other horribly in the past, but what's the point now?'

We drove on, and then, around a bend, suddenly found ourselves as scruffy extras in a scene that relatively few people in Britain have witnessed first-hand, but which nevertheless is profoundly familiar. The main field of maybe a hundred horses and riders, many in red coats, stood against the horizon, the horses snorting in the damp air. There are around 18,000 people actively involved in hunting foxes in Britain as compared with, say, 232,000 crown-green bowls players, but no one born in this country could fail to recognize this picture—if only from the huntsman's propaganda of place mats and pub signs and junk-shop prints. Aubrey wandered into mid-frame, incongruously, asking the whereabouts of the hounds.

'We sold 'em!' said a hunt supporter. 'You satisfied?' (There is something about sitting on a horse, in hunting pinks, that seems—as every huntsman's favourite author R. S. Surtees observed in his *Jorrocks* books—to require you to speak only in exclamations.)

'What are your lot going to do next, Aubrey?' shouted a large woman on a chestnut horse. 'We've seen you in your ABOLISH ANGLING T-shirts!'

'You haven't seen me in one,' Aubrey said.

This exclamatory impulse was further excited when, from across the road the pack of foxhounds appeared and the horses set off at a gallop, with a certain amount of restrained whooping, and we followed, occasionally sharing narrow paths with the riders, Aubrey in his easy stride, me running full tilt.

A good part of hunt sabbing involved being lost in wild places. The saboteurs had maps, but they were not much use. The roads around here were often estate tracks, and once you had followed a hunt for a short while it was easy to lose your bearings. Aubrey talked of a few occasions in the early days, before mobile phones, where he had been left on his own, in woods miles from any village, with dark coming down, and had to find his way home. Like the hunters he followed—and despite his protestations that it was just 'a job'—the hunt for him had been a weekly adventure, fuelled in part by such stories. On this occasion, though, and perhaps from now on, the stories looked like having no satisfactory ending. The Vale of Aylesbury with Garth and South Berks Hunt had no intention of breaking the new law visibly, and after an hour or so of chasing Aubrey—somewhat to my relief—made a call on his mobile: abandon this and do the beagles.

On the way to Sandhurst in my car, Jerry, the Seattle detective, and Aubrey told stories about foxes saved and foxes lost. They recalled a particular pacifist saboteur in Oxford who, in the event of violent confrontation, always rolled up in a ball in the woods and got beaten by terrier-men. This happened most weekends. Aubrey suggested it was all like that in the early days, when the saboteurs were mostly hippies. He remembered an otter hunt in the Seventies when a saboteur blew a hunting horn and it was taken off him by a huntsman who then broke his jaw with an otter pole. The rest of the saboteurs sat down in silent protest. Aubrey recalled evaluating that approach. 'Next season I chucked the hippy stuff out of the window. I would never start anything. But if you hit me from then on, I was going to hit you back.'

At Sandhurst, we drove around the kennels, in what felt to me like a debatably cavalier fashion, given that there were three of us, and this was private military land, full of angry huntsmen doubling as army officers. Fortunately there were no beagles or beaglers in evidence so we carried on to Hampshire, to a hunt that Aubrey had been sabotaging for nearly three decades.

The further we went the more this seemed like a typically English day out: muddy and frustrating and dogged. There are fox-hunts in many other countries—in most parts of the former British Empire, but also, notably, in France and the United States. In France the fox is just one of ninety species that are hunted, and though there are protests, they involve letter writing rather than running about in woods. In America, there were maybe 200 fox-hunts, Jerry told me, but things were a little different there: no terrier-men, for a start, so if the fox goes to ground it is left alone. Hunting with dogs has been banned in Germany and Switzerland, too, but Britain, Jerry suggested, led the world in its concern for the welfare of foxes.

'Excellent,' I said.

This sense of fair play did not, in his experience, always extend to the welfare of hunt saboteurs. He recalled the first time he was held in jail, not far from here, after being arrested. He told the police officer that he was a vegan and the next morning a little slit in the prison door opened, with his breakfast: a metal tray on which there were three frozen potatoes. 'I thought, Jesus, Jerry, maybe you should reassess your life. My girlfriend was in Hawaii at that time, on holiday, and here I was in prison in a wintry English village trying to defrost potatoes by rubbing them in my hands.'

As he and Aubrey laughed at this I tried to work out exactly why you would spend all your life trying to save animals from being killed by a pack of dogs rather than being killed by two dogs and a man with a gun. As a very crude shorthand for the explanations Aubrey and Jerry offered, I wrote the words *Maoism* and *minkhounds*, in my notebook at a set of traffic lights, but that did not really get it. 'It is part of a continuum,' Jerry said. 'If you start valuing foxes—or rats— then I believe you are going to start valuing children in Iraq more, too.'

Then Aubrey suggested we turn off the road. The afternoon was losing its shape and like any hunt leader it was his responsibility to give his followers the sense of an ending, to make the long day and the run and the hanging around in fields worthwhile. We ducked down a road near Moundsmere Manor, another monumental country house, this time designed on the principles of Hampton Court, which was home to several generations of the joint master of the Hampshire Hunt, Mark Andreae. There could, Aubrey suggested halfway down this single-track road, be an element of risk in this: there had been 'a bit of a scrap' with the terrier-men from this hunt a fortnight before. As Aubrey was describing this battle we drove into a farmyard full of farmhands and hunt supporters.

In this enclosed space, Aubrey was recognized immediately, and three men standing on a quad bike blocked our exit. A group of a dozen or so large men then gathered around the car. I had recently been reading my daughter Roald Dahl's book *Fantastic Mr Fox*, about terrier-men who fail to outwit a family of foxes. Looking at the three men in front of the car, standing on their bike, the words of a little rhyme my daughter had enjoyed chanting at bedtime came into my head, not entirely helpfully:

> Boggis and Bunce and Bean
> One fat, one short, one lean,
> These horrible crooks
> So different in looks
> Were none the less equally mean.

Sitting next to me, Aubrey looked straight ahead. 'Open the windows,' he suggested, 'otherwise they will smash them.'

The real life Boggis and Bunce and Bean hadn't had a sniff of blood on the fox-hunt all day, and if the government had anything to do with it, they never would again. Who should now have arrived in their farmyard but the man who had for the last three decades made it his life's work to spoil their fun, the man who only two weeks ago had, apparently, been doing a little hunt-ban victory dance on the impossibly green grass outside Moundsmere Manor, home of their hunt master. A man who might well have helped to put half of them out of work.

I opened the windows and Boggis or Bean or Bunce reached in quickly and took my car keys. Then there was a short moment of calm when everyone in the farmyard considered his options. No one, not the terrier-men, not Aubrey, and not me, could quite believe his luck. In this moment of silence, I found myself getting out of the car and mumbling something about being a journalist.

He's not a journalist, someone said, pointing at Aubrey.

No, I said, but he is with me.

While the men considered the implications of this remark, and traded threats, and studied in somewhat bemused fashion the British Library readers' pass I had proffered in lieu of a press card, three things happened. An attempt was made to open Aubrey's door and pull him out. The camouflaged Land-Rover containing the rest of the saboteurs came crashing into the farmyard, the driver being pulled through its open door by a couple of hunt supporters and, out of nowhere, the police arrived.

Then, I had the sense, it was all just like old times. The saboteur women screamed murderous abuse at the terrier-men while the terrier-men tried to knock video cameras from the women's hands, there were scuffles and a good deal of debate about who started what, and vicious, well-rehearsed arguments about the bloody business of killing foxes. I wandered around asking if anyone happened to have seen my car keys.

Eventually the police sorted the two tribes into different parts of the yard: men in green waxed coats on one side, saboteurs in combat jackets on the other. My keys miraculously reappeared and, under Aubrey's instruction we set off, watching our mirrors, to meet up in a pre-arranged hotel car park, where everyone talked at once. There was a sense of occasion in the air as some of the saboteurs remembered the importance of the day, and realized how much they might miss all this, the crisp winter afternoon, the cross-country runs, the sense of purpose in saving foxes' lives, the self-righteous adrenalin of confrontation. Someone handed round a bag of home-made muffins.

A saboteur who had a hunting horn around his neck, which had been 'donated' to him by a huntsman at a neighbouring hunt, was looking somewhat mournful, knowing perhaps that things might never be quite as good again.

He must have been pleased that this was all over, though, that the ban was in place?

'In a way,' he said, 'but this has been my life. I'm not sure what happens next.'

2. The perfect day

There is some debate among zoologists as to whether the British Red Fox is a subspecies of its own. Darwin's most passionate disciple, Thomas Huxley, in a fifty-page treatise on the classification of dogs, in 1880, split his canids into two groups: the alopecoids (true foxes) and the thooids (hunting dogs, wolves). The former tended to be loners; the latter were commonly pack animals (it was in this divide that fox-hunters found their sport). Huxley formally classified the fox native to Britain as *Vulpes vulpes crucigera*, distinct in its head size and dentition from the common North American and European foxes, plain old *Vulpes vulpes*. Recent DNA work has questioned this distinction, however.

There are around 240,000 red foxes in Britain, a number that has remained nearly constant since the first population surveys of the 1960s. Foxes can live to be ten years old, though their average life expectancy in Britain is about two years. They eat pretty much anything, from mice and game birds to nuts and berries. A few foxes will attack lambs. A rural fox's territory is generally around two square miles, and there is a good deal of evidence to suggest that the population is self-regulating (during the recent foot-and-mouth crisis, when there was no hunting, the fox population remained static). About 25,000 foxes have been killed most years by fox-hunting. Around 100,000 are killed on the roads. In an NOP poll in the year 2000, the fox was voted the nation's favourite land mammal.

The first time I saw a fox I was five years old. I was in a tiny cottage in Warwickshire and the fox, as I remember it, was running around the little sitting room, about a foot off the ground, as if on a wall of death. The cottage belonged to an old friend of my Dad's who, in retrospect, must have been undergoing some kind of midlife crisis. He had left his wife, given up his job in the car industry and come to live here as a poacher off the big estate up the road. One morning he had found a fox cub by the side of the road, only a day or two old, its mother nowhere to be seen. He had bottle fed it, walked it on a lead, kept it in the house, and here it was, running around the walls, looking for a way out like a goldfish in a bowl.

I was thinking about this fox while driving down to see Bob Collins, the huntsman at the Hampshire Hunt, where I had been so warmly greeted a week or so before. These days, you saw foxes in London all the time, walking among wheelie bins at dusk; I'd come downstairs early a few mornings last summer and seen a dog fox and his two cubs playing on my back lawn—we had eyed each other curiously—but still, none of these foxes had quite the memorable impact of that first one.

Bob Collins had also seen his first fox when he was five years old, though in his case it was a dead one—on his first hunt—and he'd had, in the custom of the time, his face smeared with the blood from its tail. Bob Collins's father was a farmer and a whipper-in with a hunt in the West Country. He took his two boys out early and neither of them had ever lost that scent of fox. Bob, now sixty, had been a huntsman all across England and Wales, for the last fifteen years at

Hampshire. His younger brother had recently become huntsman at the famous Quorn Hunt, in Leicestershire. On the day of the hunt ban the brother had been pictured on the front of the *Daily Telegraph* with tears rolling down his cheeks.

Having witnessed some of the dedication of the more extreme hunt opponents, I had wanted to get some proper understanding of what they had been protesting against. Talking to Aubrey and the other saboteurs, the name Bob Collins had come up several times. He was widely held to be the most worthy opponent, both of the fox and of themselves. He was, in Aubrey's terms, the best of a dead breed.

Reading about the history of hunting in Hampshire—in the letters of Jane Austen, who lived just up the road—and elsewhere, I had come across a note written by the poet Robert Southey about this part of the world in 1804, the year in which these kennels were bought by the Hunt. Even then, it seemed, the breed that Bob Collins represented was under threat. 'The fox-hunter,' Southey wrote, 'of the last generation was a character as utterly unlike any other in society, and as totally absorbed in his own pursuits, as the alchemist. His whole thoughts were respecting his hounds and horses; his whole anxiety, that the weather might be favourable for the sport; his whole conversation was of the kennel and stable, and of the history of his chases... But this race is now extinct, or exists only in a few families, in which the passion has so long been handed down from father to son, that it is become a sort of hereditary disease.'

Two hundred years later, if the Countryside Alliance and the 400,000 people who had marched in London to protest against the Hunting Bill were to be believed, Southey's diagnosis looked a little premature. Certainly there was good evidence for this hereditary disease in Bob Collins's cottage. Every inch of wall space was covered with pictures of favourite hounds, lovingly line-drawn, and of caricatures of foxes, wisecracking. There were fox key-rings and fox ornaments and fox vases, some ready for packing in piles of boxes. This last season of fox-hunting happened also to be Bob's retirement year. He was moving out to an estate house, that had been offered to him and his wife in the traditional way by a landowning hunt follower at a much reduced rent.

Propped next to the boxes were pictures of Bob in his hunting coat, on his strong horse, outside various stately homes including the palatial Moundsmere Manor, recently sold by the hunt master for nearly £7 million. There were also cartoons of the huntsman in his prime sailing over houses on Albert, the best chaser he ever owned, who could, he told me, jump the moon. In his little living room, he looked a bit diminished compared to the straight-backed man in these pictures; he walked with a limp from various falls, about three bad ones a year he reckoned, and particularly from a recent injury to his hip that now left him, after a day's riding, almost lame.

On the last day of hunting, Bob vowed never to get on a horse again if he could not hunt in earnest. Since the law had come into force there had been a series of drag hunts, by which the hounds follow an artificially prepared scent line, but Bob had stayed at home. 'I can't lie to the hounds. I tried this scent thing. But the good hounds knew. My best hound just ran behind my horse. We did the Thursday, which was the final day. I did the Saturday, and that was that.'

Ever since, he said, he had just been at a loss. 'I cannot describe it, just the emptiness of it. The sound of hounds running in a cover of woods—so spine chilling. It is what I have lived for.'

There are, as I knew, whole books dedicated to descriptions of this sound. My favourite, at least for enthusiasm, was the Victorian Charles Kingsley's. The author of *The Water Babies* began his account of a day's hunting with a little ode to the fox, 'Oh Reinecke, beautiful art thou of a surety, in spite of thy great naughtiness...' before wondering:

Art thou some fallen spirit, doomed to be hunted for thy sins in this life, and in some future life rewarded for thy swiftness, and grace, and cunning by being made a very messenger of the immortals? Who knows? Not I, I am rising fast to Pistol's vein. Shall I ejaculate? Shall I notify? Shall I waken the echoes? Shall I break the grand silence by that scream which the vulgar call the view-halloo call? It is needless; for louder and louder every moment swells up a sound which makes my heart leap into my mouth and my mare into the air...'

It was this sound, anyhow, that I imagined the old huntsman could hear as he sat at his dining table. And as he remembered it, he could not help himself crying.

It had, he said, collecting himself after a while, at least been a great last season. The young hounds had entered the pack perfectly. And they'd had a tremendous show of foxes. 'The keepers have not been quite so hard on them as usual, not shot as many, perhaps realizing the hounds were going so well. So we have killed over ninety foxes.'

His hounds, he said, were generally the last thing he thought about at night and the first thing he thought about in the morning. They woke him up by singing, at very first light, the whole pack chiming in together, a hundred of them. From then on he was with them, or planning for them, nearly all day. Each dog had its own name and its own character. Bob came up with these names, based on pedigree. It had been lovely, he said, working it all out. He got down his bloodline books, all neatly handwritten, the names and details of dogs entered at the left margin, bitches an inch in from the left. Every dog that had ever run with him was remembered here, and he still knew all of their qualities, and their failings.

That sense of structure apparent in the hound book informed everything about the life that Bob Collins had lived. He ran the hounds, he said, and the masters ran the country. By this he meant, strictly, the hunting country, but it might just as well have been the rest, too. Since he had been in hunt service, forty years, he had never had a cross word with any of his masters. And that sense of the orderly world of the hunt extended far beyond his yard. It included the most junior terrier-man and went right up to the future King of England, beside whom Bob had dined several times at huntsmen's lunches. 'I've also been to a few dos at the Beaufort Hunt,' he said, 'where Prince William and Harry bring along some tins of beer in plastic bags, same as anyone else.'

If it had not been for the outside world, this structure might have carried on forever. For Bob, the most visible sign that it had not had been the emergence of the saboteurs, who had insisted on bringing news from elsewhere to his door. 'We've had the antis here a lot,' he said. 'I personally believe they have no interest in the fox whatsoever. When I first arrived they did give me some stick. But over the years there have been a couple I have had some respect for. Aubrey Thomas in particular is one who really believes in what he is doing.'

Even Aubrey, though, always dragged the atmosphere of the hunt down a little. Still, Bob recalled, the only time that he had felt moved to violence against the saboteurs was the day his father died, four years ago. The master had asked him if he felt up to hunting that day, and he said he knew that it was what his father would have wanted. But the saboteurs, he said, must have heard of his news. By lunchtime they were standing at the side of the road as he was riding past, shouting about how some sad old huntsman had died in the West Country that night and did he know anything about it. If Bob had had something in his hand he would have lashed out, no doubt. 'Luckily,' he said, 'there were one or two policemen who knew what they were about, and immediately they heard this stuff they locked the saboteurs up.'

Overall though, he could not say that the antis had ruined things for him; they were just another thing to worry about when the wind was blowing and the scenting was hard. And, anyway, there had been more than enough magical days to make up for that nuisance.

Curious to have him describe this magic once again, I asked him if there was one day in particular, out of all the days, that had stood out for him.

His voice broke again as he described it. 'We had one day in Wales that I will never forget,' he said, 'up near Chepstow. The feelings you get as a huntsman when your hounds are running well are like nothing on earth. In the afternoon we ran for nine or ten miles as fast and true as an arrow, after a straight-necked fox, through the most beautiful country. When we got close to him it was pitch dark in this forest, and the hounds were streaming through the trees. We could see hardly anything, but I said to the master, we are going to kill this fox, any second now, Sir. He said: how do you know that? And I said I could hear it in the hounds' voices. Their tonguing had changed. It was complete darkness but they knew they were on to the fox and their voices went up again, and I knew they had him. You can't count a fox dead unless you have seen the body. It was eight o'clock at night and you could not see the hand in front of your face and the master said, we won't be finding this fox. He knew that once the hounds had killed they will tend to bury the body of the fox under leaves, and walk away. Anyway I had this one wonderful old hound, Relish, and I could just hear his voice over the noise, calling to me—a high bark—*oohoohooh*—and I went and found him in the dark, and he was there beside the dead fox, just nosing some leaves on to it.' In his cottage, Bob looked down for a moment, as if at the hound and the fox in the middle of the dark wood. 'It just felt like the end of a perfect day,' he said.

3. Hunting vicars

Anyone interested in the nature of the English character should set aside some time to read through the Burns Report into hunting with dogs. In the millennium year Lord Burns was invited by the Blair government to set up an inquiry in order to settle, once and for all, the question of whether hunting was unnecessarily cruel, and to consider the likely effects of a ban. In preparing its report, his committee invited interested parties to submit evidence, and to write further with any anecdotal material they considered relevant. What followed were hundreds of carefully collated observations by those for and, primarily, those against the ban. There were distraught vintners suggesting a fatal drop off in sherry sales, rural psychiatrists predicting a dramatic rise in male suicide, carnivorous libertarians quoting Gandhi, MBAs writing on behalf of lurchers, a vet named Baskerville misty-eyed at the skill of hounds, a petrol-station owner who feared the loss of fuel supply to knacker wagons, and a number of impassioned accounts of the particular joys, and ethical necessities, of ratting.

Nearly all of the authors of these submissions, imagining, presumably, that their work would be scrutinized by great legal minds, had a wild stab at a tone that might appeal to such an audience. The statements thus tended to lose themselves in dense footnotes and appendices; some occasionally caught the scent of an argument only to abandon it in a thicket of scientific jargon and emotional hyperbole. The more I read of them, though, the more I understood two things: that there were no rational or moral arguments for the killing of foxes by chasing them with hounds, on horseback; and that there was a small, but significant, body of people in rural England who believed that chasing foxes with hounds, on horseback, was not only an inalienable human right, but also the chief pleasure known to mankind, the denial of which would rob their lives of all meaning, purpose and clarity.

Far from clearing up the questions he had been asked to resolve, Lord Burns' conclusions, based on this evidence and long days of cross-examination of animal-welfare groups and hunt supporters, further compounded them. Both sides seized on the report as a moral victory, and Lord Burns' one legacy to the debate was a classic euphemism. Having considered all the evidence, his committee announced itself convinced that being hunted for hours on end and ripped apart by a pack of hounds 'seriously compromises the welfare of the fox'.

The Hunt Saboteurs Association, after suitably protracted internal debate, had decided not to cooperate with the Burns Report on the grounds that it believed the committee had a pro-hunt bias. As a result, the only long-standing saboteur to offer evidence was a man named Dave Wetton who supplied a handwritten account of the life and death of a particular fox killed by the terrier-men of the Surrey and Burstow Hunt in 1973, before ranging over related human cruelties in the Falklands War and Kosovo.

The word that most respondents to Lord Burns eventually fell back on when their scientific and ethical arguments tripped over each other, was tradition. Dave Wetton and his wife Cee, who had accompanied him in his saboteur activities for thirty-five years, represented a different but equally robust version of that word: they felt themselves part of an English tradition of imaginative dissent. I met them not far from their home in rural Kent.

If Aubrey Thomas was the great strategist and survivor of the hunt saboteurs' movement, then Dave and Cee Wetton formed part of its conscience and character. Dave Wetton had been connected with the League Against Cruel Sports for as long as he could remember. His life changed one afternoon in 1964 when he went out with a newly formed group from Brixham in Devon that was ruining otter hunts. That group had persuaded a few men from the Brixham fishing boats to become involved. 'The first scene I remember is this huge trawlerman, Shipman Evans, wading down a Devon stream with two smoke distress-flares going off in each hand to confuse the hounds. I thought: this is for me.'

When the original Devon group were beaten up by the otter men, and then bound over to keep the peace for a year, Dave Wetton and his friends moved the headquarters of the Hunt Saboteurs' Movement, of which there were maybe a dozen members, to Tooting in south London, where he lived with his mother. His Mum had taken his Gran away on holiday and they returned to find their terraced house painted with letters six feet high: HUNT SABOTEURS HQ.

Transport was the main problem. The saboteurs had a little Dormobile called Doris which, every weekend, they would coax up to Norfolk or down to Dorset mainly to disrupt otter hunts. They would lay aniseed and creosote along the river-banks, or dried blood, or if all else failed they would pee around gates and stiles.

The object of those days out was to save the lives of otters or foxes, but in their minds they were part of a wider global struggle against tyranny: Vietnam, the civil rights movement, women's liberation. They organized demonstrations against circuses, but their main focus was hunting. 'We were determined to upset the domination the hunters had over the countryside,' Dave said. 'We thought we would have it cracked in a couple of years.'

Wetton and his friends would advertise for supporters in the *Vegetarian*, and *Private Eye* and the *Melody Maker*. They felt their natural constituency was vegetarian rock and rollers with a sense of humour. They drew up a constitution, which had two central points: i) avoid harming the hounds or the horses in any way, and ii) if it comes to violence, run away.

In the early days they did not know quite what to expect. Sometimes they would be greeted with banter—most huntsmen seemed to believe a rumour that they were getting paid by the Kremlin, or, worse, by Linda McCartney—and other times they had their Dormobile turned over with a forklift truck. On occasion terrier-men would chase them halfway back to London.

When Dave married Cee, a small, spirited woman now in her late fifties, they planned a series of awareness campaigns alongside the direct action. At one point they decided to concentrate their efforts on clergymen who hunted. They would put crucified otters on one vicar's altar. Or they would have someone dressed up as Francis of Assisi in a congregation on a Sunday, shouting 'there is nothing sicker than a hunting vicar' through the sermon.

Their favourite target was a senior clergyman in Preston, Lancashire, who rode with the hounds whenever he could. On his retirement day the church was full of local dignitaries for a big reception afterwards. About a dozen hunt saboteurs got in, too, led by Dave and Cee, and when there was a little break in proceedings they all went to the front and faced the congregation. 'We started singing "All Things Bright and Beautiful",' Cee recalled. 'I always remember a little Brownie pack down the front joining in.' All things wise and wonderful, they carried on: *your vicar kills them all.* 'There was a sudden realization that all was not well,' Cee continued. 'The canapés were abandoned, the vicar was hustled out through a side door, and that was that.'

In many ways, the meetings that Dave and Cee attended to discuss tactics reflected the spirit of their times. At vegetarian suppers they would debate the parameters of their philosophy, decide whether tapeworms and pubic lice had rights. Dave recalled some early, more extreme, hunt saboteurs who went on to form the Animal Liberation Front having tortured misgivings about the use of incendiary devices against the fur trade. They worried about collateral damage to spiders.

The saboteurs developed strange obsessions. In 1976, three of Dave and Cee's friends became determined to dig up the body of John Peel, who was buried along with his wife and thirteen children in his local churchyard at Caldbeck in the Lake District. It was, apparently, very hard going. They dug all night in the graveyard, and believed they had got down to the bones of a favourite hound that reportedly rested on the top of the huntsman's coffin. At this point, with dawn appearing they were forced to give up having broken all of their spades. Another group made an attempt on the grave of the first Duke of Beaufort. There were plans, Dave believed, to send the Duke's skull to Princess Anne in the post, but they came to nothing.

Over the years, and particularly through the late Eighties and early Nineties, the violence Dave and Cee experienced on their campaigns got far more systematic. On certain hunts, if a saboteur group or a gang of hunt supporters came off worst one week, the next week they would be back in greater numbers: everything escalated. There were occasional pitched battles between a hundred or so saboteurs and an equal number of hunt followers. Eventually, inevitably, in the early Nineties two young saboteurs were killed in accidents with cars. In retribution there were sustained campaigns against the hunts involved. It all seemed quite a long way from hunting vicars.

It was at about this time, too, that Dave Wetton was convicted for assault. A horse in a field ran him down and when he got up he lashed out, hitting a female hunt master. He felt, after that, he could not really be involved in the leadership of the saboteurs so he and Cee 'retired', though they continued to go and disrupt hunts if any passed near their village.

In retirement Dave became involved in other causes. He became leader of the local ramblers' association, insisting on the right to roam. But he never lost his global vision. When the Chinese leader Jiang Zemin visited Britain in 1999, Dave Wetton remembered all his hunt training and broke through a police cordon at the Millennium Dome to shout 'Free Tibet' into the startled premier's car. When the pictures of his solo protest appeared on Channel 4 News, he lost his job at London Underground. 'We only have one life,' Dave said, 'and everyone should have a cause.'

Last year, the fortieth anniversary of the Hunt Saboteurs Association was celebrated in Peckham, south London. Old sabs and sympathizers came from all over the world. Dave received a signed photo from Brigitte Bardot congratulating the saboteurs on all their work on behalf of foxes (and deer and mink). There were speeches, and dancing, and it was widely acknowledged that the global militant animal-rights struggle had begun with creosoting river-banks in Devon.

Dave and Cee were among the few hunt protestors who ventured into London on the day the Countryside Alliance marched. Police reinforcements were called to protect them from the more angry sections of the crowd in Parliament Square. 'No one could believe it, watching the police going in hard, whacking heads,' Dave recalled, 'but for once it was not the heads of people on our side, it was masters of foxhounds and young toffs.' It had taken a little longer than two years, but at that moment Dave and Cee Wetton had a sense that they were finally getting close to the kill.

4. Friend of the lobster

On Remembrance Sunday in 2004, a week before the Parliament Act was invoked to force the Hunting Act into law, at the Cenotaph in Whitehall the Queen led a silent prayer for the dead of two World Wars. As the old soldiers and politicians prayed, an urban fox strolled past the memorial and nosed among the wreaths of poppies, in daylight, as if to remind politicians of their current priority. The following day, the fox made all the front pages.

A cynical historian of the Blair years in government may well begin to tell the story of New Labour with a simple statistic. While 275 hours were spent arguing about the question of whether foxes enjoy the challenge of being chased by dogs, only seven hours were spent debating the decision to invade Iraq, with the United States.

Even in debate, it was sometimes hard to see which of these issues the respective sides cared about the most. In arguing against the Hunting bill in the House of Lords, Viscount Astor quoted the words the Prime Minister had used to the US Congress when he ratified the decision to take the country to war. 'We are fighting for the inalienable right of humankind...to be free,' he said. 'Free to be you so long as being you does not impair the freedom of others. That's what we are fighting for. And that's a battle worth fighting.' The pursuit of global democracy had become, in some minds, indistinguishable from the pursuit of foxes.

I arranged to meet Tony Banks MP on the last day of his parliamentary career, when the Prime Minister was closing the House for the May election; Banks was stepping down after twenty-two years representing the east London constituency of West Ham. He was leaving with at least one ambition realized: in the long parliamentary war between hunt supporters and opponents, it was Banks who had finally called the hounds towards him and set off across the fields with them. Five minutes before the end of a debate that would have ratified a compromise Bill to delay a decision on hunting into the next parliament, he had proposed an amendment for a total ban that outfoxed even his Prime Minister.

When we had spoken on the phone to arrange to meet he'd suggested that I read a short pamphlet biography of the man he described as his inspiration in his anti-hunt campaign, the Labour MP Peter Freeman, who had represented the Welsh constituency of Brecon and Radnor from the 1920s until after the war. Freeman had been widely known, by Tories, as 'friend of the lobster' after a debate in which he had tabled a motion to prevent the boiling of live lobsters in the House of Commons' kitchens. He had also raised the question of banning hunting back in 1928—the year of the publication of Siegfried Sassoon's hugely popular *Memoirs of a Fox-hunting Man*— when the idea had been unconscionable, and he had been laughed out of the debate.

Tony Banks, who had once recommended government support for the CrustaStun, a device which paralysed lobsters before boiling, saw himself as finishing off Freeman's work. He had stood up to talk about foxes several times in the Thatcher years, only to be greeted with muffled hunting *halloo*s from the dominant Conservative benches. With the end of his parliamentary career in sight, he had been determined to at least do this.

Oddly when I met Banks, at the next table in the Westminster tea room was Sir Nicholas Soames, the well-lunched grandson of Winston Churchill and the House of Commons' most prominent hunt supporter. Banks rather enjoyed the proximity. 'Of course Soames can't hunt himself,' he explained, in a stage whisper. 'There is no horse big enough to take him.'

Banks had, he said, come to the point, an unusual one for a politician, where he loathed the human species. 'We are the most vulgar life form on the planet. I could happily take a machine gun to people who perform these terrible cruelties to animals.' He looked around the room. 'If you can take pleasure slaughtering an animal, it is not long before you can take pleasure slaughtering a human being. Who is to say,' he said, 'we are a higher life form than elephants say, or great whales?'

Not me, I said, certainly not.

I wondered if he saw the Hunting Act as, in any sense, a pay-off to back-bench MPs for their support of the Prime Minister over Iraq, a gesture towards class war, when real war was going on.

'Absolute bollocks,' he suggested. 'The reason it took so long is that dear old Tony Blair is one of those people who believes that to every problem there is a solution whereby you can keep everyone happy. But there are certain issues where the two sides are so far apart it is impossible to satisfy them both. As I told Tony, about the hunt followers, the Countryside Alliance, in this room: They hate you, they loathe you, they would not vote for you if you brought back slavery and witchburning.' Banks smiled at his own candour. 'I have to say the Prime Minister looked a little disappointed at that news, but it was the truth.'

The West Ham MP had never seen a fox-hunt but then again, he said, he had never seen a person starve to death in front of him, and that did not mean he could not talk about poverty. He was brought up with animals. His father raced pigeons.

5. The old huntsmen

In the last week of what might well have been the last hunting season in Britain, I keyed the words *fox* and *pub* and *Hampshire* into Google. I was looking for an appropriate place to meet with Aubrey Thomas the hunt saboteur, and Bob Collins the huntsman. Both men were retiring, and I had invited them out for a drink. Google came up with a choice of Foxes and Hounds and many plain Fox Inns. There was a Fox and Dogs and a Hungry Fox. In the end I suggested the Fox and Goose, which was about halfway between Aubrey and Bob, but Aubrey said it sounded too much like a hunting pub, so we met instead at a place called the Earl of Derby.

The huntsman and the saboteur had met before, of course, on hundreds of Saturdays. They had competed for the attention of hounds, seen foxes killed and seen foxes escape, had more than the odd stand-off. Though they had each spent a good part of their life wondering what the other was thinking, they had never really thought to ask.

They made curious drinking partners in a country pub. The huntsman, who I had picked up from his cottage and driven here through the lanes of Hampshire, was in his good tweed jacket and cap, his maroon hunt tie. The saboteur, head shaved, was wearing a surfing sweatshirt. When they saw each other, to start with they just laughed. Then like all old huntsmen, they began to share stories.

Bob recalled the first time he ever saw Aubrey, jogging across the field. It was the first Saturday of his first season in Hampshire and his young hounds were in extremely thick bramble. 'You came over with all your cronies, shouting and hollering, and said to me: What does it take to ruffle your feathers? I'm a firm believer that if my dogs are in thick cover with saboteurs all around I say nothing. In my experience with all the noise you made you would put the fox out anyway, and the hounds would be on it in a flash.'

Aubrey smiled. 'Before Bob came we had a lot of violence at Hampshire. We were scrapping with terrier-men all the time,' he said. 'I remember pulling a girl called Janice, a saboteur, off him, literally, early on. After that, we had a kind of unspoken agreement that things would not get out of hand.'

Bob agreed. 'Every time I saw Janice after that, I'd give her a kiss. They used to wait outside my house every morning for me to leave so they could follow me. One morning, I gave Janice a fixture card. I said she might as well know where we were going to save her getting up so early.'

Aubrey wondered what the hunt had been up to since the ban.

'Funnily enough,' Bob said, 'we have accounted for more foxes since we finished hunting than we did before. On the drag hunt the hounds mark an earth and we dig the fox out and shoot him. We boil up these foxes to make this scent for the drag. Shoot one, boil him up. And then drag it round.'

Aubrey winced a little. He told Bob about his own retirement plans. He was going to attempt the Three Peaks Challenge, running up Snowdon and Sca Fell and Ben Nevis, the highest mountains in Wales and England and Scotland, in one day. Even if the Tories got in at the May election and the Hunting Act was overturned he would not go out again. He felt he had seen it through, that his job was over.

The huntsman marvelled a little at Aubrey's stamina, not only his ability to keep up with the horses, but also the fact that he always came back, week-in and week-out. 'In a strange way, I glory what you have done,' he said. What he could never understand, though, was the saboteurs' lack of respect for private property. In his view of the world, where land was everything, he had no comprehension of trespass. Have you never been arrested, he wondered, guardedly, of Aubrey.

'Only about a hundred times,' Aubrey said. 'But I have had no convictions. I've always defended myself in court. I have sued the police on many many occasions for wrongful arrest. I have three going against them at the moment. One for torture.'

Torture?

Aubrey said that on a hunt earlier in the season in Surrey, the police handcuffed him and held him down on the ground while the terrier-men dug the fox out, for thirty minutes, then killed it in front of him. 'They then made me walk in handcuffs through the crowd of hunt supporters who were jeering and pushing me around. So: torture.'

Bob was not quite sure what to say to this. 'That would not happen at our hunt,' he said, eventually. And then, incredulous, 'A hundred times?'

'It's never been for violence or anything,' Aubrey assured him. 'Just trespass or breach of the peace. I got arrested once at the Waterloo Cup. On that occasion I was quite relieved. I ran on to the hare coursing ground on my own, chased by about five hundred drunken Irish hare coursers.'

'A hundred times,' Bob said again.

Did it feel odd that it is all over? I wondered.

'Oh hunting will carry on,' the huntsman said, with certainty. 'But it will be a different thing if it is illegal. I think even now a lot of hunts have just carried on as normal, as if nothing had happened.'

Aubrey agreed. 'I think we all know that the Welsh hunts are a law unto themselves.'

'Will you miss us?' Bob asked.

'No, not really. But I will miss the other saboteurs. There is comradeship. You act as a group, as a pack almost. It's been my way of life.'

'And mine,' Bob said.

The saboteur looked into his pint, 'I have to ask this Bob, how do you view foxes, what do you think of them?'

The huntsman considered the question: 'I love foxes. Love them,' he said. 'My two best days this year—you were not at either—I have never seen so many foxes in my life. We killed fifteen but far more got away. I respect the fox. He is a very clever animal. I do. I love them. The thing is,' he said, sadly, 'now there is a ban there will be far fewer foxes. A lot more will be shot. You get gamekeepers and farmers who have always been hunting minded, who wouldn't pull the trigger every single time. If they knew the hounds were coming, they would leave one or two foxes for us.'

Aubrey thought about this. 'So the argument that without the hunts we will be overrun with foxes, none of that was ever true. The gamekeepers can shoot all the foxes they want. The hunt was only ever for enjoyment?'

'Certainly I love it,' Bob said. 'I do.'

'So why did people make all these arguments, all this back and forward in the House of Lords. It makes no odds now, because there is a ban, but I'd like to know that the only reason people hunt foxes is because they enjoy doing it.'

'Certainly we always loved it,' Bob said. 'It is that spirit that holds hunting people together.' He looked as if he might cry again. 'It was a sad day for me when we had to pack up.'

'For me, I have to say,' Aubrey said, 'it wasn't.'

The huntsman and the saboteur then talked, with the affection of old adversaries, of some of the mutual 'friends' they had known in the time that they had been out with the hunt. Aubrey had recently been to the funeral of a former chairman of the Hunt Saboteurs; Bob had attended a couple of funerals of hunt supporters in the last week, blowing his hunting horn for the departed.

'People have come and gone,' Bob said, 'but Aubrey hasn't. He's always been there.'

Aubrey smiled. They agreed that the countryside was not what it was. Many of the people who lived here worked in London; no locals could afford to rent a cottage. Nearly all the great characters had gone. 'They are even talking about stopping us shooting pigeons,' Bob said.

Nothing was the same. Aubrey mentioned that out of the corner of his eye, in Hampshire, he saw a black panther in a farmyard not long ago. Bob had seen one, too. They both shook their heads. The saboteur wondered if the huntsman would like another beer.

Bob looked at his watch. He really wished he could stay longer, he said, but he had to be up at five-thirty the next morning.

'Why's that?' Aubrey wondered. 'I thought you were retired.'

'Oh,' the huntsman said, 'I got a call from a farmer. Right in the back of the village, seven lambs he's lost. I've got to take my two best hounds up there in the morning and kill another blasted fox.'

I drove Bob back to the kennels that he would be leaving for the last time a couple of days later. On the way, he talked about Aubrey's one hundred arrests, and the ease of sitting down with him, even after all these years. He talked, too, of his retirement dinner and of the protests that would continue until the ban was overturned; 'There will,' he said, 'be bloodshed over this, before too long.' I watched him let himself in at his little cottage door; the dogs were settled down for the night and there was no noise in the yard. And then I headed back towards the motorway.

It was tempting to think, driving through these moonlit lanes with their high hedges, that this was some authentic version of England, cottages and village greens, sub post-offices and ancient churches, and that Bob Collins at his kennels was a vivid part of that. At Moundsmere Manor, I got out and walked a little way along the wall that surrounded the grounds of the enormous house.

It remains odd, for someone who lives in the impossible

congestion of London, to be reminded that most of Britain is still divided among people with more space than they quite know what to do with (around 150,000 people, a quarter of one per cent of the total population, still own nearly seventy per cent of all of the land). The power that once went with that land has long since shifted to the urban centres, but the great hereditary landowners, with their tenant farmers, and their traditions, and their hunts, remain largely where they have been for centuries.

Walking around these walls, looking out over the fields at the stands of woodland in the distance, trying to imagine foxes alive beneath them, I had a sudden sense, for the first time, really, of what those original hunt saboteurs in their Dormobiles, and Aubrey Thomas putting in his miles in his running shoes, must have looked like to such landowners. They were the vanguard of a world beyond their walls that was changing extremely quickly; a weekly reminder of the fact that their power to do what they pleased on the land they owned, and the land they co-opted, faced a new threat. While they ran the hunt, as Bob Collins said, the masters ran the country, and they could convince themselves that this meant what it suggested. Take away the right to ride wherever they pleased on that country, though, the weekly marking out of territory that was the hunt, their idea of fun, and suddenly they were circumscribed more than ever by a Britain that held no such respect for their way of life; a Britain that they loathed. For a moment, standing under the moon at Moundsmere Manor, the 275 hours of political debate, and the Parliament Act, and the great Countryside marches no longer seemed like an overreaction. Out here, the banning of fox-hunting was, it seemed, about as close as Britain had lately come to a revolution. □

GRANTA

WHEN GRANDMAMA WAS YOUNG

Matthew Reisz

My maternal grandmother, Winifred de Kok, was tall, angular and outspoken. I often think of the time we were playing a game with my mother and brothers and she had to define the word 'pismire'. 'Well,' she said, 'everybody knows that a mire is a bog, a horrible black smelly bog...' She continued along these lines for a while, realized she'd gone off at a tangent and hastily corrected herself: 'and a pismire is a bog that somebody has pissed in!' I must have been about twelve and was both shocked and surprised that she knew such rude words.

I was her first grandchild and she was the only one of my grandparents I knew. We spent a lot of time together. When I was very little she lived in the flat above ours; later she moved to one on the same road as my primary school in Hampstead, where I would often drop by to teach her chess and card games. I was the last person to see her alive. In August 1969, when I was nearly fifteen, I went to the cinema with her and stayed the night in her flat. I found her dead the next morning.

My grandmother was sixty-one when I was born and to my child's eye she seemed an old woman without a history. It was only long after her death that I began to appreciate her professional achievements and to understand how, as a young woman, she had created a new life for herself—and how far ahead of her time she was in doing so.

Winifred de Kok was born in South Africa in 1894, the third of nine children—two boys, seven girls—and grew up on a farm in the Orange Free State where her father was a landowner and magistrate. The family spoke both Afrikaans and English. Like several of her sisters, she started work as a teacher but later decided to become a doctor. Since no medical schools in South Africa admitted women at that time, in 1921 she moved to England to train at the Royal Free Hospital in London. She qualified in 1925 and married my grandfather in 1932. When her children were small she worked as a locum, in both hospitals and general practice. She specialized in obstetrics and childcare, and from 1939 to 1953 was the Assistant County Medical Officer for Essex, taking a particular interest in women's and baby welfare clinics. She wrote a series of best-selling books on child rearing, including *New Babes for Old*

(1932), and in 1937 she translated Eugene Marais's *The Soul of the White Ant*, a minor classic of popular science writing, from Afrikaans into English. She was also well-known as a medical journalist and agony aunt and, in 1954, became Britain's first woman TV doctor, answering viewers' questions on *Tell Me, Doctor*. British television of the time was dominated by plummy Oxbridge voices, and it now strikes me as remarkable that a woman with a slight but still noticeable South African accent was chosen for such a sensitive role.

My family knew a little of her earlier life. We knew, for instance, that she had been friends with the sexologist Havelock Ellis; she met my grandfather, the short-story writer A. E. Coppard, at his house. But we had few details about the nature of their friendship until 1980, when my mother came across a reference to 'throbbing Winifred de Kok' in a review of Phyllis Grosskurth's biography of Havelock Ellis in the *New York Review of Books*. She was even more upset by the quotation of a particularly embarrassing passage from one of my grandmother's letters to Ellis. Furious that copyright material had been used without her permission, she got my stepfather, who was a lawyer, to fire off an angry letter to Grosskurth's publisher.

There was no reply, but a copy found its way to Ellis's adopted son, Professor François Lafitte. His mother, Françoise Lafitte, was Ellis's long-term companion and after her death he inherited Ellis's papers. In 1988 he donated them to the British Library. When the curator went through the material and came across my stepfather's letter of complaint, she decided to spare the family further embarrassment by keeping much of my grandmother's correspondence in reserve, inaccessible to researchers.

Neither my mother nor I had any idea that letters from my grandmother to Ellis formed part of this collection until late 2003, when I picked up a mysterious message from the curator, Anne Summers, saying that she wanted to discuss a very delicate matter. When I phoned her back, she told me about my grandmother's letters—and that a researcher wanted to have a look at them. Were we willing to grant permission?

My mother decided that we should see them first and we arranged an appointment. I then received an anxious phone call from

Summers. Did my mother realize, she asked, that her father was already married when he met her mother? That her parents had married after the death of the first Mrs Coppard—when my mother was five? That my mother was therefore illegitimate? My mother, as it happens, was well aware of all these things and amused by this attempt to protect us from old family secrets—which weren't secrets at all—in letters we ourselves had asked to see.

My grandmother's letters—there are about sixty altogether—form one volume of the sixty-six volumes of Ellis's papers in the British Library. It is a one-sided correspondence. Only a few of Ellis's letters to her survive and they were all written in the last fortnight of his life. When I came to read the letters for myself, I was both moved and impressed by the personality that emerged, of a woman determined to achieve emotional fulfilment despite the internal voices whispering to her from a puritanical childhood. What I find far more difficult is to overlay that figure—desperate with sexual yearning, discussing masturbation or the pleasures of 'undinism'— on my image of the grandmother I knew and loved as a child.

Winifred de Kok wrote her first letter to Havelock Ellis in December 1923. She was thirty years old and a medical student at the Royal Free Hospital. She had been brought up, she wrote, in a South African family where sex was a forbidden secret, and at the age of seventeen had become involved with a young man called Edgar who believed that:

> friendship is the greatest relationship between humans + that if sex came in it spoilt things, so sex was carefully ruled out. He had sex relationships with other girls + women, about which he told me—he told me everything + I know that I really meant more to him than anyone else, but he meant so much to me that it was impossible for me to have sex relations with other men. I had a strong sex instinct, I realise now, for I used to become violently attracted to men but no one meant to me what Edgar did + if ever I kissed another man, I loathed myself afterwards. Then came the war...

Edgar was killed in an aeroplane accident in 1917. Looking back on his death, Winifred reflected:

I suppose I was 'brave' about Edgar—I think I was really regressing + I suppose that that added to my years of sex suppression proved rather too much. I came to England in 1921 + soon after had a nervous breakdown—I used to be flooded with terrible depression + fear of insanity.

She sought help in psychoanalysis and became friends with the woman doctor who treated her. She soon found herself falling in love with her friend's husband, David, who was a clergyman:

They invited me to spend a fortnight of my holiday with them + he + I were together for long walks almost every day. He wooed me as no man has ever done before + I believe as he has wooed no woman before. He won me soul + body. There came a day when I realised that to give myself to him utterly was not only the greatest thing on earth but an urgent necessity as right as ever anything could be... He had told me he needed, had called on me + I was willing to satisfy his every need + and in so doing my own need was awakened—he had stirred me to the uttermost depths of my being.

They had 'passionate meetings' almost every day for several months, but the situation became more and more strained:

I spent a few days later on with them + we again realised some decision had to be made. His wife—who is wonderful—he + I discussed things + I realised that much as he loved me his marriage of 10 years' standing was the most fundamental thing + nothing must spoil that so we decided that we'd not see each other for 3 months. The next month was the most acute hell I've ever gone through. Not only longing for him with all that meant but such sheer physical desire that it made me realise why men sometimes go to prostitutes...

This attempt at a trial separation was now over and they had agreed to continue seeing each other as friends:

From seeing him almost every day [as a] passionate lover I am now seeing him casually about once a fortnight. I have tried to immerse myself in my work but you can understand how empty life is. What hurts me so intensely is that he doesn't seem to realise how empty things must be for me. He has awakened every part of my sexual nature + I know I have awakened deeps in him that have not been touched before but for him it is more of an episode, because he leads a very busy life + loves his wife—who is 5 years older than he is. He is forty. There are no children. He loves children + I long to give him a child + to bear his child.

She signs off with a plea for help:

I feel I can't quite tackle this thing alone—I can repress but I know where that leads. There is no one I can ask advice. I wonder if you'll help me.

In 1923, Havelock Ellis was the world's leading expert on sexuality. In Britain, however, he was a notorious figure; until 1935 his major work, *Studies in the Psychology of Sex*, was available only to members of the medical profession.

Henry Havelock Ellis was born in 1859 in Croydon in south London. His father was a ship's captain who, in 1875, took his sixteen-year-old son on a trip around the world. As they were about to sail from Sydney to Calcutta the ship's doctor declared that Havelock, who had never been strong, would be unable to endure the Indian climate and his father put him ashore. Ellis remained in Australia for the next four years earning his living as a teacher. During this time he discovered the work of James Hinton, a surgeon-turned-mystic who once declared 'Jesus was the Saviour of men, but I am the Saviour of women'. Confused by his own sexual feelings, Ellis decided to 'make it the main business of my life to get to the real natural facts of sex apart from all would-be moralistic or sentimental notions' and so spare future generations 'the trouble and perplexity' his own ignorance had caused him.

On his return to England in 1881, Ellis decided to train as a doctor and it was Hinton's widow and son who paid for his medical studies at St Thomas's Hospital. He qualified in 1889 but practised for only a short time. He had a wide range of other interests; he oversaw both a series of popular scientific works and editions of plays by Shakespeare's contemporaries. But his main interest remained human sexuality and in 1894 he published *Man and Woman*, an overview of current knowledge about secondary and tertiary sexual characteristics which serves as an introduction to his great work, the *Studies in the Psychology of Sex*.

Ellis wrote the first volume, *Sexual Inversion*, with John Addington Symonds. It was published in Germany in 1896 and an English edition was planned for the following year. But Symonds had died in 1893. Since then, Oscar Wilde had been tried and imprisoned for gross indecency and Symonds's family were understandably nervous about the book's reception. *Sexual Inversion* contains the first explicit accounts of homosexuality ever recorded in Britain other than in a legal context, and the notably unjudgemental tone made a strong implicit case for changing the law. Symonds's family bought up all of the first print-run. The second was withdrawn after a bookseller was prosecuted under the obscenity laws. Ellis was always keen to avoid unnecessary controversy, so he found a publisher in Chicago and hit on the ruse of renumbering the *Studies* and making his discussion of *The Evolution of Modesty* (1899)—a much less contentious topic—Volume I of the new series.

Four more volumes followed between 1903 to 1910, exploring everything from sexual selection and sexual periodicity, to detumescence, masturbation, prostitution and 'love and pain'. The seventh and final volume, *Eonism and other Supplementary Studies*, appeared in 1928; here Ellis considered transvestism ('eonism'), flagellation, narcissism, dream analysis—and something he called 'undinism'.

The *Studies* are seldom as speculative as Freud's contemporary writings, and never as intellectually challenging. Ellis's work is notable more for its frankness and the extensive case study material (much of which was gathered informally from friends, acquaintances and correspondents) than for its scientific rigour or depth of analysis. He established once and for all the variety of common sexual feelings, fantasies and behaviour. Ellis has been described as 'the first of the yea-sayers' for offering a comprehensive and even celebratory account of human sexuality. While the *Studies* themselves were unavailable to the general public he spread his views in popular writings such as his *Little Essays of Love and Virtue* (1922). These include two lectures from the period just before my grandmother first wrote to him, promisingly entitled 'The Erotic Rights of Women' (1918) and 'The Play-Function of Sex' (1921).

Ellis attracted a mixed reaction in his lifetime. Some were shocked or disapproving. Others felt he played up to his image as a sage: Graham Greene mocked his 'fake prophet's air' which reminded him of 'a Santa Claus at Selfridge's'. But there were many who sought his advice and took it seriously. Friends would come for counselling and correspondents from all over the world sent him nude photographs or detailed descriptions of their sexual practices. In the preface to the *Studies*, he makes a point of mentioning the help he had received from 'women of high intelligence and fine character'. My grandmother was about to become one of them.

The first letter was sent to Ellis care of his publisher, A & C Black. Ellis seems to have replied with sympathy and some questions of his own. My grandmother wrote to him again on February 2, 1924:

> Regarding your question as to solitary gratification. I have, perhaps, had a certain momentary relief from it but I always realised that it was the man himself, his spirit, his mind + his body that I wanted and to whom I wanted to <u>give</u> myself.

Even in this second letter, however, she is moving beyond her intense but rather naive despair and changing her mind about David's 'wonderful' wife:

> [She] is a very <u>good</u> woman + clever too—one of those women that are so good that you feel a brute if you go against them in any way + with whom you can live in harmony only if you sink your own individuality absolutely. David is being swamped. I know what it means because the same thing happens to me if I see much of her— and yet she thinks that freedom for everyone is the ideal. I realise that at all costs their relationship must remain unbroken + yet to me it seems to be <u>death</u> to David. He is starving. I know he is, and I can do nothing; + he can do nothing because he is utterly loyal + is incapable of hurting anyone.

Matthew Reisz

Ten days later, on February 12, she writes again. She returns to the topic of her physical longing: 'What do you think is best—to let it simply burn out or to relieve it?' And she cautiously welcomes his reassurances:

> Life really would be dull if one stopped falling in love—although a few months ago I did say that I'd be wise in future + be careful not to ever fall in love again. It does hurt furiously though + I'm glad, I think, to hear you say that the physical side becomes less prominent. I told you I am 30, didn't I? I suppose that accounts for the acuteness of the sheer physical strain. Especially as I more or less repressed all the sexual side of me from about 19 to two years ago.

A similar sentiment emerges from the fourth letter of February 18:

> Last year when we both were strung [out] to an enormous pitch it seemed to me that if only we could let ourselves go utterly on the physical side—instead of always trying to sit on ourselves + keep the lid on—that we would get through to an affectionate friendship. I was positive of it + am still positive that it was the solution at the time, but he had some absurd idea about it not being good for me...

My grandmother's words here, particularly the notion that sex is something one 'gets through' on the way to something else, and perhaps better, echo Ellis's recently published *Little Essays of Love and Virtue*. While promoting 'the free spontaneous erotic activity of women', he also argues that 'sexual pleasure, wisely used and not abused, may prove the stimulus and liberator of our finest and most exalted activities'. There is much about 'uplifting of the soul', love as 'something unspeakably holy' and 'the sacramental chalice of that wine which imparts the deepest joy that men and women can know'. The importance of contraception is that it allows 'the complete liberation of the spiritual object of marriage'.

Ellis's own experience of sex was probably very limited. In 1891 he married the novelist Edith Lees who, to his great surprise, turned out to be a lesbian. He later described their marriage as 'a union of affectionate comradeship, in which the specific emotions of sex had the smallest part'. After Edith's death in 1916 her French translator, Françoise Lafitte, contacted Ellis about some outstanding payments. She soon became his companion and was so devoted to him that she adopted the surname Delisle (an anagram of 'de Ellis').

Throughout his life Ellis formed intense attachments to a number of women, including the South African novelist Olive Schreiner and Margaret Sanger, the American birth control pioneer. There is no evidence that any of these relationships were ever consummated. As Ellis himself put it, 'I am regarded as an authority on sex, a fact which has sometimes amused one or two (but not all) of my more intimate women friends. But, after all, it is the spectator who sees most of the game.' This claim reflects the cold, even voyeuristic nature of his work; he often seems to be classifying sexual behaviour with the doggedness of a stamp collector. Ellis played an important role in altering attitudes but it was people of a less icy temperament, like my grandmother, who tried to live out the consequences.

In the same letter of February 18, my grandmother continues the process of rethinking her own role in the triangle:

> I know you'll smile when I tell you that he had never really tasted
> passion before. But it is true. He is a clergyman + started off by
> being very orthodox + married a woman 5 years older than
> himself, whom he worships, but I am positive he's never been
> passionately in love with her + he has deliberately kept out other
> women. I sometimes wonder whether I'm being unfair to her, but
> honestly I've taken nothing—can take nothing—that belongs to her.
> In fact, I think he's been able to give her more because of me. But
> you see how things stand between us...it is difficult to decide
> deliberately not ever to see each other especially when we realise
> that in about a year's time I'll be going back to South Africa.

She responds to another request from Ellis about her masturbatory history and begins to look back more calmly on the early phase of her relationship with David:

> At first although passionately in love I did not feel the strain but
> afterwards I found it absolutely necessary to masturbate. I really

don't think I could have gone on without. In itself it meant
nothing, but after David had left me longing + blazing for only one
thing, it helped to just continue. I'd daydream all the rest + then
get the climax + it was a relief. There were occasional times when
it was so bad that the thing seemed so pitiful in contrast with what
I wanted (which wasn't only the physical but everything else) that I
simply couldn't + there was consequently no relief + these times
were really terrible...

In spite of still wanting the same thing quite definitely I really
am quite sane again. I wasn't last year. For at least 9 months I was
obsessed by the one thought + desire. But now I am interested in
my work + other people + I think I've taken hold of life again.

By March 3 she is writing in a very different vein to accept Ellis's
invitation to visit him, and complaining about the problems of her
medical training: 'I'm quite near the end of my course + still an
operating theatre makes me feel quite sick.' She has also begun to
see David's invocation of altruism as opportunistic or cruel:

I am glad you agree with me about the things we don't do + as for
selfishness—we are sometimes most selfish when we think we are
most unselfish...

Look at last year. I think that ultimately the only reason why
David felt that he had to set limits was because it would not be
good for me + he probably thought he was being very unselfish—
but really he was being much more selfish than if he had been
selfish!! I had faced every probable or possible issue for myself +
would have been glad to accept any one except perhaps the
possibility that he might regret it afterwards + yet I was almost
sure that even if he did regret it just afterwards, he'd live to be glad
of the experience. But it seemed to me wicked, wicked to have the
cup brimming + running over, put into one's hands + then refuse to
drink. I still think it wicked + now when in cooler moments I say
'Perhaps it was better so' I realise I have fallen from grace + rather
despise myself. I think it despicable to calculate costs in such
things—whatever the cost surely one should be glad to pay.

On March 16, as the date for their first meeting approaches, she writes again, saying that she wants to postpone it. She says that only midwifery makes her medical course bearable. This leads to a reflection on what childbirth means for women and the cost to her of repressing her own nature:

> I still have periods when I think sex is a confounded nuisance. I am still swayed at times by the years when I thought that if there was such a thing as sex feeling, I certainly had nothing to do with it. It is getting its own back now.

By the date of her next letter, March 25, Ellis and my grandmother have met up for the first time, but she has been too overawed to say much and is left with 'almost 5000 things I want to ask you':

> Is monogamy right? What do we mean by monogamy—surely nothing to do with legal marriage. If a man finds he loves 2 women at the same time, what is to happen if both love him?... I wish sometimes that David had felt free to set no limits at all last year. It would have helped me to decide whether when once such a physical relation is set up it is so very difficult to do without afterwards when it becomes necessary— + whether the restraint isn't more harmful. It seems to me that it was a great chance of experimenting missed. It is so important to know what a woman feels like in a case like that.

The same letter touches on prostitution and homosexuality. Although 'not conscious of any homosexuality in myself—I mean more than normal', she takes issue with the psychoanalysts and moralists:

> The wrong thing to me in almost everything (if there is such a thing as wrong) is holding back from life in such a way that one becomes stunted + dead.

My grandmother wrote seven letters to Ellis between December 1923 and March 1924. They must have had more meetings: when the letters resume in 1925 my grandmother is no longer seeking advice but writing in the tones of an ecstatic disciple:

Matthew Reisz

You are very beautiful, O Great God Pan, and yesterday was
beautiful—and words are meaningless.

On July 7, 1925:

It is as if you have shown me how beautiful life really is, as if you
are all the beauty of life and of everything. You make me want to
embrace life and kiss it. And that has made me think: am I now
like those women who want to die when Havelock dies? And for a
moment I thought 'Yes' but then I knew 'No'. All you stand for
can't die. I'd want to die perhaps selfishly but because of you I
couldn't die but would want to go on still embracing the beauty of
life, which is you, and after that the beauty of Death too.

Towards the end comes an enigmatic passage:

It has been such a happy time, everything beautiful, every little
commonplace act and even acts that some think not clean made
divine because done by you and for you.
    It gives one quite a new viewpoint. One is taught to do good
deeds + become good, now I see that any and every deed is good if
done 'goodly'.

The following letter doesn't make matters any clearer: my
grandmother had spent almost a week with Ellis; her stay overlapped
with that of another female visitor, Josephine Walther, Curator of
the Detroit Institute of Arts, 'who seems very sweet—I like her voice
in spite of the American accent—which generally I don't care for...'
She added, not wholly convincingly, 'I'm so glad you decided to have
Josephine... You know I once said to you I wished every woman in
the world could know you—even if only for an hour or two.'
    Much of the next letter, which is also undated but probably
written in August, is newsy and amusing: about revising for finals,
the psychoanalytic scene in Vienna and a friend's efforts to find an
osteopath. It contains the first reference to the writer A. E. Coppard
whom my grandmother had recently met at Ellis's house near
Henley-on-Thames:

I sent back Coppard's book + told him which [stories] I liked +
how sorry we were it rained on Sunday + this morning had a very
nice little letter from him, saying how sorry he was + saying that
the girl he dedicated the book to was (as we know) called Winifred
too + that strangely my writing is much like hers. He also said he
once lent the book to a parson's widow who marked all [the
stories] she could make nothing of with a ? + then gave him a
lecture on the entire absence of moral uplift in them all!

I may ask him to come + have tea with me if he ever comes to
London. Do you think I might?

This sounds like—and was—the beginning of a romance. (By
September 16, Coppard was writing to her to 'bless dear Havelock
Ellis who gave you—who are all I ever dreamed of in woman—to
me'.) But then she veers off in a strikingly different direction:

It seems lonely + strange to be making golden streams all alone +
and not in a lovely garden <u>with</u> the great god Pan in loving
attendance.

With love from Your Dryad

My grandmother's earlier reference to 'acts that some think not
clean' is now explained. These were the words my mother was so
startled to read in the *New York Review of Books* in 1980. Ellis took
pleasure from watching women urinate in front of him, an activity he
called 'undinism' (after 'undine', a female water spirit). He referred to
himself as the woodland god Pan, and to the women who agreed to
urinate before him as naiads or dryads (the nymphs Pan traditionally
lusts after). Ellis was reasonably frank about this in his autobiography
and in the third volume of his *Impressions and Comments* (1924) he
describes an undinist afternoon with the poet HD (Hilda Doolittle).
He devoted a long section to the topic in the last volume of the *Studies*.
With footnotes citing German scholarly sources, he discusses the
cultural differences in positions adopted for urination, Roman bath-
prostitution, a Swiss waterfall called La Cascade de Pisse-Vache, the
unconscious links between urine and holy water, the effectiveness of
urine in coffee as a 'love filtre', and much else.

Matthew Reisz

Despite her developing attachment to Coppard and undinist
relations with Ellis, my grandmother still had to tear herself away
from her tangled relationship with David and his wife. In a letter
probably sent in September or October 1925, she begins dramatically:

> Pan dear. I've just been so <u>vile</u> that I must tell you about it or
> burst. You know you've made me see things in such a wonderful
> new way that it seemed to make me love everyone + everything
> more, because you were you + I loved you so much...

David had sent her a note inviting her for a talk and she had gone
to see him at home where they were later joined by his wife:

> I was expecting her + was quite pleased to see her. Well, she was
> very charming but I felt her freeze up, you know I always feel
> things, then she started saying about how busy he was that he
> hardly had a minute to spare, then fussed over the tea, which was
> cold, then said 'Well, I don't think I can stay down here to have
> my tea as I know you're so busy'—everything to make one feel
> <u>awful</u> unless you had a skin like a rhinoceros, + all interspersed
> with pleasant remarks until I simply dashed from the room + said
> 'I simply can't stay a moment when you behave like this, I'm going'
> + then she came after me and held the front door when I was
> trying to get out + said sweet things + all I did was say 'Why
> pretend you want me + David to be friends when you know you're
> <u>jealous, jealous, jealous</u> + don't want me? Let me out. Let me out'
> + she said 'You baby' + I said 'Well, I know I'm a baby + don't
> mind confessing it but you go on pretending to be a saint when
> you know you hate me + are jealous' + by that time I managed to
> get out and go! Havelock, isn't it awful + yet I meant it all, she <u>is</u>
> jealous + I hate her jealousy + she ought to know that it isn't
> pleasant for me to go there. You'd think a woman would know
> what another woman in my place would feel like. You see how
> horrid I am when I am <u>myself</u>.

It's hardly surprising that David's wife was jealous of a much
younger woman who was in love with her husband. But it was then
one of the sillier articles of faith in progressive circles that sexual

jealousy, as Ellis was to put it, was an emotion 'chiefly felt by degenerates and imbeciles'. Shortly after the stormy tea party, my grandmother reports to Ellis:

> I had a most charming note from Mrs David the next morning saying 'You know I do want you + you know D. hates saying how busy he is' etc. etc. I wish she wouldn't pretend she wants us to be friends when I know she doesn't.

Matters came to a head when David's wife told him he had to chose which of them he wanted as his 'mate'. David 'said he thought "mate" was too exclusive a word + he didn't feel he could'. Later, just as my grandmother was about to go to France, he changed his mind and made his choice:

> he told me he didn't think he + I would make each other happy + lots of other things which hurt me dreadfully, but he said that he was quite willing for me to prove that I was his mate + suggested that we should have sexual relations if I wished, but also telling me that he loved his wife + was happy to have sexual relations with her. So I was left to make the decision + of course there was only one thing to do, that is tell him I couldn't possibly set out to try to take a man from his wife.
>
> I was very unhappy while away chiefly because my trust in him was shaken + he didn't write.

They met again when she was back in England, but David remained evasive. They tried not seeing each other, but David found he was desperate and couldn't work—although it was left to the two women to struggle towards a solution:

> His wife + I talked over things + she said that she thought anything ought to be tried that would break the strain of things. She saw 2 alternatives: either we never saw each other or else he accepted me as his wife i.e. I went + lived with them + was his wife in all but name...
>
> I had got to the stage when I could accept anything or nothing + she had [too]—so it was left for him to make the choice. And

yesterday he chose i.e. he wants us to have full sexual relations. We all 3 talked together last night + it appears that he has never until now told her how much he cares for me + has even told her things which she might interpret to mean that he cared for me only as a friend...

I feel that he has proved he really loves me by the decision he has made now and yet I am faced with the fact that it may be only a physical obsession + that after a few weeks or months the experiment may prove a failure. On the other hand, the experiment means going to live with them, which is going to make things terribly hard for her + all of us, so that even if it is more than a physical obsession it seems to me that the experiment will never work...

In the next surviving letter, March 16, 1926, my grandmother describes their initial attempt at living together:

I've been with them for the weekend + I realise now what I've never realised before that, however much he loves me—I don't doubt that—he really has no place in his life for me + really does not need me. He is trying to fit me in but it really is impossible. But the only thing seems to be to go ahead + let him find this out for himself in spite of what I know is going to happen + in spite of the unhappiness. They already are closer than before because he thinks quite truly how fine she has been + of course he'll end by hating me, but I suppose I must go on. I too feel that it can't last long + I'm horribly afraid of the future.

Is it possible for a man to live with two women in the fullest sense sexually? It doesn't seem to me possible. If only one knew what to do, but I simply can't see clearly + feel nearly dead.

The lack of dates makes it impossible to determine how long they all tried to live together under the same roof. Although my grandmother seems to have got bogged down in a situation which can bring her nothing but pain, she is actually about to end it for good. She was to devote only one more letter to her relationship with David and his wife—and then she simply drops the subject:

I am feeling much happier the last few days. Before that I seemed quite possessed by a Devil. Horribly jealous of her— + I see you say jealousy is chiefly felt by degenerates and imbeciles. But I see that it was the only thing to do even if the experiment does not last long. My chief source of perplexity is that I can't see how he can need me at all. His work fills up his life enormously + she has always helped him with that + it seems to me that all he wants me for is to be a sort of relaxation at times. I am the champagne (a poor brand!) + she is the good plain food.

At this point, as I read the letters in the British Library, I wanted to cheer. There could hardly be a clearer statement of the down side of being 'the other woman'. 'It is not a position,' she adds, 'I consider I am able successfully to fulfil.'

My grandmother's correspondence with Ellis continued until his death. There are letters describing her marital problems, the thrill of a one-night stand and the birth of her first child (my mother). She gives an extremely acerbic account of her work at the Peckham Pioneer Health Centre (then considered a bold experiment in bringing the latest ideas in childcare to the urban poor) and an equally sharp analysis of A. S. Neill's famous progressive school at Summerhill.

Many people have written to strangers they consider experts asking for help with sexual or emotional problems. No doubt there are other cases where such initial contact has led to friendship or romance. But the arc of this particular relationship is surely unique since it ended with Ellis asking my grandmother to help him die.

By the time of his eightieth birthday, on February 2, 1939, he was clearly weakening. He was distressed by the state of the world but proved a poor prophet in his final published article 'World Peace Is Our Next Upward Movement'. On April 18, my grandmother wrote that she was sorry to hear that he was now an invalid and recommended halibut oil for his companion Françoise Lafitte's neuritis. With the next item in the British Library's box, a messy typewritten letter dated June 26, I heard Ellis's voice for the first time. He asks for an 'adequate and reliable opiate or other remedy' in case he reaches the point where life is no longer worth living. 'In one sense the matter is far from urgent,' he explains, 'but as regards *my feelings* it is *very*

145

urgent.' He also mentions that he is being looked after by his sisters Laura and Edie—Françoise, ill and exhausted, has gone away for a fortnight's break. All of my grandmother's letters to him at this point were destroyed by Ellis or his estate as potentially incriminating.

Three days later, he writes again saying that a turn for the worse has made him even keener to obtain 'the consolation of a last resort'. The next letter is wrongly dated Friday, June 29: 'I am anxious to settle it at once before F. [Lafitte] returns. The idea is hers, quite as much hers as mine.' He then discusses the options of insulin and morphia suppositories, and his plans to obtain the latter by instalments from a wholesaler.

His final letter is dated July 4 and mentions a sedative called Omnopon which he plans to take with suppositories: 'In my present slight[ly] muddled mental state it means a great deal that you are thus helping me... If you do all this I shall certainly feel easy in my mind.' By this stage, Ellis was hardly able to read and write, and he seldom left his bed. He died on the night of July 8.

Even though we have only one side of the correspondence and Ellis was getting confused, it is pretty clear what is going on: he wanted the option of euthanasia and, from a distance, she was providing help and advice. A concrete plan had been decided upon, but he had still not obtained all the drugs he needed. My grandmother had been quite willing to commit a crime, but in the event (unless he acquired and used the sedative between July 4 and 7) Ellis died of natural causes.

Years later, Ellis's companion Françoise Lafitte/Delisle took a different view. On June 1, 1947 my grandmother wrote to congratulate her on *Friendship's Odyssey*, her recently published memoir of her life with Ellis:

> What you received to the full from Havelock every other woman to whom he gave friendship glimpsed potentialities of. He shaped the vision of what love should be in their minds + he enlightened the path—bitter at times—they had to tread without turning back. In a way—in a very great way—Havelock too was a father to my children. For without the vision he kindled in my soul I could not have given them the love and understanding I was able to do.

She also enclosed Ellis's final letters to her:

I did not know how near he was to death + looking back, I
wonder if I failed him in being slow to realise how urgent his need
was. I cannot even now remember whether eventually I solved the
problem for him. I thought you would like to see these letters
(which please return) for they show how tenderly he thought of
you, to spare you, even then when his need was so urgent.

The question of 'Who/What Killed Havelock Ellis?' became an
obsession for the increasingly eccentric Lafitte. She returned the letters
my grandmother had sent her but made copies, complete with her
own odd annotations, which found their way to the British Library.
She wrote savage attacks on biographers who did not share her
idealized view of Ellis, describing one in her idiosyncratic English as
'a complete stranger dropped on us from the blues'. And she was
particularly distressed by another writer's account—which drew on
an interview with my grandmother—of Ellis's end.

The result is two crazed, guilt-ridden letters from Lafitte to my
grandmother in which she poses a series of questions: When Ellis
dated a letter Friday 29 June, did he mean Thursday 29 June, Friday
30 June or perhaps even Wednesday 28 June? Could the heart trouble
he mentions have been caused by Elasto, a medicine for 'the
unswelling of the legs', which she had 'left by mistake where it
shouldn't have been, i.e. side by side with the vitamin tablets'? Could
one of his sisters have been stupid enough to have given him 'at least
3 of these pills daily in place of the vitamin tablets'? And what was
the significance of the piece of paper, torn from one of de Kok's letters,
in a box of suppositories? Delisle signs off with a mad flourish:

May no more ghastly puzzle face either you or yours in this life.
Yet there are so many leering at Mankind!!!
    My best wishes for your heroism

When my grandmother first wrote to Havelock Ellis for advice,
she could never have imagined that the correspondence would
lead here. The letters marked a turning point in her life which
allowed her to put the past behind her and embark on an impressive

career in medicine and childcare. They touched on some of the crucial questions about sex we are still struggling with. And they also helped forge the warm, unshockable woman I remember so well. Ellis's writings are intriguing and of great historical importance but also full of unintentional comedy. Yet I can only be grateful for what he did, in his own peculiar way, for my grandmother. In a letter she wrote eight years after his death, she described him as 'the man who understood woman and love and tenderness to a greater extent than any other person who has lived'. □

OMEGA
INSTITUTE

Writers & Poets Learning Vacations.

Omega offers simple, comfortable rooms; gourmet, mostly vegetarian meals; activities such as tennis, basketball, and swimming and boating on our lake; and optional morning and afternoon classes in yoga, meditation, and tai chi. Omega is less than two hours north of Manhattan in Rhinebeck, New York, and is easily accessible by car, train, or bus.

July 29–31
The Literary Life:
A Retreat on Writing and Writers
Gregory Maguire, Nancy Slonim Aronie,
Susan Orlean, Pam Houston

August 21–26
Celebration of Poetry
Fran Quinn, Paul Muldoon, Sharon Olds,
Sapphire, Chase Twichell

August 28–September 2
Story Seminar
Robert McKee

October 14–16
Fearless Fiction: A Weekend With Writers
& Actors From the NPR Series Selected Shorts
Isaiah Sheffer, Percival Everett, Julie Otsuka,
David Strathairn, Dawn Akemi Saito

Rhinebeck, N.Y. • 800.944.1001 • eomega.org

GRANTA

THE DEATH
OF A CHAIR
Doris Lessing

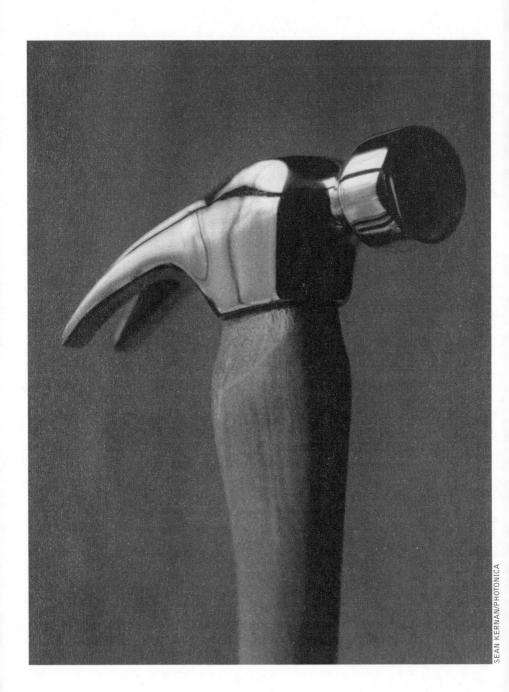

I once owned a farm cottage on Dartmoor, on the heights a mile or so above the country town of Okehampton, where every month were held auctions of furniture, kitchen equipment and farm machinery. The auctions filled the two big market-halls where also were held fêtes and fairs and all kinds of local events. It did seem as if the whole county of Devon was engaged in buying and selling farms and houses to each other, for the farm sales and auctions were popular with people coming from miles around—sometimes from Cornwall and Somerset, too—not necessarily to buy or sell, but to meet neighbours, and wander around to have a good look at how the other half lived.

In the centre of one of the halls was the better furniture, arranged into makeshift dining rooms, sitting rooms, bedrooms, each piece displayed on appropriate rugs and carpets, and there the dealers from London and Exeter arrived before anyone else. This part of the auction, which began first, was an affair of dealers bidding against each other while the rest of us looked on. But when the dealers had taken their prizes and left, there were plenty of bargains, particularly at the end of the day. All day the auctioneers and their assistants moved around among the lots, their voices sounding like a song or a chant if you were at the back of the crowd and, even close to, you had to listen hard. Meanwhile out in the yards other auctioneers were selling the farm machinery and their voices rose and fell in counterpoint. As the furniture in one part of the hall was sold, the buyers moved in to carry away their goods or sent in the men who waited outside with vans all through these days of opportunity; sofas and chairs and bric-a-brac were in constant movement outside the central drama dominated by the auctioneers. A scene of movement and impermanence.

I needed to furnish my cottage. I had the basics but the sitting room was a bit bare. I knew exactly what I wanted, I had spotted them early in the day: a sofa and an armchair. They would be sold much later than the good furniture and I knew that the later they were sold, the better the chances of my getting a bargain. The crowds thinned, as people got bored or stayed too long in the hotels and conviviality won out over bargain-getting. At the very end of the day, when it might be as late as eight or nine o'clock, when the lights were on, and the auctioneers' voices were slowing, unbelievable bargains could be had for a few shillings—perfectly good fridges and stoves and baths which had been thrown out because their owners wanted newer models. A friend of mine had equipped the kitchen and bathroom of her farm cottage for half of what a single item would have cost new.

It would be a long time before my lot was reached, up there in the hundreds, six-hundred-and-something I think it was. I went off to lunch in the hotel with friends and came back and there would still be a couple of hours before the auction reached my sofa and chair. On the old cretonne sofa now sat a middle-aged woman, and I told her I was going to bid for it, hoping she didn't intend to. No, she was selling, and went on to tell me the history of the sofa, taking her time. Her voice was all Devon, and she was a large, fair, red-cheeked woman who had to make you think of her probable Saxon forebears. 'I'm sorry to see it go,' she said, 'but I'm moving to a smaller house, now the children are grown and gone. I've had this old sofa since I married. That's forty years. It was cretonne then, a rose pattern, and it's had a good few covers since. It's as solid as a rock. My old man took his afternoon nap on it every afternoon of his life, and I've kipped down on it myself often enough when I was tired and didn't fancy climbing the stairs to my bed.'

And so she went on, talking about the sofa, and the chair too, which she had acquired at the same time. The chair now had an old labourer sleeping on it, but he was nothing to do with her because a youth, his grandson probably, came to wake him when the auctioneer reached a near lot. The woman I was sitting with, who by now seemed an old friend, I knew so much about her life on her dairy farm, got up, and sighed, and patted the sofa, and said, 'But it's no use holding on to things, not when it's time to see them go.' And she stood to one side, to see what happened.

The crowd that accompanied the auctioneer was not like the smart one that had been with him earlier in the day, bidding for the better stuff. These were mostly farmers, from the look of them, and not the rich sort. The bidding began for the sofa, and the man bidding against me dropped out when we reached three pounds. What would that be now? Then the average wage was still under twenty pounds a week. No one wanted the chair. It was very large and heavy and did not move easily over the cement floor. And the cover, of faded brown corduroy, was ripped and shredded by the claws of many cats.

The Death of a Chair

The auctioneer started the bidding at ten shillings, and that was what I got it for. Half a pound. The price of a pub lunch.

The farmer's wife, or widow, gave the sofa a final pat as she went off, but did not say goodbye to the chair, which she told me had lived for years in a back room used by the farm dogs and cats. 'And I had a lamb on it once, when it was sick. I made a barrier with a fender and there it stayed, on some sacking, until it decided to live, and I put it back with the ewe. She did accept it, though they don't always.'

That night the old sofa and the old chair arrived at my cottage. The delivery man and his assistant dragged the chair in, grunting and groaning for effect, which they hadn't done for the easier sofa.

So there was my sitting room, all set up. The sofa acquired a dark-blue cover, and the chair I covered with a new dark-brown linen, and the cats at once appropriated it. Not without protest from the humans. It was a comfortable chair.

Then I had to sell the cottage, and the sofa and chair went up to London. The chair might easily have been left, because of its weight and size, but people protested that it was too comfortable to throw away and so it joined the sofa in the movers' van. No one disputed about the sofa, which was deep and soft and long enough to sleep on. Many people had.

I was moving to a little flat, and I sawed the legs of the sofa to make it fit a certain space. The chair earned the curses of the men who carried it upstairs—not many stairs, but they said I should get rid of it. Ten years later I moved again, and this time that chair nearly was left behind, the movers hated it so much. In its new home it had to go up many flights of stairs and then up narrow stairs with a twist in them and I had to give the movers extra money. Their advice to me was to burn it: what do you want that old white elephant for, when you could buy a nice new chair?

The great chair sat in the corner of my bedroom, and the various cats sharpened their claws on it. I caught glimpses of former covers through the shreds, and many different colours. Well, I had bought the thing in the mid-Sixties, and the farm woman had had it for forty years. It wasn't new then, she said. She had married in the mid-Twenties. If you looked at it like that you could dignify the chair by calling it an antique, which sounds better than very old. Clearly, people had more room then. What a monster it was, that lumbering great chair. And I was right at the top of the house, in a room that had my bed lengthwise against the french windows. The chair was at its foot. You had to push your way past it or climb over it to get to the windows. There came a time when I decided I must get rid of it. But no one was going to buy it, I could be sure of that. And how would I find someone to take it downstairs, down to the dustbin area? It would cost money to pay someone to get it down, much more than it was worth.

Meanwhile, if the chair was a problem, the sofa had done well. Whenever I had had someone re-cover it, or move it, they exclaimed that no one made furniture like it now: so solid, so strong, so wonderfully sprung. When I did get it re-sprung, the upholsterer said that any time I wanted to sell, I must telephone him, but I would be mad to sell it, it was such a prize of a piece.

Now, the chair. Would it be possible to put ropes around it and sling it out on to the balcony beyond the french windows? And from there down on to the roof? But the roof was of slate, and that monstrous weight would dislodge slates, or even crash through the roof. I postponed and put off and continued to dodge my way over and around the chair until at last I came up with the solution. I would saw the old chair into pieces. I would dismember it, and then I could pack the pieces into rubbish bags which I could easily carry down to the bins. To attack the chair I equipped myself with a saw, sharp scissors and a claw hammer. I began by ripping off the brown cover I had put on: easy. I had used furniture tacks and glue and had roughly stitched it together at the back where no one would see the big stitches. Under that was the brown cover of thick corduroy it had had when it lived in Devon and was the home of farm dogs and cats. Not to mention the lamb.

Under the brown corduroy was another cover: flowery blue, properly fitted, not an amateur job like the two top layers. That blue layer had had a long life. It was frayed and faded. What year were we at now? Forty years, she had said. No way of knowing—but there were clues. Under the blue was an orange cover with a 'jazz' pattern: that was how this type of pattern was described in the Thirties. I remember curtains and cushions advertized as 'jazzy', a word that guaranteed modishness: 'Smarten up your furniture with our new jazzy patterns. We have them in orange, yellow and green, the fashionable colours.' This material was 'slub' linen—there was a fleck in the weave. The cover was clearly a professional effort, and so was the next, which was in grey sateen, piped and pleated, with tiny flowers. The material was thick and smooth, it had not had much wear. What would I find under it? It was hard to cut through that layer, so well did it fit on the padding. I still could not feel the wood of the frame. I decided I would start sawing at the back of the chair. I stood behind it and began. How stupid of me to think this whole business would be finished in an hour. The saw would not go through the thick pads. I tried the scissors again, pushing back layers of stuff until I found the wood, inches down. The wood was smooth—it had been planed and sandpapered and my fingers slid over it easily, but could not get very far inside, because the padding had been tacked down with those fine nails that look like cloves.

I was not doing so well with this obstinate old chair. They certainly made things solid in those days—all that trouble for a chair which would spend at least part of its life as a bed for farm animals. I finally got the saw down through the thick layers to the wood beneath and went on until I could see I was through the top back. I now regretted ever having started though I did not yet understand just what was there under my hands. I decided to saw through an arm, thinking at least *that* should come away cleanly. The difficulty was all that padding. I got some of it away, but the bottom layer was under a fine calico cover and I couldn't get it off. My claw hammer was too large and clumsy to be of any use.

I returned to the centre back which was still firm even though I had cut through it. I began cutting off wads of the layers of material, until I reached the grey sateen, and there saw—no, it was not the calico of the bottom layer of padding, this was something pale and shiny but not flashily shiny like the sateen cover. This layer, the one the chair had had when it was new, was of the palest pink silk. And now I began to suspect the truth. Pink silk! What had this chair been, in its youthful days, before it had been covered over and over with materials that were crude and clumsy, foreign to its real nature?

I used my scissors ruthlessly, and soon the delicate pink back of the chair was revealed. There the chair stood, under my roof at the top of the house, most of it covered in the rags and shags of its many torn and cut layers, but all I could see now was how it must have looked once, palely shining—and standing where? I bundled up the material I had managed to cut off, took it all down to the dustbins and returned to contemplate my wonderful chair, this once wonderful chair, now wounded in two places. How had it begun its life? When did people have chairs covered in pale pink silk in their drawing rooms? Or perhaps this was a bedroom chair, perhaps it had stood near a fireplace in a room full of the kind of furniture we do not have room for now, and had witnessed the kind of life we read about or see, let's say, in an Oscar Wilde play. It had stood on thick carpets that had rugs lying here and there, and...perhaps it was a nursing chair?

It was not too late, I could still call in a dealer. But the frame had been badly hacked, in two places, and the silk was torn and jagged. The frame could easily be mended but nothing could save that silk, and the whole point of that chair was the shining perfection of its silk. It was too late to call in a dealer. If only I had taken off the covers before beginning the sawing... I had no choice but to go on with my act of vandalism, and destroy that wonder of a chair.

First, the back, and I was immediately struck by a question: why was this silk perfect, as if it had just come from the shop? Silk quickly gets roughened, and loses its shine, but there was no sign of that here.

Under the pink silk was a layer of fine lining, in cream, which made me think of the gauzy linen the old Egyptians wore. It was firm and did not stretch, even on the bias. Under that was the thin calico, and under that the padding which consisted of three layers: the top one fine, like down, and under that a coarser one, and then a cotton-wool padding. I stripped it all off the chair back to reveal a wood the colour of weak tea. The wide strips that held the padding in place were of firm white tape and crossed each other in a basket weave, the ends fastened to the wood with tiny nails, rows of them, making a pattern outlining the chair back. My claw hammer could not get anywhere near those nails. Each layer of the padding had been tacked on to this web, with great running stitches that also made a pattern of aligned chevrons. I imagined the craftsman who had made the chair kneeling by it on a stool, with his great shining curved steel needle, making that chevron pattern which no one would ever see, tapping in those perfect little nails...but wasn't *I* seeing it and thinking of him? He was long dead, but his patterns of nails were still there glittering like silver, and the threads of the stitches were gleaming in the light from my big windows.

And now the arms. First I stripped the arm I had already cut through—a solid flat arm, nearly a foot wide. The stuffing on it was deep and thick. The arms, like the back, had the same linen-like cover that enclosed the calico to keep the padding in place. The pink silk of the arm covers had been fitted and stitched with stitches so fine I could hardly see them. Had the man who did those big clever running stitches done these fairy stitches as well? The needle he used must have been as fine as a hair, and the silk thread even finer. But enough: off with the silk cover and the padding and the shreds of the layers of its various incarnations. There stood the frame, its back filled in with webbing, but hacked through, and the bare arms. There was a lot of rubbish to stuff into bags, and it was painful to see the pieces of beautiful pink silk. But I remembered the farmer's wife saying, 'It's no use holding on to things, not when it's time to see them go.'

Now for the seat. As soon as I lifted the silk cushion, I saw that it had once been turned over: the underside was stained with something black—a big stain, filling almost the whole surface. I imagined I could still smell an acrid and corrosive substance, strong enough to burn the silk, which in the area of the stain was flaking and shredding, like burnt paper, and rotting round the edges. Some sort of medicine? Oil for a lamp?

So this glorious chair early in its life had suffered an accident and that was why the silk had never roughened and dulled. The owners of this chair had turned the cushion over, because of the stain, but then had decided—well, what? Cushions can be covered. Why had the owners not called in the experts and got their cushion made new? I let my imagination go to work. Had something bad happened? A divorce?—not likely, in those days. A death? The home had been dispersed? There had been some awful illness? Someone, wrapped in blankets, had sat in this chair to die? Associated with calamity, the chair had had to go? How many stops had this chair made in this house or that before it became a farm chair in Devon, and a place of rest for dogs and cats, and the lamb?

This chair had lived through the First World War, let us say in London, but during the Second World War it was in Devon and well out of the way of the bombing. For some reason this stain had disgraced the chair, which had found itself cast out—perhaps even to a junk shop, where it was bought by somebody attracted by the pale silken gleam, but who had then decided that pink silk was too much of a good thing, and had re-upholstered it with the shiny grey sateen patterned with little flowers.

I wished I had the address of the farm woman from Devon, so I could write and tell her what I had discovered but it was getting on for forty years since the auction in Okehampton, and she had owned the chair for forty years before that.

I put the shameful cushion into a rubbish bag, and went on with the demolition job. The cushion did not sit on wooden slats or any common sort of base. Instead, there was a looseish layer of white lining, and under that, a lattice of webbing, and on the webbing nine fat springs, each stitched down with strong thread, and bedded in handfuls of sheep's wool so that it could not bang against its neighbours. No matter how heavily anyone sat down not a sound would have been heard of clashing or squeaking springs.

How long had it taken to make this chair? I imagined a mature craftsman and his apprentice, kneeling together by the chair frame. They had planed and sandpapered the wood and beside them on the floor on newspapers were the already cut-out pieces of pink silk. A box held the hammers, pincers, scissors and springs. Smaller boxes held the minute silver nails, the nails like tiny cloves, the reels of different thicknesses of pink silk thread, pink cotton, white thread. The young man would have looked at the tiny nails, the needles, curved and straight, and then at the big hands of his mentor, confidently handling these tools, the wadding, the lining; he was wondering, 'Will these clumsy hands of mine ever be able to…?' This scene, in those days of craftsmen and their apprentices, must have taken place every day, in dozens of places. And the older man would say, 'Just watch, you'll get the hang of it, you'll see.'

Long ago this scene had taken place, by this chair, a hundred years ago at least. The chair had a stately, calm, confident air—but not an assertive one, no. It was capacious. It was designed for big skirts and ample people.

Another plastic bag of rubbish went down to the bins.

Then I took up the saw and went to work.   □

GRANTA

BLIGHT
Robert Gumpert

Robert Gumpert

At the beginning of 2004, a freelance photographer living and working in America, I lost my biggest client after a disagreement over politics. For most of that year, without much work, I had more time than usual to think, read, listen to the news and walk. With less money and fewer resources, even my own projects—which were usually done on a shoestring anyway—had to be put on hold. Current events were and are depressing in this country. Back then we were having elections (primaries, conventions and then the national) and the conservative right and the armies of God seemed very much on the move. At some point, after a period of not taking any photos at all, let alone something that meant anything to me, I was out walking, wandering round my neighbourhood in San Francisco, and some of the leaves that had fallen caught my eye because of the way they were decaying. It seemed right to try taking photographs of them, so I took a couple home. I put them between two sheets of glass, back-lit them and photographed them. As it happened, I wasn't so much interested in the shape of the leaf but more in the patterns, the way decay showed up on them. I'm not sure of the right words to describe them, but I found the patterns beautiful, exciting, somehow a tonic for the depression I was fighting. They offered a sanctuary of sorts from the insanity of current events. So I carried on. It was done pretty much at random. What was photographed depended on where I was walking: to the post office, the bookstore, the grocery, or just walking to walk. I picked up what was in my path, whatever had fallen on the ground.

I know what some of them are: magnolia blossom, geraniums, oak leaves, for example, but in most cases I have no idea. At first I kept the leaves and flowers with the intention of going through a plant book to find out what they were, but after a while I realized that my interest in them wasn't so much in what they were called, as with what they made me feel. So they all went into the compost. Somewhere I read of a scientist, or maybe it was a philosopher, who observed that we are all made up of the same matter that's been around since the big bang. In some way I can see and feel that evolution in these patterns of decay. □

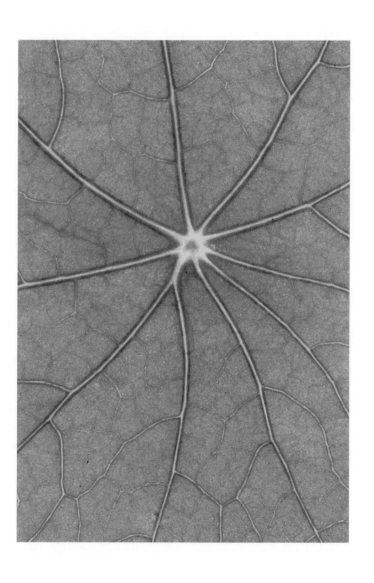

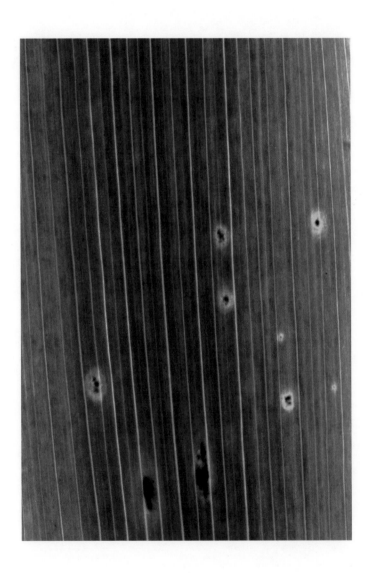

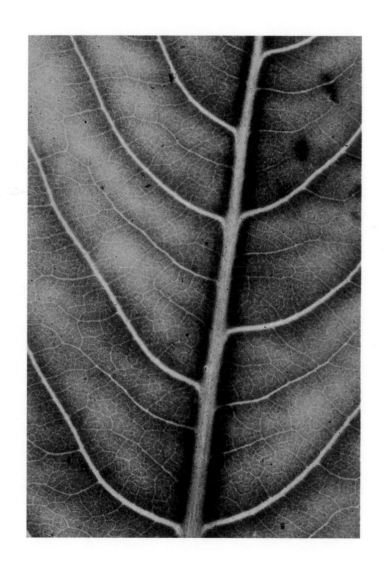

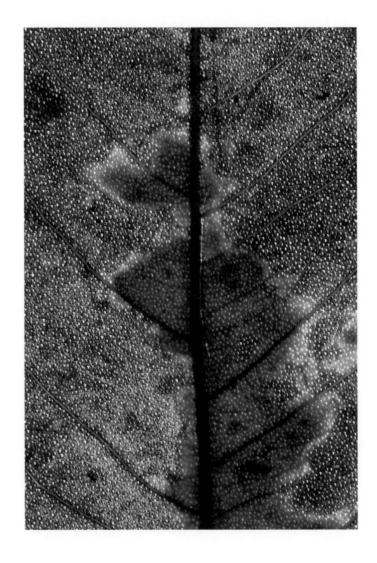

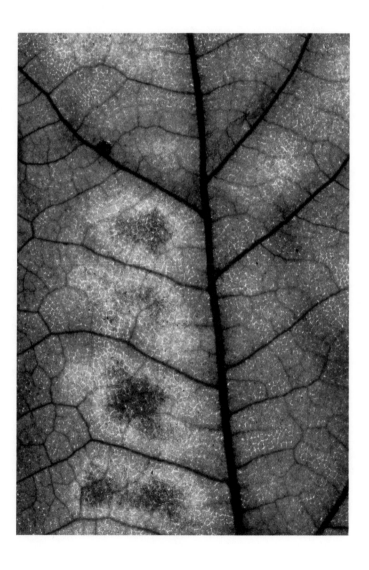

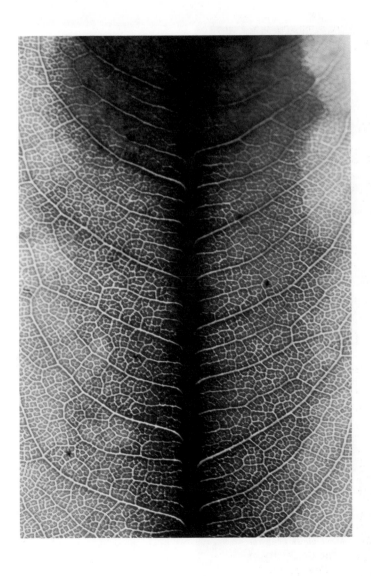

THE NATURAL WORLD

Wildlife Spectacles

Russell A. Mittermeier, Patricio Robles Gil, Cristina Goettsch Mittermeier, Thomas Brooks, Michael Hoffman, William R. Konstant, Gustavo A.B. da Fonseca, and Roderic Mast

Wildlife Spectacles captures in brilliant full-color photographs the force and mystery of mass assemblages of animals. The volume features thirty-six chapters written by biodiversity scientists that explain the history, geographic distribution, and daily lives of various animal species, as well as the conservation efforts employed to ensure their survival. The compelling core of the volume, however, lies in the breathtaking images that document these vast gatherings.

Distributed for Conservation International
Cloth $50.00

Dancing at the Dead Sea

Tracking the World's Environmental Hotspots
Alanna Mitchell

"A powerful narrative on the critically important topic of the world's environmental hotspots. This is not a pessimistic tirade, but instead a factual commentary that will convince many, written by a gifted writer with an independent mind. I recommend this book without reservation."—Richard Leakey

"A lively, impassioned ecological travelogue."—*Audubon*
Cloth $25.00

GRANTA

SHOWTIME

FARMING PHOTOGRAPHS FROM
THE DAILY HERALD ARCHIVE
TEXT BY LIZ JOBEY

Liz Jobey

It was the Victorians, with their enthusiasm for trade societies and public exhibitions, and Queen Victoria and Prince Albert in particular, with their willingness to patronize so many of them, who turned local summer shows into major annual events. During the 1830s and 1840s, many of the smaller agricultural societies amalgamated to form county-wide organizations which every summer ran a programme of events over several days. Often they kept to the local 'feast' weeks, the days around a popular local saint's day which had been celebrated since medieval times. Farmers exhibited their livestock, manufacturers showed off their latest farm machinery, experts in breeding and cultivation demonstrated their ideas. This basic formula survived the industrial and technological revolutions, as well as two world wars and several outbreaks of foot-and-mouth disease. Today, the Royal Show (first held in 1839) offers 'hospitality opportunities', 'networking facilities' and a chance to meet 'major players' in the agricultural world. But inside the ring, the core activities are still the same: men and women proudly leading their animals around on foot.

These days every agricultural show has a web site showing photographs of last year's winners. But apart from being in colour, they are not so different from the ones on the following pages. These photographs come from the archive of the *Daily Herald*, launched in 1911 as a trade union paper, and eventually, in the 1960s, becoming the *Sun*. The photo archive was given to the National Portrait Gallery in the 1970s and is now kept at the National Museum of Photography, Film and Television in Bradford.

Picture archives are places of easy nostalgia. When you look through files marked 'Industry: Agriculture', pulling out black-and-white prints of haystacks, cart horses and harvest suppers, it can seem that life was so much simpler then. Common sense tells you that this is nonsense: farming was, for the most part, hard, unprofitable and, particularly in the 1930s, under threat from cheap foreign imports of grain and meat that almost put British farmers out of business. In the future was mechanization and mass production, Europe's common agricultural policy, milk and butter mountains, mad cow disease, GM crops. But faced with a series of pictures of cheerful London families working in the Kentish hop fields which unfolds like a Pathé newsreel, you can find this future is easy to forget. □

'Mathrafal', a Welsh Cob stallion, owned by blind farmer Evan Richards of Bridgend, led by Dillwyn Thomas, Royal Welsh Show, Carnarvon, July 1952

Tavistock Agricultural Show, Devon, August 1948

'Chapel Margaret 108th' led by Miss Jennie Spence,
Great Yorkshire Show, Harrogate, July 1951

Miss Betty Ching with 'Escott Topper', Royal Agricultural Show,
Tavistock, Devon, August 1948

A cattleman asleep in one of the stalls at the Olympia Dairy
Show, London, September 1938

Miss Elizabeth Rochford of Little Berkhampstead with two of her
Anglo-Nubian goats, Bath and West Show, May 1956

Shepherd Harold Rush with his champion Suffolk ram,
Royal Show, Cambridge, July 4 1951

Stilt men, on 15 ft stilts, repairing the broken strings
on hop poles, Waterbury, Kent, June 1927

London families arriving for the hop-picking season,
Paddock Wood, Kent, August 31 1946

Hop pickers at Whitbread's Farm, Beltring, Kent, August 1935

Hop stringer Bert Parks with his daughter, Phyllis, as his wife
finishes off the banding, Kent, April 1954

Children helping to collect and destroy a plague of Colorado beetles, which threatened to destroy potato crops, Jersey, the Channel Islands, June 1950

A visit to Mrs Harrison Bell's farm, Welwyn, Hertfordshire, February 1933

At the Ovaltine Farm, Kings Langley, Hertfordshire, June 1937

Dustmen from Tottenham Borough Cleansing Department set up the first wartime pig club with a consignment of forty piglets, December 1939

GRANTA

CONSTITUTIONAL
Helen Simpson

'I just think she's a bit passive-aggressive,' said the woman to her friend. 'In a very sweet way. D'you know what I mean?'

This is so much the sort of thing you hear on the Heath that I couldn't help smiling, straight from Stella's funeral though I was, standing aside to let them past me on to the pavement. Even five minutes later, almost at the ponds, I'm smiling, but that could be simple relief at being outside in some November sun.

The thing about a circular walk is that you end up where you started—except, of course, that you don't. My usual round trip removes me neatly from the fetid staffroom lunch hour, conveniently located as the school is on the very edge of the Heath. And as Head of Science I'm usually able to keep at least two lunch hours a week free by arranging as many of the departmental meetings and astronomy clubs and so on as I possibly can to take place after school.

Because I know exactly how long I have—quick glance at my watch, fifty-three minutes left—and exactly how long it takes, I can afford to let my mind off the lead. Look at the sparkle of that dog's urine against the dark green of the laurel, and its wolfish cocked leg. In the space of an hour I know I can walk my way back to some sort of balance after my morning-off's farewell distress before launching into sexual reproduction with Year Ten at five past two.

When the sun flares out like this, heatless and long-shadowed, the tree trunks go floodlit and even the puddles in the mud hold flashing blue snapshots of the sky. You walk past people who are so full of their lives and thoughts and talk about others, so absorbed in exchanging human information, that often their gaze stays abstractedly on the path and their legs are moving mechanically. But their dogs frisk around, arabesques of pink tongues airing in their broadly smiling jaws. They bound off after squirrels or seagulls, they bark, *rowrowrow*, into the sunshine, and there is no idea anywhere of what comes next.

STEPHEN GILL

This walk is always the same but different, thanks to the light, the time of year, the temperature and so on. Its sameness allows me to sink back into my thoughts as I swing along, while on the other hand

195

Helen Simpson

I know and observe at some level that nothing is ever exactly the same as it was before.

It's reminding me of that card game my grandfather taught me, Clock Patience, this circuit, today. I'm treading the round face of a twelve-hour clock. Time is getting to be a bit of an obsession but then I suppose that's only natural in my condition. So, it's a waiting game, Clock Patience. You deal the fifty-two cards in the pack, one for each week of the year, face down into a circle of twelve, January to December, and there is your old-fashioned clock face. I didn't find out till last week so that's something else to get used to. Stella would have been interested. Fascinated. The queen is at the top, at twelve o'clock, while ace is low at one.

Forty-nine minutes left. From that hill up there to my right it's possible to see for miles, all over London, and on a clear day I'm pretty sure I can pinpoint my road in Dalston. A skipper on the Thames looked up here at the northern heights three centuries ago and exclaimed at how even though it was midsummer the hills were capped with snow. All the Heath's low trees and bushes were festooned with clean shirts and smocks hung out to dry, white on green, this being where London's laundry was done.

So you deal the first twelve cards face down in the shape of a clock face, then the thirteenth goes, also face down, into the middle. Do this three times more and you end up with four cards on every numeral and four in a line across the clock.

As I overtake an elderly couple dawdling towards the ponds, these words drift into my ears—'...terrible pain. Appalling. They've tried this and that but nothing seems to help. Disgusting...' The words float after me even though I speed up and leave the two of them like tortoises on the path behind me.

Start by lifting one of the four central cards. Is it a three of hearts? Slide it face up under the little pile at three o'clock, and help yourself to the top card there. Ten of spades? Go to ten o'clock and repeat the procedure. Ah, but when you turn up a king, the game gains pace. The king flies to the centre of the clock and lies face upwards. You lift his downturned neighbour and continue. Nearly always the kings beat the clock—they glare up at you from their completed gang before you have run your course, four scowling tyrants. But occasionally you get the full clock out before that happens, every hour completed; and that's very satisfying.

'Patience is more of a woman's card game,' said Aidan, who prefers poker. 'The secretaries at work got hooked on computer solitaire. We had to get the IT department to erase it from the memories.'

We were lying in bed at the time.

'Have you noticed how on rush-hour trains,' I countered, 'A seated man will open up his laptop in the middle of the general crush and you'll think, *He* must have important work to do. Then you peep round the edge of the screen and he's playing a game of exploding spaceships.'

I don't know when I should tell him about this latest development. Pregnancy. Or even, whether.

One thing the doctor asked my grandfather to do early on, before his diagnosis, was to draw a simple clock face on a piece of paper and then sketch in the hands at five past ten. He couldn't do it. I was there. His pencil seemed to run away with him. His clock had wavy edges, it had gone into meltdown, the numerals were dropping off all over the place and the whole thing was a portrait of disintegration.

Forty-five minutes. I can't believe my body has lasted this long, said Stella the last time I visited her in her flat. When you think (she said), more than ninety years, it seems quite incredible. She had few teeth, three or four perhaps, and didn't seem to mind this, although one of them came out in her sandwich that day while we were having lunch, which gave us both a shudder of horror. When she had the first of her funny turns and I visited her in hospital, she said, 'I don't care what's wrong with me. Either they put it right or not. But what's the point? Just to go on and on?'

For some reason the fact that she was ninety-three when she died and that her body was worn out did not make her death any more acceptable to this morning's congregation. The church was rocking with indignant stifled sobs at the sight of the coffin in front of the altar, and her old body in it. She had no children but hundreds of friends. Her declared line had always been that since death is unknowable it's simply not worth thinking about. She didn't seem to derive much comfort from this at the end, though.

Prolongation of morbidity is what they're calling this new lease of life after seventy. I turned to the sharp-looking woman brushing away tears beside me in the pew this morning, and said, 'You'd think it would be easier on both sides to say goodbye; but ninety-three or not, it isn't.'

'That's why I won't allow myself to befriend old people any more,' said my sharp neighbour. 'I can't afford to invest my time and emotion in them when the outcome's inevitable.'

'That's hard!' I exclaimed.

'So's grief,' she growled. 'Don't give me grief. I'm not volunteering for it any more.'

Look at these benches, inscribed with the dates of the various dear departed, positioned at the side of the path so the living can rest on the dead and enjoy the view. There seems to be a new one every time I go for a walk. They're the modern version of a headstone or a sarcophagus. DAVID FORD—A KINDLY MAN AND A GOOD CITIZEN. How distant he must have been from the rest, to have this as his epitaph. Or here, equally depressing, MARJORIE SMITH—HER LIFE WAS DEVOTION TO OTHERS. We all know what *that* means.

The sharp woman this morning, she had a whiff of therapy-speak about her. What she said, the way she said it, reminded me of my father in some way. Let the past go, he declares; what's the point in raking over the past, chewing over old news. As my mother would say, How *convenient.* And when, precisely, does the past begin, according to him? Last year? Yesterday? A minute ago?

My father, living in Toronto at the moment, has a deliberately poor memory and refuses nostalgia point-blank. There has been a refreshing lack of clutter in the various places he's lived since leaving home when I was five. He treats his life as a picaresque adventure, sloughing off old skin and moving on, reinventing himself on a regular basis. He lives with the freshness and brutality of an infant. He can't see the point of continuity, he feels no loyalty to the past. What he values is how he feels now. That phrase, 'Where are we going?', he's allergic to it, and from the moment a woman delivers herself of those words to him she's on the way out as far as he is concerned. Goodbye Sarah, Lauren, Anna, Phoebe and countless others, the women whom he refers to as romantic episodes.

I don't see my life in quite the same way, though I have a certain sympathy for that nonchalant approach. Aidan, for example, likes to identify his objectives and be proactive at taking life by the scruff of the neck; whereas I prefer to nose forward instinctively, towards some dim but deeply apprehended object of desire which I can't even put into words. He says that's our age difference showing: I've got a touch of the old hippy still whereas he's free of those sentimental tendencies. Anyway, I used to say to him, what if nothing much happens to you, or lots of different disjointed things? Does that make you any less of a person? I suppose I was being aggressive-passive.

At least I was being open, unlike Aidan who has a selective memory and failed to mention he was married. When I found out, then it was time for me to let the past go, to move on, despite his talk of leaving. I wasn't born yesterday.

My mother could not be more different from my father. Why they married is a mystery. She is perpetually at work on weaving the story of her life; she sees herself as the central figure in her own grand tapestry. She carries her past with her like a great snail shell, burnished with high-density embellishments. She remembers every conceivable anniversary—birthdays, deaths, first kisses, operations, house moves—and most of her talk starts, 'Do you remember?' There is quite a lot I don't remember, since I left home and Scotland as soon as I could, not popular with my stepfather, the Hero in her quest, her voyage-and-return after the false start that was my father. I was heavily abridged in the process. I'd be willing to bet a thousand pounds that her main concern once I tell her about the baby will be how to incorporate the role of grandmother into her carefully woven narrative. Still, Aberdeen is a long way off.

Helen Simpson

I'm finding more and more when I meet new people that, within minutes of saying hello, they're laying themselves out in front of me like scientific diagrams which they then explain—complex specimens, analysed and summed up in their own words. They talk about their past in great detail, they tell me their story, and then—this is what passes for intimacy now—they ask me to tell them mine. I have tried. But I can't. It seems cooked up, that sort of story. And how could it ever be more than the current version? It makes me feel, No *that's* not it and *that's* not it, as soon as I've said something. Perhaps I'm my father's daughter after all. It's not that I'm particularly secretive—it's more to do with whatever it is in us that objects to being photographed.

And here's the oldest jogger I've seen for a while, barely moving, white-bearded—look, I'm going faster than him even at walking pace. It's hard not to see a bony figure at his shoulder, a figure with a scythe.

I was on the tube this morning minding my own business when I realized that the old fellow standing beside me—not quite Zimmer-frame, but bald, paunchy, in his early seventies—was giving me the eye. I looked back over my shoulder instinctively. Then I realized that it was *me* he was eyeing and couldn't restrain a shocked snort of laughter. The parameters shift once you're past forty, it seems, when it comes to the dance of wanting and being wanted. Though that was always very good with Aidan, whatever else was wrong between us, and he's seven years younger than me.

You would think that a science teacher and tutor of sex ed would know how not to get pregnant. You would think so. Once again it was to do with my age. My GP noticed that I'd just had another birthday and advised me to stop taking the Pill. It was time to give my system a rest, she suggested, time to get back in touch with my natural cycle again now that I was so much less fertile because of the years. There are other methods of contraception far more natural, she continued, and far less invasive than stroke-inducing daily doses of oestrogen and progestogen. She sent me off to a natural family-planning guru.

I learned to chart the months, colouring my safe days in blue and my fertile days in red, in advance, thanks to the clockwork regularity of my cycle. It was pretty much half-and-half, with the most dangerous time from day thirteen to day seventeen, day one being the first day of my period. I took my temperature with a digital thermometer every morning and believed that I was safe once it had risen by 0.2 degrees from a previous low temperature for three days in a row. The onset of a glossy albuminous secretion, though, meant I had to be on red alert.

Emboldened by contact with my own inner calendar, its individual ebb and flow, I took a pair of compasses and made a circular chart for each monthly revolution on tracing paper, with several inner circles all marked with the days of my private month, recording dates of orgasm, vivid dreams, time of ovulation, phases of the moon and so on. I was steadier and more pedestrian during the first half of my inner month, I noticed—and more thin-skinned, clever and volatile in the fortnight before my period.

When after several months I placed the translucent sheets of tracing paper on top of each other, I was able to see both the regularly repeated events and also the slight variations over time as a wheeling overlap, so that looking back down the past year was like gazing into a helix with seashell striations.

'My cycle seems rather disturbed,' I said to the Wise Woman at one of our consultations.

'Two teaspoons of honey daily should regularize that,' she said. And I nodded and smiled. No kidding. Me, with a biology degree from a good university and a keen interest in neuroscience. Then, of course, three weeks after saying goodbye forever to Aidan, I found I was pregnant. Talk about the biological clock.

Thirty-six minutes left. See the sun on the bark of this sweet-chestnut tree, and how it lights up the edges of these spiralling wrinkled grooves. Our brain cortex looks like wet tree bark, as I was telling Year Eleven only yesterday. This expansive outer layer with its hundred billion nerve cells has to contract itself into tightly concertinaed ripples and ridges, it has to pleat and fold back on itself in order to pack down far enough to fit inside the skull.

It's hard to think of Stella this morning in her coffin, her bones, her skull with the brain annihilated. She could remember ninety years ago, as many nonagenarians can, as though it were yesterday; but—

unusual, this—she could also remember yesterday. That is a great thing in extreme old age, to be both near- and far-sighted. Once I asked her what was her earliest memory, and she thought it might have been when she was one or possibly two, sitting outside the post office in her pram on a snowy day. She was watching the boy in the pram on the other side of the doorway as he howled and howled—'And I thought, "Oh do be quiet! They're coming back, you know. It's really ridiculous to make a noise like that. They haven't left us here forever." He was wearing a white fur bonnet which I wanted for myself.'

This memory of hers sent some messenger running in my brain, zigzagging along corridors and byways of the mind, and triggered the retrieval of my own earliest memory, which she heard with a hoot of incredulity. I was standing outside my parents' bedroom door, and for the first time felt flood over me the realization that they were not part of me. They were separate. And I thought of my own selfish demands, and wanted to go into them and say how sorry I was for being a burden to them and how considerate they would find me now that I had realized I was not part of them. The bedroom door was tall as a tree in front of me.

'Very guilty,' I told Stella. 'I feel guilty generally. Don't you?'

She paused and we both waited to see what she would come up with. Talking to her was like mackerel fishing, the short wait and then the flash of silver.

'I don't feel guilty *enough*,' she said, with emphasis, at last.

When her doorbell rang, she would open the front-room window of her first-floor flat and let down a fishing line with a key attached to the end of it where the hook would otherwise have been. That way her visitors could unlock the front door and let themselves in, saving her the stairs.

She listened with interest while I tried to describe the latest theories about memory, how they now think that when you try to remember something you are not going to your mental library to take a memory-book off the shelf or to play back a memory-videotape. No, you are remembering the original memory; you are reconstructing that memory. The more frequently you chase a particular memory and reconstruct it, the more firmly established in the brain that memory track becomes.

Constitutional

This short cut I've just taken—thirty-one minutes, I'm watching the time—at first it was nothing but that the grass had been walked on once or twice; but it's obviously been trodden over again and again, hundreds of times, and has become an established path. Repetition—repeated reconstruction of the memory—strengthens it.

'So, Stella,' I said, 'You remember that fur bonnet from ninety years ago because you've remembered it so often that by now it's an established right of way, it's on all your maps.'

'I am not aware of having called up that memory more than once or twice,' said Stella. 'In fact I could have sworn it appeared for the first time last week. But you may be right.'

Occasional Bentleys used to glide down our mean street and disgorge a superannuated star or two—a fabled ex-Orsino, a yesteryear Hamlet. Stella had been a well-known actress, she had travelled the world with various theatre companies, she had never married; nor apparently had she ever made much money, for here she was in extreme old age living in a rented room on next to nothing. She was still working, for heaven's sake. Three times a week she would creep painfully down the stairs a step at a time, allowing a good twenty minutes for the descent, then wait for the bus to take her into Gower Street, where she introduced her students to Beatrice and Imogen and Portia and the traditional heartbeat of the iambic pentameter. She remained undimmed, without any of the usual inward-turning self-protective solipsism, open like a Shakespearean heroine to grief and chance and friendship even in her tenth decade.

If it is true that each established memory makes a track, a starry synaptic trail in the brain, and that every time we return to (or as they insist, *reconstruct*) that particular constellation of memory, we strengthen it, then so is the following: Stella's billion lucent constellations may have been extinguished at her death, but she herself has become part of my own brain galaxy, and part of the nebulous clusters of all her myriad friends. Every time I remember Stella, I'll be etching her deeper into myself, my cells, my memory.

Twenty-nine minutes until I'm due back at school. That staffroom yesterday was like a rest home for the elderly. The young ones had all gone off to leap around at some staff-pupil netball match, leaving the over-thirties to spread out with their sandwiches. I sat marking at a table near to where Max, Head of Maths, was chatting with Lower-School-History Peter and the new Geography woman.

'It's on the tip of my tongue,' said Max, his eyes locking hungrily on to Peter's. 'You know, the one that looks like...'

'In Year Eight?' said Peter.

'Bloody hell, I've got that thing,' groaned Max, 'You know, that disease, what the hell's it called, where you can't remember anything...'

'No you haven't!' snapped Peter. He fancies him.

'I went to get some money out on Sunday,' he fretted. 'I stood in the queue for the cash machine for ten minutes then when it was my turn I couldn't remember my PIN number. I'm Head of Maths, for pity's sake. So I tapped in 1989—in case I'd used my memorable date, because that's it—but apparently I hadn't because the machine then swallowed my card.'

'You read about people being tortured for their PIN number,' said the new Geography woman—what *is* her name—'Well, they could torture me to within an inch of my life and I still wouldn't know it. I'd be dead and they still wouldn't have the money.'

'What happened in 1989?' asked Peter keenly.

'Arsenal beat Liverpool 2–0 at Anfield,' said Max.

'Did they?' said Peter.

'You're not into football, then,' said Max as he turned to the crossword, shaking out his newspaper, and Peter's face fell.

It reminded me of that scene in the restaurant last time I was out for a meal with Aidan. The couple at the neighbouring table were gaping at each other wordlessly, silent with frustration. Then he electrified everyone within earshot by softly howling, 'It's gone, it's gone.' I thought he'd swallowed a tooth, an expensive crown. His expression seemed to bear this out—anguish and a mute plea for silence. But no—it was merely that he had forgotten what he was halfway through saying. He was having a senior moment.

I've always had a very good memory. It used to be that any word I wanted would fly to me like a bird; I'd put my hand up and pluck it out of the air. Effortless. Gratifying. Facts, too, came when called, and when someone gave me their phone number I would be able to hold it in my head till later when I had a pen—even several hours later.

Thanks to this, I never had any trouble with exams, unlike my GP cousin who spent her years at medical school paddling round frantically in a sea of mnemonics. 'Two Zulus Buggered My Cat,' she'd say. 'Test me, I've got to learn the branches of the facial nerve.' And what was the one she found so hideously embarrassing? See if I can remember. It was the one for the cranial nerves.

Oh	Optic
Oh	Ophthalmic
Oh	Oculomotor
To	Trochlear
Touch	Trigeminal
And	Abducent
Feel	Facial
Veronica's	Vestibular
Glorious	Glossopharyngeal
Vagina	Vagus
And	Accessory
Hymen	Hypoglossal

Not that she's prudish, but she was in a predominantly male class of twenty-two-year-olds at the time, and that's her name—Veronica.

The minute I hit forty, I lost that instant recall. I had to wait for the right cue, listen to the cogs grinding, before the word or fact would come to me. Your brain cells are dying off, Aidan would taunt.

Even so, I sometimes think my memory is too good. I don't forget *enough*. I wish I could forget *him*. It's all a question of emotional metabolism, whether you're happy or not. You devour new experience, you digest and absorb what will be nourishing, you let the rest go. And if you can't shed waste matter, you'll grow costive and gloomy and dyspeptic. My mother always says she can forgive (with a virtuous sigh); but she can never forget (with a beady look). She is mistaken in her pride over this. Not to be able to forget is a

Helen Simpson

curse. I read somewhere a story that haunted me, about a young man, not particularly clever or remarkable in any way except that he remembered everything that he had ever seen or heard. The government of whatever country it was he lived in grew interested, thinking this might be useful to them, but nothing came of it. The man grew desperate, writing out sheets of total recall and then setting fire to them in the hope that seeing them go up in flames would raze them from his mind. Nothing worked. He was a sea of unfiltered memories. He went mad.

Max is worried that forgetting his PIN number is the first step to losing his mind but really his only problem is that he knows too much. How old is he? Near retirement, anyway. Twenty years older than me. After a certain age your hard disk is much fuller than it's ever been, thanks to the build-up of the years. Mine has certainly started refusing to register anything it doesn't regard as essential— I frequently find myself walking back down the road now to check I've locked the front door behind me. Your internal organs stop self-renewing at a certain point, and at the same time your mind begins to change its old promiscuous habits in the interests of managing what it's already got.

I sometimes taunt Max with the crossword if I'm sitting near him in the staffroom in the lunch hour. 'It's on the tip of my tongue,' he moans. Last week there was a brilliant clue, tailor-made for a mathematician too—'Caring, calm, direct—New Man's sixty-third year. (5,11; 9 Across and 3 Down).' He rolled his eyes and scowled and moaned, followed various trails up blind alleys, barked with exasperation, and his mind ran around all over the place following various scents. It was interesting to observe him in the act.

Twenty-five minutes, and I've reached the tangled old oak near the top fence with its scores of crooked branches and thousands of sharp-angled twigs. I use trees to help me explain to my sixth-form biologists how the brain works. 'Neurons are the brain's thinking cells,' I say, and they nod. 'There are billions of neurons in everyone's brain,' I say, and they nod and smile. 'And each one of these billions of neurons is fringed with thousands of fine whiskers called dendrites,' I continue, while they start to look mildly incredulous— and who can blame them? The word *dendrite* comes from the Greek for tree, I tell them, and our neuron-fringing dendrites help create the brain's forest of connectivity. Dendrites are vital messengers between neuron and neuron, they cross the little gappy synapses in between, they link our thoughts together. It's as though several hundred thousand trees have been uprooted and had their heads pushed together from every direction—there is an enormous interlocking tangle of branches and touching twigs.

While I waited for Max as he wrestled with that clue, I could almost hear the rustle and creak of trees conferring. 'I'll give you another clue,' I said. 'You're in it.' But even that didn't help him.

It's not that my mind is going, it's more like my long-term memory is refusing to accept any more material unless it's really unmissable. When I was young I remembered everything because it was all new. I could remember whether I'd locked the door because I'd only locked it a few hundred times before. Now I can't ever remember whether I've locked it as I've done it thousands of times and my memory will no longer deign to notice what is so old and stale.

My short-term memory is in fact wiping the slate clean disconcertingly often these days. Like an autocratic secretary, it decides whether to let immediate thoughts and impressions cross over into the long-term memory's library—or whether to press the delete button on them. 'I've got an enormous backlog of filing and I simply can't allow yet more unsifted material to accumulate,' it snaps, peering over its bifocals. 'It's not that there isn't enough space—there is—but it's got to the point where I need to sort and label carefully before shelving, or it'll be lost forever—it'll be in there somewhere, but unretrievable.'

The thing about my sixth formers—about all my pupils, in fact—is that it is not necessary for them to commit anything to memory. Why should they store information in their skulls when they've got it at their fingertips? Yet Stella's decades of learning speeches by heart meant that when age began its long war of attrition her mind was shored up with great heaps of blank verse. I have noticed myself that if I don't continue to learn by repetition, even just the odd phone number, then my ability to do so starts to slide away. I will not, however, be trying to learn Russian in my old age as I once promised myself. No, I'll follow the progress of neuroscientific research, wherever it's got to. I've learned from Jane Blizzard's example that you have to find a way to graft new stuff on to old in order to make it stick.

My ex-colleague Jane had been teaching French and Latin for as long as anyone could remember. She decided when she took early retirement at fifty-five last year that she wanted to study for the three sciences at A level, and came to me for help in organizing this. Forty years ago she had not been allowed to take science at her all-girls school, even at a lower level, and felt this was a block of ignorance she wanted to melt. She's clever, and passed the three A levels with flying colours, but to her horror discovered a few months later that all her newly acquired knowledge had trickled away. She had not been able to attach it to anything she already knew, and her long-term memory had refused to retain it.

As I overtake a couple of pram-pushing mothers in their early thirties, I hear, 'Her feet were facing the wrong way.' Would this mean anything to a girl of seventeen? Or to a man of sixty-three? My pupils will baulk at my pregnancy. The younger ones will find it positively disgusting. I speed up and pass two older women, late fifties perhaps, free of make-up, wrapped in a jumble of coloured scarves and glasses on beaded chains, escorting a couple of barrel-shaped Labradors as big as buses. 'She was just lying on the pavement panting, refusing to move,' one of them announces as I pass. They have moved on from the dramas of children to the life-and-death stuff of dogs. And I, I who am supposed to be somewhere between these two stages, where am I in this grand pageant? My colleagues will say to each other, So why didn't she get rid of it?

Eighteen minutes left, and I'm making good time. If I'm lucky I might even catch Max groaning over his unsolved clues and help put him out of his misery.

It was my grandfather again who introduced me to crosswords—first the general knowledge ones, then, as I left childhood, the cryptics. He had an acrobatic mind and a generous nature. I used to stay with him and my grandmother for long stretches of the school holidays, as we liked each other's company and my parents were otherwise involved.

When my grandfather started to forget at the age of eighty-one—by which time I had long since finished at university and was on to my second teaching job—it was not the more usual benign memory loss. It was because his short-term memory, his mind's secretary, was being smothered and throttled by a tangle of rogue neurofibres.

Since different sorts of memory are held in different parts of the brain, the rest stayed fine for a while. He could tell me in detail about his schooldays, but not remember that his beloved dog had died the day before. It reminded me of the unsinkable *Titanic* with its separate compartments. In time, his long-term memory failed as well. The change was insidious and incremental, but I noticed it sharply as there would usually be several months between my visits.

Talking to someone whose short-term memory has gone is like pouring liquid into a baseless vessel. Your words go straight through without being held at all. That really is memory like a sieve. While I was digging the hole in his back garden in which to bury the dog, he stood beside me and asked what I was doing.

'Poor Captain was run over,' I replied, 'So I'm digging his grave.'

'Oh that's terrible,' he exclaimed, tears reddening his rheumy old eyes. 'How terrible! How did it happen?'

I described how Captain's body had been found at the kerbside on the corner of Blythedale Avenue, but he was examining the unravelled cuff of his cardigan by the time I'd finished.

'What's this hole you're digging, then?' he asked, a moment or two after I'd told him; and I told him again, marvelling to see new grief appear in his eyes. As often as he asked I answered, and each time his shocked sorrow about the dog was raw and fresh. How exhausting not to be able to digest your experience, to be stalled on the threshold of your own inner life. For a while he said that he was losing himself, and then he lost that.

Finding his way back into a time warp some fifty years before, he one night kicked my terrified old grandmother out of bed because, he said, his parents would be furious at finding him in bed with a stranger.

'I'm not a stranger,' she wept. 'I'm your wife.'

'You say so,' he hissed at her, widening his eyes then narrowing them to slits. 'But I know better.'

From then on, he was convinced that she was an impostor, a crafty con-artist who fooled everybody except himself into thinking that she was his eighty-year-old wife.

In the evenings he would start to pace up and down the length of their short hallway, muttering troubled words to himself, and after an hour or so of this he would take the kettle from the kitchen and put it in the airing cupboard on the landing, or grab a favourite needlepoint cushion from the sofa and craftily smuggle it into the microwave. He wrote impassioned incomprehensible letters in their address book, and forgot the names of the most ordinary things. I mean, *really* forgot them. 'I want the thing there is to drink out of,' he shouted when the word 'cup' left him. He talked intimately about his childhood to the people on the television screen. He got up to fry eggs in the middle of the night. He accused me of stealing all their tea towels.

'I want to go home,' he wept.

'But you *are* home,' howled my grandmother.

'And who the hell are *you?*' he demanded, glaring at her in unfeigned dismay.

But, because muscle memories are stored in quite another part of the brain, the cerebellum at the back, he was still able to sit at the piano and play Debussy's *L' Isle joyeuse* with unnerving beauty.

Thirteen minutes. It always surprises me how late in the year the leaves stay worth looking at. November gives the silver birches real glamour, a shower of gold pieces at their feet and still they keep enough to clothe them, thousands of tiny lozenge-shaped leaves quaking on their separate stems. That constant tremor made them unpopular in the village where I grew up—palsied, they called them.

Trees live for a long time, much longer than we do. Look at this oak, so enormous and ancient standing in the centre of the leaf-carpeted clearing, it must be over five hundred years old. It's an extremely slow developer, the oak, and doesn't produce its first acorn until it's over sixty. Which makes me feel better about the elderly *prima gravida* label.

They have been known to live for a thousand years, oak trees, and there are more really old ones growing on the Heath than in the whole of France. Look at it standing stoutly here, all elbows and knees. When the weather is stormy, they put up signs round here—BEWARE OF FALLING LIMBS. It was these immensely strong and naturally angled branches, of course, which gave the Elizabethans the crucks they needed for their timber-framed houses and ships.

Stella was like seasoned timber, she stayed strong and flexible almost until the end. When she had her second stroke, three weeks after the first, she was taken to a nursing home for veterans of the stage and screen, somewhere out in Middlesex. In the residents' lounge sat the old people who were well enough to be up. They looked oddly familiar. I glanced round and realized that I was recognizing the blurred outlines of faces I had last seen ten times the size and seventy years younger. Here were the quondam matinee idols and femmes fatales of my grandparents' youth.

Then I went to Stella's room. I held her strong long hand and it was a bundle of twigs in mine. There was an inky bruise to the side of her forehead. Her snowy hair had been tied in a little topknot with narrow white satin ribbon.

I talked, and talked on; I said I'd assume she understood everything—'Squeeze my hand if you can to agree' —and felt a small pressure. I talked about Shakespeare and the weather and food and any other silly thing that came into my head. Her blue eyes gazed at me with such frustration—she couldn't move or speak, she was locked in—that I said, 'Patience, dear Stella. It's the only way.'

Her face caved in on itself, a theatrical mask of grief. Her mouth turned into a dark hole round her toothless gums, a tear squeezing from her old agonized eyes, and she made a sad keening, hooting noise.

Afterwards, in the corridor, I stood and cried for a moment, and the matron gave me automatic soothing words.

Helen Simpson

'Not to worry,' I said. 'I'm not even a relative. It's just the pity of it.'

'Yes, yes,' she said. 'The pity of it, to be sure. Ah but during the week I nurse on a cancer ward, and some of those patients having to leave their young families...'

I really did not want to have to think about untimely death on top of everything else, and certainly not in my condition; so I returned to the subject of Stella.

'Walled up in a failed body,' I said. 'Though perhaps it would be worse to be sound in body but lost in your mind, dipping in and out of awareness of your own lost self. Which is worse?'

'Ah well, we are not to have the choice anyway,' she said, glancing at her watch. 'We cannot choose when the time comes.'

The trouble is, old age has moved on. Threescore years and ten suddenly looks a bit paltry, and even having to leave at eighty would make us quite indignant these days. Sixty is now the crown of middle age. And have you noticed how ancient the parents of young children are looking? Portly, grizzled, groaning audibly as their backs creak while they lean over to guide tiny scooters and bicycles, it's not just angst at the work-life balance that bows them down—it's the weight of the years. Last time I stopped for a cup of tea at the cafe over by the bandstand, I saw a lovely new baby in the arms of a white-haired matriarch. Idly I anticipated the return of its mother from the Ladies and looked forward to admiring a generational triptych. Then the baby started to grizzle, and the woman I'd taken for its grandmother unbuttoned her shirt and gave it her breast. No, it's not disgust or ridicule I felt, nothing remotely like—only, adjustment. And of course that will probably be me next year.

My baby is due early in summer, according to the dates and charts. If it arrives before July, I'll still be forty-three. Who knows, I might be only halfway through; it's entirely possible that I live to be eighty-six. How times change. My mother had me at thirty-two, and she will become a grandmother at seventy-five. Her mother had her at twenty-one, and became a grandmother at fifty-three. At this rate my daughter will have her own first baby at fifty-four and won't attain grandmotherhood until she's 119.

I'd better take out some life insurance. I hadn't bothered until now because if I died, well, I'd be dead so I wouldn't be able to spend it. But it has suddenly become very necessary. I can see that. Maternity leave and when to take it; childminders, nurseries, commuting against the clock; falling asleep over marking; not enough money, no trees in Dalston; the lure of Cornwall or Wales. I've seen it all before. But it's possible with just the one, I've seen that too.

I'm not quite into the climacteric yet, that stretch from forty-five to sixty when the vital force begins to decline; or so they used to say. And a climacteric year was one that fell on an odd multiple of seven (so, seven, twenty-one, thirty-five and so on), which brings me back to my glee at that crossword clue last week, and the way I taunted old Max with it—'Caring, calm, direct—New Man's sixty-third year. (5,11; 9 Across and 3 Down).' Grand climacteric, of course. The grand climacteric, the sixty-third year, a critical time for men in particular.

To think that my grandfather had three more decades after *that*. Towards the end of his very long life—like Stella, he lived to ninety-three—it was as though he was being rewound or spooled in. He became increasingly childish, stamping his feet in tantrums, gobbling packets of jelly babies and fairy cakes, demanding to be read aloud to from *The Tale of Two Bad Mice*. He needed help with dressing and undressing, and with everything else. Then he became a baby again, losing his words, babbling, forgetting how to walk, lying in his cot crying. Just as he had once grown towards independence, so, with equal gradualness, he now reverted to the state of a newborn. Slowly he drifted back down that long corridor with fluttering curtains. At the very end, if you put your finger in the palm of his hand, he would grasp it, as a baby does, grab it, clutch at it. When at last he died, his memory was as spotless as it had been on the day he first came into the world.

Seven minutes left, and I'll pause here at the home-run ash tree to pull off a bunch of keys, as children do, for old time's sake. So ingenious, these winged seeds drying into twists which allow them to spin far from the tree in the wind; nothing if not keen to propagate. I have a particular liking for this ash tree; it's one of my few regular photographic subjects.

I'm careful how I take photographs. I've noticed how you can snap away and fail to register what you're snapping; you can take a photograph of a scene instead of looking at it and making it part of you. If you weren't careful, you could have whole albums of the years and hardly any memories of them.

I take my camera on to the Heath, but only on the first of the month, and then I only take the same twelve photographs. That is, I stand in exactly the same twelve places each time—starting with the first bench at the ponds and ending with this ash tree—and photograph the precise same views. At the end of the year I line up the twelves in order, the February dozen beneath the January dozen and so on, and in the large resultant square the year waxes and wanes. You don't often catch time at work like this. Aidan was quite intrigued, and soon after we met he was inspired to add a new Monday morning habit on his way to work. He left five minutes early, then paused to sit in the kiosk near the exit at Baker Street to have four of those little passport photos taken. He stuck these weekly records into a scrapbook, and after eighteen months it was nearly full. It was what I asked for in September when I found out that he already had a wife and child. He refused. So, in a rage, I took it. I was going to give it back, it belonged to him; but now of course it doesn't belong to him in the same way any more. It's his baby's patrimony.

I have a feeling that this baby will be a girl. In which case, of course, I'll call her Stella. If the dates are accurate, then she'll be born in early summer. I might well be pushing her along this very path in a pram by then, everything green and white around us, with all the leaves out and the nettles and cow parsley six feet high.

Four minutes to go, and I'm nearly there. Walking round the Heath on days like this when there is some colour and sun, I can feel it rise in me like mercury in a thermometer, enormous deep delight in seeing these old trees with their last two dozen leaves worn like earrings, amber and yellow and crimson, and in being led off by generously lit paths powdered silver with frost. It must be some form of benign forgetfulness, this rising bubble of pleasure in my chest, at being here, now, part of the landscape and not required to do anything but exist. I feel as though I've won some mysterious game.

Two minutes to spare, and I'm back where I started, off the path and on to the pavement. That got the blood circulation moving. It's not often that I beat the four scowling kings. There's the bell. Just in time.

□

150 NYRB CLASSICS

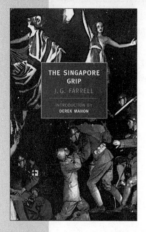

The 150th NYRB Classic has just been published

The Singapore Grip

By J.G. Farrell

Introduction by Derek Mahon

For over five years, *New York Review Books* has been reissuing many truly remarkable works of literature that have gone out of print. *The Singapore Grip* is the 150th book to appear in the NYRB Classics series.

The Singapore Grip is a love story and a war story, a tragicomic tale of a besieged city and a dying way of life. It offers a further expansion of the daring historical vision revealed in Farrell's earlier masterpieces, *Troubles* and the Booker Prize–winning *The Siege of Krishnapur.*

Paperback • $17.95

Also by J. G. Farrell in *NYRB Classics*: ———————————
Troubles • Introduction by John Banville
Paperback • NYRB Classic #87 • $16.95

The Siege of Krishnapur • Introduction by Pankaj Mishra
Paperback • NYRB Classic #132 • $14.95

There are 147 other books in the NYRB Classics series, by such writers as Thomas Flanagan, Georges Simenon, Richard Hughes, Alberto Moravia, Henry James, Edmund Wilson, James Schuyler, Helen Keller, Peter Handke, Rebecca West, J. R. Ackerley, and Jessica Mitford.

In the NYRB Classics series you'll find old favorites and make new discoveries, too.

NEW YORK REVIEW BOOKS

nyrb CLASSICS

Available at your local bookstore or call (601) 354-5306 or visit www.nyrb.com

GRANTA

NIGHTWALKING
Robert Macfarlane

Moonrise woke me at one that morning. The blizzard had blown over, the cloud cover had thinned away, so when I opened my eyes there was the moon, fat and unexpected above the mountains. Just a little off full, with the shape of a hangnail missing to black on the right side, and the stars swarming around it.

I scrambled up and did a little dance on the snowfield, partly to get warm, and partly because if I looked backwards over my shoulder while I jigged, I could see my moon-shadow dancing behind me on the snow. It was that bright.

That moonlight had made quite an effort to reach me. It had left the sun at around 186,000 miles per second, then proceeded through space for eight minutes, or 93 million miles, then bounced off the moon's surface and proceeded through space for another 1.3 seconds, or 240,000 miles, before pushing through troposphere, stratosphere and atmosphere, and arriving with me: trillions of lunar photons pelting my face and the snow about me, giving me an eyeful of silver, and helping my moon-shadow to dance.

Snow perpetuates the effect of moonlight, which means that on a clear night, in winter mountains, you can see for a distance of up to thirty miles. I know this because I saw that far that night, and because I have seen that far on several previous occasions. Several, but not many, because you require the following circumstances in unison: a full moon, a hard frost, a clear sky—and a willingness to get frozen to your core.

The previous day, the weather forecast had spoken of a 'snow-bomb'—the remnant of a polar low, dragged south by other fronts—which would hit north-west England, before quickly giving way to a high. When the snow-bomb landed, temperatures over high ground were expected to drop to fifteen degrees below zero Celsius, and the wind would gust at speeds of up to fifty miles per hour.

It seemed too much to hope that I would be rewarded with such conditions. But I drove north the next morning on the chance that the forecast would hold true. I passed through snow and sleet, and reached the mountains by the afternoon. The path to them switch-backed up through old oak woods from the lake-shore.

Snow lay between the trees. Black snow-clouds were starting to hood the earth from the east. An hour up the mountain, I crested a rise into a hanging valley, and the lake below became invisible. I had left early spring and walked back into winter. All I could see were white mountains. Sunlight fell like bronze on distant snowfields. The wind was satisfactorily cold, and already so strong that I had to lean into it at a ten-degree vaudeville tilt.

Beyond the hanging valley, the path was thick with hard snow. The small rocks on the path were grouted with ice. By the time I reached the ridge, the blizzard had reached me. Visibility was no more than a few metres. The white land had folded into the white sky. It was harder to stand up in the wind. I cast about for sheltered, flat ground. There was none.

Then I found a small tarn, roughly circular, perhaps ten yards across, pooled between two small crags, and frozen solid. The ice in the tarn was the milky grey-white colour of cataracts and noduled in texture. I padded out to its centre and tested the ice's strength. It did not even creak beneath my weight. I wondered where the fish were. The tarn was, if not a good place to wait out the storm, at least the best place on offer. I liked the thought of sleeping there, too: it would be like falling asleep on a silver shield, or a giant clock face.

Noctambulism is usually taken to mean sleepwalking. This is inaccurate: it smudges the word into somnambulism. Noctambulism means walking at night, and you are therefore etymologically permitted to do it asleep or awake, just as, etymologically, you can somnambulate at high noon. I recommend awake for noctambulism, and night for somnambulism, but those are just my preferences.

Generally, people noctambulize because they are seeking melancholy. Thus Kafka, a regular noctambulizer, who wrote in his diary of feeling like a ghost among men. 'Walked in the streets for two hours weightless, boneless, bodiless, and thought of what I have been through while writing this afternoon,' he noted of a winter night.

There is another reason for being out at night, however, and that is the mix of strangeness and wildness which the dark confers on a place. Sailors talk of the eerie beauty of seeing a familiar country from the sea: it turns the landscape inside out. Something similar happens at night, except the landscape is turned back to front.

Night, though, is a diminishing resource. Among the many resources which modernity is exhausting is darkness. Look at a satellite image of Europe taken on a cloudless night. The continent gleams. Italy is a sequinned boot. Spain is trimmed with coastal light, and its interior sparkles like a rink. Offshore, Britain burns brightest and most densely of all.

This excess of light pollutes night with what is known as skyglow. Artificial light, inefficiently directed, escapes upwards before being scattered by small particles in the air, such as water droplets and dust, into a generalized photonic haze. The stars cannot compete, and are invisible. Energy worth billions of pounds is wasted. Migrating birds collide with lighted buildings. The leaf-fall and flowering patterns of trees—reflexes which are controlled by perceptions of day-length—are disrupted. Glow-worm numbers are dwindling because their pilot lights, the means by which they attract mates, are no longer bright enough to be visible. Towns tint their skies orange: from a distance it seems as though something is on fire over the horizon.

Up on the ridge, the blizzard thrashed for two hours. I lay low, got cold. I watched red reeds in the tarn's frozen water flicker in the wind. Hail fell in different shapes: first like pills, then like tiny jagged icebergs, then in a long shower of rugged spheres. It clustered in dents in the tarn ice.

Lying on the tarn, I remembered August Strindberg's experiments with night photography in the 1890s. Strindberg had become convinced that photography, despite its relentless reliance on surface for its effects, might in fact see through exteriors to reveal the essences of people and objects. First, he tried to photograph the human soul with a large and lensless camera which he built himself. He failed. Next, he tried to photograph snow crystals, hoping to reveal the central monadic form of the universe: the repeating structure which, at all scales, determined the world's appearance. He failed. Finally, he tried to photograph the stars. On cold nights, he laid large photographic plates, primed with developing fluid, out on the earth, hoping they would take slow pictures of the stars' movement.

He failed. But the resulting plates carried exquisite evidence of the stars: dots of white and silver light, constellated into strange astral patterns. Strindberg named the plates 'celestographs', and he sent them and an account of their making to the French astronomer, Camille Flammarion. Flammarion did not reply. It is likely that the astral patterns were caused either by dew or dust settling on the plates, creating a nebula of micro-oxidations.

On the tarn, slowly over half an hour, the hail turned to snow, which had the texture of salt, and fell on to the ice with a soft granular hiss. Then the snow stopped altogether.

After moonrise had woken me that morning, and after I had danced, I looked around. I was in a metal world. The unflawed slopes of snow on the mountains across the valley were fields of iron. The deeper moon-shadows had a tinge of blue to them; otherwise, there was no colour. Ice gleamed like tin in the moonlight. Everything was neuter greys, black and sharp silver-white. The hailstones which had fallen on me earlier lay about like shot or ball-bearings, millions of them, drifted up against each rock or nested in snow-hollows. My face felt burned by the cold. The air smelled of minerals and frost.

Looking south, the mountain ridge was visible, curving gently round for two miles. It was as narrow as a pavement at times, at others wide as a road, with three craggy butte summits in its course. To east and west, the steep-sided valleys, unreachable by the moonlight, were in such deep black shadow that the mountains seemed footless in the world.

I began walking the monochrome ridge. These were the only sounds I could hear: the swish of my breathing, the crunch my foot made when it broke through a crust of hard snow, the wood-like groans of plate ice cracking and sinking as I stepped down on it. Once, stopping on a crag-top, I watched two stars fall in near-parallel down the long black slope of the firmament.

When the ground became steep, I moved from rock to rock. On the thinner sections I walked out to the east, so I could look along the cornice line, which was fine and delicate, and proceeded in a supple phosphorous curve along the ridge-edge, as though it had been engineered.

At one point, several small clouds drifted through the sky. When one of them passed over the moon, the world's filter changed. First my hands were silver and the ground was black. Then my hands were black, and the ground was silver. So we switched, as I walked, from negative to positive to negative, as the moon zoetroped the passing clouds.

Robert Macfarlane

In 1979 three scientists, Lamb, Baylor and Yau, performed what is agreed to be among the most beautiful experiments in the field of optics. They used a suction electrode to record the membrane current of pieces of toad retina with high rod-cell density. They then fired single photons at the retinal pieces. The membrane current showed pronounced fluctuations, proving that a rod cell could be tripped into action by the impact of a single photon.

The human eye possesses two types of photo-receptive cells: rods and cones. The cone cells cluster in the fovea, the central area of the retina. Further out from the fovea, the density of cone cells diminishes, and rod cells come to predominate. Cone cells are responsible for our acute vision, and for colour perception. But they only work well under bright light conditions. When light levels drop, the eye switches to rod cells. It takes rod cells up to two hours to adapt most fully to the dark. Once the body detects diminished light levels, it begins generating a photosensitive chemical called rhodopsin, which builds up in the rod cells in a process known as dark adaptation. So it is that at night, we become more optically sensitive. Night sight, though it lacks the sharpness of day sight, is a heightened form of vision. I have found that on very clear nights it is possible to sit and read a book.

Rod cells work with great efficiency in low light-levels. However, they do not perceive colour: only white, black and the greyscale between. Greyscale is their approximation of colour: 'ghosting in' is what optic scientists call the effect of rod-cell perception. It is for this reason that the world is drained of colour by moonlight, and it is also for this reason that night is the natural home of the melancholic.

The brightest of all nightscapes is to be found when a fat moon shines on a landscape of winter mountains. Such a landscape offers the maximum reflection, being white, planar, tilted and polished. The only difficulty for the night-walker comes when you move into the moon-shadow of a big outcrop, or through a valley, where moon-shadow falls from all sides and the valley floor receives almost no light at all. The steep-sidedness of the valley is exaggerated: you have the powerful sensation of being at the bottom of a deep gorge, and you long to reach the silver tide-line of the moonlight again.

After two hours, I reached the flat-topped final summit of the ridge. I cleared some space among the rocks, and slept. The cold woke me just before dawn, and I was grateful to it. I cut a snow-seat facing east, and sat watching as the dawn broke, polar and silent, and then colour returned to the world.

The first sign of it was a pale blue band, like a strip of steel, tight across the eastern horizon. The band began to glow a dull orange. As the light came, a new country shaped itself out of the darkness. The hills stood clear. Webs of long, wisped cirrus clouds, in a loose cross-hatched network, became visible in the sky. Then the sun rose, elliptical at first, red as a snooker ball, astonishing in its colour.

Within half an hour the sky was a steady tall blue. I stood up, feeling the early sunlight warm my cheeks and fingers, and began to make my way down. As I got lower, the land began to free itself from the cold. I could hear the gurgle and chuckle of meltwater moving. Yellow-green tussocks of grass showed through the snow. I found a waterfall which was only part frozen. Its turbulence was surprising and swift after the frozen night-world. I stood for a while watching it, then drank from the stone cistern it had carved out beneath it and snapped off an icicle to eat as I walked.

The shoreline forest, as I came back through it, was dense with dawn birdsong. I felt tired, but did not want to sleep. Near the head of the lake, just downstream of a small stone-and-timber bridge, where the river widened, there was a deep pool, glassy and clear, with a bank of turf next to it.

I sat on the turf for a while and watched light crimp on the water and flex on the stones which cobbled the streambed. I undressed and waded into the water. It felt like cold iron rings were being slid up my legs. Dipping down, I sat in the water up to my neck, huffing quietly with the cold. The current gently pushed at my back. I listened to the whistles and calls of a shepherd, and saw sheep streaming across the tilted green fields on the lake's far shore. In an eddy pool a few yards downstream, between two dark boulders, the curved rims of sunken plates of ice showed themselves above the surface. The sun was now full in the eastern sky, and in the west was the ghost of the moon, so that they lay opposed to each other above the white mountains, the sun burning orange and the moon its cold replica.   □

What do we do? How should we act?

THE PARIS REVIEW

$12.00   172 $16 IN CANADA

WWW.THEPARISREVIEW.ORG

GRANTA

THE END OF THE PROVINCES

PROVINCES

Jeremy Seabrook

The End of the Provinces

In a global economy, with instantaneous worldwide communications networks, there are no longer any outlying areas, distant settlements, remote places, since everywhere is brought into contact with the ubiquitous metropolis. If provincial life still exists, it does so only residually and is doomed to eventual extinction. Provincialism may be associated with narrow-mindedness, bigotry and parochialism; but it has also signified rootedness, belonging, and a local distinctiveness not yet inflected by the universalizing claims of globalism. The experience of the decay of provincial life in Britain in the period after the Second World War is being repeated today all over the world, but at an even faster pace.

In the years after 1945 our town was a drably functional place, an industrial suburb based on the leather industry in the national division of labour. The only people ever seen in the central area during working hours were the aimless retired and women with very young children. No one else had a good reason for not being in a place of work. There were a few oddities, whose histories were well-known to everyone—the couple grimly called Sickness and Diarrhoea, elderly women with bleached hair, said to have been prostitutes, who clung together for support and spoke only to each other. Of the woman who had been a resident of the private hospital, with her short hair and pebble glasses, and never seen without her companion, more knowing townspeople said 'Cheese and cheese'. The war-wounded from 1914–18 were still conspicuous, selling matches and bootlaces, although their wares were only a pretext for begging charity. Late in the afternoon, a small queue formed outside the casual ward of the workhouse—officially abolished along with the Poor Law in 1948, but which still aroused fear and revulsion among those who had seen its thick walls absorb generations of the sick and infirm of the surrounding streets. The few sleepers in the casual ward were unkempt men, feet wrapped in sacking, who remained on the tramp long after an uprooted restless population had been settled— definitively, or so it seemed—on the long journey into industrialism.

Most people went sedately about business that was transparent and blameless. They changed their library books, took their clothing coupons to the haberdasher's and formed a line in the Home and Colonial store where women in snoods wielded spatulas like

227

sculptresses, changing the mass of butter into four-ounce oblongs. Days were long and eventless, the energy of the town securely captive in its hundreds of factories. Shops were plain and unadorned; faded blue holland blinds, evaporated rain-splashes on the glass and the desiccated remains of insects shrivelled on sun-drained crêpe paper. There was little enough in the windows—square-shouldered dresses and baggy double-breasted suits, sensible shoes, timeless uniforms of an austerity without ornament. Wartime rationing still prevailed. The only animated places were those where some vital commodity was rumoured to be in stock—tins of snoek, a consignment of bananas. Shopping was a sober, considered activity, and coins left a metallic trace in the hand which had weighed them against the cost of an object. No one bought on impulse or, indeed, did anything on impulse. No one wasted a penny, or bought any item that could be had more cheaply elsewhere in town.

The rural past had not been effaced even in the town centre. Sheep still cropped the grass on the graves behind the rusty railings of the Church of the Holy Sepulchre. In the main thoroughfare a few private houses remained, remembrance of the notable families who had had an establishment in this, the county town: eighteenth-century sandstone, with a small garden in front where a lilac and a lime tree still flourished; a wooden fence separating the gold-knocker on the heavy front door from the dusty street. These dwellings of notaries and doctors were overshadowed by the sombre grey brick of Notre Dame Convent, a school where ambitious working-class families placed their girls, so that they might lose their accent but not their virginity. It was run by bony-fisted nuns who pummelled ladylike virtues into their raw countrified charges without leaving too many traces of bruising. Opposite the school the New Theatre displayed its stone portico with steps leading to a foyer, where coloured lights provided a hint of lubricious celebration in a sober time. Behind the facade, it was only a blank pile of red brick. In the late 1940s it hosted shows with titles like 'This Was the Army'—revues in which former war heroes, dressed in fishnet stockings, mimicked The Andrews Sisters. There was always an audience for these spectacles but the general wisdom was that the performers had a screw loose. But they are harmless, aren't they? I once asked my mother. She said tartly, Don't you believe it; and this set me wondering why men dressed up as women, and what possible risk there could be in such entertainments. The theatre, which had been built in the Edwardian period, lasted only until the late 1950s, when it was replaced by a spare, geometric construction called a supermarket, opened with great fanfare by one of the new celebrities created by television—in this instance, a woman famous for the girth of her bust, and who drew crowds such as had not been seen in the town since the death of the late king.

The Co-op arcade suggested something sylvan and leisured. Built in the 1930s, in white and green tiles, it was enclosed and always in need of the scant artificial light provided by bulbs behind fluted metal shells. It provided a place to shop safe from rain and wind, a rudimentary precursor of later shopping malls. Then, of course, it provided strictly purposeful facilities: it was where you went to get your bread and milk tokens, which guaranteed you would receive your divvy, your Co-op dividend, each quarter. There was also a soft-furnishing shop—something of an exaggeration for the spindly products that were on sale. The funeral parlour displayed a marble slab, some ornamental gravel and plastic flowers, where the subdued bereaved were consulted on the degree of affection they wished to announce to the world in their choice of memorial. In the hardware shop, durable, serviceable, you could buy galvanized buckets, scrubbing brushes and enamelled colanders, emblems of the penitential work of women, which did little to attract frivolous purchasers. Indeed, shopping as significant leisure activity had not yet touched our town. People bought seriously, and wondered whether they might not make do and mend for a little longer, or whether some homemade substitute might not serve instead of the goods on sale. Sales staff were older men with flaky skin and dry hands which they rubbed together in eager anticipation of pleasing customers who had not yet emerged into the confident splendour of consumers. The arcade linked two of the principal shopping streets, one of which was where the middle and professional classes made their sedate purchases. Its superiority lay in the restraint, good taste and high quality of the merchandise. Here, women who didn't disdain the word *housewife* sank, exhausted from their shopping, into the leather chairs of a bright cafe with chromium mirrors, sipped tea from fluted teacups and nibbled confectionery from a silver-gilt stand—objects of envy and rancour to those who feigned pity for them for having nothing better to do.

Jeremy Seabrook

The landlord of The Vine pub was a relative of ours. There, theatricals gathered; racy, exciting and forbidden to respectable people. Actresses on tour drank gin and, from time to time, men met for purposes other than going to the football match, comparing their losses on the horses or playing cribbage together. After closing time at 10.30, interesting exchanges took place between glamorous transients to the town and the rare Bohemian individuals who actually lived there: people who habitually used words stronger than *bloody*, *bugger* and *sod* told jokes about sex, and anecdotes about people who had had relationships with minor royals or Ivor Novello. The interior of the pub smelled of cigarettes and scandal; rather than permit his daughter to grow up in such an atmosphere, our cousin sent his daughter to be raised by her grandmother in the innocence of a brand-new council house where people, delighted with their purpose-built bathroom and labour-saving kitchen, had little time to dwell on the seamier side of life.

Entertainment was, in any case, limited; and at 10.30 each night, a whistle was blown by a functionary of the bus company, as a warning to seekers after pleasure—those pioneers of the time to come—that the last buses were about to depart; which they did a couple of minutes later, leaving the town centre deserted, the street lamps contemplating the depth of their undisturbed reflection in the wet road.

The Electricity Showroom retained an aura of mildly exciting modernity, especially for those who were finally seeing the gas fittings removed from their small houses (often leaving a truncated metal pipe sticking out of the living-room wall), to be replaced by brighter lights that dispelled shadows from dark over-furnished rooms, and prepared the way for the even brighter moon-glow of TV which would swiftly become a basic necessity. I remember my grandmother, then in her eighty-fifth year, climbing on to a wooden chair to light the gas mantle, and the ghostly greenish flicker playing on the waxed dado. At this time, the gas lamps in the streets were also replaced, and our town briefly gained the reputation of being the best lit in Europe—although they illuminated nothing more dramatic than a drunk committing a nuisance in a doorway, or a woman lifting up her skirt for a customer in the shrubbery at the edge of the park.

The radiant white tiles and glass of the Fifty Shilling Tailors was a place for male ceremonial dressing—suits for funerals, weddings, confirmations and first communions which frequently outlived their owners, in a style that did not change and was not subject to anything so volatile as fashion. Here, discreet men in double-breasted suits with tape measures around their neck, and scissors which lent them an air of mild menace, enquired politely which side their customer dressed, the better to mask the contour of genitals that might otherwise have been perceptible through the coarse cloth. Clothing had not yet contracted to accentuate the shape of bodies which still shrank from any public avowal of sexuality.

The main road opened out into the Market Square, where a sixteenth-century coaching inn, redolent of archaic travels and ancient luxury, stood until it was torn down in the 1950s for the more compelling urgency of retail outlets. The Market Square was paved with cobbles; each Wednesday and Saturday primitive trestles were erected in the form of irregular improvised streets. Market days still generated an air of excitement which was absent for the rest of the week. Everyone used the market and, especially on Saturdays, it became an informal meeting-place where you ran into acquaintances and relatives you hadn't seen for weeks or even months. People would stop, 'hello stranger', and fall into conversations which embraced scores of people, their illnesses, marriages, relationships and deaths. It was still possible to know almost every family in the town. At that time, although the population was around 90,000, the working portion was split into perhaps 5,000 extended families who lived in four or five distinctive industrial areas, separated by main roads and the railway. As they spoke together, extensive networks of relationships sprang to life, conjured back from the dead who mingled with the living in the afterlife of the unforgotten.

Nineteenth-century slums lingered in pockets behind the main streets. These small courts and terraces were dank with moss where sunlight never reached, a broken gas lamp in the middle, window-frames warped and paintless, front doors scratched, windows replaced by plywood or cardboard. Lace curtains had hung so long they had fallen into cobwebby rags. Here and there a geranium survived on a window sill, but willowherb and grass forced their way through the irregular paving stones, and buddleia rooted in choked gutters and crumbling masonry.

Jeremy Seabrook

Most produce in the market was local. In winter, frozen swedes lay with carrots, parsnips, turnips and potatoes that had been in the pits since autumn; savoy cabbages, the outer leaves a filigree of snail-eaten silvery holes, plump white cabbages from which the green had seeped away, stems of Brussels sprouts, each hard knot enclosed in its bright casing. This was the staple fare from late autumn till early summer. Only seasonal vegetables were eaten, augmented from time to time by peas or butter beans steeped overnight in salt water with a pinch of bicarbonate of soda. But in summer, the rough wooden display counters were piled with fruit and vegetables—so many varieties of apple, some windfallen and bored by grubs, misshapen and irregular, pears ripened in drawers among underwear and linen, plums and damsons, tomatoes, lettuce and spring onions, dewy cucumbers and new carrots still with their feathery plumage, fresh peas in squeaky pods, broad beans in white downy casings, runner beans succulent with summer rain, plump pink radishes, cherries and strawberries, wicker boxes of redcurrants, blackcurrants and even pale bitter whitecurrants. The provincial summer was a perpetual feast and you gorged on the fresh fruits in anticipation of the bland monotony of winter's root vegetables. Nor were the free fruits of the countryside neglected—horse mushrooms gathered from the meadows around town in the early morning while the dew was still on them, sloes taken from the dark spiny foliage in the hedgerows, crab apples made into jelly, elderberries which weighed down their trees in thick black clusters, blackberries that children gathered in porous, blue sugar bags that leaked an indelible purple ink on to hands and clothing.

On the clothing stalls, the only locally made stuff was scraps of lace which industrious women in the adjacent countryside still produced as they sat on their doorsteps and placed their pins on the worn cushions before dextrously winding the cotton in its intricate patterns. The bric-a-brac and the second-hand goods came from recently cleared houses—ewers and basins, tea sets, bone-handled fish knives and forks tarnished from lack of use; silver-backed mirrors and brushes still with a few wisps of the hair of the dead in their bristles; tiered cake stands redolent of languid tea-times in the conservatories of the middle class, glassware and tureens, china fit only to be locked away in the cabinet that stood in hundreds of front rooms; flowerpots and mementos of Great Yarmouth or Bognor Regis; the sentimental knick-knacks of the early-genteel—the figurines and wide-eyed dogs and cats, a coy plaster girl tugging at the side of her skirt. It was as though the contents of houses had been poured out for public view, pale tender objects of private consumption promiscuously displayed, much as happened with lives themselves when the stories of their adulteries, their conjugal violence, and their sexual misdeeds were reported daily in the local paper.

The offices of the newspaper stood on the Market Square, too, in a Victorian defilement of the architecture, which prefigured the later obliteration of its country character. The paper was delivered to almost every household that could afford it; and it served less as a disseminator of news than as a vehicle for gossip—the decrees nisi, the man in the cinema observed to have changed his seat fourteen times, the importuners in the public lavatories, those bound over for being drunk and disorderly or for keeping a house of ill fame—one of which was identified at the top of our street. Its occupants were always being 'pinched', but they paid the fine and continued to keep their disorderly house which, however, showed little sign of the discomposure attributed to it by the law but continued to stand, serene and shabby as any of its neighbours.

The newspaper was also a means of extra-judicial punishment. People in the provincial town had long memories; and these they stocked abundantly with details of those they knew and even, if the crime were spectacular enough, of those they had never heard of; so that whoever had had the misfortune to see her or his name in the paper was marked for life. The people accumulated knowledge, and a name, a reminder, a nudge would be enough to retrieve every particular. It was good for the oral tradition, but hard on those regarded as evil-doers. Twenty years afterwards, someone would be sure to know of the man who had stolen items of women's wear from a garden clothes line; who had been bound over for indecent exposure by the river; or even who had permitted the chimney to catch fire and been fined two pounds ten shillings. The local newspaper was a contemporary equivalent of the stocks: shame and disgrace remained constant; only the technology was different.

Serious crime was sufficiently rare to contaminate the landscapes touched by it. Walking from our house, we would sometimes go as far as Hardingstone, a village on the opposite side of the Nene river valley from our red-brick suburb. In the churchyard, among the lichen-covered tombstones stood a plain wooden cross; on it the words IN MEMORY OF AN UNKNOWN MAN. This was the burial place of the victim of a notorious murder in 1930, known as the blazing-car murder. The murderer, Rouse, having previously insured his life, picked up a hitch-hiker in his car and killed him. Having dressed him in his own clothes, in order to make it appear that it was he who had perished, he set fire to the vehicle. The charred corpse was found at the wheel of the car. Rouse was denounced by a former lover he had slighted; and at his trial, it emerged that he had had several mistresses, and that two of them had borne his illegitimate children. The presence of this bare, unvisited mound inspired us with a strange terror, since it was a murder that clearly prefigured the future. It could not have occurred without wider access to the motorcar, the maintenance of roads, the construction of showy road-houses, pubs with winter gardens decorated with potted palms. The ability of the murderer to transfer his identity to another, the fact that it was never known who the dead man really was, suggested a future of lost or stolen existences, identities sloughed off or left behind. This disturbed our regular and ordered childhood, with its fixed bedtime, its bland nutritious mealtimes, and its ritual celebrations. It foreshadowed mobility, undiscovered bigamies, people who chose to define themselves rather than submit to the limited cast-distribution of a provincial town—boot and shoe operative, father, sister, Methodist, shopkeeper.

The streets where we lived, built in the mid-nineteenth century, had been named by the builder after his family—Alfred, Edith, Ethel and Cyril. There was also an Upper Thrift and a Lower Thrift Street, which celebrated this virtue. Steps led up to the front door, plaster scrolls, modest ornamental carving over the windows, even a sculpted tympanum and some restrained stained glass. They exuded a sense of secular piety, a commitment to frugality and a sparing retentiveness. These were built for the modestly prosperous of the mid-Victorian boom, people whose greatest concern was not to fall back into the poverty from which they were fugitives. They lived a parsimonious existence in which nothing went to waste; grease scraped thinly on bread, tea leaves reused until the liquid they produced was palest grey, suet puddings with a meagre filling of scrag-end, and the water in which vegetables were boiled drunk as a medicinal accompaniment to meals. They knew better than to waste shoe leather or to burn daylight, and they saved their breath to cool their porridge. Every conceivable object would come in handy—in an old chocolate box, memento of a moment of extravagance long ago, hatpins, buttons, glass beads, stubs of pencil, brooches, thimbles, scraps of leather, lengths of cotton and the end of skeins of wool for darning. They knew how to make and mend, patch and repair, and stitch and sew. Hands were never still, but itched to be doing something useful: knitting, making rag rugs, darning thin fabric over a wooden mushroom.

They didn't grow flowers in the back garden, but rows of potatoes, scarlet runner beans, cabbages and Brussels sprouts. Many gardens had a fruit tree—plum, Bramley apple or pear; and every fruit was picked, apples stored in the cold cellar, so that even in the middle of winter a faint sour breath of fruit pervaded the house. Women bottled fruit and made jam, while the men contrived to lengthen the life of the most sorry down-at-heel shoes on the metal last that every shoeworker possessed, and on which were made the family's shoes with a piece of leather secreted from the workplace under the eyes of vigilant foremen and bosses. A nostalgia for self-reliance persisted, an obstinate resistance to growing dependence upon the market for most of their needs.

Reminders of their country origins remained, even after life had become thoroughly urban. Going for a walk was a modest adventure. Children still learned to read the season in the landscape, the feathery green of cow parsley, the wood anemones and celandines of March, the faint scent of bluebells, pale in the dark woods, cobalt under sparser trees, the acrid smell of hawthorn. The tiny planes of dog roses opened their shallow pink cups to the solstitial light of June. In autumn we gathered burrs of sweet chestnut, hazelnuts and sour blue-black sloes, even gleanings in the harvest fields, although the corn was only fed to the hens. And the skies over the valley were full of drama—the flat-bottomed cumulus of June, the anvil clouds and bursting thunderheads of August. In winter, frost blossomed on the inside window panes of the houses and froze the piss in the night jar under the bed. A summer afternoon on the allotment was a holiday, tart redcurrants and raspberries lighting up the bushes with their ripeness, the only sound the clash of spade against pebble as the men dug the rectangle of stony ground, from which sprang fare sanctified by the label 'home-grown', which they had not yet become wise enough to understand was a stigma that would render everything local inferior and shameful.

If we turned in the other direction, we passed the leather factories on each street corner, the feral smell of hides and the machines that had stolen the skills of shoemakers and locked them in metal presses and cutters. At the top of the road stood the gaunt shell of the Church of St Edmund the Martyr, named after a fifteen-year-old king of East Anglia in the ninth century, victim of invading Danish warlords. Its congregation never exceeded thirty people even on Easter morning. Facing it was the workhouse, by that time transformed into a hospital but still displaying raw, blank, brick walls which overlooked the yard in which its disgraced uniformed captives had exercised in the hour between work and the rations of hard bread, porridge and thin broth.

People expected little and got less; and they reconciled themselves to their choiceless frugality with an extensive lore of resignation—the certainty that things would get worse before they got better, that those who forbore to ask questions would hear no lies, that nothing was to be done without trouble but letting the fire go out, that there was no profit to be got from pigs but their muck and their company, and the best that could be said of life was that at least you hadn't yet been put to bed with a shovel, and it would be time enough to be sorry when you were singing alleluia to the nettles.

The consolation of this bleak material and social landscape was that we knew our place: not in the hierarchical sense, although there was a highly developed consciousness of the nuances of class, but, more significantly, that our function in the national division of labour was clear and incontestable. Everyone needed shoe-leather; demand for military boots ensured that the town prospered in times of war, although less flamboyantly than those which grew rich through the making of weaponry and armaments. Like all the industrial cities, the mill towns, pit villages, there could be no doubting the reason for existence of the places where people lived. Indeed, the break in the link between locality and function dealt a severe blow to the identity of British people, from which the ruined industrial areas of Britain are still suffering.

Of course, beneath the order and the undisturbed sense of performing a vital task lay another, secret life. Women hid their bruises and denied the cancer eating their body until days before it killed them; people endured years of intolerable relationships, sometimes retreating into total silence against their partner. None of this was ever avowed in public. The incestuous child, the orphaned and the unloved, sat in thin summer clothes outside the pubs late in the evening, as the sky turned pale green in the chill summer air. The homosexual man stood as the water trickled down the rusty pipes in the cracked ceramic of the public lavatory, cigarette burning his lips, looking without moving his head to see if the occupant of the next stall also had an erection or if he were a policemen sent to entrap him. My aunt's husband had been compelled to leave his job in the police force when he got her in the family way; he left his native Coventry in disgrace and worked in a tannery in Northampton. Their daughter, at the age of fourteen, was raped in a park one Sunday morning, and never spoke of it to anyone for the next fifty years. The young man who stole women's clothing from a washing-line was jailed, while the divorced woman was both ogled by men and shunned by decent people. The woman who put her head in the gas oven, but failed to end her own wretched life, was also taken before the magistrates as a criminal. Magistrates exuberantly condemned the weak, the vulnerable and the wicked in righteous enunciations of unselfconscious class prejudice. If life was often unkind, people nevertheless recognized that an outer conformism smothered individual tragedies which, whatever the formal disapproval they were bound to express, still left space for private compassion and tolerance.

It is impossible to judge the heroic and, often, lost battles against insufficiency, the perpetual eking out of an inadequate diet, mending sheets and darning fabric worn into holes, the borrowed shilling and the unpaid rent, the moonlight flit and the fear of the moneylender's hands. Yet the consolations of the labouring poor were not negligible either—the confidences on the doorstep, the woman who knew what to do in any emergency, the sense of suffering shared—this made more bearable lives which posterity regards as insupportable. If the pain of the passing of provincial life has been denied, it is because everything that succeeded it has been tendentiously and insistently portrayed not as the mixture of the gains and losses that accompany all social change, but as an irresistible progress towards a beckoning future over which dispute is not possible.

When this way of life had finally been effaced, there was—and continues to be—much public discussion about whether what replaced it was 'better'. Much of this missed the point. Societies evolve and change; economic systems mutate; and as they do so, some are benefited, leaving others stranded and confused, unable to adapt to the exigencies of the hour which are always painted in the rosy colours of progress. Because it was clear that what people most desperately wanted was a way out of poverty, when that road was indicated to them, they scarcely reflected on where it might lead, or on what undervalued luggage might have to be shed on the journey.

The only option then was to look back in regret. And here lie the roots of peculiarly British nostalgias: a persistent conviction that everything is getting worse is a subterranean popular corrective to the constantly reiterated official assertion that we are engaged on broad avenues of mobility and improvement, and that these lead only upwards. It is not difficult to know what you are being delivered from; what you are being liberated into is another matter. In that stifling provincial town, unopened to other ways of life, to cultures and to peoples that would both spoil and enrich it, we knew exactly where we stood. There was no need to look for meaning, because it was there all around us. Function and purpose were in the leathern tang of the air we breathed. It stood to reason that everybody needed a strong piece of local shoe-leather in which to walk to work, to fight in distant battlefields, to migrate to the dominions in search of a better life or to accompany relatives and friends on a last journey to the grave.

It appeared permanent and enduring; and in that lay its poignancy, for it was already, in the circumspect and inexcitable 1950s, on the edge of dissolution. How fragile the common wisdom, the penurious and penny-pinching existence which the townspeople had seen as the only imaginable shape for a human life; how transient that illusion of rootedness in a fierce Nonconformist morality and Puritan heritage of want, work and woe; and what moral bewilderment its passing engendered. And with how little understanding, with what meagre recognition it was dismissed; as though anyone who sought to salvage one particle of such an oppressive past must be a perverse lover of poverty, a Luddite or wrecker of the people's progress!

It was destined to disappear in a very brief space of time. The erosion of the distinctive life of our town was most dramatically enacted in what were called slum clearance programmes: terraces, courts and yards which had housed people for a hundred years were unfit for human habitation—a judgement which their unhappy inhabitants had made as long as the buildings had stood. Only when this was issued by government officials, it appeared to cast retrospective doubt upon the humanity of the three or four generations who had lived in them. As the houses were demolished, people moved on, leaving behind sometime treasures that had clearly become as worthless as the homes they were leaving: shoeboxes of family photographs, deal chairs and tables, the stopped clock and the scuffed oilcloth—all the paraphernalia of life, suddenly exposed, along with the blackleaded fire grate and the fluttering wallpaper where only the wall of a house remained. Their old occupants had fled without even finding time to pack for the new life they expected in a better elsewhere.

They could not leave behind the associations with poverty quickly enough. Only later, they wondered what had become of the brass candlesticks given as a wedding present, the tarnished cruet donated to a woman in service by a grateful employer. Later still, a piercing sense of regret that what was gone was indeed irrecoverable; and an increasing tendency, in the quiet times, to dwell on the past as though the past were a cantankerous relative who had died, but from the contemplation of whose serene features in death you cannot, nevertheless, tear your gaze.

The lives of people were being bettered. They did not, perhaps, realize, amid the urgency of the flight from want, that this was a verb in the passive voice. If an obscure resentment later arose, this was when it dawned upon them that the roots of belonging had also been disturbed, the networks of kinship broken and the neighbourhoods dispersed and, as the factories were taken over and then closed down, that the reason for the existence of the provincial town itself was being expunged. At the time, there was no obvious defect in the promise of free gifts, prizes and rewards that filled the air; only when we got home with our purchases, as it were, did we become aware of the uncounted losses that had figured nowhere in the prospectuses of perpetual gain. The transformation had occurred, behind our back, on terms over which we were not consulted. It had all been a transaction, the true costs of which did not appear at the time the contact was signed, the bargain (between whom?) struck.

The division of labour which had assigned our town a specific role was being redistributed globally. If we had seen the places to which the work which had slipped so mysteriously through our skilled fingers was being reassigned, we might have observed that the lives of the industrial suburbs of Asia and South and Central America bore a strong resemblance to what we had known; and that the new work was welcomed in these places as a deliverance.

But something continued to tug at the heart, in the remembrance of a life where everything was in its place. The uniqueness that distinguished our town from all other places exercises over us now that peculiar poignancy of things we know to be irrevocably past. We can see the other people we were then, and we pity them for their innocence and unknowing; and weep for the selves we were, before we were altered, before our consciousness had changed forever.

There was not, and could not have been any political acknowledgement of unease at the passing of those scenes of oppression. Feelings of disquiet could be expressed only obliquely, in 'kitchen-sink' literature, exhibitions in local museums of 'the way we were', evocations of our town as it was before the War, memories of duty and duress, of the consolations of kin and the charity of neighbours poured into microphones and tape recorders. Only in an indirect and sublimated form could we recognize that the life of constant improvement and increase was also a time of unspeakable dispossessions, of which we had then no inkling.

Here, too, is the origin of sullen resentment over the absence of discussion on what we might have chosen, had we been consulted; a resentment that darkens our apprehension of changes we never sought among those we surely welcomed. This is where the roots of xenophobia, racism, the distrust of the perpetual strangers we have become to each other, are to be sought: in the silence over inadmissible dissatisfactions with what had replaced the dour, torpid inertia of provincial life. We became discontented with our flawed purchases, when the workmanship of the shining goods proved to be shoddier than we had believed, when things fell apart and the glittering toys lost their lustre; our relationships, too, were spoiled, and pervaded by a sense of inadequacy, leaving the obscure ache that can be assuaged by drink, drugs, the neediness that expresses itself in taking and getting, the avarice of the disinherited, a sulky disengagement from a world we never made, which promised everything and yet strangely withheld the benefits it was to have showered upon us.

There are no longer any provinces in the bland topography of globalism. Even the regeneration of provincial cities in Europe transforms these into outposts of global culture: it is not because of their sense of community or shared function that Manchester, Barcelona or Strasbourg are celebrated, but because of their art galleries, their shops, their clubs and entertainment. The intensity of their revival depends upon the extent to which they have become aspects of metropolitan culture.

Contemporary communications systems, global cultural convergence, information conglomerates and transnational providers of entertainment have made deep inroads into worlds that remained for centuries bounded, enclosed and self-reliant. These were characterized by networks of kin, work and neighbourhood, networks which have been torn apart and scarcely exist now in that particular form. They have not disappeared, however, but have been reconstituted in global networks of far wider scope and reach. Relationships constituted through the new networks are based upon instant access to a whole world; careers articulated to the global economy, elective relationships, often at a distance, that give their participants the freedom to remain where they please, for they are never out of touch. If the provinces exist now, they are social rather than geographic, a class rather than a place—the province of poverty, where those people excluded from the privileged networks remain in a state of semi-carceral impotence, starvelings of worldwide markets.

If the death of the self-serving orthodoxies of provincial life is a cause for rejoicing, the loss of its depth and rootedness remains a source of bitter and sorrowing regret; especially when these are replaced by global suburbs of unbelonging and the slums of permanent exile. □

INHERIT THE LAND

FAMILIES IN THE DUMPS OF TIJUANA

Jack Lueders-Booth
PHOTOGRAPHS

'Above us, the infinite swirl of gulls. And garbage hurricanes lift off all around us: the photographer thirty yards away from the young woman and me is dwarfed by a whirlwind of trash—it rises twenty, thirty feet above his head, and he stands at the apex, shooting us with our arms around each other, holding on in the wind.' Luis Alberto Urrea

'More than one viewing is necessary to understand that the photographer is not where we expect him to be, out here with us looking in. He's in there with them, looking out at us.' Frank Gohlke

80 duotone photographs • Introduction by Luis Alberto Urrea • Afterward by Frank Gohlke • Publisher: Pond Press www.pondpress.com • Consortium Book Sales and Distribution www.cbsd.com • ISBN: 0 9761955 0 X

GRANTA

POUNDING A NAIL
Studs Terkel talks to Bob Dylan,
1963

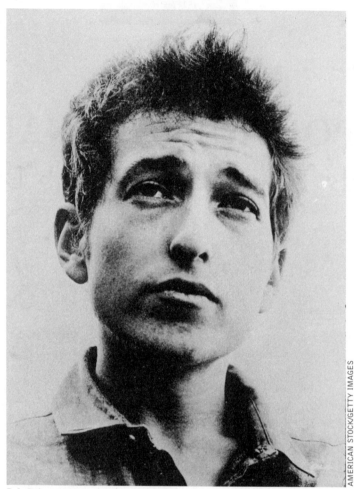

Bob Dylan, 1963

Nineteen forty-five, early autumn. A month before, the Second World War had ended in Japan with a flash and a bang. Four Sundays later, I began as host of a one-hour weekly radio programme of recorded music called *The Wax Museum*. The phrase *disc jockey* had not yet entered our working vocabulary. In effect, though, that is what I was. In the ensuing months, it captured an audience in Chicago that was limited but fervent. What surprised me was the nature of the listeners. I had expected a teacher or two, a social worker, somebody living alone and sitting in the second balcony of a play on a Saturday matinee, or anyone of the 'educated class'—the usual suspects. But— out of nowhere, it seemed—came a few fan letters from other kinds of people: a truck driver, a shipping clerk, a waitress, a housewife.

Of all the works in which I have ever been engaged, it was that one- hour weekly radio programme that was the most revelatory to me. (The name of the programme was something of a pun; the recordings, 78 rpm, were wax-based and highly breakable.) Some eight years later, after a roller-coaster experience with jobs—what with 'Tail Gunner Joe' McCarthy, and Edgar Hoover being sainted as well as feared, and me occasionally uttering unfashionable thoughts—I astonishingly latched on to a classical music FM radio station, WFMT. The station's owner made me an offer I could under no circumstances refuse. It was a one- hour daily programme, during which I could do any damn thing I pleased. I began, naturally, as the eclectic disc jockey I had been. From there the programme grew into something else. I read short stories I liked, whether they were by Flannery O'Connor, Ring Lardner, Chekhov, you name it. Guests somehow came about. Authors, musicians, of course—classical, opera, jazz, and folk of all cultures— and certain neighbourhood people that I found of interest. It was the latter assemblage, the 'ordinary' people, that attracted the attention of a New York publisher, André Schiffrin. From that moment on, the matter of putting forth interviews described as 'oral history' occupied most of my working days. Nonetheless, during my forty-five years on WFMT, although there was a considerable conversation, a piece of music was invariably included, if merely to italicize what the guests had to say. It could be a pop trifle, a show tune, a folk song, or any art song; it could be a passage from a symphony or concerto. It wasn't as though I was seeking music in the words of my visitors; it was simply my talisman—a fetish, some would say.

Studs Terkel and Bob Dylan

Bob Dylan was a young folk poet at the time I spoke to him, one of the most exciting singers of songs around—rumpled trousers, curly hair, wearing a skipper's cap, twenty-two years old. He walked into my studio in May, 1963. It wasn't his first radio interview—he'd done a few in New York the previous year—but certainly among his earliest.

Studs Terkel: Where did you come from, Cotton-Eyed Joe?

Bob Dylan: The beginning was there in Minnesota. But that was the beginning before the beginning. I don't know how I come to songs, you know. It's not up to me to explain—I don't really go into myself that deep, I just go ahead and do it. I'm just sort of trying to find a place to pound my nails.

Studs Terkel: Woody Guthrie, is he a factor in your life?

Dylan: Oh yeah. Woody's a big factor. I feel lucky just to know Woody. I'd heard of Woody, I knew of Woody. I saw Woody once, a long, long time ago in Burbank, California, when I was just a little boy. I don't even remember seeing him, but I heard him play. I must have been about ten. My uncle took me.

Terkel: What was it that stuck in your mind?

Dylan: It stuck in my mind that he was Woody, and everybody else I could see around me was just everybody else.

Terkel: If I may venture an opinion, that could apply to you, too, Bob. Unique. It's hard to separate you from the songs you sing. You write most of the songs you sing, don't you?

Dylan: Yeah, I write all my songs now.

Terkel: There's one song, the only way I can describe it is as a great tapestry—'A Hard Rain's A-Gonna Fall'.

Dylan: I'll tell you how I come to write that. Every line in that really is another song. Could be used as a whole song, every single line. I wrote that when I didn't know how many other songs I could write. That was during October of last year and I remember sitting up all night with a bunch of people someplace. I wanted to get the most down that I knew about into one song, so I wrote that. It was during the Cuba trouble, that blockade, I guess is the word. I was a little worried, maybe that's the word.

Terkel: You're right. Each one of those lines, each one of the images could be a song in itself. You know why I asked you to sing that live? I have this letter from a kid who's about your age, he's twenty-one. He was wondering what this new generation is really thinking of. We hear so much. At the very end he says, 'America's heard the story of the bright, straight-A student, the fraternity-leading good guy Charlie. But there's a quiet group that remains. One that has no overwhelming crusade that is outwardly on the make, but one that is uneasily discontented. Thoughtfully or restless, young people of this sort may eventually determine future directions... Outwardly we seem to be cool, but there's a rage inside us.'

Dylan: I've got a friend who wrote a book called *One Hundred Dollar Misunderstanding*. I don't know if it's around Chicago. It's about this straight-A college kid, you know, fraternity guy, and a fourteen-year-old Negro prostitute. And it's got two dialogues in the same book. A dialogue is one chapter and the other chapter follows with just exactly what he's thinking and what he does. The next chapter is her view of him. The whole book goes like that. This guy Robert Gover wrote it. That would explain a lot too. That's one of the hippest things nowadays, I guess. I mean, it actually comes out and states something that's actually true, that everybody thinks about. I don't know if this fellow who wrote the letter was thinking crusades. This guy who wrote it, you can't label him. That's the word. You understand what I mean?

Terkel: I follow you, I think. Back in the 1930s there were young people feeling passionately under one label or another. They were pigeonholed. What you stand for, it seems to me, and the fellow who wrote this letter and the guy who wrote that book, they belong to nobody but themselves. But we know something is there. Outwardly cool... I suppose you have to be that because the chips on the table are so blue.

Studs Terkel and Bob Dylan

Dylan: Maybe it's just the time, now is the time maybe you have to belong to yourself. I think maybe in 1930, from talking with Woody and Pete Seeger and some other people I know, it seems like everything back then was good and bad and black and white and whatever, you only had one or two. When you stand on one side and you know people are either for you or against you, with you or behind you or whatever you have. Nowadays it's just, I don't know how it got that way but it doesn't seem so simple. There are more than two sides, it's not black and white any more.

Terkel: 'A Hard Rain's A-Gonna Fall'—I think it will be a classic. Even though it may have come out of your feelings about atomic rain...

Dylan: No, no, it wasn't atomic rain. Somebody else thought that too. It's not atomic rain, it's just a hard rain. It's not the fallout rain, it isn't that at all. I just mean some sort of end that's just gotta happen which is very easy to see, but everybody doesn't really think about, is overlooking it. It's bound to happen. Although I'm not talking about that hard rain meaning atomic rain, it seems to me like the bomb is a god in some sort of a way, more of a god and people will worship it actually. You have to be nice to it, you know. You have to be careful what you say about it. People work on it, they go six days a week and work on it, you have people designing it, you know, it's a whole new show.

Terkel: These are all pretty good people too, in everyday life.

Dylan: Yeah, I don't believe they're bad people. Just like the guy that killed this fella hitch-hiking through Alabama. The guy that killed him. I forget his name.

Terkel: It might have been the storekeeper. We don't know if he did it, but this is the fellow—

Dylan: Yeah, who might have killed him. Even if it's not him, if it's somebody else that actually shot the bullet. There's nothing more awful, I mean, shot right in the back. I seen so many people before I got to New York, that are good people, that maybe are poor, and there are other people telling them why they're poor, and who made it so that they are poor. To take their minds off of that they are poor, they have to pick a scapegoat—

Terkel: But do you believe, Bob, in good and evil? There is a basic good—

Dylan: Oh, I'm sure.

Terkel: Obviously you do from the songs you write. One of the lines of the song that got me...earlier you said things are not quite as simple as they were. 'The executioner's face is always well hidden.' That's on the button.

Dylan: Yeah, oh golly. All over the place it's hidden.

Terkel: It's so impersonal today. You said it's gonna happen. What's gonna happen?

Dylan: What's gonna happen, there's got to be an explosion of some kind. The hard rain that's gonna fall. In the last verse when I say, 'When the pellets of poison are flooding the waters,' that means all the lies, you know, all the lies that people get told on their radios and in their newspapers. All you have to do is think for a minute. They're trying to take people's brains away. Which maybe has been done already. I hate to think it's been done. All the lies I consider poison.

Terkel: I'll be fifty-one soon. My generation has had it. I'm talking about you, you know, and your friends, nineteen, twenty, twenty-one. How many feel as you do?

Dylan: Oh, there's an awful lot of them. Well, I don't know, you said my friends—

Terkel: I don't mean just your circle, 'cause you've travelled a good deal.

Dylan: I can tell you something about my friends, I can tell you about people I growed up with, that I knowed since I been four or five. These same kind of people I knew when I was ten and twelve. Little small-town people. This was in Hibbing, Minnesota, and some other places I lived before I finally split for good. These people were my friends, I went to school with them, I lived with them, I played with them, I ate with them. We did good things, bad things, we went through all kinds of things together. As I stand here right now, the last time I saw any of them was maybe two or three years ago, and you know, either me or them has changed.

Terkel: What's happened to them?

Dylan: They still seem to be the same old way. Like when they seen me, they heard I was in New York and they have words like—I can just tell by their whole conversation it's not a free feeling that they have. They still have a feeling that's tied up, where it's tied up in the town, in their parents, in the newspapers that they read which go out to maybe five thousand people. They don't have to go out of town, their world's very small. You don't have to, really. If you leave one town into another town it's the same thing. I'm not putting them down. It's just my road and theirs, it's different. Like a lot of them are married, maybe some are going to school. Some are working, you know, just working. They're still there. They're not thinking about the same things I'm thinking about.

Terkel: They're not thinking what you're thinking. You spoke of those poison pellets on the water. Maybe it hit them too...?

Dylan: Oh, yeah. It hit me, too. I just got out of it. I just got out of it, that's all.

Terkel: You were ten years old when you saw Woody, and it was about five years ago that you took to the guitar and singing.

Dylan: No, about five years ago I just sort of never really did go back home. I've been in New York City for the past almost two years. Before that I was just all around the country, to the southlands, and I was in Mexico for awhile.

Terkel: You've been influenced not only by people like Woody but by blues singers as well.

Dylan: Oh yeah. Big Joe Williams, I think you might know him. He lives here, I guess.

Terkel: Yeah, he does. I know him.

Dylan: He's an old friend of mine.

Terkel: You also take traditional songs and make them your own.

Dylan: Not any more. [*Laughs*]

Terkel: You did 'Man of Constant Sorrow', the white spiritual. You took that and made it something wholly different. But not any more, you say?

Dylan: Two or three years ago I was singing folk songs that I'd learned. Now I don't sing any of them any more.

Terkel: Has it occurred to you that your own songs might be considered folk songs? We always have this big argument: what is a folk song? I think 'Hard Rain' certainly will be one, if time is the test.

Dylan: Yeah, yeah, time will be the test.

Terkel: It seems you can write about any subject under the sun.

Dylan: Anything worth thinking about is worth singing.

Terkel: Any subject. A love song, let's say, like 'Boots of Spanish Leather'. There we have a song of a lover's farewell. This is far, far removed from the June-moon-spoon-theme way of writing. I suppose it's difficult for you to answer, Bob: what led you to the idea of writing these songs? Was it always with you?

Dylan: Yeah, it's always been with me. I can't really say what led me to them. I'm one of those people that think everybody has certain gifts, you know, when they're born, and you got enough trouble just trying to find out what it is. I used to play the guitar when I was ten, you know. So I figured maybe my thing is playing the guitar, maybe that's my little gift. Like somebody can make a cake, or somebody else can saw a tree down, and other people write. Nobody's really got the right to say that any one of these gifts are any better than any other body's. That's just the way they're distributed out. I had seen that this is exactly what my gift is, maybe I got a better gift. But as of right now, I haven't found out what it is. I don't call it a gift, it's only my way of trying to explain something that is very hard to explain.

Terkel: There's a piece you wrote called 'My Life in a Stolen Moment'. You say, 'I wrote my first song for my mother and I titled it "Mother". I wrote that in fifth grade and my teacher gave me a B-plus. I sat in a science class and flunked out for refusing to watch a rabbit die.'

Dylan: That's my college days. I only was there for about four months. But I really did get to see it. If I talk about college I ain't talking about 'em just from anything people have told me. I was actually there. I seen what goes on. I started smoking at eleven years old, I stopped once to catch my breath. I don't remember my parents singing too much, at least I don't remember swapping any songs with them. I just write. I've been writing for a long time.

Terkel: Some will say: listen to Bob Dylan, he's talking street mountain talk now, though he's a literate man, see.

Dylan: [*Laughs*] I don't think I am.

Terkel: How do you answer that when they say it?

Dylan: I got no answer. If they want to think I'm literate, it's okay by me.

Terkel: Probably it's just easier for you to express your feelings this way. I suppose the influence of a great many singers—

Dylan: Woody.

Terkel: Woody, the fact that Woody, more than college, was the big influence on you. Did Woody hear you sing some of these songs?

Dylan: Every time I go sing these songs I wrote for Woody, he always wants to hear 'A Song for Woody'. Even when he was in the hospital. [*Laughs*] He always wants to hear that.

Terkel: The tribute of a young folk poet to an older one who has meant so much to him. Do you remember the words to that one?

Dylan: Yeah, but I never sing it. Only to Woody.

Terkel: I'm thinking of the Irish anti-war song 'Johnny I Hardly Knew You'. You're saying the same thing in your own way.

Dylan: Somebody's come to the end of one road and actually knows it's the end of one road and knows there's another road there, but doesn't exactly know where it is, and knows he can't go back on this one road.

Terkel: He knows there's something else.

Dylan: He's got all kinds of stuff which just doesn't add up, you know, all kinds of thoughts in the head, all about teachers and school, and all about hitch-hikers around the country, all about— These are friends of mine, too, you know, college kids going to college. These are all people that I knew. Every one of them is sort of a symbol, I guess, for all kinds of people like that. In New York it's a different world, you know, especially 'cause I never been to New York before and I'm still carrying their small-town memories with me, so I decided I oughta write it all down. The road is very hard to find now. Maybe sometimes I wish this was 19-something else.

Terkel: Nineteen-thirties?

Dylan: Before that. You know like I was talking about pounding a nail in a board, it seems like there's a board there and all the nails are pounded in all over the place, you know, and every new person that comes to pound in a nail finds that there's one less space, you know. I hope we haven't got to the end of the space yet.

Terkel: You're looking for a fresh piece of wood.

Dylan: No, I'm content with the same old piece of wood, I just want to find another place to pound in a nail.

Terkel: Isn't that what most of them are looking for? A place to pound a nail.

Dylan: Yeah. Some of the people are the nails.

Terkel: You mean they're being pounded. [*Laughs*]

Dylan: Yeah.

Terkel: Your new album has 'Oxford Town' in it. That deals with the James Meredith case. Was he one of the nails?

Dylan: Yeah, it deals with the Meredith case [*James Meredith, a black youth, was denied entrance to the University of Mississippi*], but then again it doesn't. Music, my writing, is something special, not sacred. Like this guitar, I don't consider sacred. This guitar could bust and break, it's pretty old now. I could still get another one. It's a tool for me, that's all it is. It's like anybody else has a tool. Some people saw the tree down, you know, or some people spit tacks. When I go to saw the tree down, I cut myself on the saw. When I spit tacks, I swallow the tacks. I've just sort of got this here tool and that's all I use it as, as a tool. My life is the street where I walk. That's my life. Music, guitar, that's my tool, you know. □

NOTES ON CONTRIBUTORS

Tim Adams was deputy editor of *Granta* from 1988 to 1993 and is now a staff writer at the London *Observer*. His piece, 'Benjamin Pell versus The Rest of the World' appeared in *Granta* 87.

Robert Gumpert has been working as a photographer since 1974, when he documented the coal miners' strike in Harlan County, Kentucky. Since then he has worked on a series of long-term projects, including studies of the US criminal justice system and emergency health care in the United States.

Clifford Harper is an illustrator whose work regularly appears in the London *Guardian*. His website is www.agraphia.uk.com.

Kathleen Jamie is the author of a travel book, *Among Muslims* (Sort of Books/Seal Press) and several collections of poetry. Her latest, *The Tree House* (Picador), won the 2004 Forward prize. She lectures at St Andrews University.

Doris Lessing's recent books include a collection of essays, *Time Bites* (Fourth Estate/Perennial) and a novel, *The Story of General Dann and Mara's Daughter, Griot and the Snow Dog* (Fourth Estate). She has received numerous awards including, in 2005, the David Cohen British Literature Prize.

Barry Lopez is the author of a number of books including *Arctic Dreams* (Harvill Press/Vintage), for which he received the National Book Award, and, most recently, *Resistance* (Vintage), a collection of short stories.

Robert Macfarlane's book about mountaineering, *Mountains of the Mind* is published by Granta Books in the UK and by Pantheon Books in the US. He is a Fellow of Emmanuel College, Cambridge.

Richard Powers is the author of eight novels including *Plowing the Dark* and, most recently, *The Time of Our Singing* (Vintage/Picador), which won the W. H. Smith Literary Award in 2004. He lives in Illinois.

Matthew Reisz is the editor of the *Jewish Quarterly*. He is writing a book about his grandparents. He lives in London.

Jeremy Seabrook's most recent book is *Consuming Cultures: Globalization and Local Lives* (New Internationalist). He is a contributor to *The Statesman* in Kolkata, *Third World Resurgence* in Malaysia and the London *Guardian*.

Helen Simpson's short-story collections include *Hey Yeah Right Get a Life*, (Vintage), published in the US as *Getting a Life* (Knopf). 'Constitutional' is the title story from her new collection to be published by Jonathan Cape.

Craig Taylor produces two photocopied magazines: *The Review of Everything I've Ever Encountered* and *One Million Tiny Plays about London*. His writing has appeared in the London *Guardian* and the *New York Times Magazine*.

Studs Terkel's 'Pounding a Nail' is taken from *And They All Sang: Adventures of an Eclectic Disc Jockey*, which will be published by Granta Books in the UK next spring and by The New Press in the US this autumn.

NORTHERN COLORADO SKI TOURS

by TOM AND SANSE SUDDUTH

The Touchstone Press
P.O. Box 81
Beaverton, Oregon 97005

Northern Colorado Ski Tours

I.S.B.N. No. 0-911518-44-4

Library of Congress Catalog Card No. 76-26311

Copyright © 1976
Tom & Sanse Sudduth

PREFACE

Without a doubt, northern Colorado contains some of the most beautiful wilderness in the United States. Few summits reach such heights or display such deep glacial cuts as those in the Front Range, the mountain chain along the Continental Divide which first rises from the eastern plains of Colorado. Few sights dazzle the eyes as much as the Ten-mile Range in Summit County where one pointed peak after another juts skyward to form a snow-capped sawtooth range. North of Vail Pass, the rugged Gore Range, ribbed with rock outcroppings and streaked by avalanches, forms an inaccessible barrier in winter and stands proudly aloof from other northern Colorado ranges. Farther north, the terrain becomes more rolling, the contours more gentle as the North Gore Range ends at Rabbit Ears Pass and the Park Range begins, producing a more subtle beauty of broad snowfields and interlaced drainageways.

Besides the scenic grandeur, a main delight for the ski tourer in northern Colorado is the long skiing season and excellent, dependable snow conditions. This area, in fact, produced many of Colorado's first skiers, some of them by choice, most by necessity. In Summit County there was Father John L. Dyer, the famous "Snowshoe Itinerant" who first learned to ski in 1862 to be able to reach the scattered mining camps for preaching sessions and who later carried the mail from Buckskin Joe over the Mosquito Range to California Gulch near Breckenridge, skiing the 37 miles once a week. Even more incredible are the skiing exploits of Bill Kimball, "the best showshoe man ever known in Middle Park." In the winter of 1875 he carried 70, 80, even 105 pound sacks of mail from Empire over the newly-constructed Berthoud Pass Road, continuing night and day with no sleep all the way to Hot Sulphur Springs. In the Steamboat Springs area beginning in 1913, Carl Howelsen, a Norwegian-born cross-country and jumping champion, taught an entire community that skiing could be fun as well as functional. With the innovation of a binding that would hold skis on their feet better, "literally every able-bodied citizen in town of both sexes between the age of seven and seventy" began to join Howelsen on his Sunday *langlaufs,* skiing to a scenic destination for lunch and then gliding through open slopes of powder back to town.

This book is an invitation to see the spectacular mountain ranges in northern Colorado, to ski the same snowfields and valley bottoms that have been crossed by miners, mail carriers, and early ski enthusiasts, and to experience, quietly and profoundly, the beautiful backcountry in winter.

SKI TOURING IN NORTHERN COLORADO

The general techniques of ski touring and winter camping are not within the scope of this book. However, several important points on ski touring in northern Colorado are briefly noted.

TRAILS AND CABINS: Of the many varied ski routes researched for this guidebook, the great majority either contained freshly broken trails or showed evidence of recent ski touring use, hence providing easy skiing and giving no problems with orientation. Several Forest Service Districts have now marked special routes for ski touring and a few, including the Dillon Ranger District, have available brochures with maps and ski touring and snowmobile trail information. In an effort to prevent conflict with snowmobiles, all major snowmobiling areas such as the Mt. Evans Road, Stevens Gulch near Silver Plume, Dillon Reservoir, and the Swan River valley near Breckenridge have been left out of this book, even though those areas include excellent ski touring terrain.

Cabins for overnight use—some quite rustic but many thoughtfully fixed up with cots, stoves, and tables—are mentioned in this book with the appropriate tour text. It is hoped that these cozy winter refuges will continue to be renovated and cared for, and that each tourer who uses a cabin will keep it clean, obey all posted regulations, and contribute food staples and camping supplies. Besides the cabins described here, many Colorado Mountain Club cabins are available also for overnight use. For information, contact: Colorado Mountain Club, 2530 West Alameda, Denver, Colorado 80219.

LIFE ZONES: On any particular ski route the most useful indicator for weather and snow conditions, and for the type of wildlife, is the life zone or elevation range through which it travels. In the lower reaches of the Canadian Life Zone (8,000-10,000 feet elevation) mild weather prevails and snow cover melts more rapidly, staying longest along shaded, north-facing slopes. This area offers the best chance of seeing large game such as deer, elk, and even Rocky Mountain Bighorn sheep and Rocky Mountain goats in the Front Range. (Please do not startle big game; observe from a distance. See Winter Backcountry Ethics.) In the Hudsonian Life Zone (10,000 feet elevation to timberline) snow cover is generally dependable from December through April on all hillsides. Although wary and difficult to spot, many small mammals such as coyotes, foxes, cottontail rabbits, and snowshoe hares inhabit this area. In spring especially, the warm, windless days and crusted snowpack create ideal touring and camping conditions in this zone. The Arctic-Alpine Life Zone, from timberline to the tops of the high mountain peaks, holds winter's spell longest, often receiving snow when spring rain falls in the lower regions. Here, white-tailed ptarmigan hide in the wind-stunted brush, while mountain chickadees can be seen in the spruce trees near timberline. Large snowbanks remain through May and early June in this area.

WAXING: Wax, like snow, is crystaline in structure. It forms a bond with snow when the ski is motionless and weighted, creating grip; it releases the bond when the ski is moving and unweighted, allowing glide. Consistent snow conditions in northern Colorado allow the use of only two waxes for most of the winter—for cold days Rex or Swix "green" (or a similar hard wax), for warmer days Rex or Swix "blue." "Purple" or "red" wax are needed as the days become warmer in late February and March and klistervok and klister are used for the hot, wet, icy or slushy conditions in April and May.

HOW TO USE THIS BOOK

The information capsule preceding the text lists nine important facts about the tour and provides a means for quick comparison with other tours.

First, tours are divided into half-day trips, one-day trips, and overnights according to distance and type of terrain. A **half-day trip** allows a morning or afternoon of exercise and fresh air and measures 2.5 miles one way or less, except when the tour route follows a downhill, and hence, faster course. A **one-day trip** usually proceeds to a scenic destination for a lunch stop, and then returns over the ski tracks or makes a loop return, a trip requiring the greater part of a day. An **overnight** reaches a suggested point too far into the backcountry to allow a safe return in the same day. For these ambitious trips, pack sleeping bag, tent or snow-cave shovel, other winter camping equipment, and food.

Next, the tours are rated according to the difficulty of the trail or terrain and given a classification of Easiest, More difficult, or Most difficult. This system, first proposed by the Holy Cross Ranger District, Minturn, Colorado and now recommended to all Forest Service Districts within the Rocky Mountain Region, uses the same code and language as is used for alpine runs at ski areas. As applied in this book, **Easiest** tour routes follow level or rolling terrain, well-cleared of trees, rocks, ditches, and other obstacles. They average not more than 6 percent grade overall but can contain short downhill runs and uphill climbs of up to 10 percent slope. **More difficult** tour routes contain within their length slopes as steep as 20-25 percent but which are short enough so that momentum can be controlled, and contain fairly sharp turns but with wide, obstacle-free run-outs for those who overshoot them. Tour routes rated **Most difficult** indicate slopes up to 40 percent (about the same as an intermediate or more difficult *alpine* ski run) and/or tighter curves with less turning area.

Tour **distance,** listed in both miles and kilometers, is measured one way only for tours that return over the same track. For loop tours the total round trip distance is given. Steep switchback areas on cross-country trips, either uphill or downhill, are calculated as twice their linear distance.

Skiing time, suggested as a guide for skiers who are not sure of their pace, corresponds to the one way or round trip distance. For tour routes over Easiest terrain, it is figured at 1-1½ miles per hour, a comfortable rate which allows time for rest stops, re-waxing and picture taking. For More and Most difficult tour routes, skiing time is determined from a basic rate of 2 miles per hour and adjusted according to the steepness of the terrain. Lunch breaks and driving time are not included.

Elevation gain or **loss,** the single most important factor in determining tour difficulty, measures the difference between the highest and lowest points on the tour. If the route contains significant drops and climbs within its length, each uphill increment is added together for an *accumulated elevation gain,* each downhill increment added together for an *accumulated elevation drop.*

Each life zone or elevation range holds unique and predictable rewards and hazards for ski touring, a topic reviewed in Ski Touring in Northern Colorado (see above). The **maximum elevation** or highest point along the tour route is a useful indicator of these conditions.

Although the amount of snowfall varies significantly from year to year in northern Colorado, several other factors such as exposure to wind, side of the hill, average elevation, even skier use contribute to a tour route's ability to hold snow. The **season** listed for each tour suggests those months where adequate snow usually covers the tour route to insure good skiing conditions. This information represents a consensus of Forest and Park Rangers and experienced ski tourers.

All appropriate **U.S.G.S. topographic maps** are listed with publication dates and series classification in the order that the tour route crosses them. These maps provide extremely useful information for ski touring, especially for the longer and more difficult tour routes. Based on aerial photographs, they show the shape and elevation of the terrain, plot major trails, roads, creeks, and lakes, and differentiate between woodland, scrub, and open areas. U.S.G.S. topo maps are available for purchase at most mountaineering shops or may be obtained from the U.S. government by sending the map name and $1.25 per map to the Central Region-Map Distribution, U.S. Geological Survey, Denver Federal Center, Bldg. 41, Denver, Colorado 80225.

Each ski tour description is organized into a paragraph or two of introduction, a paragraph of driving directions, and several paragraphs of specific trail information. The introduction discusses prominent features of the tour such as interesting history and the origin of place names, spectacular viewpoints, outstanding ski runs, and prevalent hazards. The paragraph of driving directions provides instruction from the nearest major town, suggests a parking area, and notes variable conditions such as likely snowdrifts and unplowed roads. The remaining paragraphs of trail information summarize the tour route and include good vistas, promising alternate routes, unique trail features, and common tree types. Directions are based on true north as they appear on the topo map rather than on magnetic north as they would read on a compass. For example, a peak sighted at a 346° bearing from a vista point would be checked at 0° (346° + approx. 14°) on the topo map and would appear due north of the vista point. All sightings were checked in this manner and then rounded to the sixteen points of the compass. Specific ski terms such as "glide," "telemark," "double pole," etc. are given in the trail information not to prescribe a certain technique for a certain part of the trail but to provide a better understanding in ski touring language of the terrain.

The map photos in the book, enlarged or reduced sections of U.S.G.S. topographic maps used for each tour, correlate closely with the tour description. Symbols that have been drafted onto the map such as "starting point," "avalanche danger," and "alternate route" are listed in the LEGEND. The zig-zag line used to indicate cross-country switchbacks represents a symbol rather than the exact tour route. For best understanding of the tour, it is best to read the text and at the same time, follow the trail along the map, noting each prominent feature as described.

WINTER BACKCOUNTRY ETHICS

Once a domain crossed only by a solitary visitor or two, the winter backcountry now is receiving more and more use by recreationists. Parking areas spill over with cars on busy weekends, popular trails receive constant skier traffic, and regions even remote to summer hikers and backpackers are now entered in winter, suddenly made accessible by the natural pathway of snow. In the 1975-76 winter season alone, Colorado received a calculated one million "tour-skier days." Thus the potential for environmental abuse is great. But, the solution is obvious: minimize to the greatest extent possible the impact upon the land. The following list of winter backcountry ethics will help assure that the sport of ski touring will be as enjoyable in the future as it is today.

RESPECT PRIVATE PROPERTY. Road closures in winter sometimes create problems of access to public lands and private-but-open lands and problems of sufficient parking area, a situation antagonized by the ever increasing numbers of ski tourers. *Always seek permission before crossing any private land; never assume access; respect "No Trespassing" signs.* Use common-sense consideration in parking at trailheads. Be careful to avoid blocking private driveways and other cars. Also, be self-sufficient in handling car problems and muddy or slick road conditions.

PACK IT OUT. In winter the pristine beauty of the backcountry conveys a particularly refreshing feeling to its viewers, especially when a blanket of new snow covers the ground. Few things mar this natural splendor more than the sight of city-waste, garbage and litter. Make a habit of putting every scrap of trash—bottles, cans, orange peels, tin from wax cans—into a litter bag, then pack it out. *Remember: trash and snow don't mix.*

DO NOT DISTURB WILDLIFE. The influx of ski tourers into elk and deer wintering ranges threatens the survival of these magnificent animals more than do hunters. A startled elk, for example, will often run until exhausted; then wet and overheated, it will die from pneumonia. Or die from starvation and disease, unable to find enough food for its enormous 1000-pound body to replace the precious calories lost while fleeing. Dogs can easily kill elk and deer in winter by simply chasing them. Therefore, observe wildlife from a distance, perhaps with the aid of binoculars. Avoid elk and deer wintering grounds; pass quietly or detour if you should happen to spot some animals. Leave dogs at home.

CAMP WITHOUT A TRACE. Gone are the days of chopping, digging, lashing, splicing woodcraft, of the ingenious backwoods artisan who can fashion three types of firepits and build several assorted tree-bough beds. The goal for nature-sensitive ski tourers today is to camp so simply that later visitors to the site will find no trace of human use. To keep from scarring the environment, use gas stoves and foam pads instead of wood fires and bough beds. Leave the attractive dead branches on the trees.

OBSERVE WILDERNESS SANITATION RULES. Keep in mind that there are no sanitation facilities in the backcountry and make a point of using toilets before beginning the ski tour. If you must relieve yourself, find a screened spot away from travel and water routes, bury all waste, and burn then bury the toilet paper.

KNOW THE HAZARDS. Remember that pain, anguish, frustration, and despair belong to the world of man. *The mountains don't care.* Every ski tourer who enters the backcountry takes with him the individual responsibility for his comfort and safety. Know the symptoms and prevention of hypothermia; learn proper route selection around potential avalanche sites; become skilled with map and compass in case of disorientation or whiteout conditions. Rescue parties frequently must endure severe risks—often unnecessary if those needing help had taken the basic precautions.

Educate others in the winter backcountry ethics; ski softly in the wilderness and . . . PLEASE LEAVE NOTHING BUT YOUR SKI TRACKS.

AUTHORS' NOTE

One of the true delights of ski touring (and of writing ski touring guidebooks) is the opportunity to meet exceptional people. To all those who shared our enthusiasm for this guidebook and contributed their valuable thoughts and ideas, to the fellow ski tourers who helped us break the many miles of trail, we extend a sincere thanks.

We especially would like to express our gratitude to the many veteran ski tourers who contributed directly to the tour selection. *In the Fraser Valley:* Ben Beauregard of Sulphur Ranger District, Allen Gingery of C & G Touring, Ken Hoornbeek and Paul Schmitz of Rocky Mountain Outfitters, Inc., and Clint Roberts of Ski Idlewild Lodge. In *Rocky Mountain National Park:* Wendell Funk of Recreation Rentals and Jim Liles, manager of the Park's West Unit. *In the Colorado State Forest:* Larry Fairleigh and Mike Widler, State Park managers. *In Summit County:* Burnie Arndt of Copper Mountain Ski Area, Ann Cullen of The Pathfinder, Breckenridge, Gene Dayton of Breckenridge Ski Area and Bob Kluge of Gore Range Outfitters. *In the Vail area:* Bruce Batting of Vail Ski Touring & Guide Service, Jim Gregg and Terry Skorheim of Holy Cross Ranger District, and Steve Rieschl of Vail Ski Area. *In Steamboat Springs:* Phil Eggleston and Bill Gilbert of Mountaincraft, Lynn Jones of Hahn's Peak Ranger District, and Don Quinn and Sven Wiik of Scandinavian Lodge. *In Georgetown:* Chad Simonds of Crystal Cave Hostel. *In Denver:* Bob Braddock of Mountain World and Steve Cornwell of Holubar Mountaineering Ltd. *In Boulder:* Gary Neptune of Neptune Mountaineering.

We also wish to thank Lou Bowlds, President of the Rocky Mountain Division, United States Ski Association, for the endorsement and promotional support of the project. And finally, a sincere thanks to Horst Klea, Eastern Sales Manager of Fischer of America, Inc. for the financial assistance in the route-scouting.

All tours in this book were skied by the authors in the 1974-75 and 1975-76 seasons. In an effort to make future editions of this book up-to-date and useful, we invite any comment, correction, or suggestion. Please direct correspondence to the authors in care of: COLORADO SKI TOURS, Box 636, Steamboat Springs, Colorado 80477.

Good touring!

T.S.
S.S.

Contents

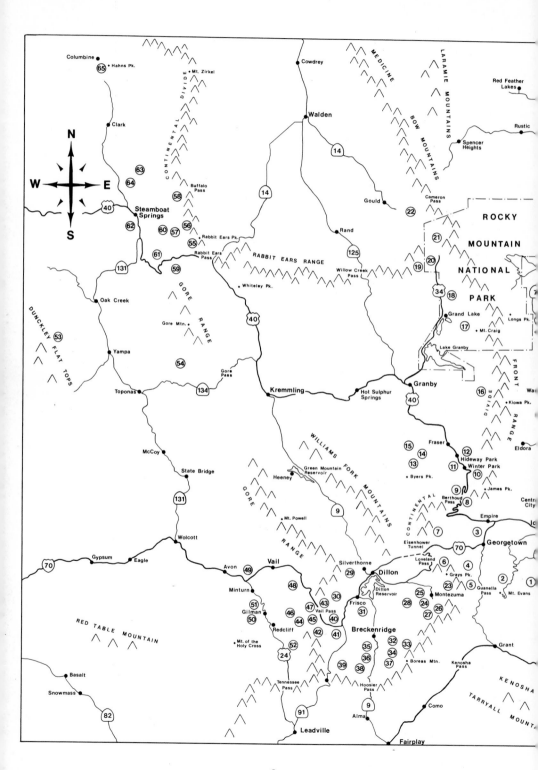

LEGEND

STARTING POINT	●
TRAIL	– – – – –
SWITCHBACK	-ᴧ-
ALTERNATE ROUTE	– –➤
MILEAGE	**3.0**
AVALANCHE DANGER	✳
STOPPING POINT	○

1

MT. EVANS WILDLIFE AREA

One day trip
Classification:
   More difficult to most difficult
Distance: 4.6 miles one way (7.4 KM.)
Skiing time: 3-3½ hours one way
Accumulated elevation gain: 1,010 feet
Accumulated elevation loss: 730 feet
Maximum elevation: 9,229 feet
Season: Late December through March
Topographic maps:
   U.S.G.S. Meridan Hill, Colo. 1957
   U.S.G.S. Harris Park, Colo. 1957
      7.5 minute series
Colorado State Wildlife Area

The Mt. Evans Wildlife Area, managed by the Colorado Division of Game, Fish and Parks as a reserve for elk and other big game, provides public access through private land to the Arapaho National Forest. In winter this designated Camp Rock Road is closed to all motorized vehicles and itself becomes a very popular ski touring route. The snow-packed roadbed climbs and drops throughout its entire length, reaching good lookout points after 1.9, 2.4 and 4.0 miles. The Truesdell Road, another much-used ski touring route, climbs south from the parking area and soon crosses a saddle to the Bear Creek and Grass Creek valleys. Due to lower elevation, the skiing season is relatively short on either the Camp Rock or Truesdell Road, with best conditions coming after the heavy snowfalls in late February and early March. An extended trip into the Arapaho National Forest in April will usually require hiking.

Please keep in mind that the Game, Fish and Parks personnel operate the Mt. Evans Wildlife Area primarily as a reserve for big game—that they extend the land use to ski tourers as a courtesy. If you should spot any of the elk, mountain goats, bighorn sheep, or mule deer that winter near this area, pass quietly or detour.

Drive on I. 70 and Colo. 74 to Evergreen and turn west onto the Upper Bear Creek Road (Jefferson County 74), a junction 0.4 mile north of the middle of Evergreen and in front of the Upper Bear Creek Inn. Proceed on this main road through Brookvale and follow the signs reading "State Wildlife Area," staying right after 6.1 and 6.5 miles. Turn left after 8.1 miles, pass the private

Wildlife Headquarters buildings, and proceed another 0.5 mile up the road to a large parking area, a total distance of 9.5 miles from Colo. 74.

Pass through a red gate and begin gliding west-northwest over the wide, often ski-packed Camp Rock Road. Curve left and double-pole to the bottom of a shallow drainage, then bend slightly right and begin an easy, steady climb, soon heading west through the open ponderosa pine forest. After 0.5 mile the snow-filled road drops on a long, thrilling run into another drainageway, then climbs steeply up the mountainside, bending sharply left, then right. Maintain a steady climb southwest past the 1.0 mile mark, curve gradually right and eventually proceed through a left, then right switchback. In another few yards the road levels and conifers open to reveal the surrounding countryside. Squaw Mountain, to the north, topped with radio relay towers, is the most conspicuous landmark across the wide Vance Creek valley.

Bend left on a short, gentle drop after 1.9 miles and continue west on a gradual, rolling climb, reaching the junction with the Bear Creek Guard Station road at the ridgetop. At the 2.4 mile mark this second viewpoint, a good lunch spot on non-windy days and a turnback point, looks down upon the deep Bear Creek valley south and gives vantage to the rolling alpine fields which suround Mt. Evans west-southwest. For a tour to the Camp Rock Campground, as figured in the information capsule, proceed west on a gradual drop, glide through a long curve right, and soon begin to descend more quickly, finally slowing to a stop in a drainage bottom at the 3.3 mile mark. Climb and drop through two more prominent drainageways, each filled with exquisite, silvery-blue spruce, and follow the wide roadbed to another high point. A white, sparsely-covered range southwest, part of the acreage devastated by the Shelter House Fire of September 1962, shows clearly from this spot.

Ski through a series of winding, exhilerating downhills on the final 0.6 mile descent to the Camp Rock Campground, passing the Camp Rock Fire Road left, then proceeding down two last switchbacks to the picnic area. Here the well-blazed Beartrack Lakes Trail cuts west into a forest of thick, towering spruce and leads to several overnight camping sites: the Beaver Meadows with three-sided shelters at mile 6.0, the clearing around the burned Mt. Evans Shelter House at mile 8.2, and the largest Beartrack Lake itself at mile 10.8. This advanced, extended ski route, most accessible during the warmer months of March and April, requires a good knowl- edge of winter camping and orienteering skills. For the return trip on the Camp Rock Road, plan on more than half the skiing time as the trip in, and control speed carefully with a snowplow and pole drag through the long drops.

Starting out

2 IDAHO SPRINGS RESERVOIR

One day trip
Classification:
  More difficult to most difficult
Distance: 2.5 miles one way (4.0 KM.)
Skiing time: 2-2½ hours one way
Elevation gain: 1,060 feet
Maximum elevation: 10,600 feet
Season: Mid-December through March
Topographic maps:
  U.S.G.S. Idaho Springs, Colo. 1957
  U.S.G.S. Georgetown, Colo. 1957
  U.S.G.S. Mt. Evans, Colo. 1957
          7.5 minute series
Arapaho National Forest

A steady, rolling climb through a lodgepole pine-filled valley, the snowy road to the Idaho Springs Reservoir offers dependable midwinter touring conditions within an hour's drive from Denver. On weekends the cacophonous roar and grind of snowmobiles on the Mt. Evans Road echo faintly in this valley but snowmobilers usually do not venture up the reservoir road itself. Although the advanced, extended tour over the Chicago Lakes Trail has a steep section which requires a short hike, it leads to a panoramic view of the Chicago Lakes and Mt. Evans amphitheaters, one of the most spectacular wintertime vistas along the Front Range.

Drive on I. 70 to the town of Idaho Springs. Take Exit 50 onto Colo. 103, the Mt. Evans Road, and proceed just under 9.0 miles to the trailhead, marked by a large sign reading "Idaho Springs Reservoir" and 0.2 mile beyond the South Chicago Creek parking. Park on the plowed side of the road.

Begin skiing east up the wide, wind-swept Idaho Springs Reservoir Road, climbing above and right of Colo. 103. After about a hundred yards enter a lodgepole pine forest where the snow becomes deeper and more protected and soon stay right as a branch road, unmarked on the topo, forks left to private property. The tall conifers block any long view as the ski route makes a steep climb, moderates for several yards, then climbs again on a winding, southerly course into the midday sun. Spruce begin to compete for habitat with the longer-needled pine after 0.8 mile, and the snow-packed roadbed soon rounds a small bend right, bringing into view the windblown hillside of Rogers Peak far ahead.

Pass the Shwayder Camp entrance sign left, make another steep climb past a snowy baseball field, then glide on a delightful, near-level run south, bypassing the private camp cabins on the left. The grade alternates again from steady climb to level to rolling climb as the ski route passes through a corral gate and winds south through the forested valley. Ski by several gigantic boulders near the 2.4 mile mark, very probably "glacial erratics" transported to their present location by the large glaciers that helped carve this valley. Bend right, then left on another steady climb and come to the north end of the Idaho Springs Reservoir, a good spot for lunch or turning back.

With an additional 2.4 miles and 880 feet elevation gain, the tour may be continued up the valley to the north Chicago Lake via the Chicago Lakes Trail. Glide easily over the roadbed along the west side of the ice-covered reservoir and as soon as a small, red cottage appears at the end of the road, angle right on a traverse up the hillside, avoiding the private property left. Follow the trail southwest into the trees, climbing above a willow-filled meadow in the creekbed. Pass the trail register right and after several easier climbs and drops, break out of the trees above another willow-choked park. In several more yards the trailcut becomes too steep and narrow to ski and requires a hike of about 0.1 mile through thick trees and over windfalls.

Turn left at the 4.0 mile mark after the grade has moderated and immediately glide into the middle of an open park, the first viewpoint of the Chicago Lakes amphitheater and the summits of Mt. Spalding and Mt. Evans. A ragged, glacial-carved summit—the ridgetop between Gray Wolf Mountain and Mt. Spalding—protrudes southwest from the amphitheater wall, and behind and farther left another sheer rock wall rises to the 14,264-foot top of Mt. Evans. Glide back into the trees on the south side of the park, pass a blazed tree right, then bend slightly to the right. Continue southwest on easy drops and climbs over the obvious trailcut and after 4.5 miles begin breaking onto an open hillside. Yellow pitch snags, gnarled and weathered, remain from an ancient forest fire here, and five-needled limber pine, characteristic of high, windy places, find root in the rocky soil. The landscape is dominated, however, by the cold, blue amphitheater wall which encircles the Chicago Lakes bowl, frosted with snow, streaked with deep shadows, and indeed an awesome sight.

For the return trip, retrace the ski tracks. Proceed on foot again through the steep grade on the Chicago Lakes Trail and control speed carefully through the other steady drops with a pole drag and snowplow.

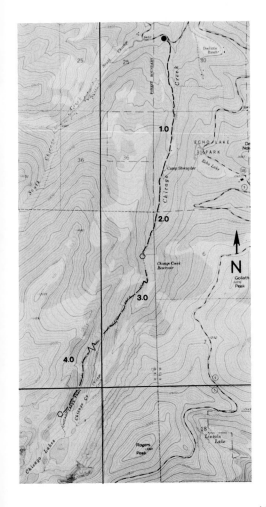

3 BARD CREEK

One day trip
Classification: More difficult
Distance: 4.6 miles one way (7.4 KM.)
Skiing time: 3-3½ hours one way
Elevation gain: 1,740 feet
Maximum elevation: 10,840 feet
Season: December through late April
Topographic maps:
 U.S.G.S. Georgetown, Colo. 1957
 U.S.G.S. Grays Peak, Colo. 1958
   7.5 minute series
Arapaho National Forest

In 1859, a Dr. Richard Bard from Iowa, for whom Bard Creek is named, came into the valley of West Fork of Clear Creek and built a lonely, hand-hewn log cabin on the south side. The following summer Dr. Bard met with other prospectors at the only other cabin in the valley and helped establish the Union District Valley City Company, the beginning of today's town of Empire. Besides gold, the topic of the day was national politics, and Bard's neighbors stated clearly their convictions by naming the nearest mountain in honor of the popular presidential candidate, Abraham Lincoln. Bard, a staunch Democrat, answered this political statement by naming the mountain behind his cabin for Stephen A. Douglas, Lincoln's eminent opponent. To underscore his views Bard also named the opposite mountain Democrat. Another prospector, from Kentucky but a loyal Union man, entered the fervent debate by conferring the name Republican to the mountain adjoining Democrat. And so the debate went on.

Drive on U.S. 40 to Empire. Turn south at the middle of town, cross the West Fork of Clear Creek, and proceed toward Empire Pass. Curve west onto the high, narrow Bard Creek road and continue as far as possible, usually a total of 2.2 miles from U.S. 40. Parking is limited to a small turn-around area at the end of the plowed road.

Begin skiing west over the snow-covered Bard Creek roadbed and soon pass two private cabins on the hillside to the right. Bend right, bearing toward the forested, 11,074-foot mountain west-northwest, then enter a grove of aspen and cross to the north side of the creekbed. Here, on the south-facing hillside, splashes of sun penetrate the tree cover, sometimes melting the snow from the patches of dark green kinnikinnik. Begin a more

noticeable climb up the snowy roadbed; swing back toward the creek and continue beneath another private cabin. Stay left as a sawmill road turns right up Lincoln Mountain, pass a deep gulch that drops into Bard Creek from the right, and glide west through the willows and aspens near the creekbed. Throughout this first one-half mile you will see several rare bristlecone pine among the more common aspen and lodgepole. These ancient, gnarled conifers have needles in groups of five, conspicuously marked with gray droplets of sap.

Begin a steepening climb west-southwest up the roadbed, now suddenly wide and smooth. (On the return trip this short section, the most challenging of the entire tour, must usually be negotiated with a strong snowplow or pole drag.) With the climb the two forested tops of Columbia Mountain come into view across the valley south, and in a few more yards the open, wind-blown range of Republican Mountain shows through the roadcut west-southwest. Proceed through delightfully easy drops and climbs, weaving between black-trunked lodgepole and cream-colored aspen. Pass a branch road, unmarked on the topo, which forks left and eventually ski into a small, willow-filled park. From here the tour route maintains a gradual, rolling climb through the open valley, allowing a good view of the surrounding mountains.

At 1.9 miles come to the weathered ruins of the Bard Creek Mine, an excellent place either to end the tour or to stop for lunch. First in sight is a large mound of ore tailings, topped with the skeletal remains of a wooden loading chute.

As outlined in the information capsule, the tour can be extended another 2½ miles up the valley, ending at a spectacular timberline vista. Climb 40 feet above the creekbed, pass a switchback right, then another branch road left, and continue by a large log cabin, almost hidden in trees near the creek. Begin another steady climb near the 3.0 mile mark, eventually gaining a partial view of the long, arcing range of Sherman Mountain south and the snow-blanketed Engelmann Peak west-northwest. Follow the roadcut until snow becomes so deep that you are raised to a level with the tree branches and the cut becomes hard to find. Then stay on the north side of the creekbed and continue cross-country on a gradual climb up the valley.

From the third large meadow the view encompasses a vast amphitheater of treeless, wind-blown peaks. Robeson Peak, a bulky, rounded mound, rises behind a protruding knoll due west. Two high points in the range southwest comprise Bard Peak. Silver Plume Mountain shows south-southeast.

Return over the ski tracks.

Mine ruin exploration

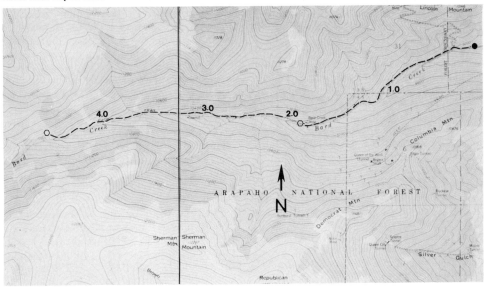

4 WALDORF ROAD

One day trip
Classification: Easiest
Distance: 3.5 miles one way (5.6 KM.)
Skiing time: 2½-3 hours one way
Elevation gain: 1,170 feet
Maximum elevation: 10,730 feet
Season: December through March
Topographic maps:
  U.S.G.S. Georgetown, Colo. 1957
  U.S.G.S. Grays Peak, Colo. 1958
        7.5 minute series
Arapaho National Forest

On August 1, 1906 a golden spike was driven into the last rail of the narrow-gauge Argentine Central Railroad at its alpine terminus on McClellan Mountain, heralded as *"the highest point in the world* reached by a regular railway." Built both as a transport for silver-rich ore from the Waldorf mines and as a scenic ride for tourists, the Argentine Central was expected to become one of Colorado's most popular attractions. Today only the old railroad grade still remains, which, like the crumbling cabins in the Waldorf mining camp, serves as a reminder of the adventurous mining days in Colorado.

Take the down ramp from I. 70 into Georgetown, turn right at the first intersection and continue to the Guanella Pass Road at the south end of town. Pass through several switchbacks up Leavenworth Mountain, then proceed south to the junction with Waldorf Road, a total of 2.5 miles from George-

town. Park in the cleared area on the right side of the road.

Glide south-southwest over the obvious cut of the Waldorf Road and immediately cross under a power line. Continue the easy climb through a switchback north, cross under the high voltage line, then bend toward a high point on Leavenworth Mountain ahead and ski into a stand of lodgepole pine. These trees become more and more scattered as the smooth roadbed bends west and contours to a crossing with Leavenworth Creek at the 0.3 mile mark. With a gradual climb up the Leavenworth mountainside the ski route holds an excellent vantage of the South Clear Creek Valley. The south summit of Independence Mountain with its conspicuous rocky clearing marks the skyline east-southeast, and then the forested range continues south through a saddle and rises to the snowy cone of Sugarloaf Peak, so-named because it is shaped like the loaf of sugar of pioneer days.

Follow the jeep-size road past the snow-covered mounds of tailings near the Kirtley Mine, turn left on a switchback and climb gradually back into the sheltering pine. Proceed straight after 0.8 mile where a branch road switchbacks right to the old railroad grade higher on the mountainside, and ski with long, easy glides to a meeting with the creekbed. Another jeep road, unmarked on the topo, soon joins from the left and the ski route continues on a delightful run through a section of willows, then aspen. At 1.5 miles begin an easy climb above the creekbed. Look for the beautiful and rare bristlecone pine through this section, easy to identify with its sappy, resin-marked needles, five per fascicle.

Follow the snow-covered road on an obvious cut through thick willows, climb again up the Leavenworth mountainside, then ski through creek crossings at 2.3 and 2.5 miles and wind southwest in and out of scattered clumps of spruce. The ski route stays above the right side of the creek for the next mile and climbs gradually through the tree clumps to a good midwinter stopping point at the Sidney Tunnel. First in view at this site is a cabin ruin with only one wall still standing on the hillside (right). Farther beyond on the left sits a rusty steel building which contains old pipes, flywheels, rods and pistons, the machinery used in the early 1900s to mill silver ore. A large mound of tailings, topped with the picturesque ruins of an old flume, marks the location of the Sidney Tunnel. All these buildings are private property so leave everything untouched and be especially careful not to litter.

For those skiers with a strong glide and good endurance, the tour over the Waldorf Road can be continued to the actual site of the Waldorf mining camp. This extension, still over "easiest" terrain, adds another 2.6 miles and 880 feet elevation gain to the tour and enters the wintry Arctic-Alpine Life Zone, thus requiring a day of good weather. Stay to the right of Leavenworth Creek, follow the snow-buried road as much as possible, and cross under the high voltage line at miles 4.1 and 4.5. Then contour up the open hillside through scattered conifers and pitch stumps for another 1.6 miles and intercept the Waldorf site, marked with a new Quonset hut and two remaining cabins from the mining days. A vast, barren amphitheater extends beyond, formed by the alpine sides of McClellan Mountain, Argentine Peak and Mount Wilcox. Return over the ski tracks, a descent with sufficient grade for long, double-poled coasts and easy glides.

Mine flume from Sidney Mill building

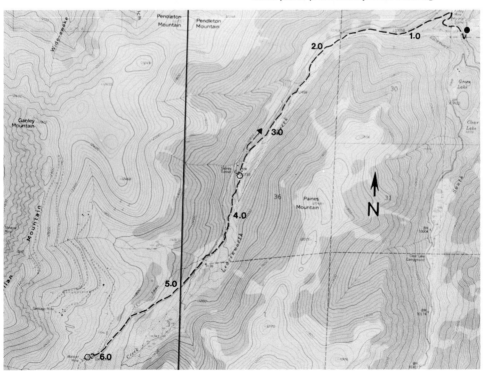

5 NAYLOR LAKE

Half-day trip
Classification: Easiest
Distance: 1.3 miles one way (2.1 KM.)
Skiing time: 1 hour one way
Elevation gain: 530 feet
Maximum elevation: 11,390 feet
Season: Mid-November through early May
Topographic maps:
    U.S.G.S. Mt. Evans, Colo. 1957
    U.S.G.S. Montezuma, Colo. 1958
        7.5 minute series
Arapaho National Forest

The high mountain road to Naylor Lake disappears under a carpet of snow by at least mid-November with several feet often remaining in early May. This long season of excellent snow conditions makes the tour one of the most popular in the area. The climb, steady but never steep at any one spot, results in a surprising elevation gain of 530 feet for the short 1.3 miles and provides a return run of one long, exciting coast. For the advanced skier a loop route to snow fields southeast of Naylor Lake via the Silver Dollar Trail is possible. However, be prepared to do some cross-county bushwacking if deep snow has obscured the trail.

The drive up the Guanella Pass Road is an adventure in itself. First it switchbacks to a high lookout over Georgetown, then proceeds south up the scenic South Clear Creek Valley. If you are making the trip for the first time in winter, be sure to continue another two miles to the top of the pass and see the rugged and spectacular Sawtooth range and the barren, 14,060-foot Mt. Bierstadt east.

Drive on I. 70 into Georgetown and intercept the Guanella Pass Road at the south end of town. Proceed through several switchbacks up Leavenworth Mountain, pass the Cabin Creek Power Station, and continue to the Naylor Lake trailhead, a point where the road makes a sharp bend left and a total of 8.8 miles from the south end of Georgetown. Park in the plowed pullout area on the right side of the road.

Climb over the snowbank and begin skiing west-southwest between the tall, snow-laden engelmann spruce, stopping at the nearby registration box to fill out an information card. Break trail on the snow-buried roadbed up a gradual, then steeper climb. Except for

the massive, 12,959-foot dome northeast, no other mountains show above the thick conifers. Bend left, then right through a hairpin turn and continue southwest on a pleasant, near-level run. Soon a long, white range, the eastern extension of Square Top Mountain, begins to show over the trees ahead left and the forested south side of Otter Mountain comes into view right. The snowy roadbed proceeds on a winding, gradual climb and, near 0.5 mile, breaks out into a long, open meadow, not indicated on the topo.

Break trail west through the deep snow in the meadow, crossing the inconspicuous Naylor creekbed, and after about 200 yards come to a sign reading "Silver Dollar Trail," near the trees at the far side. This trail, an advanced alternate route to Naylor Lake, turns left into the thick trees, winds west-southwest along a branch drainage for about one-half mile, then breaks out onto the more open hillside southeast of the lakebed. Turn north at the first meadow and drop through rolling fields of snow to the east end of the lake, a thrilling deep-powder run. *Do not follow the Silver Dollar Trail west onto the steep, treeless hillside south of Naylor Lake, an area with potential for avalanche* (see map).

To continue on the easier roadbed route, bend right in front of the Silver Dollar Trail sign, then proceed through a curve around an island of four trees. Soon turn west, maintain a steady, winding climb up the obvious roadcut, and after 1.0 mile, ski out onto the open, sometimes wind-crusted lee side of the lake. The vista from this east side is magnificent, encompassing a vast amphitheater of towering, snow-capped peaks. Highest and most eye-catching is Square Top Mountain southwest, carved with a deep, rocky chasm on its north side. Steep, rocky outcroppings above, then a protruding ridge below which holds Murray and Silver Dollar Lakes mark the eastern reaches of Argentine Peak due west. Mt. Wilcox, named after owner and president of the famous Argentine Central Railway, Edward John Wilcox, appears west-northwest as a high, rounded knoll.

In spring only, after the snow has settled and avalanche danger has diminished, the tour can be extended west to Silver Dollar Lake, adding 1.1 miles and 560 feet elevation gain to the tour. Rather than attempt to follow the snow-covered Silver Dollar Trail, ski across to the west side of Naylor Lake and climb steadily west, then south, staying directly in the bottom of the valley. The return trip from Naylor Lake backtracks over the roadbed, much faster now with the broken trail. If speed needs to be checked on the downhill run, step into the deep snow next to the track and try some telemark or christie turns.

Lunch stop at Naylor Lake

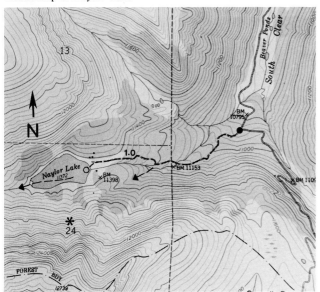

6 GRIZZLY GULCH

One day trip
Classification: More difficult
Distance: 2.6 miles one way (4.2 KM.)
Skiing time: 2-2½ hours one way
Elevation gain: 930 feet
Maximum elevation: 10,720 feet
Season: December through late April
Topographic map:
    U.S.G.S. Grays Peak, Colo. 1958
             7.5 minute series
Arapaho National Forest

Grizzly! Old Ephraim! Silvertip! The White Bear! No matter what name was used by early mountain men to describe this greatest of North American carnivores, it generally connoted fear and respect. The grizzly bear seemed almost as undaunted by lead from the white men's muzzle-loaders as he was by the Indians' stone-tipped arrows, and the fury of a wounded animal has been told and re-told in countless stories. Once widely distributed throughout the Colorado Rockies in habitat much like Grizzly Gulch, this magnificent beast is now very close to extinction in Colorado. The last reliable sighting occurred in the San Juan Mountains of southern Colorado in 1967.

The tour along Grizzly Gulch penetrates between the windswept Baker and Kelso mountaintops, finally stopping at the northern reaches of Grizzly Peak on the Continental Divide. Torreys Peak, named for the renowned botany professor John Torrey who compiled a classic book on Rocky Mountain flora, reaches its regal size on the skyline south, the eleventh highest peak in Colorado.

Proceed on I. 70 to the Bakerville Exit 41 several miles west of Silver Plume. Continue straight ahead from the overpass, cross the frontage road, and park in the plowed area north of the trailhead reserved for public use.

Ski straight south from the parking area for about 25 yards, passing several private buildings on the right. Turn left onto a roadcut where the trailhead sign reads "Stevens Gulch/Grizzly Gulch" and begin a gradual climb into the shadows of aspen and conifers. Soon the road switchbacks right and proceeds through several sections of steady climb, more tiresome if snowmobiles have worn washboard ruts into the snow. Bend left, then right at a second set of switchbacks and glide another few yards to the first view of the surrounding mountains. Baker Mountain ahead and right appears as two massive mounds, the first thickly forested and the second, behind, a snowy alpine peak. Straight down the road the pointed, 14,267-foot top of Torreys Peak juts into the clouds, then a long ridge leads left to the steep, rocky wall of Kelso Mountain, the most absorbing part of the vista.

Glide over the gently-climbing roadbed as each opening in the trees brings a new view of the snowy mountain. Double pole through a slight drop and continue past the 1.0 mile mark to the turnoff into Grizzly Gulch, an obvious right fork in the road. Pass above a log structure near Quayle Creek, bend slightly right in the direction of Torreys Peak, and coast down a long, fun drop, ending amid the tattered shacks of an old mining camp. Here the wide road ends and the ski route drops on a straight, willow-lined course to the creekbed, then climbs steadily for a few yards onto a narrower trailcut. Continue on a steady, then very gradual climb through thick trees, eventually coming to a point overlooking the picturesque San Juan Tunnel cabin in the snow-filled gulch below. High on the hillside, a double-decked mine building rises to the protruding shaft of the Grizzly Tunnel.

Contour along the hillside on a gentle climb at 2.0 miles as the deep gulch below fills with conifers. Ski past a snowy couloir on the Kelso mountainside left, the steep avalanche run-out area now covered with new, young seedlings, and soon break out onto an open hillside. Two trail-like cul-de-sacs climb and traverse the hillside at the point where the main trailcut drops left through scattered willows and crosses the creekbed, then proceeds south-southwest onto a quiet, snow-covered meadow. Here in the sheltering trees on the north side you can stop for lunch and gaze across the rolling snowfields to magnificent Torreys Peak, sometimes gleaming brilliantly with sunlight, other times enveloped in clouds.

For a longer, more advanced trip, continue cross-country through the meadow, passing the site of a solitary cabin—now burned—marked on the topo map. Stay several yards above and right of the creekbed and climb steadily through sub-alpine fir over an easily-lost, narrow trailcut. Ski quickly across each avalanche run-out area and proceed no farther than timberline, an extension that adds another 1.6 miles and 850 feet elevation gain to the tour. This high point, just over the range from the Arapaho Basin Ski Area, gives view finally to the rocky, corniced summit of Grizzly Peak, a mountain as rugged and wild as its name.

Torreys Peak

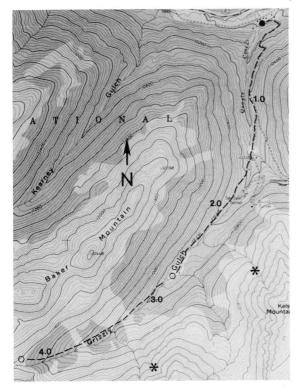

21

7 HERMAN GULCH

One day trip
Classification: More difficult
Distance: 2.9 miles one way (4.7 KM.)
Skiing time: 2½-3 hours one way
Elevation gain: 1,260 feet
Maximum elevation: 11,560 feet
Season: December through late April
Topographic maps:
    U.S.G.S. Grays Peak, Colo. 1958
    U.S.G.S. Loveland Pass, Colo. 1958
            7.5 minute series
Arapaho National Forest

Thousands of travelers on Interstate 70 speed past the entrance to Herman Gulch daily but few realize how close they come to some of the wildest, most unspoiled country in Colorado. The tour begins with obstacles: snow obscures both the trailhead and the first few yards of the trail on a course which circumvents private property. And once on the road itself, the climb is discouragingly steep for several hundred yards. Soon however, thick conifers muffle the whine and rattle of Interstate traffic and the tour route climbs very gradually into a beautiful, secluded valley, a passageway that leads to a timberline view of Continental Divide mountains.

The best touring weather for Herman Gulch comes with the warm spring days of March and April. In midwinter, several avalanche chutes and run-out areas must be carefully avoided and, after periods of wind and snow when avalanche danger is high, the gulch should not be toured.

Drive west on I-70 to the exit for Herman Gulch, marked only with an "Exit 35 mph" sign, 2.8 miles west of the Bakerville Exit 41. Proceed to the bottom of the down ramp near the old U.S. 6 roadbed, the starting point for the tour. Turn left (south), cross under the two lanes of I. 70, and continue to a designated parking area to the right of the eastbound I. 70 up ramp. Pack skis back under the Interstate to the starting point.

Ski east along the old U.S. 6 roadbed for about one hundred yards, passing to the left of the I. 70 down ramp. Watch closely for two half-buried signs near treeline: the first directs travel east with arrows, the second, several yards beyond, reads "Herman Gulch Trail/Watrous Gulch Trail" and marks the turn-off into the trees. Follow the tree blazes northeast on a short traverse up the mountainside, intercept the cut which extends beyond the power line right-of-way, and immediately turn left onto an obvious jeep road. This snowy path begins a fairly steep climb through an aspen grove, then curves right around a ridge, giving brief vantage first to the upper Clear Creek valley, and in several more yards to the Eisenhower Memorial Tunnel. Continue northwest on an easier grade as the white bottom of Herman Gulch shows through the conifers left and break into the open valley at 0.6 mile.

Veer to the west side of the gulch at the first avalanche path, a well-scrubbed chute that fans out from the Woods Mountain range northeast, then continue cross-country through scattered engelmann spruce and willows in the gulch bottom. Mt. Sniktau, in view to a lesser extent from the tour's beginning, now rises to a snow-capped point south, a grand memorial to the pioneer journalist, E. H. N. Patterson, who used "Sniktau" as a pen name. Break trail northwest on a delightfully gentle climb, bearing after 1.0 mile toward a flat face on the Continental Divide.

Cross through a small neck of trees and ski onto a wider valley floor, proceeding on a course well away from the second avalanche path northeast. Now in view southeast is the most inspiring vista of the tour: Kelso and McClellan Mountains, indistinguishable from this distance of over six miles, form one long, rock-ribbed wall and glow with a deep magenta hue.

Climb high along the left side of the valley as a third, then a fourth avalanche path sweeps down the Woods Mountain range. Three and four-foot seedlings stick bravely through the snow in these chutes now, doomed to destruction with the next big flood of snow. Swing to the north side of the valley after 2.0 miles, avoiding any danger from the obvious avalanche path on the Mount Bethel hillside. Weave through thicker conifers which spill into the gulch bottom, soon bend left toward the open amphitheater above Herman Lake, and continue the easy cross-country climb. A few stunted, twisted trees dot the hillside south and snow in the gulch becomes hardened from wind as the tour route pushes above timberline to a vast and lonely stopping point. In spring only, after warm days have settled the snow, a switchbacking climb can be made to the Herman Lake bowl itself, adding another 0.7 mile and 410 feet of elevation gain to the tour.

Snowy day trail breaking

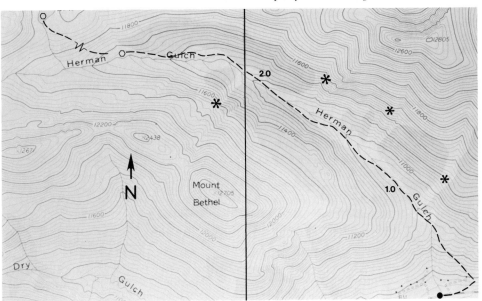

8 SEVENMILE SKI TRAIL

Half-day trip
Classification: Most difficult
Distance: 3.2 miles one way (5.1 KM.)
Skiing time: 1½ hours one way
Elevation *loss*: 1,570 feet
Maximum elevation: 11,310 feet
Season: Mid-November through April
Topographic maps:
U.S.G.S. Berthoud Pass, Colo. 1957
U.S.G.S. Empire, Colo. 1958
7.5 minute series
Arapaho National Forest

The Sevenmile Ski Trail was named by skiing enthusiasts in the 1940s who would follow the roadbed on a fast, winding descent into the Fraser Valley. It was actually part of the old Berthoud Pass Wagon Road, an important transportation link between Denver and Middle Park that was surveyed by Captain Berthoud in 1863 and finally opened for travel on October 1, 1875. The distance from the top of the pass to the first stage station at Spruce Lodge (now gone) measured seven miles, hence the unofficial name for the ski trail. During the first winter after its opening the snowy roadbed became a route for skiing, or "snowshoeing" as it was called in those days. According to a story in *The Olden Days* by Mary L. Cairns, Bill Kimball, "the best snow-shoe man ever known to Middle Park," carried 70 or 80, even as much as 105 pounds of mail per trip from Empire over the pass to Hot Sulphur Springs during that winter, often going night and day without sleep.

The tour as described in the text will challenge even the best of "skinny" skiers. There are, however, several other tour possibilities that are much easier, recommended for beginning skiers. With arrangements for a car pick-up, the wide Fraser riverbed can be toured, beginning from the fourth switchback of U.S. 40 and continuing for several miles down the valley toward Winter Park. Or, an out-and-return trip can be made from the fourth switchback up the valley for about a mile.

Drive on U.S. 40 to the top of Berthoud Pass and park in the large parking lot in front of the Berthoud Pass Lodge. Arrange for a shuttle or second car pick-up at the fourth switchback on the west side of the pass, a distance of 6.3 highway miles from the top. This switchback, plowed widely along the lower east side, also serves as a parking area for the tour up and down the Fraser Valley. However, do not park here when highway maintenance crews are working to remove the snow.

The tour begins from the north end of the Berthoud Pass parking lot with a breathtaking plunge onto the open hillside below. Known as "Hell's Half Acre" by the many skiers already initiated to the Sevenmile Ski Trail, this steep, concave slope provides superb powder skiing following a winter snowstorm. However, after periods of wind or warm weather, it can be hard-packed, sometimes icy and crusty, and at these times perhaps the most challenging tour route described in this guidebook. Ski to the U.S. 40 switchback, also another possible starting point which would eliminate the drop down Hells Half Acre. Continue under the telephone line, traverse the long snowbank below the highway, and then either follow the old wagon road left, the Sevenmile Ski Trail itself, or turn right and head into the thick spruce and fir toward the Fraser riverbed route.

The Sevenmile Ski Trail maintains a steady drop on a contour below the U.S. 40 highway and passes through two thick groves of conifers. Bend gradually right, then left around a protruding ridge; soon break out below another open hillside left which was burned several decades ago, and continue across the Current Creek drainage. Double pole back into the trees and after 1.7 miles come to a long avalanche path, now filled with small aspen and alder. Although the continual plowing of snow on U.S. 40 above usually triggers any possible slide here, do not cross this steep hillside if avalanche danger is present. Glide back into the trees near 2.2 miles; control speed with a snowplow or a pole drag and follow the roadcut on a fast and thrilling mile-long coast to the fourth switchback of U.S. 40, a good point for a shuttle pick-up.

The alternate route down the Fraser riverbed offers more skiing variety than the Sevenmile Ski Trail. Follow the drainage bottom through a bend left and drop steadily for several hundred yards, skiing over many sudden bumps from the snow-covered logs and boulders. Soon bend left again, glide below a run-out area from the avalanche paths on Colorado Mines Peak, and near 1.3 miles begin a switchbacking descent down the steep basin. Cross a large meadow at the junction with Current Creek, drop more slowly through a second open area, and after 2.0 miles pass a tiny log hut, only six by twelve feet in size and nearly buried in the snowdrifts. Continue down the snowy river-bed until the timber becomes too thick to penetrate, then contour left to the Sevenmile Ski Trail and drop quickly to the stopping point at the highway switchback.

1940s Ski Course Marker

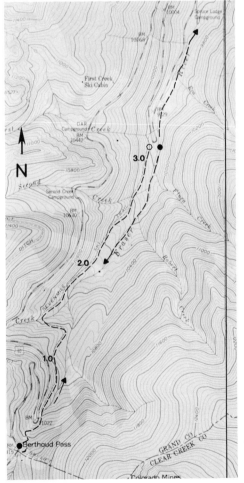

9 SECOND CREEK BOWL

Half-day trip
Classification:
More difficult to most difficult
Distance: 1.2 miles one way (1.9 KM.)
Skiing time: 2-2½ hours one way
Elevation gain: 735 feet
Maximum elevation: 11,320 feet
Season: Mid-November through April
Topographic map:
U.S.G.S. Berthoud Pass, Colo. 1957
7.5 minute series
Arapaho National Forest

Nestled high on a ridge between the First and Second Creek valleys, the picturesque "Second Creek cabin" makes a cozy lunch spot and rest area for the tour up Second Creek bowl. Uniquely constructed, the center ridge of the small A-frame extends out of the roof where it is lashed to a nearby spruce. Inside the cabin there is a top loft with sleeping space for four persons; below is another large sleeping bench and an adjacent area for chopping and storing wood. A cute, two-plate wood stove sits near the front. If you use the cabin, pack in wood, matches, and donate staple foods. Be sure to clear snow away from the door carefully before entering the cabin and share with the cleaning and maintenance.

The recommended route to the cabin climbs steadily along the north side of Second Creek for 0.5 mile, then turns northwest and makes a switchbacking ascent to a safe course along the ridgetop. In view west during most of the tour is a source of danger: a magnificent, snow-and-rock wall, usually corniced and awesome with its potential for avalanche. Deep powder snow often fills Second Creek bowl during the cold mid-winter months, creating perfect conditions for a return run of linked telemark and parallel turns.

Proceed on U.S. 40 to the old Second Creek Campground area, almost 3.0 miles west of Berthoud Pass. Park in the plowed space on the west side of the highway.

Sidestep over the bank of plowed snow at the start, contour on a gradual climb toward the creekbed, and immediately pass to the right of a red outhouse. Stay on the north side of the drainage and proceed on a cross-country climb west, skiing across the open mountainside between clumps of conifers above and below. Many giant engelmann spruce soon fill the creekbed, then eventually thin to a few scattered trees. With this openness and with the steady increase in elevation the view takes in a greater panorama of the large Second Creek bowl. Twisted, weathered snags cover the hillsides everywhere. On the horizon south a series of white avalanche paths contrast vividly with the dark trees; north the mountainside rises to a sharp, rocky ridgetop, then dips west into a shallow saddle.

Follow the northernmost drainage where the creek divides near the 0.5 mile mark. Soon turn northwest and begin a switchbacking climb up the most gradual part of the mountainside, intercepting the ridgetop at the west end of the saddle. The brown, wind-blown summits of Parry Peak, Mt. Eva, and Mt. Flora form a rolling skyline east, and with the last climb, Colorado Mines Peak, topped with a huge FAA radar installation building, shows over the forested range south-southeast. Contour west around a slight knoll, then swing north and follow above a deep ravine of smooth snow. This high route, sometimes with crusted, wind-eroded snow, avoids the avalanche danger from the sheer amphitheater wall west. Continue north to the Second Creek cabin, neatly tucked in a conspicuous island of fir and spruce on the ridgetop.

For a return trip down the opposite side of the bowl, schuss south from the cabin and double pole onto a large, wind-swept mesa. Stay well below the avalanche run-out west, obvious by its scrubby seedlings with stripped branches, and continue the contour south into open fir and spruce. Before starting the downhill run, look directly north at Peak 11,527 just beyond the First Creek valley. It appears unmistakably like a gigantic Saint Bernard dog: rocky outcroppings form the eye, nose, and large jowls, beneath the ear another rock ledge shapes the front foot, the skyline range outlines the back and the tail disappears into the ridgetop. Continue the return trip by turning downhill and making the long, exhilerating drop into the creekbed. Follow the ski tracks to the parking area.

Second Creek A-Frame

10 JIM CREEK

One day trip
Classification:
  Easiest to most difficult
Distance: 4.2 miles one way (6.8 KM.)
Skiing time: 3-3½ hours one way
Elevation gain: 1,560 feet
Maximum elevation: 10,760 feet
Season: December through early April
Topographic maps:
  U.S.G.S. Fraser, Colo. 1957
  U.S.G.S. East Portal, Colo. 1958
  U.S.G.S. Empire, Colo. 1958
    7.5 minute series
Arapaho National Forest

An old favorite among old ski tourers, the ski route along the Jim Creek valley usually remains well-packed throughout the winter. Those who want an easy half-day tour follow the roadbed for less than a mile, staying on land owned by the City and County of Denver and open for public use. Snow-cavers dig overnight shelters in the open hillside near mile 2.0 and the more ambitious tourers reach the upper meadow near the end of the tour route, another excellent spot for overnight camping. The Winter Park Ski Area graciously permits ski tourers to park near their east entrance but this parking privilege must not be abused by blocking traffic to the Ski Area.

Drive on U.S. 40 to the east entrance of the Winter Park Ski Area, about 10.2 miles from the top of Berthoud Pass and immediately opposite the Jim Creek valley. Park in the open area next to the highway, making sure that access to the Ski Area is unobstructed. If this area is full, additional parking may be found near the gravel pit another mile up U.S. 40 (when the gravel pit area has been plowed open). The ski route from the gravel pit to Jim Creek follows the Fraser River Canal road (see map photo).

Cross to the northeast side of U.S. 40 and drop over the road shoulder into the flat bottom of the Jim Creek valley. The open starting point here provides a good introduction to the high Front Range peaks which will be companions for the tour. Straight up the valley east is the snowy range north of James Peak, a panorama which will become progressively more rugged and severe as the tour route sweeps south. Through the Fraser valley, the alpine summit of Parry Peak rises

into the skyline southeast, and then the Continental Divide continues right to the long, smooth face of Mt. Eva, flanked on either side with deep canyons. The next high summit in the range, rounded, wind-blown Mt. Flora south-southeast, makes her only appearance on the tour from this first meadow.

Intercept an obvious, often snow-packed roadbed which contours along the south side of the Jim Creek valley. Climb very gradually west over the roadbed on a course near treeline and after 0.3 mile glide under an enormous green aqueduct, part of the Fraser River Diversion Canal. With each opening in the conifers left, the wide, scenic valley comes into view: willows of orange and brown mark the creekbed and on the hillside beyond, hundreds of aspen blend together in splendid detail, casting a soft beige color over the entire area. Pass the Diversion Canal roadcut which joins from the right, ski above the Jim Creek dam near the 0.8 mile mark, and continue on a winding course through a patch of gray alders. On the white range at the end of the valley, the old Rogers Pass Road crosses the Continental Divide.

Break into a clearing after 1.0 mile, bend left, then right on a contour across the hillside, and eventually cross through a steep, stump-dotted meadow right. Snow-capped Ptarmigan and Bottle Peaks appear on the west horizon west, more than 12 miles away. The ski route curves near Jim Creek, then cuts through the middle of a long, snowy ledge between the creekbed and the sparsely-timbered hillside south. Re-enter the thick forest of spruce and fir after 2.1 miles and follow the roadcut through several rolling climbs. Cross a level open area which extends to the creekbed, giving view to a snow-slide path on the opposite valley side. The roadcut comes to an end near 2.9 miles and the ski route proceeds cross-country either directly over the snow-filled creekbed, an excellent springtime ski trail, or through the trees along the more open east side.

The tall conifers become more and more scattered until finally the ski trail breaks into a secluded meadow at 4.0 miles. Unmarked on the topo, this snowy park extends several hundred yards upstream and allows an unobstructed view of the James Peak range. Magnificent rock sculptures pattern its mile-long side and a series of ragged points rise into the skyline, hiding the actual summit of the peak beyond. *Do not ski onto the steep side of James Peak beyond treeline, an area with high potential for avalanche.* With a snow-hardened ski track the entire return trip, a delightful, rolling downhill run, takes little more than an hour.

Wax stop

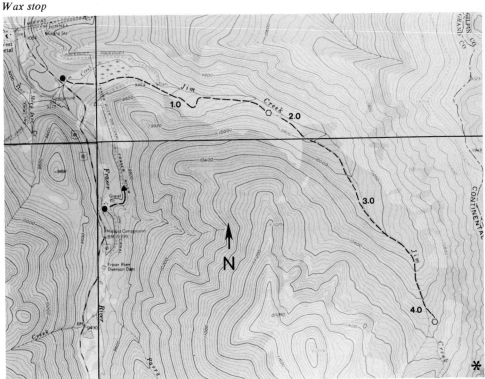

11

GREAT VIEWPOINT LOOP

One day trip
Classification: **More difficult**
Distance: **5.2 miles** *round trip* **(8.4 KM.)**
Skiing time: **3-3½ hours** *round trip*
Elevation gain: **750 feet**
Maximum elevation: **9,590 feet**
Season: **December through early April**
Topographic map:
 U.S.G.S. Fraser, Colo. 1957
   7.5 minute series
Arapaho National Forest

The Great Viewpoint Loop is only one example of the many excellent ski touring trails within the Rocky Mountain Outfitter's trail system (see map photo). Constructed exclusively for touring and ski-packed after each storm, these interconnected routes follow old logging roads and jeep trails and are marked with easy-to-spot signs, color-coded according to trail difficulty. With a commanding view of the mountains that surround the Fraser Valley, the Great Viewpoint Trail rates as the most popular tour, recommended however only on windless days. Check at the Ski Touring Center for trail regulations and further information.

Drive on U.S. 40 to the Beavers Ski Chalet at the south end of Hideaway Park. Proceed to the Ski Touring Center on the right side of the Chalet to obtain instructions about the ski touring parking and pay a small parking fee which helps defray the cost of plowing the snow. Park about 100 yards beyond the Ski Touring Center in the stable area.

Register your tour at the Ski Touring Center and pack skis across U.S. 40 to the west trailhead, marked with a sign reading "Ski Touring Trail." Begin skiing on a very gradual climb along the left side of a drainage, pass under a high voltage line, and follow the ski-packed trail on a gradual climb near treeline. Soon the trail curves right, makes a short, fast drop down the backside of the hill, then passes through a barbed wire

fence and crosses the railroad tracks. "Stop, look, and listen" for the Denver and Rio Grande Western train here which comes very fast around the curve south. Cross the tracks, continue south over the easy-gliding ski trail, and stay left where the Ice Hill Trail, which ends the tour loop, turns right. Several yards before the 0.5 mile mark the trail loop forks right onto the Cherokee Trail where the Tracks Trail continues along the telephone line toward Winter Park. Then the trail loop begins an easy climb along an old logging road, staying right as the Serenity Trail turns left through a natural gate of two magnificent blue spruce.

Follow the Cherokee Trail through an easy curve west past 1.0 mile, glide south again through groves of aspen and lodgepole pine, and climb through two switchbacks to the wide, snowy Aqueduct Road, a near-level ski route which leads to the alpine slopes of the Winter Park Ski Area south. Turn north onto the Great Viewpoint Trail itself, where Tunnel No. 1 cuts under the hill, and climb gradually up the hillside. From each open logging cut here a splendid panorama of peaks comes into view. Colorado Mines, Mt. Flora, Mt. Eva, Parry and James Peaks all stack up along the skyline southeast and the snow-capped Front Range continues north beyond Corona and Devils Thumb Passes. The view increases even more at the hilltop near 2.0 miles and includes the Indian Peaks Range north-northeast, the Never Summer Mountains north-northwest, and on a clear day even the faint spire of Rabbit Ears Peak 58 miles southwest.

Switchback left through stumps and seedlings on the hilltop, pass a turnoff right to the steeper North View Trail, and immediately come to the second part of the "Great Viewpoint." Here a beautiful vista opens to the west, stretching beyond the forested Vasquez Creek valleys to the shining summits of Bottle and Ptarmigan Peaks due west and the glacial-carved Byers Peak a few more degrees left. The pace of the tour picks up as the ski route makes a mile-long descent down the west-facing hillside. Take the lower road near the 3.0 mile mark, turn right onto the Little Vasquez Road after several more yards, then ski north under the large, silver aqueduct and continue straight ahead where the wider roadbed, a designated snowmobile route, turns right. After 3.4 miles the ski route crosses Little Vasquez Creek, passes the cement spillway of another aqueduct, and proceeds north into the shadows of a spruce and fir forest.

Pass the Chickadee Trail which angles back left, wind through two creek crossings, then begin a slight drop on the snowy road-cut. After 4.1 miles come to the junction with the Blue Sky Trail, a delightful, unpacked powder run. Turn northeast, cross the snowmobile route on Little Vasquez Road, and glide over the downhill trail to a fast schuss across Ice Hill, a slushy section with the spring thaw and frozen on cold days. Continue straight where the trail branches right to the Cherokee and Serenity Trails, close the loop near the railroad tracks and follow the main trail on an exciting, packed drop back to the trailhead.

The great view

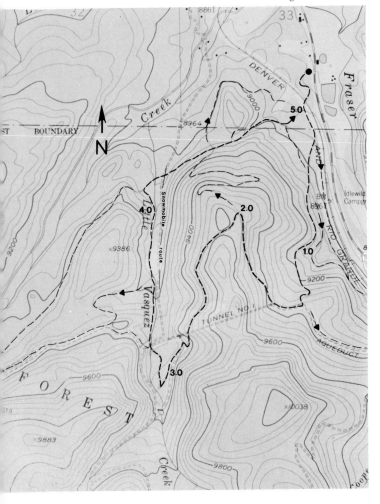

12 HOMESTEAD MEADOW LOOP

One day trip
Classification: More difficult
Distance: 5.4 miles *round trip* (8.7 KM.)
Skiing time: 3-3½ hours *round trip*
Accumulated elevation gain: 420 feet
Accumulated elevation loss: 720 feet
Maximum elevation: 9,260 feet
Season: December through early April
Topographic map:
    U.S.G.S. Fraser, Colo. 1957
              7.5 minute series
Arapaho National Forest

With a variety of trails in the "Easiest" and "More difficult" classifications, the ski touring trail system at the Idlewild Ski Area is especially popular with beginning tourers and with tour groups. As a recommended all-day tour route, the Homestead Meadow Loop first takes advantage of the Ski Area chairlift for an energy-saving gain in elevation and then proceeds through many easy drops and some gradual climbs, linking different trails into one large loop. The feature attraction comes mid-tour as the route breaks into a meadow where the picturesque ruins of an old privately-owned homestead still stand. For trail regulations and further information, see the ski touring personnel at the Ski Touring Barn.

Drive on U.S. 40 toward the north end of Hideaway Park. Turn west at the Idlewild Ski Lodge sign and proceed another 0.4 mile on the Ski Area road to the parking area.

First, register the tour at the Ski Touring Barn where trail regulations, a trail map, and a one-ride lift ticket can be obtained. Then ride the chairlift to the top of the alpine hill, turn left from the unloading ramp and immediately enter the trees to the right of the alpine run on the well-marked Serendipity Trail. This northeasterly trail soon passes the Turkey Trot Trail, an alternate course which bypasses the chairlift, and then continues on easy climbs and relaxing drops through the conifers and aspen. Turn right onto the Winterwoods Trail after 0.5 mile, begin a gradual climb through a climax forest of lodgepole pine, and after several hundred yards of easy gliding, ski over the Crosstrails Trail, often packed by snowmobiles, which links up with the Moffat Road south.

Follow the Winterwoods Trail past 1.0 mile on an easy downhill of long glides. Turn sharply right (east) onto the Ditch Trail fork where the South Fork Loop Trail turns left, and after a few more yards turn left again onto the Ditch Trail itself (see map photo). A superb ski touring trail, this snow-filled ditch maintains a near-level grade as it winds south and west through two shallow gullies, then swings north and intercepts the Homestead Passage Trail at 2.5 miles. Glide north over the Homestead Passage roadbed on a gentle downhill. Soon cross onto the private land of Diamond Bar Tee Ranch, open for public access in cooperation with Operation Respect. Begin a faster and faster drop and suddenly break out of the trees into the Homestead Meadow.

Turn left into the Homestead Meadow as the roadbed continues on a steady drop toward the basin of Ranch Creek north. A cluster of log buildings mark this clearing and provide a fascinating study of early farming life in the Fraser Valley. Built near the turn of the century, the exquisite two-story farmhouse shows refinements not found on the log cabins of the earlier pioneer days. The remains of a front porch still stand at the entrance, white sills outline each window, and even wallpaper, now tattered and flapping with any breeze, lines the sturdy log walls. Next to the farmhouse is a well, its earthen sides carefully lined with log poles, and farther beyond is another log cabin, perhaps the storehouse for food. A few yards north an old barn, roofless and near collapse, catches the drifting snow, providing a finishing touch to the picture postcard scene.

With a grand view of the nearby Front Range mountains northeast and Mounts Stratus, Nimbus, and Cumulus of the Never Summer Mountains on the distant horizon north, the Homestead Meadow serves as the most popular lunch stop for the Ski Idlewild tours. Heavy use creates a high potential for litter abuse so be sure to pack out every scrap of garbage. For a return loop via the Ridge Trail, double pole northwest past the log barn, cross a shallow drainage, then re-enter the trees on a marked trail and immediately cross through a barbed wire fence. After an easy, winding drop, the Ridge Trail begins a gradual climb west and south and eventually passes a tumble-down slab wood cabin at 4.4 miles. Ski past two right turn-offs to the Crosstrails Trail, join the Meadows Trail, and finish the tour with a refreshing downhill run southwest onto the very gentle alpine slopes of the Idlewild Ski Area.

Ski Touring Barn at Ski Idlewild Lodge

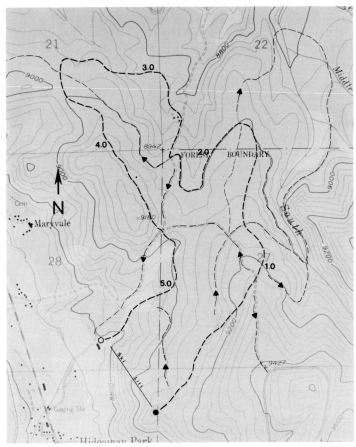

13 WEST ST. LOUIS ROAD

One day trip
Classification:
  Easiest through most difficult
Distance: 5.0 miles one way (8.0 KM.)
Skiing time: 4-4½ hours one way
Elevation gain: 1,510 feet
Maximum elevation: 10,550 feet
Season: Mid-November through mid-April
Topographic map:
  U.S.G.S. Bottle Pass, Colo. 1957
         7.5 minute series
Arapaho National Forest

Forest Service authorities have separated the snowmobile and ski touring areas in the Fraser Experimental Forest, designating the area west of the St. Louis Road for skiers only. Thus the West St. Louis Road, posted with a sign reading "Skiers Only On This Trail/No Snowmobiles," makes a peaceful, quiet tour throughout the winter. Beginning skiers can follow the gentle road for 1.3 miles to a large meadow; intermediates may want to continue to the switchbacks at 3.2 miles or loop back via the Aqueduct Road. The entire 5.0 mile trip rates a most difficult classification due to its longer length, the steeper, 7 percent grade through the switch-

backs, and the more difficult downhill technique needed for either the road or creekbed return route.

Drive on U.S. 40 to the middle of Fraser, turn west onto Eisenhower Drive and continue across the railroad tracks. Proceed another long block west, then turn left onto the Fraser Experimental Forest Road, marked by a sign. Bend right after two blocks and stay on this main road to a large parking area near the Fraser Experimental Station, a total of 4.7 miles from U.S. 40.

On the west side of the St. Louis Road a Forest Service sign, giving mileages to the Byers Peak and Bottle Pass Trailheads, marks the turnoff onto the West St. Louis Road. Stay to the right of a barbed wire fence and glide southwest over the flat roadbed, immediately passing a huge log barn (right). Cross under a power line and climb very gradually into a thick forest of pine and spruce. Except for a few glimpses of the thickly timbered range northwest, all long views are cut off by the tunnel of trees as the snow-filled roadbed curves slowly west-southwest, then back southwest. Break into a tiny clearing where the Deadhorse Creek Road, unmarked on the topo, forks right, proceed on the left fork to a sudden viewpoint of the dazzling White Bottle Peak due west.

At 1.0 mile, glide south over the delightfully easy, winding roadbed; eventually curve right, pass a southerly trail branch, and cross the snow-buried bridge over West St. Louis Creek. A long park of smooth snow, surrounded by clusters of tall spruce, now opens north, a quiet, scenic spot to stop for lunch or to end the tour. The snowy road rises out of the meadow and makes a slow curve from south-southwest to west, gradually gaining enough elevation for a view northwest of snow-capped Front Range peaks, more than 14 miles away. Shortly after 2.0 miles pass the Aquaduct Road turnoff which loops south across the creek on an alternate tour route. Continue west, passing a small meadow near the creekbed, climb on a noticeably steeper grade for several hundred yards, and begin curving southwest until the road switchbacks at 3.2 miles. On the return trip this last 1.5 miles drops steadily, providing long, easy glides and downhill coasts.

For advanced skiers, the tour may be continued through the switchbacks to the end of the road, as outlined in the information capsule. After the first switchback follow the winding roadbed on a gradual northerly climb, pass the Lexen Creek Road, unmarked on the topo, at the second switchback, and head back toward the West St. Louis valley. Avoid skiing onto the corniced lip of the road as the mountainside steepens, hook right through an obvious drainage, and begin a gradual turn right. Now on the horizon east-northeast are the Front Range mountains near Rollins Pass, the snowy white gorges dip deeply into a vast bank of forest. In view closer are the interesting logging cuts of the Fraser Experimental Forest south. Tall conifers soon block this view as the roadbed maintains a steady climb west, proceeds through a third switchback at 4.0 miles, then switchbacks again after another 100 yards. The white, blunt top of Byers Peak pops into view at the final, sixth switchback; the road then levels, crosses West St. Louis Creek, and comes to an end very close to 5.0 miles.

For a thrilling downhill run through deep, fluffy powder, return down the creekbed, usually containing sufficient snow by mid-January. Begin with a breathtaking plunge to the drainageway bottom and tunnel through the spruce and fir, skiing directly over the creekbed. The fifth and third switchbacks on the road offer escape routes and, as the terrain becomes less steep, and hence slower, the first switchback allows a way to join the faster, broken trail on the road.

Trailhead sign

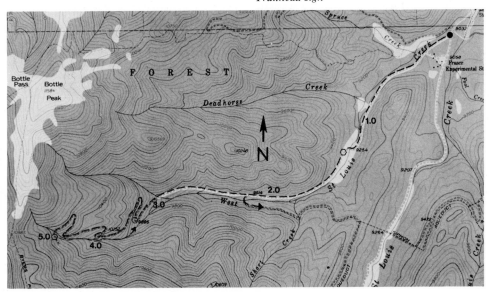

14 MORSE MOUNTAIN LOOP

One day trip
Classification:
   More difficult to most difficult
Distance: 6.6 miles *round trip* **(10.6 KM.)**
Skiing time: 4½-5 hours *round trip*
Elevation gain: 1,410 feet
Maximum elevation: 10,440 feet
Season: Mid-November through mid-April
Topographic map:
   U.S.G.S. Bottle Pass, Colo. 1957
                  7.5 minute series
Arapaho National Forest

With a new bearing every few hundred yards, the snowy roadcut south of Morse Mountain climbs over and up the undulating hillside, averaging a steady but unobtrusive 8 percent grade. Besides sufficient physical fitness, you will need an open mind toward timber-powder skiing and some knowledge of map-reading to make the entire loop. However, the spectacular vistas, especially the last-minute view of Byers Peak, and the exhilarating downhill runs more than compensate for the effort.

Drive on U.S. 40 to the middle of Fraser, turn west onto Eisenhower Drive and continue across the railroad tracks. Proceed another long block west, then turn left onto the Fraser Experimental Forest Road, marked by a sign. Bend right after two blocks and stay on this main road to a large parking area near the Fraser Experimental Station, a total of 4.7 miles from U.S. 40.

Hike back down the Fraser Experimental Forest Road for about 40 yards, returning to the sign which reads "West Saint Louis Creek." Begin skiing west-southwest over an obvious roadcut on the right side of the creekbed, swing close to the hillside right and proceed on an easy, rolling climb in and out of the black-trunked pine. Soon a flat, snowy-white wedge, the northern ridge of Byers Peak, flashes through the trees left, then shows more clearly as the road passes

to the right of a large meadow. Continue west through several yards of easy gliding, then resume the gradual climb, bend right into thicker pine, and enter the Spruce Creek valley. Glide through a long section of aspen and alder after 0.5 mile, follow the roadcut up a steep, then soon more gradual climb, and begin curving right along a deep drainageway.

Cross the northerly, conifer-cluttered drainage at 1.2 miles, bend sharply left and continue the gradual climb through soft snow on a more protected roadcut. After several hundred more yards the road turns left around a ridgetop and the trees open for a vista of Front Range mountains east-southeast. Highest and most rugged, the 13,391-foot top of Parry Peak breaks into granite outcroppings toward the viewpoint, then the rocky ribs continue left through a saddle and rise to the high point of James Peak, almost 12 miles away.

Proceed north-northwest on an easy climb over the snowy roadcut, skiing to the right of another deep branch drainage. Bend left across the creekbed, soon bend left again as the road loops around the small, tree-filled bowl, and after 1.9 miles come to a road fork. Here an alternate route turns right, climbs to the saddle southwest of Morse Mountain, then drops through the Tipperary Creek drainage to a pickup car at the Crooked Creek trailhead (No. 15), a pleasant, sheltered tour of long glides. For the loop route marked on the map photo, ski straight ahead on the left fork, turn right at the ridgetop after several yards, and near 2.1 miles switchback right up the pine-hidden roadcut. The Front Range peaks on the horizon again catch the eye as the ski route climbs around another ridge and continues through scattered pine seedlings.

Follow the road west after 2.5 miles, dip through a small drainage, then make a short, steady drop after several more yards, immediately passing a trail to Bottle Peak left. Climb steadily along the rim of a small, conifer-filled bowl left, make the final switchback right just after the road begins to drop slightly, and ski cross-country on a northeast and east contour, heading toward the saddle area on the ridgetop. With dramatic suddenness this last climb brings Byers Peak into view southwest, a jagged, corniced mountaintop flanked by three high-walled bowls and indeed the most impressive vista of the tour.

The rounded bulk of Mt. Nystrom stands behind a wide, snowy amphitheater south and tops another mountain range seven miles away.

Orient yourself on a northerly bearing before leaving the ridgetop, then enter the shadows of tall spruce and fir on the north-facing hillside and drop down the fall line to a plainly discernible branch road below.

Deep powder snow fills the hillside here, Old Man's Beard droops from the snow-laden tree branches, and this quiet, scenic timber run, about twenty minutes long, makes some of the best skiing of the tour. Follow the roadcut east to the saddle southwest of Morse Mountain, glide south for another fast half-mile to close the loop, and then return over the ski tracks.

Inquisitive gray jay

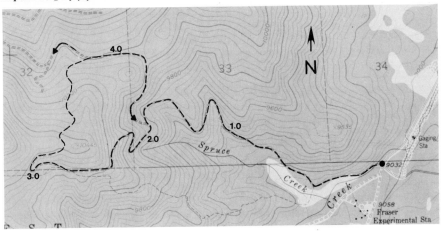

15 CROOKED CREEK ROAD

One day trip
Classification:
   Easiest through most difficult
Distance: 5.4 miles one way (8.7 KM.)
Skiing time: 3½-4½ hours one way
Elevation gain: 1,030 feet
Maximum elevation: 9,910 feet
Season: December through March
Topographic map:
   U.S.G.S. Bottle Pass, Colo. 1957
          7.5 minute series
Arapaho National Forest

Almost as serpentine as Crooked Creek itself in the valley bottom, the wide, near-level Crooked Creek Road makes an excellent route for skiers of all abilities. Beginners and families can enjoy a leisurely pace and still reach the scenic, snow-blanketed meadows at 2.5 and 3.5 miles. Stronger tourers can push ahead on a full day of skiing to the snowy island of Church Park. Good throughout the winter except on windy days, this tour is even better on the hot, klister-wax days of late March and sometimes early April when the snow crust is unbreakable.

Drive on U.S. 40 north from the town of Fraser, cross the bridge over St. Louis Creek and proceed another 0.3 mile to an inconspicuous junction. Turn west onto the road, cross the railroad tracks, and after 0.2 mile turn left (this section of the road is not indicated on the 1957 Fraser topo). Soon turn west again, eventually pass the turnoff to the Tally Ho Guest Ranch, and continue to the Arapaho National Forest boundary where the plowed road usually ends, a total of 3.2 miles from U.S. 40. Park in the large turn-around area.

Glide southwest over the snowy, near-level roadbed, immediately crossing over a buried barbed wire fence. An eye-catching snowfield along Tipperary Creek and the forested side of Sheep Mountain soon show through the trees right as the wide road curves right and enters a branch drainage. Switchback across Tipperary Creek, passing below a possible alternate route on an old logging road, then ski by a weathered post-and-pole fence left. Ski around a ridgetop after 0.6 mile, bend sharply right then left on an "S" turn which does not show on the topo map, and follow the winding roadbed southwest through an interesting section of skinny, snow-bent lodgepole pine. Several times during this first mile a panorama of distant, snow-capped peaks comes into view, encompassing an area from Rogers Pass east-southeast through the Indian Peaks range to Rocky Mountain National Park northeast.

Bend right and bear toward the forested top of Sheep Mountain near the 1.1 mile mark. Soon pass a grove of cream-colored aspen right, then follow the roadbed through a long curve left and after several hundred more yards come to a viewpoint of the snowy face on Ptarmigan Peak southwest. Maintain elevation on the road left where a branch road drops right toward the valley floor. Pass several small logging roads which lead off through the engelmann spruce on either side and loop through a prominent creek drainage at 2.2 miles. The roadbed soon passes a log loading ramp left, then bends left on a steady climb and comes to another viewpoint of the snow-topped Ptarmigan Peak and the long horizon range behind.

Curve right around a small knoll and cross a snowfield which drops left all the way to the Crooked Creek valley. Now deep with snow, occasionally wind-drifted, the road proceeds through a cluttered drainage of mountain alder and aspen, passes logging roads on the right and the left, and after 2.6 miles suddenly enters a treeless meadow and hillside, marked on the topo. In spring, when avalanche danger has subsided, this smooth, steep hillside makes an irresistible spot for downhill plunges. Continue back into the spruce on a gradual curve left, dip through another drainage and contour northwest and west around a steep, protruding knoll. Glide west over the level road after crossing Crystal Creek, bend right just below Ptarmigan Creek at 3.5 miles, and ski into the spacious park surrounding Crooked Creek. Tall spruce near the creekbed, rolling, patterned snowfields on the hillside, snow-capped Ptarmigan and Bottle Peaks south all make this place an inviting lunch spot, and possibly the turning back point.

For advanced skiers, the tour can easily be extended another 1.8 miles to Church Park as presented in the information capsule. Fol-

low the roadcut on an easy but continuous climb along the north side of Crooked Creek, a route which crosses two vast snowfields, then winds through scattered trees for several hundred yards and breaks into a third open area. Here distant landmarks can be picked out on the white band of mountains behind: the Devils Thumb spire, the white ribbon of Moffat Road, the low point of Rollins Pass. Continue on a cross-country course west as the roadcut becomes lost under deep snow. Curve left with the contour of the hillside and soon intercept the flat and trackless expanse of Church Park, a final stopping point.

Church Park

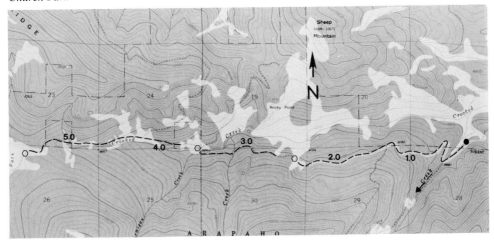

16 ARAPAHO CREEK

One day trip
Classification:
   Easiest through most difficult
Distance: 3.6 miles one way (5.8 KM.)
Skiing time: 2-2½ hours one way
Elevation gain: 374 feet
Maximum elevation: 8,720 feet
Season: December through early April
Topographic map:
   U.S.G.S. Monarch Lake, Colo. 1958
           7.5 minute series
Arapaho National Forest

The road along the south side of Lake Granby, plowed open throughout the winter, gives access to a very good ski touring area that few people know about: Monarch Lake and the Arapaho Creek valley. The tour begins on a special scenic note with a view southeast through the steep valley walls of North Arapaho Peak. Massive and rock-strewn, this 13,502-foot summit, which together with South Arapaho Peak rounds out the south end of the Indian Peaks Range, is always an enchanting spectacle, changing appearances from morning to night and from season to season. In winter it often spills a steady stream of snow into the air, an indication of the strong winds at that high elevation. In spring it shines brilliantly with the hot sun and shadows only the large glacier, a vestige of the Ice Age, which lies hidden on its east side.

Drive on U.S. 40 to the west end of Granby and turn north onto U.S. 34. Proceed 5.5 miles to a right turn onto the Lake Granby Road, marked with a sign reading "Colo. Big Thompson Project/Granby Dam and Dikes," etc. Follow this road across the spillway and along the south side of Lake

Granby, curve left across Arapaho Bay, and continue to a parking loop near Monarch Lake, the end of the plowed road and a distance of 9.9 miles from U.S. 34.

Cross through the gate at the end of the parking loop and follow the wide, snow-covered roadbed for 25 yards to the north end of Monarch Lake. Here the rocky-ribbed side of North Arapaho Peak can be seen southeast beyond the lakebed and through the "V" of Arapaho Creek valley. Pass a half-buried sign which lists several trail mileages including "Arapaho Trail 2" and then continue over either of two routes: turn left onto a jeep-size roadcut and skirt the north side of the lake or ski cross-country over the open lakebed, bearing first to the right of the island, then continuing southeast toward the mouth of Arapaho Creek valley. The route over the roadbed, as figured in the information capsule, soon enters sheltering stands of lodgepole pine, winds through gentle dips and climbs, then after 0.4 mile crosses through a wide swath of willows and re-enters the conifers.

Leave the road near 0.7 mile as it swings close to the steep southern reaches of Mount

Irving Hale left, *avoiding any avalanche danger through this area.* Stay near the lakebed for several hundred yards, then rejoin the Forest Service route left, now trail-wide, and glide past drifted snowfields at the beginning of Buchanan Creek right. Cross a slight drainage after 1.6 miles and after another 100 yards come to a sign listing "Arapaho Pass 13" and several other trail mileages. Fork right onto the Arapaho Creek Trail where the Buchanan Pass Trail, an excellent spring ski route when avalanche danger is low, continues straight ahead. The conspicuous trailcut proceeds south beneath a canopy of thick spruce and soon crosses two branches of Buchanan Creek.

Connect with the trailcut at the end of a log bridge, herringbone and straight climb a small hill for about 30 yards, then coast through a fun drop and continue southwest through easy climbs and drops. After 2.4 miles the trail reaches another trail junction where a sign reads "Arapaho Pass 10/Lake Granby 4." To stay on "easiest" terrain, turn right at this point and make a return loop northwest across Monarch Lake (see map photo). To enter the Arapaho Creek valley,

"most difficult" terrain through the switchbacks, ski behind the sign for several yards to a log cabin and pick up the trailcut heading south. Continue through six, steep but short, switchbacks on a climb along the east side of Arapaho Creek, and with the last turn left come to a high point which looks straight down into the valley bottom, providing a dramatic perspective.

Glides become long and easy as the trailcut heads south-southeast on a level contour and then begins a long, gradual descent near 3.3 miles. A slice of North Arapaho Peak, hidden by trees since the view from Monarch Lake, now reappears at the end of the valley. Pass a snowy talus field after 3.5 miles with due caution for avalanche and break into a second open area in another hundred yards, a pleasant spot for lunch or for an overnight camp. Strong skiers, equipped for winter camping and knowledgeable about avalanche, can continue the tour several more miles up the valley. On the return trip, check speed carefully with a snowplow and pole drag through the switchbacks, then retrace the ski tracks or loop northwest across Monarch Lake.

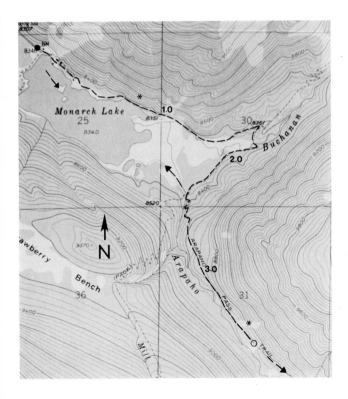

17 EAST INLET TRAIL

One day trip
Classification: More difficult
Distance: 3.2 miles one way (5.2 KM.)
Skiing time: 2½-3 hours one way
Elevation gain: 790 feet
Maximum elevation: 9,180 feet
Season: December through late March
Topographic map:
  U.S.G.S. Shadow Mountain, Colo. 1958
    7.5 minute series
Rocky Mountain National Park

Backlit in midday sun, patterned by vividly contrasting shadows and snowfields, the massive dome of Mount Craig makes an impressive sight at the end of East Inlet valley. Called Middle Mountain by the Arapahoes, it is balanced on either side with precipitous Mount Cairns and Mount Wescott. The East Inlet Trail begins in snowmobile territory east of Grand Lake but after a few hundred yards it crosses the Park boundary where motorized vehicles are prohibited, a regulation which preserves the serenity of the ski tour. After the initial steep climb to Adams

Falls the trail proceeds through easy climbs and gentle drops, eventually traversing up the north side of the valley. For a superb half-day trip on windless days, leave the East Inlet Trail where it touches the first meadow and ski cross-country up the flat valley floor, a tour which has Mount Craig in view most of the time.

Drive on U.S. 40 to the west end of Granby and turn north onto U.S. 34. Proceed toward Grand Lake for 14.4 miles, then turn right onto Colo. 278 where U.S. 34 forks left to Rocky Mountain National Park. Stay left where a main road heads to the right into the town of Grand Lake, join the Big Thompson Irrigation Tunnel Road, and continue another 2.0 miles to the circle turnaround near the West Portal of Adams Tunnel. Park on the south side of the turnaround.

Begin skiing southeast from the parking area across a gently-rising snowfield and after a few hundred yards come to the trailhead sign, posted with several trail mileages. Nearby is a box for registration of one day trips and a bulletin board with Park regulations and a topographic map. Find the blazed tree to the right of the bulletin board and glide over the rolling trail through scattered lodgepole pine. Cross a small, snowy bridge, soon turn left and begin a steep climb, passing many large, lichen-streaked boulders. Occasional foot travel on this first half mile can pack the snow into hardened ruts and bumps, making the downhill return trip more difficult.

For a wintertime look at Adams Falls, detour right where a sign marks the cutoff and ski or hike another 25 yards to a vista point, also a pleasant lunch spot. Below, darkened with shadows, the East Inlet creekbed winds between the deep, narrow chasm of the falls. Then take the left fork onto the main trail and continue the steady climb, reaching the Park boundary at the hilltop. Here the climb ends and the trail contours along the hillside through gentle ups and downs. Ski to the edge of a snowy meadow, dotted with dried weed stalks; bend left and wind through tall lodgepole pine on the northwest side. At the far end of the valley rounded, bald Mount Craig now looms into sight, soon joined by ragged-topped Mount Cairns north and forested Mount Wescott south.

Cross a bridge and veer next to the

smooth, open meadow. After several gentle rolls, the trail loops through another tributary drainage, climbs gradually around a small knoll, and drops back into thick pine. Ski along the left side of a shallow gully and continue the easy, rolling climb to another vista point of the three immense mountains at the end of the valley. Schuss a short, steep drop into trees again, follow the meandering trail beneath rock cliffs high on the hillside north, and glide through an island of lodgepole pine. Leaving the meadow behind, pass under more rock cliffs and enter a stand of pine with curious bi-color trunks, charcoal on the west-facing side, rust on the east-facing. Proceed through another drop and climb left, then turn toward a massive spire on Mount Cairns.

Ski across a branch creek next to the footbridge and continue the gradual climb past a water-stained, stratified rock wall. Glide onto a hillside and soon come to another bridge from which four pointed spires can be seen on Mount Cairns northeast. Climb through more lodgepole pine, pass the turnoff to Lower East Inlet Campground, and follow the trailcut through a rock outcropping. Bend left, herringbone a short, steep section, and continue on a steady climb, soon breaking above timberline. The mountainside becomes steeper as the trail traverses southeast, giving spectacular vantage to Mount Craig, Mount Wescott, and the deep East Inlet valley. The prominent ridge above the second falls marks the 3.2 mile mark, a good stopping point and lunch spot. Return down the trailcut, carefully controlling speed.

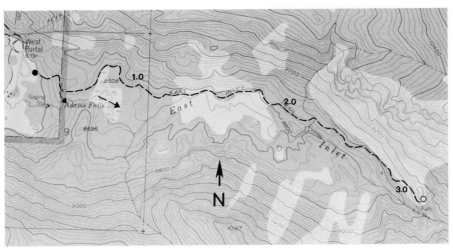

18 BIG MEADOWS

One day trip
Classification: Easiest
Distance: 4.3 miles one way (6.9 KM.)
Skiing time: 2½-3 hours one way
Elevation gain: 700 feet
Maximum elevation: 9,420 feet
Season: Mid-November through mid-April
Topographic map:
   U.S.G.S. Grand Lake, Colo. 1958
          7.5 minute series
Rocky Mountain National Park

With warmer temperatures in March and April the rolling snowfields of Big Meadows begin to melt during the day and freeze again at night until a thick crust has formed on top. Strong enough to support your weight on skis, this snow crust eliminates trail breaking and turns Big Meadows into a vast ski area. On level terrain each hard kick can propel you for a four or five yard glide. Both the Tonahutu Trail, named after the Arapaho word for the meadows area, and the Green Mountain Trail climbs steeply for Big Meadows. The longer Tonahutu Trail, recommended as the better route and described in the text, maintains a very gradual climb through sheltering groves of conifers. Shorter and also popular among ski tourers, the Green Mountain Trail climbs steeply for much of its length, linking a series of sun-splashed parks. Required technique for the downhill return on this latter trail includes a strong pole drag, a stronger snowplow, and a quick eye for soft landing spots.

Follow U.S. 40 to the west end of Granby and turn north onto U.S. 34. Proceed 15.7 miles to the Visitors Center, staying left where Colo. 278 branches right to Grand Lake. Here you can register, obtain an en-

trance permit (free), and find out about the special Park regulations. For the Tonahutu Trail, leave your car at the Visitors Center and walk to the trail access route, marked by a large "Ski Trail" sign, which begins from the southeast corner of the parking lot. For the Green Mountain Trail, drive through the Grand Lake Entrance Station (relocated north of the Visitors Center since publication of the 1958 Grand Lake topo) and continue for 2.6 miles to a large parking area.

From the Visitors Center parking lot begin skiing east over the level forest floor. False openings in the lodgepole pine and occasional criss-crossing ski tracks sometimes disguise the unmarked summer trail, especially near the start. However, the wide-spaced trees permit easy penetration and any easterly cross-country course will intercept the well-defined Tonahutu Trail in about 0.7 mile. Follow the shallow but perceptible Harbison Ditch as a guide; keep it on the left and proceed east and east-northeast on a delightfully winding course through black-trunked pine. Soon pick up a small drainage filled with aspen and alder on the right, climb up and over a small rise, and continue next to a grove of spruce, fir, and aspen. Swing southeast away from the drainage where the summer trailcut becomes visible and wind a short distance through lodgepole pine to the junction with Tonahutu Trail.

Turn left and begin an easy, winding climb on this wide trailcut. Continue straight where a spur branches right and pass a snow-buried pipe which parallels a short section of the trail. Bend left around a little rockpile, then with a few steps of herringbone make a short, steady climb up the mountainside. The snowy path eventually descends to the valley floor again, winds through a shady grove of engelmann spruce and sub-alpine fir, and re-enters the open stands of gray-barked pine. With Tonahutu Creek now in view right and an open meadow left, glide north over the near-level trail, cutting through Lodgepole Campsite. Continue near the creekbed, swing left closer to the steep side of Green Mountain, and break into another willow-covered meadow. Mountaintops come into view east and southeast and double-topped Nisa Mountain, named from Arapaho *nisi* and *nisah* meaning "two" and "twins," rises east-northeast.

Immediately beyond the meadow begin a steep climb; bend left on a steady, uphill traverse and then dip through a wide gully. A majestic, 12,804-foot peak shows north-northeast over the forested range as the trail continues into the southern reaches of Big Meadows. Either continue over the level, protected trail on the west side of Big Meadows, following trimmed branches on spruce and fir for trail markers, or ski near the meandering creek gully on a cross-country course through the open snowfields. Curve left from the meadow after passing the second protrusion of trees, very accurately represented on the topo, and rejoin the trail near the Green Mountain Trail junction, a good stopping point. Return down the Green Mountain Trail to a second car, or double back over the ski tracks.

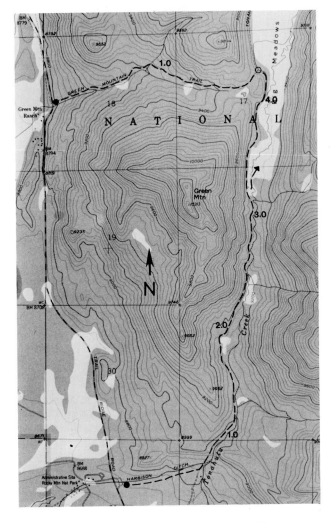

19 BAKER GULCH

One day trip
Classification: More difficult
Distance: 1.9 miles one way (3.1 KM.)
Skiing time: 1½-2 hours one way
Elevation gain: 520 feet
Maximum elevation: 9,380 feet
Season: December through mid-April
Topographic maps:
  U.S.G.S. Grand Lake, Colo. 1958
  U.S.G.S. Bowen Mountain, Colo. 1957
      7.5 minute series
Rocky Mountain National Park
Arapaho National Forest

Pointing out the peaks

The tour along Baker Gulch leaves the flat snowfields of Kawuneeche Valley and penetrates magnificent, snow-capped summits which round out the south end of the Never Summer Mountain range. In winter open meadows near the 1.9 mile mark, unmarked on the topo, make a good destination point for the tour, safe from the avalanche danger higher up the gulch. In late spring only, after the snowpack has settled and when danger from wet slides is also low, the trip can be extended along the gulch bottom all the way to the Grand Ditch. From this 10,300-foot vantage a magnificent array of alpine peaks spread across the horizon. Mount Ida, Nakai Peak, Sprague Mountain, Taylor Peak, Mount Adams and countless others loom skyward to form the high backbone of Rocky

Mountain National Park. Even James Peak and other peaks near Berthoud Pass and the ski runs of Winter Park Ski Area can be seen.

From Granby drive on U.S. 34 to the west entrance of Rocky Mountain National Park. Stay left on U.S. 34 where Colo. 278 branches right to Grand Lake and proceed to the Visitors Center. Here you can register, obtain an entrance permit, and find out about the special Park regulations. Continue through the Grand Lake Entrance Station (relocated north of the Visitors Center since publication of the 1958 Grand Lake topo) and drive another 6.3 miles to the parking area, marked by a "Ski Trail Parking" sign on the left side of the road.

Ski west from the parking area toward the flat snowfields of Kawuneeche Valley. Pass to the right of a bridge over the tiny North Fork Colorado River and follow the trail markers on an easy glide across the valley floor, skiing near a snow-buried barbed wire fence right. Known to many as simply the North Fork Valley, this vast, open basin has

46

also been called Hacquihana Valley, an Arapaho name meaning "Valley of the Wolves." Perhaps for the noticeable lack of wolves, the Colorado Geographic Board approved a final name change to Kawuneeche or Coyote in Arapaho, a name recommended "as being somewhat pronounceable." Reenter the trees on the west side of the valley, turn right where the Bowen Gulch trail forks left, then ski past a log house and a branch road (right) and glide west over the Baker Gulch roadcut.

Follow the main road north and west through a forest of black-trunked pine, begin a slight climb as the roadcut contours next to the hillside, and ski beneath a weathered, slab-wood cabin, marked on the topo map near 0.7 mile. In another few yards the ski route drops over a small rise and comes to the Arapaho National Forest boundary. Cross a small section of willows and continue on a gradual, winding climb up the mountainside, eventually reaching an elevation above the tops of giant spruce in Baker Gulch (left). Glide on a level run through a patch of gray alder, then ski back into the deep shade of fir trees and after 1.5 miles break into a meadow.

Ski cross-country through the willow and aspen as the trailcut becomes obscure. Curve left at a tree with three blazes, cross a branch gulch near a snow-covered log bridge, and continue the southerly course on a loop through another small gulch. The trail contours along the hillside to a steep dropoff into the Baker Gulch bottom, then switchbacks north and soon enters another open meadow, an excellent stopping point for the tour in mid-winter. Here the view extends to the open face of Baker Mountain northwest, girded with the white cut of the Grand Ditch, and to the burned ridgetop near the Green Knoll north.

For a longer springtime trip, continue along the north side of the gulch several yards above the bottom and switchback through steep spots at miles 2.3 and 3.1. A loop return along the Grand Ditch and down the Ditch Road bring the *round trip* distance to 11.0 miles and nearly triples the elevation gain, a total of 1,440 feet. Stay near treeline along the gulch bottom until reaching the tree clumps at 3.9 miles and do not begin switchbacking north into possible avalanche areas on the open hillside. Ski east over the level roadbed which parallels the Grand Ditch and after nearly two miles turn right onto the Ditch Road, an easy-to-miss junction 20 yards in front of the Rocky Mountain National Park boundary. Make the quick drop on the Ditch Road to Kawuneeche Valley, ski south along treeline to close the loop, and then return over the ski tracks to the parking area.

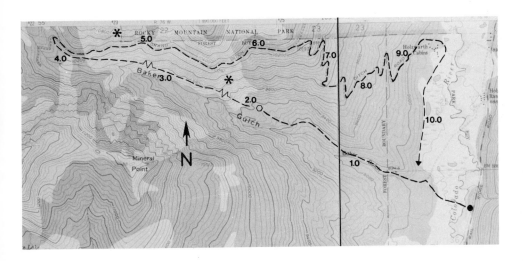

20 KAWUNEECHE VALLEY LOOP

Half-day trip
Classification: Easiest
Distance: 2.5 miles *round trip* **(4.0 KM.)**
Skiing time: 1½-2 hours *round trip*
Elevation gain: 60 feet
Maximum elevation: 8,940 feet
Season: December through March
Topographic maps:
 U.S.G.S. Fall River Pass, Colo. 1958
 U.S.G.S. Grand Lake, Colo. 1958
  7.5 minute series
Rocky Mountain National Park

Of all the ski trails in Rocky Mountain National Park, none offers easier gliding than the loop around Kawuneeche Valley. Staked out with many small "ski" signs, this short, fast course circles over flat snowfields on the valley floor, then returns through thick lodgepole pine along the east side. With no steep hills or difficult drops, the loop makes an ideal tour for beginning skiers and slow-paced families, especially on the warmer days in March. Remember, however, that the open valley provides little protection from wind, and on stormy, midwinter days consider instead the more sheltered tours to Big Meadows (No. 18) and Shipler Park and Lulu City (No. 21).

Drive on U.S. 40 to the west end of Granby and turn north onto U.S. 34. Proceed 15.7 miles to the Visitors Center, staying left where Colo. 278 branches right to Grand Lake. At the Center register your tour and obtain an entrance permit (free). Then drive north through the Grand Lake Entrance Station and continue another 8.9 miles to the parking area turnoff, marked by a "Ski Trail Parking" sign. Turn left and drive 0.2 mile more to the Timber Creek Campground. A sign reading "2 Mile Loop" identifies the trailhead at the north side of the large parking area here.

Climb over the snowbank and begin skiing north-northwest on a level run, guided by "ski" signs along the trail. Pass through a few scattered trees and immediately break out onto the wide Kawuneeche Valley floor. With long, easy glides continue between the hillside right and the snowy furrow of the Colorado River left; soon curve left and weave through brilliant vermilion and rust willows in the middle of the valley. The flat, well-marked trail first heads northwest for the bald dome of Red Mountain, appropriately named because Indians used its red earth for war paint, then swings slightly left and bears toward the forested east ridge of Green Knoll.

Enter a stand of lodgepole pine on the west side of Kawuneeche Valley and intercept a small park of smooth, unbroken snow. Hook south, follow the natural opening through the trees, and proceed down the valley, staying right of a tributary creek and flat, willow-covered snowfield. Pass a protruding clump of pine and continue south along the treeline. On the horizon ahead a cluster of shimmering, snow-capped peaks stretch between the valley walls, part of the Vasquez Mountains west of Berthoud Pass about 59 miles away. Follow the trail markers into another extension of pine, turn right and ski through a road-like swath in the trees. Soon bend left, glide along a barbed wire fence, and take a few steps of herringbone up a short, steep hill, the only climb in the entire tour loop.

Double pole down a gradual drop and come to the Ditch Road, an alternate ski tour trail described in the Baker Gulch tour (No. 19). Turn left and pass several log cabins of the old Holzwarth Homestead, recently purchased by the Park and retained as a living ranch. Glide east to a barbed wire fence, ski over the snow-buried gate, and continue back into Kawuneeche Valley. The trail recrosses the tiny Colorado River and makes a wide arc left over the smooth snow, heading for the trees on the other side. Pass an old homestead cabin which sits near treeline across a meadow east. Built near the turn of the century, this picturesque pine hut still retains its hand-hewn Dutch logs, sod roof, and board porch. Weave north through tall lodgepole pine, pass the snow-laden picnic tables in Timber Creek Campground, and end the loop at the parking area.

Colorado River headwaters

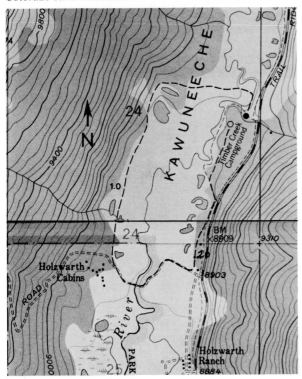

21 SHIPLER PARK AND LULU CITY

One day trip
Classification: Easiest
Distance: 3.7 miles one way (6.0 KM.)
Skiing time: 2-2½ hours one way
Elevation gain: 380 feet
Maximum elevation: 9,420 feet
Season: December through mid-April
Topographic map:
** U.S.G.S. Fall River Pass, Colo. 1958**
**   7.5 minute series**
Rocky Mountain National Park

"Gold! Silver! Get rich quick!" reads a sign along the trail to Lulu City, telling about the lure of precious minerals that brought a rush of prospectors into the valley in 1879. A post office, stores, and hotels were built and the stage arrived from Georgetown four times a week. Lulu, memorialized with a city, creek, and mountain, was the daughter of a founder of the town. She was remembered as the most beautiful girl in the valley, with lips as red as wild strawberries! No rich ore was found around Lulu City, however, and the gold seekers began to drift out of town on rumors of another big strike elsewhere. One discouraged prospector finally muttered, "Someday you'll see nothing but a foot-trail along this street. Raspberry bushes and spruce trees will be growing through the roof of the hotel yonder." Today his prophecy of demise holds true. After a delightfully easy ski tour up the North Fork valley, you will see only a serene and snow-blanketed park at the Lulu City site.

From Granby drive on U.S. 34 to the west entrance of Rocky Mountain National Park. Stay left on U.S. 34 where Colo. 278 branches right to Grand Lake and proceed to the Visitors Center. Register your tour here and obtain an entrance permit. Then continue north through the Grand Lake Entrance Station and drive another 9.6 miles to the trailhead at the old Phantom Valley Trading Post site. Parking is provided for many cars.

Drop west from the snow-covered road where a sign reads "Lulu City 3 mi." and immediately break through the scattered pine to an open park. From this point the vista extends beyond timbered valley walls to a white knoll on Jackstraw Mountain east-southeast and the frosted top of Red Mountain west. Ahead (right) three forested knobs comprise Shipler Mountain, a perspective which changes dramatically near the end of the tour. Glide north past a stand of dead, silvery gray trees, follow the "ski" signs through a curve left, and double-pole down a short, easy drop into the meadow. Ski between deep, icy pools of water in the Colorado riverbed, then continue north across another small meadow and dip through a tributary drainage. The well-marked trail bends right, climbs over a small hill, and heads into thicker conifers. Soon a log Ranger Cabin (locked) can be seen ahead through the trees, the remaining building of the historic Phantom Valley Ranch that was razed in the early 1960s.

Glide north across another flat, snowy meadow, continue straight where the Red Mountain Trail forks left, and ski back into the trees, soon passing a trail mileage sign, then another sign telling the history of Lulu City. Begin a gradual traverse along the steep hillside right, watching carefully for any signs of dangerous snow sluffs. The view of the skyline disappears for a short time as the trail rolls and drops on a delightful run through thick lodgepole, then breaks into scattered aspen. Here the bald dome of Lead Mountain rises beyond a forested range northwest and Lulu Mountain, sharp and solidly white, juts skyward at the end of the valley. Even more eyecatching, however, is Shipler Mountain east-northeast. Fringed with numerous snags from a forest fire, it appears as one massive, rugged jumble of granite boulders.

Pass a slight rise left and soon break into the huge expanse of Shipler Park. Ski cross-country through willows and open conifers on the east side of the park and come to the snow-drifted log walls of an old cabin. Built in 1876 by mountainman and miner Joseph Shipler, this cabin's sod roof lasted until 1963 before finally collapsing under heavy snows. Enter thick timber on a level, conspicuous trailcut and glide north through tall, red-trunked lodgepole pine and moss-laden engelmann spruce. Dip through a series of three tributaries and eventually ski into the open snowfields of the Lulu City site. Stay above and east of the tiny Colorado River and make a gradual cross-country climb toward the middle of the park. With a sharp eye and a little luck you may be able to spot Lulu City's old bear trap, usually the only ruins visible in winter. Needed at one time to eliminate the bears that scavenged the garbage dumps and prowled around the camp, this small log box has outlasted every store, hotel, and cabin in the area, a tribute to the priorities of civilized life. A short distance above and north of the trap is a sign eloquently describing how this once-bustling camp has "yielded to the sounds of wind and river." Return over the ski tracks.

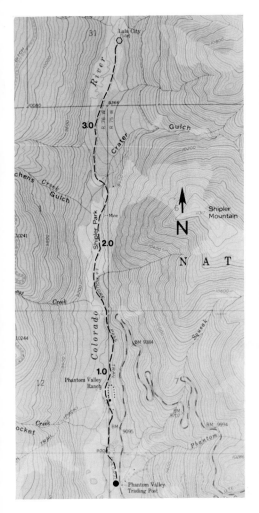

River reflections

51

22 COLORADO STATE FOREST

Half-day through overnight trips
Classifications:
   Easiest through most difficult
Season: Mid-November through early April
Topographic maps:
   U.S.G.S. Clark Peak, Colo. 1962
   U.S.G.S. Gould, Colo. 1955
   U.S.G.S. Mount Richthofen, Colo. 1957
      7.5 minute series
Colorado State Forest

One of the newest and most exciting ski touring areas in northern Colorado is the Colorado State Forest which borders the east side of North Park. Managed for recreational use by the Colorado Division of State Parks, this area now contains several well-planned winter trails, open for both ski touring and snowmobile use. However, ski tourers greatly outnumber snowmobilers within the State Forest; snowmobile convoys sometimes travel over Cameron or Montgomery Pass but pack cross-country skis with them to use while on this west side. A State Parks parking permit, valid for any State Park, is required for admission, available from the Park Ranger and from sporting goods stores at $1 per day or $5 per year.

Besides the scenic trails, a main reason for the growing popularity of the Colorado State Forest is the charming and spacious "bunkhouse" which can be reserved for overnight use, thus eliminating a long return drive in the same day. Filled wall to wall with double-bed bunks, a large picnic table, and an ingenious 50-gallon barrel stove, the bunkhouse sits between two other North Michigan Lake cabins, marked as Camp Pennock on the topo. Wood for the stove and a gas lantern are supplied through courtesy of the Park. Regulations: pack out all trash, help clean the cabin, don't chop wood inside. For reservations, usually needed one or two weeks in advance, contact: Colorado Division of State Parks, 3030 South College, Fort Collins, Co. 80521, telephone 482-2602, or Star Route, Box 91, Walden, Co. 80480, telephone 723-8366.

From Denver drive on U.S. 40 over Berthoud Pass to the junction with Colo. 125 northwest of Granby and proceed on Colo. 125 over Willow Creek Pass to Walden. From Fort Collins drive on 287 to Laramie, Wyoming and continue on Wyo. 230/Colo. 127 to Walden. Turn east from the middle of Walden onto Colo. 14 and proceed another 18.8 miles to a turnoff into the Colorado State Forest, a left turn in front of a KOA Campground where Colo. 14 bends right. Curve right after another 0.1 mile where the left fork stays straight to the Park Headquarters and maintenance building and follow the plowed road to a parking area on the north side of North Michigan Lake. Construction of an all-weather highway over Cameron Pass, a more direct route to the Colorado State Forest, is scheduled for completion by 1980, possibly sooner.

22A. BULL MOUNTAIN RUN

Classification: Most difficult
Distance: 1.8 miles one way (2.9 KM.)
Skiing time: 1½-2 hours one way
Elevation gain: 748 feet
Maximum elevation: 9,708 feet

One of the most popular trails in the State Forest, the Bull Mountain Run begins several hundred yards east of the bunkhouse and follows an old logging road on a no-nonsense climb to the top of Bull Mountain. Beautiful views of Clark Peak northeast and unnamed summits in the Medicine Bow Mountains east highlight the trip up, and a zipping return, too fast to allow a sideways glance and especially fun with powder snow, highlights the trip back down. The trailhead will be marked "if porcupines haven't eaten the sign."

22B. CANADIAN RIVER ROAD

Classification: Easiest
Distance: 2.5 miles one way (4.0 KM.)
Skiing time: 1½-2 hours one way
Elevation gain: 186 feet
Maximum elevation: 9,146 feet

This tour route follows the level, well-packed Bockman Lumber Camp Road for 1.0 mile, then turns north onto the wide

Canadian River roadbed and climbs gradually through a tributary basin. At mile 2.5, marked with a sign, a trail branches right and begins a steeper climb toward the alpine cirque of Ruby Jewel Lake, itself a possible destination point (7.5 miles) with due regard for avalanche. The Canadian River Road forks left at mile 2.5, drops gradually into a drainage of the South Fork Canadian River, and after 4.0 miles continues on a hillside contour through proven snow caving territory.

22C. BOCKMAN LUMBER CAMP ROAD
Classification: Easiest
Distance: 2.2 miles one way (3.5 KM.)
Skiing time: 1½-2 hours one way
Elevation gain: 70 feet
Maximum elevation: 9,030 feet

Stay right after mile 1.0 where the Canadian River Road forks left and a sign reads "5 miles Highway 14/6 miles Montgomery Pass." For the first-time ski tourer, the slightly-rolling course to the Bockman Lumber Camp site provides a perfect introduction to the sport. More advanced tourers can follow the easy-to-see roadbed all the way to Montgomery Pass, a 7.3 mile trip.

Trailhead leap

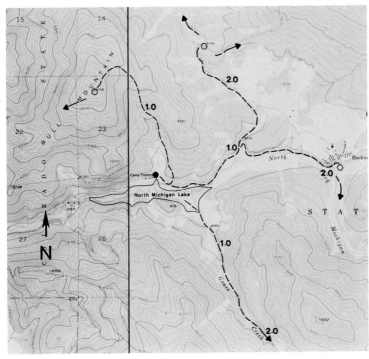

53

23 PERU CREEK

One day trip
Classification: Easiest
Distance: 4.0 miles one way (6.4 KM.)
Skiing time: 2½-3 hours one way
Elevation gain: 920 feet
Maximum elevation: 10,920 feet
Season: Late November through mid-April
Topographic map:
  U.S.G.S. Montezuma, Colo. 1958
        7.5 minute series
Arapaho National Forest

On one spring day in 1898 a massive climax avalanche suddenly broke loose near Grays Peak and surged through the Peru Creek valley, destroying the mining town of Decatur. Although climax avalanches happen infrequently, the possibility of their occurrence exists as much today as in 1898. Thus the Peru Creek valley, especially the upper valley near Horseshoe Basin, should not be toured during times of high avalanche danger. The popular and scenic tour to the Pennsylvania Mine mining camp, as described in the text, follows a route safe from avalanche danger.

Drive on U.S. 6 to the junction with Montezuma Road, a little over 1.2 miles east of the Keystone Lodge at the Keystone Ski Area. Turn south, soon fork left where a branch road turns right to the Ski Area parking lots, and proceed just over 4.6 miles to the trailhead. This trailhead is right after the sharp bend across the Snake River, 1.0 mile before Montezuma. Park in the cleared area.

Ski north through an open meadow for 50 yards, pass a brown tin shack left, then pick up the obvious Peru Creek roadbed and begin curving right with the contour of the hillside. Glide through a grove of aspen, some of which bend over the snowy road; continue the easy, winding climb and eventually curve right to an easterly bearing. From a little meadow near 0.5 mile snow-topped Morgan Peak pops into view east-southeast, and soon after, the frosted rocky face of Cooper Mountain appears across the Peru Creek valley east-northeast. The view of these beautiful alpine peaks is greatly expanded near 1.2 miles as the ski route bends left and enters the open valley floor. Here the steep side of Argentine Peak can be seen at the far end of the valley east. Brittle Silver Mountain and the west ridge of Decatur Mountain rise to magnificent summits along the south valley side, and Independence Mountain forms the high point above the forested range down the valley west-southwest.

Cross under a high voltage line near the creekbed, begin a slightly steeper climb back into a grove of exquisite blue spruce and lodgepole pine, and continue east along the Lenawee Mountainside with easy glides. An old sluice box and mine shack soon can be spotted below the avalanche chute on Collier Mountain south and then the interesting ruins of the Maid of New Orleans Mine show near the roadbed, old skeletons from the glorious silver mining days of the 1870s and 1880s. Pass a signpost listing "Argentine Pass 5" and glide onto an open hillside where once again the view extends to snow-capped summits east-southeast. Brittle Silver Mountain, surrounded by the deep Warden and Cinnamon Gulches, appears as an isolated cone and the steep alpine walls of Silver Mountain and Revenue Mountain form a broad amphitheater behind.

Follow the roadbed through a bend right after 2.1 miles, cross the wide mouth of Chihuahua Gulch, then pass a roofless log cabin as marked on the topo and begin a short gradual drop toward the Peru Creek basin. Re-enter the trees on the roadcut after a cross-country contour across the meadow, pass a cabin marked "No Trespassing" at mile 2.5, and continue under the high voltage line again to a junction with a jeep road near 3.0 miles. Fork right across Peru Creek where the road to Decatur cuts left and then make a gradual climb east-northeast along the Brittle Silver mountainside, reaching the site of the Pennsylvania Mine mining camp after another mile. A log cabin now used by the Colorado Mountain Club and the crumbling ruins of two tall lodging houses, complete with slab siding, still stand on the north side of the road. Nearby are the collapsed beams and timbers, unloading boxes, and a huge cement cylinder of the old mill.

If the day is not windy and if avalanche danger is low, the tour can easily be continued up the valley bottom to Horseshoe Basin, an extension over "easiest" terrain which adds another 2.0 miles and 560 feet of elevation to the trip. Stay in the valley bottom and ski past these landmarks: two cabins and a tin-roofed stone building at the Decatur site, posted "Private Property," at mile 4.5, a lone mine shack at the "11159" mark on the topo above mile 4.9, three old power towers in the valley basin, one crumpled by avalanche, then a sign reading "Argentine Trail/Argentine Pass 3" at mile 5.5, and a white building near the National Treasury Mine site at the entrance to Horse-shoe Basin at mile 6.0. For the easy, fast return trip, follow the rolling, gradually descending course over the ski tracks.

Pennsylvania Mine ruins

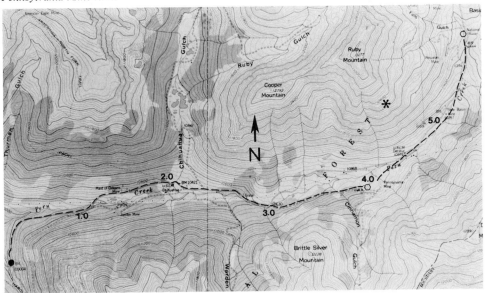

24 SAINTS JOHN

One day trip
Classification: Easiest
Distance: 1.5 miles one way (2.4 KM.)
Skiing time: 1-1½ hours one way
Elevation gain: 440 feet
Maximum elevation: 10,740 feet
Season: Late November through mid-April
Topographic maps:
  U.S.G.S. Montezuma, Colo. 1958
  U.S.G.S. Keystone, Colo. 1958
      7.5 minute series
Arapaho National Forest

The historic mining camp of Saints John, framed by the distant twins Grays and Torreys Peaks, is one of the most interesting and scenic tour destinations in the area. It was here in 1864 that a solitary prospector named John Coley made one of the first silver discoveries in the Territory of Colorado. The mining camp itself was named by members of the Free Masons for their two patron saints, Saint John the Baptist and Saint John the Evangelist.

Proceed on U.S. 6 to the junction with Montezuma Road, a little over 1.2 miles east of the Keystone Lodge at the Keystone Ski Area. Turn south, soon fork left where a branch road turns right to the Ski Area parking lots, then follow this gravel road another 5.5 miles until reaching the mountain village of Montezuma. Continue to the south end of the town and park in the large turnout area on the right side of the road.

The steep, avalanche-streaked sides of Collier Mountain east and Glacier Mountain southwest tower above the starting point for the tour, which is at a lofty 10,300 feet in elevation. A snowy cirque on Bear Mountain

rises above a range of conifers west, and a long, sweeping bowl near Grizzly Peak north-northwest marks the Continental Divide, more than 5½ miles away. Both of these latter scenes comprise part of a stunning alpine panorama that comes into view at different times on the tour. Begin skiing west on a short, double-poling descent to the Snake River basin. Cross a snow-covered bridge and follow the road up a moderately steep climb, soon passing left of a large, weathered barn. Turn northwest as the road meets the treeline and proceed on a gradual traverse up the Glacier mountainside. A few scattered blue spruce block much of the view at first, then an opening reveals the quiet village of Montezuma.

Pass a branch road which cuts back southeast to the old Equity Mine, climb gradually into more and more lodgepole pine, and eventually proceed through two short switchbacks. The increase in elevation now allows a superb view of Collier Mountain east and the precariously-perched mine shack near the Bullion Mine southeast. Follow the snow-packed road through a curve left, pick up the small ravine of Saints John Creek on the right, and soon come to the north end of a snowy, open meadow. Skirt the edge of the meadow, heading south, then pass a stump-filled clearing left and continue through a few thick clumps of engelmann spruce. From here the two tops of Bear Mountain west blaze brightly in the morning sun while the white, treeless side of Glacier Mountain south remains darkened with shadows.

Proceed south on a gradual—then steeper —climb up the Saints John valley. Re-enter the tall spruce trees on a crossing to the west side of the creek and shortly after break into the old mining camp site. First, pass a large snow-covered mound left, residue from the old smelter, *staying well clear to avoid any snow sluff danger.* Across the creek east, a half-buried pile of beams and timbers marks the site of the old silver mill. Built in 1872, it housed "machinery from the East" and boasted "the most complete and up-to-date milling available." The building finally collapsed completely in 1958 under the heavy winter snows. Above and northeast of the mill ruins, the tall chimney for the smelter, masoned with bricks imported from Wales, still can be seen. Of the many log and frame houses spotted in the valley and hillsides in the 1870s, only three or four still stand today, lonely survivors from the yearly battle against avalanches.

For a longer tour, continue up the valley to the Wild Irishman Mine, an advanced trip that totals 3.3 miles one way with 1,400 feet elevation gain. Pass left of the last building in Saints John, then turn south and drop into the creekbed. *Do not follow the road west onto the avalanche run-out,* obvious by its treeless, fan-shaped path. Climb cross-country near the creek for about one-half mile. Rejoin the road as it crosses the drainage and follow it southwest along a slight rise. The ski route continues through a snowy meadow, not shown on the topo, then enters the trees and climbs gradually southwest and west to the Wild Irishman site. Giant, red-barked spruce, some with trunks two feet thick, cover the hillside here, interspersed among twisted and slanted snags. And deep, fluffy snow usually fills the north-facing slope, creating storybook powder conditions for the return.

Atop Wild Irishman Mine cabin

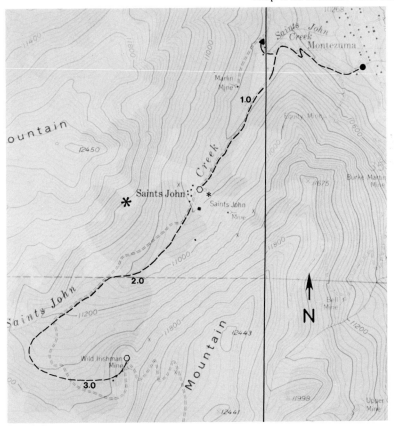

25 HUNKIDORI ROAD

One day trip
Classification: More difficult
Distance: 3.4 miles one way (5.5 KM.)
Skiing time: 2½-3 hours one way
Accumulated elevation gain: 930 feet
Accumulated elevation loss: 200 feet
Maximum elevation: 11,030 feet
Season: Late November through late April
Topographic maps:
   U.S.G.S. Montezuma, Colo. 1958
   U.S.G.S. Keystone, Colo. 1958
      7.5 minute series
Arapaho National Forest

Several very hunkydory things highlight a tour over the Hunkidori Road. For one, thick conifers shelter the road through most of its length, providing comforting protection from wind chill and keeping the snow soft and easy to ski. Another thing is that the terrain is pleasantly varied, affording gradual drops as well as climbs. And finally, the old Hunkidori Mine site itself, marked with an old log cabin and other old mining structures, makes an interesting destination point.

Drive on U.S. 6 to the Montezuma Road junction, a little over 1.2 miles east of the Keystone Lodge at the Keystone Ski Area. Turn south, soon fork left where a branch

road turns right to the Ski Area parking lots, and proceed to Montezuma, about 5.7 miles from U.S. 6. Continue to the south end of town and park in the large turnout area on the right side of the road.

Begin skiing west on a short drop to the Snake River basin, following the ski route for the Saints John tour (No. 24). Make a gradual climb up the Glacier mountainside, proceed through the two switchbacks, and after 0.5 mile curve south-southwest along the Saints John Creek. Soon branch right from the Saints John tour route and ski along the north side of a spacious, snow-covered meadow. Here an old, cylindrical mill sieve still rests on its wooden frame and a rusted iron tub lies nearby, curious relics of the mining days in this area. In view south beyond the meadow is the solidly white bank of Glacier Mountain; a half-forested knoll near the Wild Irishman site protrudes prominently, and the long, white range continues west toward Keystone Mountain.

Glide west across the meadow, crossing Saints John Creek; pick up the road to the Hunkidori Mine at the far side and continue into the shadows of thick pine and spruce. Immediately pass a branch road right, climb gradually for several more yards, then take the second sharp right, bearing toward the snow-capped top of Lenawee Mountain north. The roadcut makes a quick, then more gradual drop and proceeds on an easy climb through a thick tunnel of trees. Soon turn slightly right, schuss through a wide gully which shows conspicuously on the topo, and drop quickly again. Climb gradually for several yards, pass a junk car left, and begin another long, winding descent, eventually entering a more open forest of red-barked spruce. Pass a junked pick-up truck, bend right just after 1.0 mile, and proceed north, then northwest through easy flats and rolling downhills. It is awesome to realize that the giant engelmann spruce through this section are about 200 years old, as old as the United States.

Loop through a log-filled drainage, follow the snowy roadcut through a curve left, and begin climbing on an easy grade, now skiing with a view of the deep Snake River valley north. Continue the curve southwest into the afternoon sun, passing 2.0 miles. Various summits of Bear and Independence Mountains show above the treeline southwest as the terrain opens for the first time since

Saints John Creek. *Proceed only if the snow is stable, cross quickly in single file through an old but potential avalanche area.* Wind west over the more exposed, sometimes wind-crusted road, climbing through easy to steep grades. Cross two small drainages and glide by another creekbed, soon heading through thick trees again toward the barely-visible east summit of Bear Mountain south-southwest.

As the trees open slightly, turn west-south-west and cross Grizzly Gulch; bend right, climb steeply then more gradually, and soon turn left through a switchback at 3.0 miles. Curve west and follow the winding, snow-filled roadcut through thick trees, eventually turning south and entering the Hunkidori Mine site. An old post-and-pole corral shows above the snow and against the hillside beyond sits a weathered log cabin, resting squarely against a huge spruce tree. At the foot of Independence Mountain, farther south, a secluded, snow-filled park opens up, littered with beams of an old mine shack, a sluice box, and scattered power poles. Since the park is directly under an avalanche path down Independence Mountain, view these latter ruins from a distance. *Do not ski beyond treeline!* For the return trip, ski back down—and up—the roadbed, an exhilarating, never-boring run over varied terrain. Remember to save energy for the climb back up the east side of Bear Mountain.

Bird in the hand

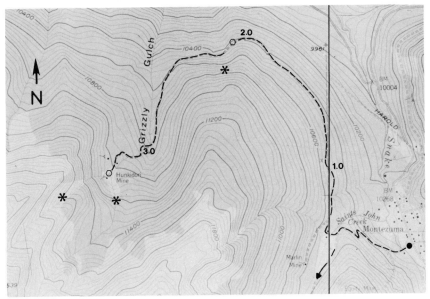

26 WEBSTER PASS TRAIL

One day trip
Classification: Easiest to more difficult
Distance: 3.0 miles one way (4.8 KM.)
Skiing time: 2½-3 hours one way
Elevation gain: 890 feet
Maximum elevation: 11,390 feet
Season: December through early April
Topographic map:
  U.S.G.S. Montezuma, Colo. 1958
      7.5 minute series
Arapaho National Forest

"The Snake River and Hall Valley Wagon Road has just been completed," reads the Georgetown *Colorado Miner* of October 19, 1878. "Hipla! Hurrah! Carry the news everywhere! . . . There is Joy in the Halls of Montezuma." Such was the excitement in the small Montezuma mining camp a century ago when an improved "Post Road" finally penetrated the great Continental Divide barrier at Webster Pass, establishing a direct route with Denver. Today this same Webster Pass Trail, unmaintained and long-forgotten, makes a delightful route for ski tourers. One note of caution, however: two Climax avalanche paths intercept the roadbed after the first mile and when heavy storms create high avalanche danger this tour route is not recommended. *Be careful!*

Take U.S. 6 to the junction with Montezuma Road, a little over 1.2 miles east of the Keystone Lodge at the Keystone Ski Area. Turn south, then soon fork left where a road branches right to the Ski Area parking lots. Drive through the mountain village of Montezuma and continue south to the end of the plowed road at the old sawmill site, a total of 6.4 miles from U.S. 6. Park in the turnaround.

Begin skiing south over the flat roadbed, bearing toward the towering, wind-blown summit of Teller Mountain. After several yards be sure to look over your shoulder toward Collier Mountain east-northeast and observe the timberline mine buildings near the Bullion Mine site. Perched safely above an avalanche chute, silhouetted against the sky, an old mine shack clings to the mountainside, still holding on despite the howling winds and fierce storms at that elevation. Enter a stand of conifers and immediately turn left onto an obvious roadcut, leaving the southerly road which continues next to Deer Creek (No. 27). Wind southeast through full-branched spruce on an easy grade, pass an obscure shortcut to Deer Creek right, and soon bend more sharply right. The roadcut, usually filled deeply with snow, climbs gradually south-southeast and after 0.4 mile comes to a small meadow, giving view to the avalanche path on Santa Fe Peak northeast.

Ski by a cabin in the trees right, climb steadily through a curve left, and soon turn back right, passing the old roadbed to the Bullion Mine on the left. Now Teller Mountain looms into view ahead, glowing in the backlit sunlight with an iridescent yellow-green cast. Loop through another left, then curve right and pass a new turnoff to mining property left, unmarked on the topo. Leave tree cover just before 1.0 mile and *proceed quickly and one at a time across a large avalanche run-out.* Ski in and out of a band of engelmann spruce, follow the roadbed beneath a hillside of pitch stumps, timber that once supplied the nearby mines, then hook toward the creek and continue southeast through fairly open terrain. Ore tailings and scattered mine buildings near the Silver Wave Mine, intriguingly high up the mountainside, soon can be seen back through a saddle on Santa Fe Peak northeast.

Cross quickly and singly through a second run-out area, passing trees which have been stripped of their uphill branches by the avalanches. After 1.5 miles re-enter the trees, now mostly on the left, and soon come to a small, wood-slab cabin, a nice stopping point for lunch and turning back. More ambitious skiers can extend the tour another 1.5 miles as figured for the information capsule. Stay near the bottom of the drainage and glide easily over the open, windswept terrain, heading toward the distant switchbacks below Webster Pass. Near the 2.4 mile mark climb onto a slight shelf which holds a network of old beaver dams and ice patches, then continue the easy climb south through clumps of low-lying, twisted evergreens. Keep a sharp lookout through this final section for the camouflaged but very tranquil white-tailed ptarmigan, often spotted in and among the shrubbery.

With the more stable snow and warmer weather in March and April, the top of Webster Pass itself is attainable, an advanced climb which adds another 1.5 miles and 710 feet of elevation gain to the tour. Bear left of the scree hilltop between Handcart Peak and the pass and follow the long switchbacks of the snow-covered road, eventually reaching the tiny Webster Pass signpost. Here the view looks down into the deep Handcart Gulch and scans the snow-topped Platte River and Kenosha Mountains on the far-away horizon southeast. Immediately east is the bulky, mostly snowbare mass of Red Cone, well-named for its colorful russet slopes. On the return trip, carefully snow-plow down the Webster Pass snowfield, then glide back on the ski track.

White tailed ptarmigan

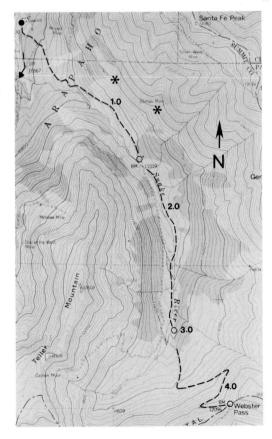

27 DEER CREEK

One day trip
Classification: Easiest
Distance: 2.6 miles one way (4.2 KM.)
Skiing time: 2-2½ hours one way
Elevation gain: 860 feet
Maximum elevation: 11,360 feet
Season: Late November through mid-April
Topographic maps:
  U.S.G.S. Montezuma, Colo. 1958
  U.S.G.S. Keystone, Colo. 1958
      7.5 minute series
Arapaho National Forest

The ski tour along Deer Creek starts out from an elevation almost two miles above sea level and then climbs still higher, ending at a lookout point near timberline. Here in this white, wintry Artic-Alpine Zone is the chief delight of the tour: a massive cliff of snow, sculptured by the wind and backlit in the midday sun. Near the lookout point a weathered miner's cabin protrudes from the snowdrifts. Built so sturdily that the roof still remains intact, it serves as a reminder of the mining boom during the 1870s and 80s when men braved this harsh climate on hopes of a rich strike. Although the climb up the Deer Creek valley maintains a fairly steady 6 percent grade, the terrain does not require advanced skiing technique, making this tour an excellent choice for beginners with good endurance.

Drive on U.S. 6 to the Montezuma Road junction, a little over 1.2 miles east of the Keystone Lodge at the Keystone Ski Area. Turn south, and soon fork left where a road branches right to the Ski Area parking lots. Proceed through the town of Montezuma and continue south to the end of the plowed road at the old Sawmill site, a total of 6.4 miles from U.S. 6. Park in the large turnaround.

Ski south on an easy climb over the snow-covered roadbed, pass by a clump of spruce on the left, and soon enter a meadow of scattered willows. Continue straight where the Webster Pass Trail (No. 26) turns left into thicker conifers, then stay to the left of the open meadow for several hundred yards, heading toward the tawny, wind-blown top of Teller Mountain. This 12,615-foot peak memorializes Henry M. Teller who helped locate the Chautauqua Mine in the Deer Creek valley about 1865 and later served for thirty years as a U.S. Senator from Colorado. Cross the valley when the roadcut becomes visible on the other side, gliding over the swath of smooth snow which covers the Deer Creek bridge. Pass the turnoff to the old Superior Mine at the 0.4 mile mark and resume the gradual climb onto a mountainside of tall spruce. Soon these thick, full-branched trees block all long vistas except for the snowy top of Lenawee Mountain on the horizon behind.

Stay above and right of the wide Deer Creek gulch and glide easily up the rolling roadcut, eventually coming to the first viewpoint of the beautiful, snow-white cliffs at the end of the valley south. An interesting and well-preserved log cabin/mine shaft and log loading box in the trees right also mark this point, making it a nice lunch and rest stop. The ski route winds left, then right at an obscure creek crossing near 1.0 mile and, as the meadows widen left, proceeds south-southwest into thicker clumps of trees. Soon pass a tattered, half-buried house trailer and follow the roadbed in and out of tree clumps on a gradual climb. After 1.8 miles leave the road, now fairly inconspicuous. Stay near treeline for better protection from wind and continue cross-country up the west side of the valley, following the route marked on the map.

Cross a west tributary of Deer Creek after 2.0 miles and as trees begin closing in from both sides, break trail south up the more open valley bottom, eventually funneling into a plainly discernible east tributary of Deer Creek. Keep this drainage on the left and begin a steady climb up the hillside, soon increasing the view north-northeast to the spectacular, alp-like summits of Torreys and Grays Peaks more than seven miles away. Curve right as the climb lessens after a couple hundred yards and cross-country south and west through the trees until intercepting the wide snow path of upper Deer Creek valley. Follow the open valley south-southwest on a gradual climb, then veer right near timberline and climb to a lookout point on top of a knoll, a good stopping place for the tour. *Stay far away from the avalanche run-out zones on the valley floor farther south and west.* A sheer, dazzling-white cliff, the source of the avalanches, surrounds this lookout point, in view now for all of its mile-long length. On the west side a thick cornice protrudes from the top and avalanche debris is often strewn below; south the bowl becomes larger and rocky outcroppings streak the sides.

The return trip doubles back over the track and usually takes little more than one hour. The drop back into the lower valley is long and steady, never uncomfortably steep, an excellent place to begin practicing the telemark and christie turns.

Teller Mountain

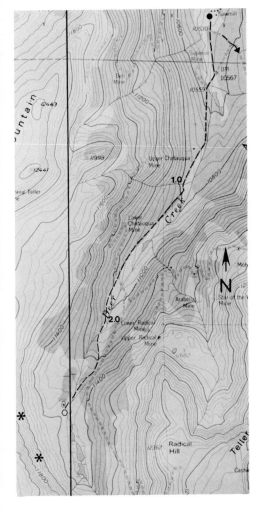

28 KEYSTONE GULCH

One day trip
Classification: Easiest
Distance: 5.7 miles one way (9.2 KM.)
Skiing time: 3½-4½ hours one way
Elevation gain: 1,565 feet
Maximum elevation: 10,800 feet
Season: Mid-November through mid-April
Topographic map:
    U.S.G.S. Keystone, Colo. 1958
          7.5 minute series
Arapaho National Forest

A little more than one-half mile east of the historic lumber and mining camp of Keystone—once an important loading station for the Colorado and Southern narrow gauge railway—the hillside opens slightly and a deep gulch penetrates the thickly-forested ranges. Sheltered by tall pine and spruce on windy days, filled with midday sun on good weather days, the road along this winding Keystone Gulch makes an easy-gliding ski tour, a route marked and recommended by the Keystone Ski Area. *Due to avalanche danger, do not ski beyond the first switchback at the 5.7 mile mark.*

Drive on U.S. 6 to the junction with the Keystone Road, the east access route to the Keystone Ski Area. Follow the Keystone Road 0.3 mile, then turn right onto the Soda Ridge Road and proceed another 0.5 mile to the trailhead, directly across from the turn-off to the Flying Dutchman Condominiums. Limited parking can be found along the side of Soda Ridge Road. If parking is unavailable, leave your car in the Keystone Village parking lot south of the Keystone Lodge and ride the free shuttle bus to the trailhead.

Glide south-southeast on the roadbed past a post-and-pole fence and house on the left, pass the first trail marker right and enter the trail proper, a wide, lodgepole-lined jeep road. This snowy path climbs gradually onto the steeper northwestern reaches of Keystone Mountain, contours around a protrud-

ing knoll, and converges near the creek basin right. Willows of vibrant yellow and orange fill the creekbed here, adding color to the green and white landscape. Follow the sunny, snow-filled road through a small drainage of aspen seedlings, proceed through a slight bend left, then right as the valley widens, and begin a short, steeper climb near the gaging station at 0.6 mile. After a level run through black-trunked pine east of the creekbed, the road begins climbing again, rising gradually to a better view of the forested range west and the snow-capped mountain behind north. From this quiet, forested refuge it is hard to imagine that on the other side of that mountain range north is the noisy, bustling west entrance to the Eisenhower Memorial Tunnel.

Continue the gradual, southerly climb past the 1.0 mile post and soon ski beneath a hillside of fuzzy lodgepole pine seedlings, an area shown as a clearing on the topo. Wind back down to creek level with long, easy glides, pass a private cabin right, and ski into a snowy meadow which opens to the west, an inviting rest and lunch spot on a sunny day. Resume the easy climb in and out of the conifers, curving left and soon passing a drainage filled with tall, cream-colored aspen. The bottom of Keystone Gulch opens again to a meadow as the snowy roadbed winds above and left, climbing through scattered, thin-trunked pine at the 2.0 mile post.

Break into a small meadow which gives view to the densely forested top of Keystone Mountain east, the backside of the ski area, then glide on an easy grade back into the tall, shady pine and soon ski onto an open, snowy lane next to the creek. The road crosses the creekbed twice within 200 yards, bends left and proceeds on a long, gradual climb 80 feet up the east side of the valley, eventually passing the 3.0 mile post. A stand of tall, dead trees, victims most probably of an old fire, marks the hillside west as the road continues across another branch drainage, then enters a meadow which opens across the gulch. In a few yards a branch road, unmarked on the topo, turns right across the creek and traverses the sparsely covered hillside west, a possible route for another tour.

Ski by a saddle in the range west which brings an end to the section of sparse timber and begin a slightly steeper climb at the 4.0 mile post. Glide easily over level terrain

again in 50 yards, passing the half-buried
ruins of a cabin near the creek, then ski into
a stand of full-branched pine which block
the view of the open gulch bottom. Proceed
southeast on an easy, rolling climb through
the conifers, curve east just before the 5.0
mile post and break again into the open
gulch. Continue the curve left until bearing
northeast, pass an inconspicuous, unmarked
roadcut which traverses the hillside northwest, and climb along a northeasterly branch
of Keystone Gulch. Soon the two high points
of Keystone Mountain, treeless and wind-
blown, come into view ahead, the first vista
of timberline since the tour's beginning. In
several hundred more yards the first switchback on the road, marked by a sign, signals
an end to the tour route.

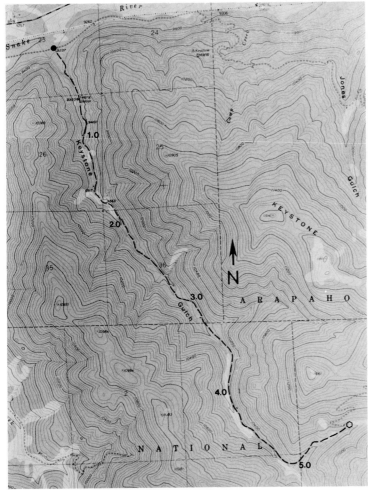

65

29 SOUTH WILLOW CREEK

One day trip
Classification: More difficult
Distance: 4.0 miles one way (6.4 KM.)
Skiing time: 2½-3 hours one way
Accumulated elevation gain: **600 feet**
Accumulated elevation loss: **270 feet**
Maximum elevation: 9,600 feet
Season: December through March
Topographic maps:
  U.S.G.S. Frisco, Colo. 1970
  U.S.G.S. Dillon, Colo. 1970
      7.5 minute series
Arapaho National Forest

For the sheer delight of ski touring, South Willow Creek is unsurpassed. The terrain varies from easy, winding climbs through thick pine to fast-gliding traverses across open snowfields to long coasting descents. A rustic log cabin, thoughtfully maintained by all its users, marks the destination point for the tour and in the cabin's log book winter experiences are shared with fellow ski tourers. An excerpt: "Arrived in afternoon, snow depth three feet, will spend the night here, donated some extra ground cloth to front door and a couple of candles. Began snowing this evening, hasn't stopped yet." Another excerpt, a sad and touching story, and a fitting memorial for the cabin: "Jan. 3rd (1975). Snowed last night about 6 inches, broke trail in this afternoon. Cabin in good condition other than the porch collapsed due to snow. Bob Hurtt spent winter '71 up here. He was killed in an avalanche in Crested Butte two weeks ago. He and Sandy loved this place. Keep it neat."

Drive on I. 70 to the interchange south of Silverthorne and exit onto the down ramp to Colo. 9 North. Proceed toward Silverthorne, soon cross the Blue River bridge, and take the next left onto a dirt frontage road. Take the following course to the trailhead: south for a little over 0.2 mile, west then south again on a climb for over 0.7 mile, north on a winding climb for 0.3 mile, back south to a parking space at the bend in the road.

Cross to the trailhead sign on the west side of the road and begin gliding over a level, well-blazed trail, staying left of a barbed wire fence. Ski over a wide road for a few yards, then separate left onto the trailcut and follow the blazes through tall lodgepole pine. The trail proceeds through a grove of small aspen and contours north-northwest across a snowy meadow, expanding the view to interlaced curves of the I. 70 exchange in the valley below, and the flat expanse of Dillon Reservoir and snow-capped peaks beyond. Break onto a road-like passage on a course near treeline, double pole down a long, easy drop, and watch left for conspicuous blazes as the trail re-enters thicker trees. With another exciting drop several yards beyond, the trail spills onto a large, snow-covered hillside, a tempting place to stop and practice a few christie turns.

Climb gradually across the meadow, passing above a magnificent, lonely pine; bear west-northwest toward sharp peaks in the Gore Range and continue across the willow-filled creek just below the main clump of spruce. Ski straight across a small hillside and weave through willows on a second creek crossing near the 1.0 mile mark. The blazed trail re-enters the red-trunked pine, switchbacks right, then left on an easy climb up the next ridge, and contours west on a fast run to the third creek crossing. Climb above and left of the drainage, passing the 2.0 mile mark. Wind north-northeast through shady trees on a near-level contour, pass a steep drainage that joins on the right, then turn left over the top of the ridge.

Wind through a faster and faster drop down the hillside and as the terrain levels, intercept a jeep trail and turn left. Ahead right a steep, snowy face on the 12,885-foot peak flickers through the trees, then ahead left the white dome of Buffalo Mountain comes into view as the trail proceeds west on an easy, rolling drop. Eventually begin climbing again, curve gradually left and, near the 3.0 mile mark, pass through a shallow, pine-filled drainage. Continue across two branches of South Willow Creek and immediately come to a mileage sign which lists destination points farther north. With a short, steady climb the trail traverses a small knoll, then heads through open, full-branched pine toward the middle of the steep valley ahead. Hundreds of aspen color the north valley wall with a soft beige hue, and in dramatic contrast, rugged rock outcroppings break out between the white avalanche paths on the south wall.

Glide along the north side of an open meadow for several yards, then turn southwest toward Buffalo Mountain and follow the blazes back into the conifers. Very soon break into a second meadow near 4.0 miles, bend slightly right and continue west to the half-buried, picturesque log cabin, a nice stopping point for the tour. Farther west the southern reaches of Red Peak crowd close to the rugged north side of Buffalo Mountain and create a narrow valley with high avalanche potential. Thus it is not advisable to extend the tour route beyond the cabin.

South Willow Creek cabin

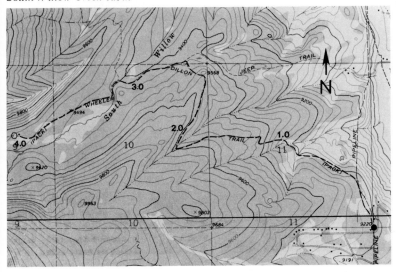

30 NORTH TENMILE CREEK

One day trip
Classification: More difficult to most difficult
Distance: 5.0 miles one way (8.0 KM.)
Skiing time: 3-3½ hours one way
Elevation gain: 1,250 feet
Maximum elevation: 10,400 feet
Season: Late November through early April
Topographic maps:
U.S.G.S. Frisco, Colo. 1970
U.S.G.S. Vail Pass, Colo. 1970
7.5 minute series
Arapaho National Forest

The grade for the first mile of the North Tenmile Creek trail averages about 9 percent, giving this tour a slow, toilsome beginning and a very fast finish. Most of the tour route, however, follows level runs and easy, rolling climbs, excellent terrain for ski touring. Although the mountain vistas are not as rugged and spectacular as on other tours, beauty can be found in the rustic buildings at the Prospect Mine site, the black holes and frosted pockets along the stream, and the tall spruce which often creak and sway in the breeze. Stay on the road for the first several hundred yards where it crosses land posted "Private Property/No Trespassing."

Drive on I. 70 to the exchange west of Frisco, exit onto the down ramp and proceed to a pullout area immediately west of the exchange. From Frisco drive west on U.S. 6 for less than a mile and pass straight under the I. 70 overpass to the parking area.

Glide west over the wide, often snowmobile-packed road for about 25 yards, then begin curving left and bear toward the barren, avalanche-streaked Wichita Mountain. Soon ski onto a narrower trailcut and climb gradually up the south-facing hillside. Royal Mountain, topped with frosted granite slabs, comes into view southeast before the trail enters a grove of aspen and lodgepole pine and continues past a large, green water tank which shows through the trees left. Bend right where another trail seems to parallel the creekbed, and cross through a small drainage, again heading toward Wichita Mountain. Cross the ditch marked on the topo, wind through a long, steady climb above the creek, and eventually break into an open meadow near 1.0 mile. At this lower end a clump of limber pine, a tree usually found near timberline, signals the change to more exposed terrain, and icy patches of the wind-scoured mill pond often show through the snow.

The smooth, steep hillside south periodically sluffs snow into the creekbed so stay well clear of this area. Ski by a roofless cabin and several shacks at the Prospect Mine site and re-enter the lodgepole pine on a long, easy-gliding run west-southwest. Break into a meadow after 1.5 miles, pass a grove of striking snags and a beaver pond left, then continue again through the sheltering pine with gradual climbs and short, coasting drops. The trail crosses an open hillside, a perfect practice area for telemark and christie turns, and proceeds just inside treeline past 2.0 miles. Soon ski into another fairly open meadow, passing a clump of beautiful blue spruce at the lower end, and wind through scattered conifers to an inconspicuous creek crossing, marked by a post and several yards downstream from a clump of impenetrable spruce.

Follow the trailcut through dense fir on an easy, rolling climb up the north-facing hillside, gaining 20 yards of elevation above creek level. After 2.7 miles the trees give way to a view of dazzling-white mountains in the Gore Range due west, and then the trail turns right and drops quickly to a second creek crossing. Stay to the right of the creekbed, look carefully for the blazes and trimmed branches of the narrow, often obscure trailcut, and in another mile come to a weathered signpost which marks the Wheeler and Meadow Creek trail junctions. Here the trail bends right, then continues the gradual climb in and out of tree clumps, reaching the first good viewpoint of the horizon range near 4.0 miles. Thickly corniced and solidly white, the range now shows straight down the trail, an area marked "GORE" of Gore Range on the topo map.

Break trail across the open hillside, following a cross-country route near the creekbed as the trail becomes completely hidden by deep snow. In good weather the tour can be extended another two miles on the same gradual climb. Near 5.0 miles the 12,736-foot high point on the white range comes into view north-northwest. Burned stumps and scraggly trees dot the mountainside north, and across the valley a snowy bowl stands out on the forested side of Uneva Peak. The return trip over the ski tracks, a thrilling, rolling ride, often takes less than an hour. Proceed carefully with a snowplow and pole drag through the steep final section.

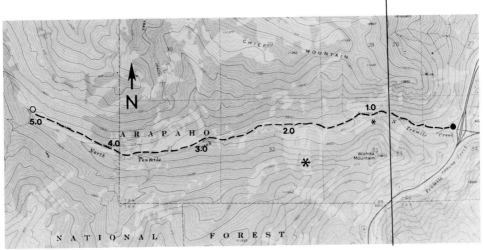

31
RAINBOW LAKE AND MINERS CREEK

Half-day trip
Classification: Easiest
Distance: 1.4 miles one way (2.3 KM.)
Skiing time: 1 hour one way
Elevation gain: 110 feet
Maximum elevation: 9,260 feet
Season: December through March
Topographic map:
U.S.G.S. Frisco, Colo. 1970
7.5 minute series
Arapaho National Forest

The tour to Rainbow Lake measures only 1.4 miles one way and follows very gentle terrain, ending with a short drop to the lakebed. Thus, it is the perfect tour for beginning skiers and slow-paced families, as well as all skiers who just want a half-day outing. For those who can manage a few fairly steep climbs and drops, the "Miners Creek" cabin serves as an excellent destination, a "more difficult" tour of 3.5 miles one way with 1,010 feet elevation gain. The small log cabin, often nearly buried with snow by spring, reflects the efforts of thoughtful maintenance by its users and contains two wooden bunks and a cute stove made from a 20-gallon barrel. In 1975-76 the Forest Service declared this route to the cabin as a designated snowmobile trail and also established a cross-country trail at the Peak One Campground near Dillon Reservoir. For more information, request the "X-C Ski & Snowmobile TRAIL INFORMATION" pamphlet from the Dillon Ranger District, P.O. Box 188, Dillon, Colorado 80435.

Drive east from Frisco on Colo. 9, continuing 1.2 miles from the junction of U.S. 6 and Colo. 9 in Frisco. Park in the Peak One Campground parking area.

Cross to the south side of Colo. 9; bend right past a sign reading "Rainbow Lake" and ski into the full-branched pine on a flat jeep road. Ahead down the roadcut Peaks 1 through 4 in the Tenmile Range, pointed and

blazing-white, stack up along the skyline, a captivating vista for several hundred yards of the ski route. Ski across the wide swath of the high voltage line, a cut which directs view toward snow-capped Buffalo Mountain northwest, and immediately take a smaller road fork on the left where a right fork contours lower on the hillside. Cross another old right-of-way swath, bend gradually right through an open area, and glide easily over the snowy roadcut past a road spur at the 0.7 mile mark. The ski route maintains a very pleasant, near-level grade, contouring next to the steeper Ophir mountainside left, then heading south to a picnic area, the turn-off to Rainbow Lake.

Ski across Miners Creek, turn right from the roadbed near the red outhouse, then wind west-northwest through the black-trunked pine to a small saddle and begin dropping toward Rainbow Lake. Take a right trail branch as the left branch contours higher along the hillside and snowplow through a steady drop to the lakebed, the most challenging part of the tour. A cozy picnic can be held in the thick pine east of the lake with a panoramic view of white peaks on the horizon. The white dome of Buffalo Mountain, carved deeply with the cirque of Salt Lick Gulch, appears again to the northwest. Farther south are several rolling alpine peaks in the Gore Range, and then jagged summit of Peak 1 shows southwest.

To continue the tour to the Miners Creek cabin, follow the flat roadbed beyond the turnoff to Rainbow Lake and glide through patches of white aspen, lodgepole pine and willow. After 1.5 miles curve close to the hillside right, contour on a very gradual climb, and after a couple hundred yards ski out of the trees into a sunny meadow along the creekbed. Pass an unusual five-trunked aspen tree, ski beyond into an open park, then continue on an easier left-hand fork where the road divides and cross over a creekbed at 2.4 miles. The road proceeds from a short climb after the creek crossing to a winding, rolling run and then passes by tall spruce and willow patches, crosses another branch creek at mile 2.9 and makes a steady climb to a knolltop. Several yards left of the road is a secluded lunch spot which affords a view of Bald Mountain southeast.

Begin another climb south-southeast on the road, soon turn right at a sign reading "Miners Creek Trail," and continue the climb west, bearing toward the pointed top of Peak 1 on the horizon. Stay right where a steep trail forks left, glide to the end of a small opening of trees, then immediately turn uphill (left) on a trailcut which also drops down the hillside. Proceed southwest through willows and long-needled fir, bend left with the contour of the hillside and follow the trailcut, now more obvious, on a gradual climb. The trail curves right around the hillside until breaking into the clearing with the cabin at 3.5 miles. Here the view extends east-northeast to snow-capped summits near Loveland Pass with two twin peaks, Grizzly Peak and perhaps Grays Peak, rising slightly higher than the rest. For the return trip, follow the ski tracks back to the parking area.

Peak 1

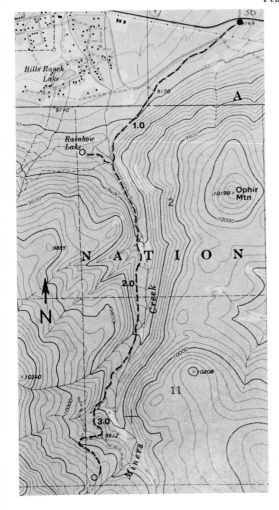

32 SALLY BARBER MINE

Half-day trip
Classification: Easiest
Distance: 1.5 miles one way (2.4 KM.)
Skiing time: 1-1½ hours one way
Elevation gain: 405 feet
Maximum elevation: 10,685 feet
Season: December through mid-April
Topographic maps:
   U.S.G.S. Boreas Pass, Colo. 1957
   U.S.G.S. Breckenridge, Colo. 1970
       7.5 minute series
Arapaho National Forest

With a starting point at the end of the plowed road in French Gulch, the ski route to the Sally Barber Mine measures only 1.5 miles, just the right distance for a quick morning or afternoon tour in an otherwise busy day. Both the drive to the trailhead and the ski route itself give views to remains from the mining days in the Breckenridge area: the mounds of smooth pebbles in the creekbed which were left from the goldboat dredging, the still-raw mine scar at the Wellington Mine site, and the scattered debris at the ghost town of Lincoln City. For a very different and beautiful ski touring experience, tour the road to the Sally Barber Mine on a moonlit night, a possible trip even in late April or early May. The famous circuit preacher of Summit County, Father L. Dyer, who lived in Lincoln City in the early 1860s, often skied at night out of necessity. In his autobiography, the *Snow-Shoe Itinerant,* he recorded one of the attempts and also gave the rational for night-skiing:

"On the third day of April (1863) I left Lincoln City and stopped at Mr. Silverthorn's in Breckenridge until about two o'clock in the morning, when I took my carpet sack, well-filled, got on my snowshoes, and went up Blue River. The snow was five feet deep. It might be asked, 'Why start at two o'clock?' Because the snow would not bear a man in daytime, even with snow-shoes. From about two o'clock until nine or ten in the morning was the only time a man could go; and a horse could not go at all."

Drive on Colo. 9 to the middle of Breckenridge, turn east onto Wellington Road and after three blocks follow the road on a curve left, then right into French Gulch. Proceed east past the Wellington Mine site and the old townsite of Lincoln City and continue to a parking area at the end of the plowed road, a total of 3.9 miles from the main street of Breckenridge.

From the turn-around area begin skiing east over the flat roadbed. Continue straight after 50 yards where a road marked "Private Driveway" forks left and in several more yards turn right onto the lower Sally Barber Mine Road. Occasionally the main road is plowed for the first 50 yards to the private driveway. Curve south toward the open, wind-blown face of Bald Mountain and drop gradually to a crossing over French Creek. Bend right through the willows in the drainage, begin a very easy climb back into the clumps of engelmann spruce, and soon ski into an open cut. Here the view expands to snowy-white Peak 7 in the Tenmile Range on the horizon west, and then as the tour continues, the flat, rolling ridge north of Peak 7 can be seen. Mineral Hill, covered with the delicate lines of aspen, also comes into view across the broad expanse of French Gulch.

Contour up the hillside near treeline as deep snow hides the roadbed for several yards. Continue into the trees above the open cut and after 0.6 mile cross Weber Gulch, a steep, tree-filled drainage. The roadbed, now wide and obvious, dips across another small drainage and winds through the trees with only a slight climb, allowing long, delightful glides. Through each opening in the trees right the white summits of the Tenmile

Range can be seen, extending to the rocky face of Peak 1 at the far north end. Soon the road passes several burned snags which are scattered through the timber on this hillside and also visible among the aspen on Mineral Hill north, the remains possibly from a devastating forest fire that swept the gold mines in French Gulch during June 1860.

Ski around a small knoll at 1.4 miles, glide through a more open area where the view extends to a cluster of distant peaks near the Loveland Pass area northeast, and in another few yards come to the ruins of the Sally Barber Mine. The dilapidated walls of a roofless cabin, often almost completely buried with snow, mark one side of the site.

Four high posts provide corners for a loading shack a few yards away, its wooden flume in back still half-filled with soil, and farther beyond lie the interesting remains of a rusted steam boiler. From the mine the tour can be continued west with a drop through Australia Gulch and then a long descent to a new road, near the "10417" mark but not included on the 1970 Breckenridge topo. Ski 0.2 mile north to the junction with another mining road, drop quickly again through Ford Gulch to the rock mounds in the French Gulch basin, and loop back east to the trailhead. Or, for the easiest return trip, gentle enough for beginning skiers, follow the ski tracks back from the Sally Barber Mine, skiing the delightful dips and rolls in the roadbed to the trailhead.

The steamboiler

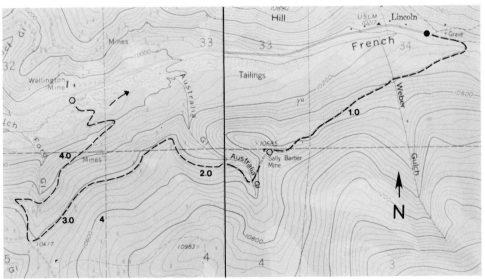

73

33 FRENCH GULCH AND LITTLE FRENCH GULCH

One day trip
Classification: Easiest
Distance: 3.1 miles one way (5.0 KM.)
Skiing time: 2-2½ hours one way
Elevation gain: 620 feet
Maximum elevation: 10,900 feet
Season: December through mid-April
Topographic map:
  U.S.G.S. Boreas Pass, Colo. 1957
            7.5 minute series
Arapaho National Forest

From the earliest beginnings of the Breckenridge gold rush in 1859 through the goldboat era in the early 1900s, French Gulch has been a major center of mining activity. Named after a French Canadian known as "French Pete" who is given credit for its discovery, the little valley contained a respectably-sized village by 1861 called Lincoln City. French Gulch was later harbor for some of the gold-dredging boats of the "Breckenridge Navy" which scraped the creekbed bottom to bedrock for the last flecks of gold. Today both the ghosted remains of Lincoln City and the high mounds of rocks from the goldboaters are visible on the way to the ski touring trailhead.

One of the most famous residents of Lincoln City was Father L. Dyer, a part-time miner, a mail-carrier when funds ran low, but mainly a preacher who traveled from mining camp to mining camp to minister to all the miners. Appointed to the Blue River Mission in 1862, Father Dyer soon found the need in his ministry for what he called "snow-shoes," actually eight-foot long skis.

Drive on Colo. 9 to the middle of Breckenridge, turn east onto Wellington Road and after three blocks follow the road on a curve left, then right into French Gulch. Proceed east past the Wellington Mine site and the old townsite of Lincoln City and continue to a parking area at the end of the plowed road, a total of 3.9 miles from the main street of Breckenridge.

With a view behind Peak 8 and the Breckenridge Ski Area begin skiing east-southeast over the flat French Gulch roadbed. Pass a jeep-size roadcut left marked "Private Driveway" and continue straight in another few yards where the Sally Barber Mine Road (No. 32) turns right toward the bottom of the gulch. Mt. Guyot, lofty and wind-blown, soon appears on the horizon southeast as the road traverses the lower reaches of Humbug Hill and then breaks out below the snow-covered mounds of tailings at 0.7 mile. Proceed on an easy, rolling climb over the roadcut, now a more obvious cut through the pine and spruce. Pass a private cabin and a half-roofed shack right and after 1.5 miles come to the turnoff into Little French Gulch, an alternate ski route when avalanche danger is low.

To continue into French Gulch, follow the roadbed southeast on a very pleasant, rolling run. Soon break out of the thick conifers, curve gradually right, then pass private cabins on both the left and right side of the road and break trail across a long, open park, shown at 2.1 miles on the topo. Be sure to observe any private property restrictions that may occur through this area. Ski in and out of scattered tree clumps for the next several hundred yards and as the roadcut becomes indistinguishable from the open meadows, pick an easy cross-country descent to the open bottom of French Gulch. Bald Mountain, in and out of view throughout the last mile, now shows clearly southeast, a steep, mammoth range, heavily drifted with snow on this north-facing side, and decorated with vivid shadows from the midday sun. On good weather days the flat gulch bottom provides a superb ski route, allowing easy gliding all the way to the bank of trees below French Pass, a 3.1 mile stopping point.

When hot spring days have created a stable snowpack and reduced avalanche potential, a tour can be made into Little French Gulch. Fork left at the 1.5 mile turnoff, climb gradually over an obscure trailcut through blue spruce and fir, and after several hundred yards contour across a steep, open hillside. *Avoid crossing this area if you have doubts about the snow stability.* Instead enter the gulch via a steep climb through trees along the south side of the creekbed. Pass a picturesque log cabin often buried in snow above the roof after 2.4 miles and continue up the gulch to treeline. Ahead the steep side of Mt. Guyot can be seen, crossed with a

74

road to a high mine shack, and behind, Bald Mountain and then the Tenmile Range show on a wide horizon. A tour extension onto the steep, barren mountainside of Mt. Guyot is recommended only for experienced ski mountaineers. For tours up both French Gulch and Little French Gulch, make a return over the ski tracks.

Campfire group

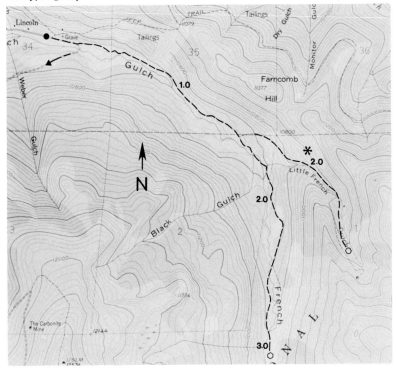

34 BOREAS PASS ROAD

One day trip
Classification: Easiest
Distance: 3.4 miles one way (5.5 KM.)
Skiing time: 2½-3 hours one way
Elevation gain: 510 feet
Maximum elevation: 10,860 feet
Season: December through mid-April
Topographic maps:
    U.S.G.S. Breckenridge, Colo. 1970
    U.S.G.S. Boreas Pass, Colo. 1957
           7.5 minute series
Arapaho National Forest

When the day is sunny, the wind calm and the snow packed, then there is no better tour in the Breckenridge area than the Boreas Pass Road, an excellent choice during the months of March and April. On many winter days, however, high winds and snow blast the unprotected roadbed and provide convincing proof that Boreas, Roman god of the north wind, still lives within the Breckenridge mountains. The route follows the old Denver, South Park and Pacific Railroad bed and hence climbs at a very easy, 2.8 percent grade, gentle enough for uphill glides. From this high vantage on the east side of the Blue River Valley, a stunning panorama of the Tenmile Range unfolds, expanding as the tour contours south. Bakers Tank at mile 3.4 makes a good destination point for an all-day tour, as described in the text, but strong, ambitious skiers can continue above timberline to the top of Boreas Pass at mile 7.1 and then ski the long course downhill toward Como.

Drive on Colo. 9 to the south end of Breckenridge and proceed south to the junction with the Boreas Pass Road, the first main turnoff left (east). Follow the Boreas Pass Road up Illinois Gulch, switchback left and loop right around Barney Ford Hill, then continue to the end of the plowed road, a total of about 3.4 miles from Colo. 9. Park in the small turnaround area or in limited spaces along the side of the road, making sure access is provided to the driveways of the private residences.

Begin gliding over the smooth, snow-filled Boreas Pass roadbed on a curve left. Ski through a small cut, pass a branch road on the right, and continue through several more yards of tall spruce until coming to an unobstructed viewpoint. Sharp and dazzling-white, Peak 10 juts highest into the skyline a few degrees right of west-southwest. The snowy, pointed summit of Crystal Peak appears immediately to the left, and then Pacific Peak comes into view farther left, easily distinguished with its black-ribbed, triangular face. The smooth, flat side of Mt. Helen, half hidden by trees, completes the beautiful vista to the southwest. Follow the wide roadbed across a shallow gully, bend gradually right then left, and after 0.4 mile ski through a large cut at Rocky Point, the first place to become snowbare in spring.

Proceed through a second cut at Rocky Point and immediately break out of the trees to an extraordinary panorama of the entire Tenmile Range. Now Peak 9 and Peak 8, banded by the alpine runs of the Breckenridge Ski Area, can easily be picked out across the valley west. From this middle point the white, wavy range extends for many miles on both sides, south to Quandary Peak and Hoosier Ridge, north all the way to distant peaks in the Gore Range. Also visible from this lookout point, Goose Pasture Tarn, flat and snow-covered, creates a distinct arrowhead shape in the valley below.

Curve southeast to a greater view of Hoosier Ridge and climb along the steep mountainside on a very gradual but steady grade. The Tenmile Range becomes screened by a grove of yellow aspen for several hundred yards as the roadbed passes 1.0 mile. Soon bend left around a slight ridge, then bend left again, heading east toward the vast, barren range of Bald Mountain. After 1.4 miles enter a large, open basin, the site of a bustling mining settlement in the early

1880s called Conger's Camp. Either loop north and west around the basin on the roadbed or drop slightly and climb on a fun shortcut and then proceed into the trees on the east side. From this point the wind-blown summit of Red Peak, streaked with tiny avalanche paths, comes into view on the Hoosier Ridge south.

Ski through a cut of red sandstone, curve right, then break out of the trees and pass beneath the ruins of an old flume on the hill-side left. Pass a tree-filled drainage that leads to Indiana Creek, bend left around the ridge marked "10741" on the topo, and head east again toward Bald Mountain. After winding around the bowl of another drainage, loop northwest around one final ridge and then break into the large meadow where Bakers Tank stands, a good stopping point at 3.4 miles. The 15-foot-high tank was used to store water for steam locomotives of the Denver, South Park and Pacific Railroad. It served from 1882 to 1937 and has now been restored as a permanent memorial, complete with its movable spout. For the easy, fast-gliding return trip, follow the ski tracks back down the road to the parking area.

Boreas Pass Road

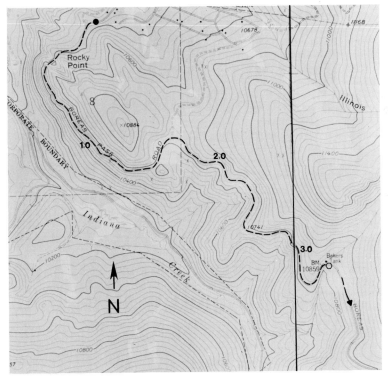

35 THE BURRO TRAIL

One day trip
Classification: Easiest
Distance: 5.2 miles one way (8.4 KM.)
Skiing time: 3-3½ hours one way
Accumulated elevation gain: 435 feet
Accumulated elevation loss: 970 feet
Maximum elevation: 10,600 feet
Season: December through early April
Topographic map:
U.S.G.S. Breckenridge, Colo. 1970
7.5 minute series
Arapaho National Forest

The Burro Trail begins in the Blue River subdivision south of Breckenridge and follows a rolling downhill course north to the Breckenridge Ski Area at Peak 9. Except for a steep schuss or two near Carter Gulch which might be classified "Most difficult," the tour route contains only easy drops and short climbs, varied terrain for some of the best ski touring in the Breckenridge area. Stands of pine and spruce line the route for much of its length and serve as a good windbreak, protecting the tourer on stormy days and keeping the snow soft and skiable. Reportedly, the Burro Trail was often traveled by prospectors and their trains of "jacks" during the mining boom in Breckenridge over 100 years ago.

Drive on Colo. 9 about three miles south of Breckenridge. Pass a sign marking the boundary of the Blue River subdivision and turn right (west) after several more yards onto a dirt road. Follow this road for 1.3 miles as indicated on the map and stop where the unplowed road forks south and the plowed road curves west. Park in the limited spaces along the side of the road here but be careful not to block the driveways to Blue River residences. In spring be prepared for very slick road conditions from the mud and ice.

Begin skiing southwest over the unplowed roadbed, following the tour description for Spruce Creek Road (No. 36). Turn right onto the steep Crystal Creek trail fork to the Burro Trail after 0.9 mile, a turnoff point where the steep rocky ridge east of Pacific Peak first comes into view. Or, for a slightly longer but easier route, stay on the Spruce Creek Road for another 0.2 mile to the junction with the Burro Trail itself, a turnoff which again coincides with a brief view of the rugged ridgetop southwest. Follow the Burro Trail east-northeast on a gradual, winding descent, curve slightly left after 1.5 miles as the hillside drops steeply below the trailcut, and eventually come to the junction with a road which drops steeply right to the tour starting point. This junction, at 2.2 miles, gives views of the distant Williams Fork Mountains near Loveland Pass north-northeast and makes an excellent spot for lunch.

Turn left after the junction, follow the trailcut through a shaded, north-facing hillside of spruce and fir, and soon curve back right on a pleasant, gradual drop. The terrain levels on either side after 2.6 miles and the trail proceeds north from green, full-branched conifers through a grove of gray-barked pine. Continue with long, easy glides beneath this canopy of evergreens, passing occasional glimpses of Buffalo Mountain and the Gore Range north-northwest, Bald Mountain east and after 3.1 miles Peak 8 west-northwest. Drop and climb through a prominent gulch after another hundred yards, bend left on a rolling course to a beautiful view of Peak 10 and Crystal Peak, and soon make a fast schuss to the bottom of Carter Gulch, the 3.5 mile mark.

Re-enter the lodgepole pine on the north side of the gulch, follow the trailcut on a gradual climb north-northwest, then bend left and make another short climb west-southwest. Soon the trail curves right, funnels through a gully of smooth snow, and passes above more willow-covered snowfields in the bottom of Carter Gulch right. Ski around a final ridge at 4.0 miles and double pole onto the wide, snowy bottom of Lehman Gulch, joining the Lower Lehman Ski Run of the Breckenridge Ski Area. Follow this flat, well-packed course for another mile; drop very gradually north to the "A" chairlift and continue to a stopping point at the Peak 9 Ski Area base.

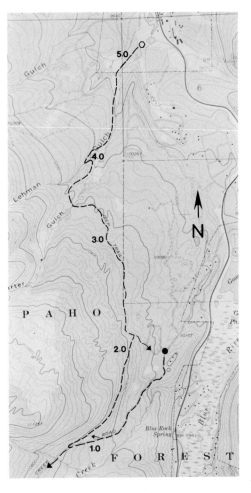

Traveling companions

36 SPRUCE CREEK ROAD

Half-day trip
Classification: More difficult
Distance: 2.2 miles one way (3.5 KM.)
Skiing time: 1½-2 hours one way
Elevation gain: 795 feet
Maximum elevation: 10,960 feet
Season: December through early April
Topographic map:
U.S.G.S. Breckenridge, Colo. 1970
7.5 minute series
Arapaho National Forest

For beginning ski tourers who pale at the mere sight of a slight drop, who understand well the theory behind the snowplow but are baffled by its actual practice, a tour over the wide Spruce Creek Road provides the perfect remedy. On the return trip the route descends from one rolling drop to another where speed can easily be contained, a terrain feature which helps build confidence in a tourer's ability to handle downhill. Advanced skiers can easily extend the tour route as described by either skiing farther southwest to the Colorado Mountain Club cabin below Mohawk Falls or contouring back north to the Crystal Lake drainage.

Drive on Colo. 9 about three miles south of Breckenridge. Pass a sign marking the boundary of the Blue River subdivision and after several more yards turn right (west) onto a dirt road. Follow this road for 1.3 miles as indicated on the map photo for The Burro Trail (No. 35) and stop where the unplowed road forks south and the plowed road curves west. Park in the limited spaces along the side of the road here but be careful not to block the driveways to Blue River residences. The Summit County highway department may soon begin plowing the road farther south to a parking area for ski tourers. In spring be prepared for very slick road conditions from the mud and ice.

Glide southwest on a very pleasant, near-level grade over the unplowed roadbed. Pass branch roads to the right then left, ski for several yards through a cut with snowy banks, then curve right and continue the easy, winding climb through the mixed coni-

fer forest. With each occasional opening in the trees through this first section, Pacific Peak sends flashes of sunlight from the horizon west-southwest, appearing like the massive, pointed tip of an iceberg. The rocky face of the ridge east of Pacific Peak, purple with shadows from the midday sun, comes into view after the curve right, and beyond the ridgetop, Quandary Peak, fourteenth highest in the state, makes a slow arc across the skyline.

Except for brief glimpses of the open, rolling face of Bald Mountain east, all vistas are soon blocked by aspen and pine as the snow-filled roadbed continues on a gradual climb above the Spruce Creek drainage. Curve right after 0.6 mile, then curve right again in another hundred yards, bearing toward the white, flat face of Mount Helen. Soon begin a slightly steeper climb on the road, bringing the rugged amphitheater wall below Pacific Peak into view for the first time on the tour. Pass a switchback right at 1.1 miles, the turnoff to The Burro Trail. Glide across a short fill area where the hillside drops slightly on both sides and proceed on a steady climb, angling a few degrees right. Through the trees other landmarks soon show on the horizon from this section, including the barren summit of Red Peak west-southwest and higher still, the long, wavy range of Hoosier Ridge.

Glide through a short, very gradual drop after 1.4 miles, then bear southwest toward the snowy mound on the ridge southeast of the Mohawk Lakes, and continue the easy climb into more open terrain. Pass a junction near mile 2.0 with the wide aqueduct road, a good alternate route which contours north into the Crystal Creek drainage. Maintain elevation on a contour as the roadbed becomes difficult to discern and after another 200 yards come to a flat, open area which makes a scenic lunch spot and good turning back point. In view ahead is the rounded, snowy mound and spectacular ridge wall which extends east from Crystal Peak. The tip of 13,951-foot Fletcher Mountain, part of the Mayflower Gulch amphitheater, shows through the trees at the far west end of the ridge. For the return trip, glide back down the wide Spruce Creek roadbed, controlling speed if necessary by skiing the deeper snow on the sides of the road. With fast, packed snow in spring, a snowplow or pole drag might be necessary.

Spring tour with the kids

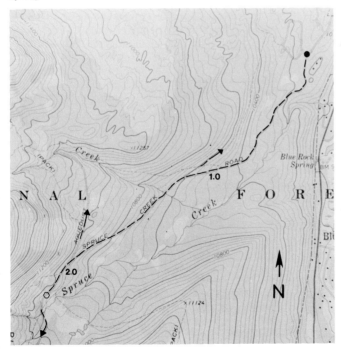

37 PENNSYLVANIA CREEK

One day trip
Classification: More difficult
Distance: 4.0 miles one way (6.4 KM.)
Skiing time: 3-3½ hours one way
Elevation gain: 1,340 feet
Maximum elevation: 11,640 feet
Season: December through mid-April
Topographic maps:
  U.S.G.S. Breckenridge, Colo. 1970
  U.S.G.S. Boreas Pass, Colo. 1957
          7.5 minute series
Arapaho National Forest

Once past the steep climbs in the first half-mile, the tour up the Pennsylvania Creek valley settles into an easy-gliding, very gradual climb, slowly but steadily gaining elevation to a high lookout into Horseshoe Basin at the valley's end. Here in this wintry Arctic-Alpine Life Zone the evergreens become stunted and scraggly and the surrounding valley walls, wind-packed with snow, appear very cold, almost hostile to life. The feeling of desolation is reinforced on the climb to the lookout point as Summit 12,331, empty and wind-scoured, rises like a huge moon above the forested range east. This interesting destination point is reached after a fairly slow, 4.0 mile trek, often requiring a full day of trail breaking with the deep snow in winter. In spring, however, the hard crust on the snow permits long, effortless glides and makes the tour much easier. Occasional snowmobile convoys also tour the valley on weekends and pack the snow into hard trails, creating a faster track for the tourer on the return trip.

Drive south from Breckenridge on Colo. 9 to the turnoff into Blue River Estates, marked by a sign. Turn left (east), proceed straight past two roads that branch right, then take the third main right and continue up and over a hill on a bend left. Turn sharply right at the next branch road, bend left across Pennsylvania Creek, make a steep right turn after 0.2 mile and continue to limited parking places near the end of the plowed road, a total distance of 1.1 miles from Colo. 9. Be especially careful not to block the driveways to the private houses.

From a 10,300-foot elevation mark on the side of Mount Argentine, the starting point provides a splendid view west across the Blue River Valley. The massive dome of Mount Helen rises in the foreground, covered with smooth snowfields on the right side and rocky outcroppings on the left. Farther north the deep Crystal Creek valley divides the range and leads to an amphitheater beneath Crystal Peak, south of the sharp, snowy summit of Peak 10. Climb over the snowbank at the turn-around area and begin skiing on a very steep grade up the roadbed, the most difficult part of the tour. Skinny, black-trunked pine soon screen the vista west as the road switchbacks left, passes a steep cut through the trees, and then switchbacks right where another road, unmarked on the topo, extends down the mountainside left.

Follow the road east-southeast on a rolling, sometimes fairly steep climb. Continue into more scattered pine, begin an easy, re-freshing drop near 0.5 mile, and in another few yards break into a small meadow. The open snowfields soon expand toward the creekbed below and bring a panorama of mountains into view. Old posts near a mine site mark the northern reaches of Red Mountain on the horizon south and a mountaintop, covered conspicuously with tall, black snags and marked as 11,307 feet on the topo, shows southeast. Behind, the rocky, shadowed north side of Quandary Peak is added to the beautiful vista of the Tenmile Range.

Pass through a shallow gully near 1.1 miles, drop right to the valley bottom as the roadbed becomes hard to find, and continue on an easy climb southeast over the snow-fields. Curve gradually right into a narrower valley after 2.0 miles and eventually pass below another hillside of dead trees left. With the view of the Tenmile Range soon sealed off by the contour of the hillside, the ski route becomes lonely and isolated, continuing south toward the sheer face of Red Peak for the final mile. Curve right as the conifers give way to open snowfields and climb to a small shelf in the middle of Horseshoe Basin, at 4.0 miles, a good destination point for the tour. With this climb the 12,331-foot summit on Hoosier Ridge rises into view over the forested range east and appears as rounded and barren as a huge moon. For the return trip, follow the valley bottom to the roadbed and continue over the ski tracks to the parking area.

Timber run

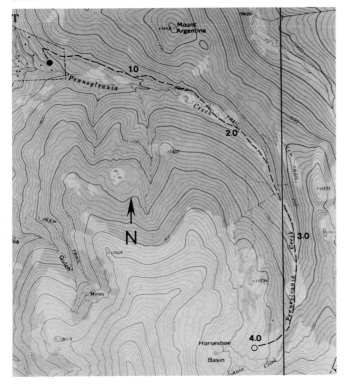

38 McCULLOUGH GULCH

Half-day trip
Classification: More difficult
Distance: 1.5 miles one way (2.4 KM.)
Skiing time: 1-1½ hours one way
Elevation gain: 520 feet
Maximum elevation: 10,820 feet
Season: December through early April
Topographic map:
   U.S.G.S. Breckenridge, Colo. 1970
       7.5 minute series
Arapaho National Forest

The wide basin of McCullough Gulch separates Pacific Peak and its eastern ridge from the massive dome of Quandary Peak, spreading like a fan at its upper, western end. There the gulch contains many alpine tarns, created during the last of two glacial periods that marked much of the entire Blue River Valley area. Although those snow-covered lakebeds make intriguing destination points for tours, they lie above timberline within the Arctic-Alpine Life Zone, a region of wind-scoured snow, white-outs, and possible avalanche. An extended trip into the treeless "high country," most possible in spring, requires extensive ski mountaineering skills and proper equipment.

The sub-alpine forests near the mouth of the gulch offer much more congenial touring conditions in winter than do the snowfields above timberline. The special delight of this tour route, as described in the text, is the spectacular view of Quandary Peak, a 14,265-foot Colorado Fourteener, fourteenth highest in the state. Formed from ancient Pre-cambrian granite, the peak was named by early miners who were "in a quandary" to identify some unusual rocks found near its summit. In spring the broad, east-facing ridge of Quandary provides a ski route for advanced ski mountaineers who attempt a climb to the top of the peak.

Drive on Colo. 9 several miles south of Breckenridge to the entrance of McCullough Gulch, directly across the highway from the Shangri-la Inn. Either park along the side of the highway or park in the Shangri-la Inn parking lot after first securing permission from the manager.

Begin on the west side of the highway near a sign reading "McCullough Gulch." Ski past a storage rain gauge and glide northwest on a rolling run across the meadow, heading toward the low point of the gulch. Soon enter scattered conifers and willows and continue on a northerly bearing until intersecting the McCullough Gulch Trail. Then turn left through more willows and follow the trail past a blazed tree which marks the Arapaho National Forest boundary. In several more yards the snow-filled trailcut begins a steady climb above the creekbed left, a more difficult section if snowmobiles have worn washboard ruts into the snow. Then the trail curves left, climbs gradually to the right of a small ridge, and near the 0.5 mile mark bends right and proceeds on another short, steady climb.

First only a slice of Quandary Peak, steep and rocky, shows down the tree-lined trailcut west, and then the entire mountainside comes into view as the trail breaks onto an open hillside. Glide easily over a near-level section through scattered conifers, cross another small snowfield, and after 0.7 mile maintain elevation on a right trail fork where a left fork drops toward the creekbed. Pass a small cabin in another hundred yards, nestled just inside a small band of conifers right, and then continue the easy contour west through more scattered tree clumps, some higher on the hillside with tall snags from a fire. Soon the gulch bottom flattens and makes good terrain for a cross-country course all the way to the timberline McCullough Gulch Lakes.

For a closer stopping point, climb through the rolling snowfields as far as the Blue River Diversion Road at mile 1.5. From this point the snowy summit of Red Mountain with its deep, west-facing drainage and the high wind-blown mountains in Hoosier Ridge show well through the gulch mouth east-southeast. And the rock-strewn side of Quandary Peak, the most captivating part of the vista, looms into the sky across the gulch southwest, sometimes casting colors of browns, maroons, rusts, and grays with the backlit sun, sometimes frosted with new snow and impassively cold. For the return trip, either follow the ski tracks back along the trail or drop through the dips and rolls along the creekbed and then contour back to the trail when trees begin to block passage in the gulch. Control speed carefully through the steady, often fast drop to the gulch bottom.

Water fill up

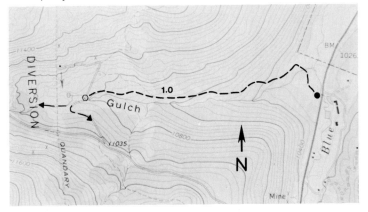

39 MAYFLOWER GULCH

One day trip
Classification: Easiest
Distance: 2.6 miles one way (4.2 KM.)
Skiing time: 2-2½ hours one way
Elevation gain: 1,000 feet
Maximum elevation: 11,540 feet
Season: December through mid-April
Topographic map:
    U.S.G.S. Copper Mountain, Colo. 1970
        7.5 minute series
Arapaho National Forest

The stunning beauty of the Mayflower Gulch amphitheater, often featured in magazine and newspaper articles, attracts more and more viewers each winter. The tour route first crosses the private land of the Climax Molybdenum Company via a public access route provided as a courtesy by the Company. Large groups which plan to tour the area are requested to inform the Company's Public Relations Department, Climax, Colo. 80429 of their plans. The cabins of the old Boston Mining Camp are a good stopping point. Be extremely careful of the corniced Gold Hill ridge and other potential avalanche areas beyond.

Drive on I. 70 to the Wheeler Junction interchange near the Copper Mountain Ski Area. Proceed south onto Colo. 91 and continue another 5.3 miles to the entrance of Mayflower Gulch, marked by a sign on the east side of the highway. Park beside Colo. 91, avoiding any possible hazard areas from the mining operations of the Climax Molybdenum Company. (Colo. 91 will be relocated in 1976 and 1977).

Begin skiing up the open snowfield on the south side of Mayflower Gulch, cross under a power line and immediately bend right onto a snowy roadcut. Follow this road on a short, steady climb into the pine and spruce forest and after the road levels, bend back left on a gradual traverse across the mountainside. Soon intercept a wide, rolling cut on the hillside, unmarked on the topo; pass a sign in the trees right reading "Public Access Road/Climax Molybdenum Company," and climb steadily up the cut for about 100 yards to another branch road. With each opening in the trees through this first 0.8 mile the view extends north to the two wind-blown summits of Tucker Mountain, its steep face divided by Tucker Gulch and banded by several old mining roads.

Ski south-southeast over the designated public access road for several hundred yards, contouring on a gradual climb toward the open drainageway of Mayflower Gulch. After an easy-gliding downhill run near 1.0 mile, enter the open west side of the gulch where the large Mayflower amphitheater comes into view for the first time, a magnificent, spine-tingling sight. A rounded ridgetop west of the 13,841-foot peak shapes the left side of the amphitheater from this viewpoint, and then the sheer, rock-ribbed wall drops right into a slight saddle, a point where several rock spires protrude into the air. The pointed peaktop of Fletcher Mountain, only 49 feet short of qualifying as a Colorado Fourteener, sits squarely in the middle of the vast bowl and a third high peaktop, unnamed and unmeasured but equally impressive, balances the vista on the right side.

Stay near treeline on the southwest side of the valley and ski cross-country on an even, gradual climb over the snowfields, a course which keeps the rock amphitheater in view most of the time. After 1.3 miles the summit of the 13,841-foot peak breaks into view over the wind-blown range south-southeast, and then the sharp Pacific peaktop begins to show above the Mayflower Hill ridge due east. Ski in and out of a scattering of trees, curve slightly right with the contour of the hillside, and eventually break trail across a slight shelf that parallels the lower cut of the creekbed. As the ski route proceeds beyond 2.0 miles, the massive, pyramid-shaped Pacific Peak dominates the panorama east, seen clearly through the large cirque which surrounds the Pacific Creek drainage.

Continue the gradual, cross-country climb to a stopping point at the cabins of the old Boston Mining Camp, in view at the end of the valley during the last half of the tour. The ruins of a large lodge mark the lower end of the camp, a crumbling structure with walls twelve logs high, now roofless and filled with snow. Farther beyond this lodge ruin are three picturesque log cabins, identical in design and built one above the other on the hillside. The metal-roofed cabin at the far end has been carefully restored by members of the Mayflower Mountain Club and contains a woodburning cookstove, a picnic table, a toilet, sleeping area for about eight people, and various camping supplies. Reservations for overnight use of the cabin and donations toward maintenance can be made by writing Mayflower Mountain Club, P.O. Box 535, Climax, Colo. 80429. A donation of at least $2 per person on weeknights and $3 per person on Saturday nights is requested upon receipt of the reservation confirmation. Please protect the cabin and pack out trash.

Spring nap at Mayflower Gulch cabins

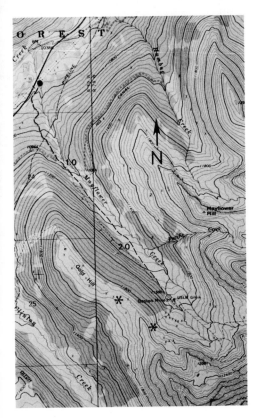

40 WHEELER LAKES

One day trip
Classification: Most difficult
Distance: 2.8 miles one way (4.5 KM.)
Skiing time: 2½-3 hours one way
Elevation gain: 1,320 feet
Maximum elevation: 11,080 feet
Season: Early December through early April
Topographic map:
  U.S.G.S. Vail Pass, Colo. 1970
      7.5 minute series
Arapaho National Forest

Oromaniacs who love to climb will love the cross-country trek to the Wheeler Lakes, a lofty, near-timberline destination point. The route climbs at a heart-pounding 12 percent grade for the first 1.7 miles, then finally settles into easy, rolling climbs of under 5 percent for the remaining 1.1 miles. And what goes up with switchbacks and herringbone, often comes down with a wide-tracked, lightning-fast downhill plummet. With midwinter powder snow the steep descent invites sweeping downhill runs, good terrain for the telemark and christy turns. In early spring, however, the open, south-facing snowfields begin to form a heavy, often breakable crust which creates even more challenge for the return trip. Although the route follows roughly a summer hiking trail, soon to be abandoned by the Forest Service, few trail markers are evident and a topo map is needed for orienteering.

Drive on I. 70 or Colo. 91 to the Copper Mountain Ski Area turnoff south of Wheeler Junction. Proceed on the Ski Area road to the parking lots and park as directed by the attendant. This parking privilege is a courtesy of the Copper Mountain Ski Area.

Pack skis north across the Copper Mountain complex to U.S. 6/I. 70 and cross very carefully over the highway at the point where the opposite hillside is the most gentle. A "chain station" shack on U.S. 6 and a Forest Service sign reading "Arapaho National Forest Trail/Wheeler Lakes" now mark this starting point but both will change with construction of I. 70. Stay to the left of a small gulch near the start and climb cross-country up to the open hillside with four or five long switchbacks. Look for a blazed tree along the west side of the hillside after about 0.5 mile and 200 feet elevation gain. Continue west-northwest past this marker, climb steadily through the open conifers, and after another 200 yards come to the edge of a deep, aspen-filled ravine. Here the trail turns right, climbs through aspen for several yards, then switchbacks left to a crossing with the ravine near the 0.7 mile mark.

Follow the blazes along the left side of the ravine; ski in and out of several clumps of red-barked spruce and maintain the steady climb northwest, using herringbone or short switchbacks to gain elevation through the steep spots. Several times during this climb the view opens toward the Copper Mountain Ski Area, covered with dipping, swaying dots of alpine skiers, and also toward the rugged, avalanche-streaked Tenmile Range, interesting places to peruse while waiting to catch your breath. After 1.5 miles the ski route proceeds along a small ridge between two branches of the drainage and soon reaches an open saddle, the low point between Wheeler Lakes and the mountain directly south. This flat snowfield, itself a satisfying tour destination point, provides an expansive view of the terrain west and south, including the Black Lakes ridge above Vail Pass, the deep, serpentine Stafford Creek valley, and steep-faced Jacque Peak, highest point along the skyline.

Ski to the right of the saddle area, follow blazes through a bend right, then left, and continue the very gradual climb along a conspicuous, spruce-lined trailcut. Break trail west-northwest across another large snowfield, contour along the hillside on a gradual curve right and after 2.4 miles come to a half-buried sign which reads "Wheeler Lakes ½." Head north from this sign, leaving the North Tenmile Creek summer trail; pass by several more blazed trees, then glide across the open snowfield for several hundred yards to the southern end of South Wheeler Lake. Continue across the flat, snow-covered lakebed and climb a small rise at the north end, a final stopping point for the tour which looks down into the rolling Officers Gulch valley. Return through the snowfields near the ski tracks on a thrilling downhill run and use long traverses through the open conifers for the steep final mile.

Snow burial

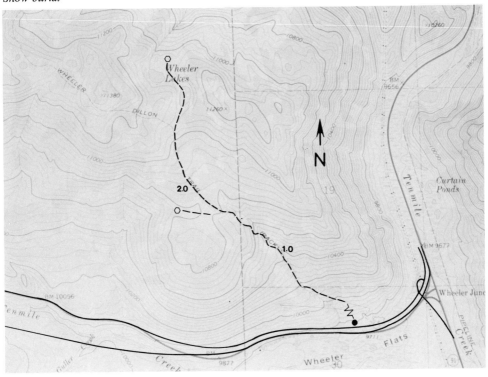

41 GULLER CREEK LOOP

One day trip
Classification: More difficult
Distance: 5.8 miles *round trip* (9.3 KM.)
Skiing time: 2½-3 hours *round trip*
Elevation gain: 1,000 feet
Maximum elevation: 10,720 feet
Season: December through early April
Topographic maps:
U.S.G.S. Vail Pass, Colo. 1970
U.S.G.S. Copper Mountain, Colo. 1970
7.5 minute series
Arapaho National Forest

For the rare skier who has mastered the skills of both nordic and alpine skiing, the Guller Creek loop makes the perfect tour, a route which combines the best of both ski worlds. The tour begins at the base of the Copper Mountain Ski Area amid the flash and fanfare of alpine skiers and then travels west to the snow-filled Guller Creek gulch, a quiet and scenic pathway that proceeds for many miles toward the Elk Ridge mountains. Halfway up the gulch the loop route turns east and contours back to the ski area, ending with a fast run down the alpine slopes. The completion of the I. 70 highway and possible construction of a new ski lift near Union Gulch will change the trailhead and tour route slightly in the coming years. For further information, contact the Ski Touring Director, Copper Mountain Ski Area, P.O. Box 397, Frisco, Colo. 80443.

Drive on I. 70 or Colo. 91 to the Copper Mountain Ski Area turnoff south of Wheeler Junction. Proceed on the ski area road to the westernmost parking lot or park as directed by the attendant. This parking privilege is a courtesy of the Copper Mountain Ski Area.

Proceed to the ski touring trailhead west of The Center complex at the Copper Mountain Ski Area, ski west into a stand of huge, red-barked pine, and immediately pass a sign which identifies the "A," "B," and "C" trail loops. These three ski-packed tour routes all begin with several hundred yards of easy, rolling gliding along the west Tenmile Creek valley, this section a very pleasant warm-up before the slower-paced climb into Guller Creek. Follow the markers left onto the "A & B" trail where the "C" trail forks right, ski past the mouth of Union Gulch, and soon bend left up the mountainside on a short, steady climb. Continue through several more winding climbs and near 1.5 miles contour

onto the open side of a small ridge, a nice spot to rest and to view the expansive West Tenmile Creek valley.

The view extends farther east to the stark, white avalanche paths along the Tenmile Range as the trail drops in and out of a shallow gulch and then proceeds across the open mountainside on a westerly traverse. As soon as the white banks of Guller Creek show ahead, begin a snowplow descent to the treeless drainage bottom, a steep, breathtaking schuss especially when the snow is fast. Turn up the gulch at 2.1 miles where the "C" loop, marked by a sign, drops back to the Tenmile Creek valley. Glide easily on a cross-country course up the gulch bottom, climbing very gradually and bearing for the bald, blunt top of Jacque Ridge on the horizon. After 2.8 miles the ski route passes under an open, rolling hillside right, then soon enters the site of an old sawmill, in spring marked only by the bottom logs of the mill building. Here the loop tour route turns left up the hillside.

The tour can easily be extended up the Guller Creek drainage for another 3.0 miles one way as shown on the map photo. Easiest and most enjoyable in March and April after the snow has formed an unbreakable crust, this route climbs gradually but steadily southwest up the gulch bottom and passes interesting half-buried cabin ruins at the 4.0 and 5.1 mile marks. Throughout these last two miles Peaks 4, 5, and 6 of the Tenmile Range form a scenic backdrop northeast, a stunning vista of avalanche paths and snow-capped summits that you ski toward during the long, continuous return coast. Be sure to stay high in the trees on the north side of the gulch when crossing the Jacque Ridge avalanche run-out at 4.2 miles.

To continue the loop tour, climb steadily east and northeast up the open hillside from the sawmill site and follow the trail markers on a gradual, 1.0 mile contour to the ski runs of Copper Mountain. Break out of the trees near the bottom of the "I" chairlift, drop northeast through the last unpacked snowfield to the Woodwinds Trail, and for the easiest descent, follow the Woodwinds, Scooter, and Loverly Trails to the bottom of the mountain. Or for a more challenging descent, climb from the bottom of "I" lift to the top of "G" lift via the Miner Matter trail and ski down the steeper "G" lift runs. With the smooth, packed snow these alpine slopes create very fast skiing conditions for the tourer and require concentration on edge control and unweighting for the turns. The easier slopes can be negotiated with snow-plow turns and also provide an excellent place for stem christies, parallel christies, and wedel turns, better terrain usually than the unpacked hillsides.

First lesson

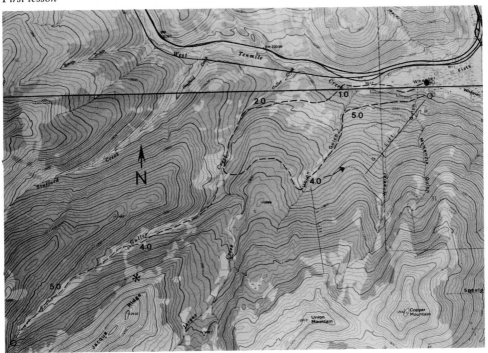

42 STAFFORD CREEK

One day trip
Classification: Easiest
Distance: 6.0 miles one way (9.7 KM.)
Skiing time: 3½-4½ hours one way
Elevation gain: 1,440 feet
Maximum elevation: 11,160 feet
Season: December through early April
Topographic maps:
U.S.G.S. Vail Pass, Colo. 1970
U.S.G.S. Copper Mountain, Colo. 1970
7.5 minute series
Arapaho National Forest

A smooth, wide highway of snow completely covers the bottom of the Stafford Creek valley by early December and provides an excellent ski tour route, free from any major orienteering or avalanche problems. The warm weather in spring improves this route even more by melting the top layers of snow into an unbreakable crust, a condition which facilitates long, effortless glides and greatly reduces the skiing time for the tour. With the construction of the new I. 70 highway, the access route to Stafford Creek along the West Tenmile Creek valley will change, either paralleling higher on the hillside south or following the proposed bicycle path. See the map photo for the I. 70 route.

Drive on I. 70 to Colo. 91 to the Copper Mountain Ski Area turnoff south of Wheeler Junction. Proceed on the ski area road to the westernmost parking lot or park as directed by the attendants. This parking privilege is a courtesy of the Copper Mountain Ski Area.

Ski into the trees on the west side of the Copper Mountain base area and immediately pass a trailhead sign which designates the "A," "B," and "C" trail loops. Follow the "C" trail west to the West Tenmile Creek valley and glide easily over the rolling snowfields near the creekbed, a course used in part for the Copper Classic Citizens Race. Pass a shallow, tree-filled drainage left after 0.8 mile, the rather obscure entrance to Union Gulch, and continue west-northwest with long, easy glides along the West Tenmile Creek. Near 1.5 miles the Stafford Creek route proceeds straight where the "C" trail loops left into the Guller Creek valley. Then after another mile of easy gliding, the ski route turns left and heads into the wide, conspicuous valley of Stafford Creek.

Begin climbing south-southwest on a very easy grade up the open valley bottom, bearing toward the corniced, wind-blown heights of Elk Ridge on the skyline ahead. The view behind for most of this third and fourth mile is channeled toward Peak 1 only in the Tenmile Range, a steep, rocky summit over four miles away. Pass the scattered snags and stumps of an old burn on the hillside left, cross to the left side of the creekbed as the hillside becomes steeper right, and wind through a short section of scattered spruce which spill into the valley bottom. Begin curving to a westerly bearing after 4.0 miles, ski through another grove of spruce that closes in from both sides, and soon break out below a sparsely-covered hillside right. Like so much of this Copper Mountain and Vail Pass area, pitch stumps and fire-blackened snags also mark this hillside, scars that remain from the logging activity in the early 1900s.

Head southwest toward a conspicuous tree-filled drainageway after 5.0 miles and maintain the gradual climb for another mile, eventually intersecting a thick wall of trees that cross the bottom of the valley. This area provides shelter for a lunch stop or an overnight camp and marks a final end to the Stafford Creek tour route. The terrain steepens considerably beyond this last band of trees and the possibility of avalanche exists above timberline near the steep side of Elk Ridge, conditions that discourage an extension of the tour. For the return trip, follow the tracks back down the valley on an easy, rolling descent. With the fast, unbreakable snow crust in spring, an eye-watering, leg-shaking trip down the entire Stafford Creek valley can take as little as 20 minutes, an average speed of over ten miles per hour.

Spring sunbathing

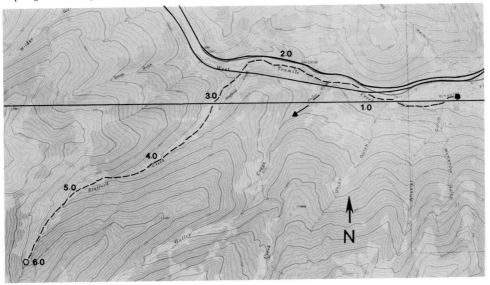

43 CORRAL CREEK

Half-day trip
Classification: More difficult
Distance: 1.8 miles one way (2.9 KM.)
Skiing time: 1-1½ hours one way
Elevation gain: 680 feet
Maximum elevation: 11,280 feet
Season: Mid-November through mid-April
Topographic map:
U.S.G.S. Vail Pass, Colo. 1970
7.5 minute series
Arapaho National Forest

The Corral Creek valley on the east side of Vail Pass has become a favorite touring area with tour guides and ski instructors as well as the ski touring public for two main reasons. First, the valley offers excellent tour opportunities for both snowy and sunny days: a sheltered logging road above the west side of Corral Creek, an open route along the snowy creek bottom, a high scenic climb and exciting drop through the scattered tree clumps beneath Uneva Peak. Second, the valley has been closed to snowmobiles by the Forest Service, blessfully confining the noise and smell of the internal combustion engine to U.S. 6/I. 70.

With construction of the new I. 70 highway, the old trailhead south of Vail Pass will be closed and the ski route will begin from the top of Vail Pass. A new road to mining claims, shown on the map photo, is scheduled for construction along with I. 70 and should make a good access route into the Corral Creek valley. The Forest Service now provides trail markers for the access route and will continue to mark the trail after I. 70 construction. For the most current information on the tour route, contact the Holy Cross Ranger District, P.O. Box 0, Minturn, Colo. 81645.

Proceed on the new I. 70 highway to the top of Vail Pass and park in the Rest Area parking lot on the west side. Until construction of I. 70 is completed, the old parking area and trailhead on U.S. 6 may be used. Drive on U.S. 6 to the east side of Vail Pass, continuing 1.2 miles from the top, 4.1 miles west of Wheeler Junction. Park along the side of the road.

For the entrance to Corral Creek from the top of Vail Pass, pack skis to the east side of I. 70 and begin skiing away from the highway interchange on a newly constructed roadbed, a route with an even grade that eventually loops south and east to private mining claims. Climb northwest on a gradual traverse to the open ridgetop, at 0.5 mile, and leave the mining road for tour routes with more variety. Either follow a cross-country route north toward the Uneva Peak mountainside or turn south and begin an exhilarating, rolling drop over the old logging road west of Corral Creek. On a clear day the vista from the ridgetop here encompasses a beautiful array of mountain peaks. Most spectacular are the sharp summits in the Tenmile Range, including Crystal and Pacific Peaks on the distant horizon southeast. In view north-northwest is the ragged, glacial-carved spine of the Gore Range, a cluster of unnamed peaks within the Eagle Nest Primitive Area.

The tour route along the ridgetop north climbs gradually over a 10,810-foot high point and then drops through the open snowfields to a shallow saddle. Contour next to the Corral Creek drainage after 1.3 miles and continue north and northwest through the scattered clumps of spruce. *Do not ski above timberline toward the summit of Uneva Peak unless the snow pack is very stable.* Although this south-facing hillside often has wind-packed or sun-crusted snow, the return trip carries enough elevation drop to make memorable skiing under all conditions, excellent terrain for the telemark turn. The tour can be continued with a long, gentle drop to the old sheep camp at the bottom of the valley, then ended with an uphill loop back to the summit above Vail Pass, an extension which doubles the tour length.

The old logging road above the west side of Corral Creek provides a sheltered tour route, a good choice on days when the weather is less than perfect. From the ridgetop above Vail Pass turn south and contour on a gentle cross-country drop until intercepting the snowy cut. Coast on the logging road past a hillside of pitch stumps and continue the easy descent into more and more conifers. After several more rolling drops, break out into a large meadow at the south end of the valley, just around the bend from the old U.S. 6 roadbed. Here the weathered posts and poles and the rough-wood shack of the old sheep camp sometimes show above the snowdrifts, the corral for which Corral Creek is named. End the tour with a leisurely climb to the top of Vail Pass.

Ski touring class

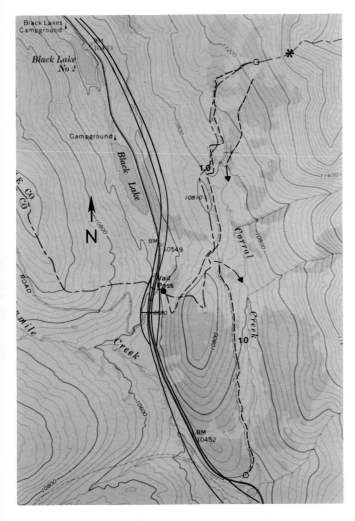

44 WILDER GULCH AND WEARYMAN CREEK

One day trip
Classification: Most difficult
Distance: 10.9 miles one way (17.5 KM.)
Skiing time: 4-5 hours one way
Accumulated elevation gain: **680 feet**
Accumulated elevation loss: **2,620 feet**
Maximum elevation: 11,280 feet
Season: Mid-November through mid-April
Topographic maps:
    U.S.G.S. Vail Pass, Colo. 1970
    U.S.G.S. Red Cliff, Colo. 1970
          7.5 minute series
Arapaho and White River National Forests

Like the well-traveled Shrine Pass Road tour (No. 46), the ski route along Wilder Gulch and Wearyman Creek begins at Vail Pass and ends in the mountain village of Redcliff near U.S. 24. This route is shorter and faster but more difficult, requiring a knowledge of map and compass for orienteering over the saddle crossing and secure downhill technique for the steep drops into the Wearyman Creek valley. An out-and-return trip up either Wilder Gulch or Wearyman Creek make excellent, "easiest" tours in themselves and eliminate the need for a pick-up car. If snow conditions are stable, the Wilder Gulch tour can be continued to the top of Ptarmigan Pass for a spectacular overlook of the Resolution Creek valley. This route also is the first leg in a very advanced, extended trip from Vail Pass to Aspen.

Drive on U.S. 6 to the top of Vail Pass and park in the large plowed area on the west side of the highway. After the new I. 70 highway has been constructed over Vail Pass, park in the Rest Area parking lot (see map photo). Arrange for a pick-up car in Redcliff.

Ski southwest over the snowy Shrine Pass Road for about a hundred yards and then contour cross-country to the West Tenmile Creek basin where the road switchbacks north. Climb gradually through the scattered clumps of conifers on the east-facing hillside, break trail south across a slight shelf and after 0.9 mile curve right on an easy drop to the bottom of Wilder Gulch. On a powder-snow day a steeper line on this descent creates just the right momentum for exhilarating telemark and christy turns. Proceed southwest on an easy climb up Wilder Gulch, paralleling a telephone line on the hillside right. Pass several wireless posts of another line near the creekbed, ski under more and more conifers on the hillside right, and then begin to wind past trees in the gulch bottom near 2.5 miles.

Begin a short, noticeably steeper climb up the gulch bottom, break out of the trees after 2.9 miles and glide across a flat, open meadow, marked as "11084" on the topo and an important point for orientation. For a tour toward Ptarmigan Pass, ski southwest along an old telephone line cut on a gradual then steep climb and soon break out of the thick spruce to a view of snowy, rounded Ptarmigan Hill and a sheer, corniced ridge left. *Do not continue up the open snowfield unless the snow pack is extremely stable.* Ptarmigan Pass itself, well into the Arctic-Alpine Life Zone at 11,765 feet, provides a broad survey of mountain ranges in all directions. Most spectacular are the jagged, blue Gore peaks in the Eagles Nest Primitive Area north-northwest.

For the tour into the Wearyman Creek valley, cross the meadow at the 2.9 mile mark, curve right into dense spruce and fir, and hold a westerly traverse on a fairly steep then gradual climb. Cross over the flat saddle to the right of a power line, stay in the low point of the drainage, then begin a gradual drop northwest and intercept a large meadow after 3.5 miles. If snow pack is stable, contour west across the open, steep hillside beyond 4.0 miles. After periods of wind and snow or with wet slide conditions in spring however, turn south and switchback to a safer course along Wearyman Creek. A narrow roadcut on the south side of the creekbed provides easy access through the conifers for a half-mile. And after 5.3 miles there are two route possibilities: a sheltered, sometimes obscure roadcut on the south valley side, unmarked on the topo, or a cross-country course over open snowfields north of the creek.

Soon pass under aspen-covered hillsides to the north, some showing sedimentary rock strata of the Minturn Formation. Cross an open hillside after 7.2 miles, then drop near the creekbed and cross into the trees on the south side. With long glides and easy, coasting runs follow the roadbed through three more creek crossings and join the Shrine Pass Road at the 8.3 mile mark. This wide, ski-packed road maintains a steady drop from the Wearyman Creek junction, passes under several more interesting outcroppings of sandstone, then becomes a near-level grade and crosses under a power line. Ski by the deep Lime Creek drainage north after 8.9 miles and come to a large, green water tank in Turkey Creek after another mile, marked "WT" on the topo and usually the junction with the plowed road. During midwinter months the final mile to Redcliff is often skiable but from mid-March on, the roadbed is usually snowbare, sometimes muddy.

Linked Christies

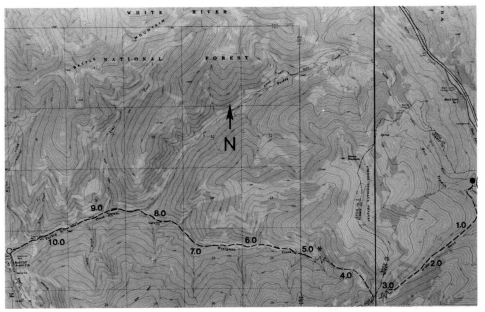

97

45 SHRINE BOWL

One day trip
Classification: More difficult
Distance: 6.3 miles *round trip* **(10.1 KM.)**
Skiing time: 3½-4 hours *round trip*
Elevation gain: 930 feet
Maximum elevation: 11,530 feet
Season: Mild-November through late April
Topographic maps:
  U.S.G.S. Vail Pass, Colo. 1970
  U.S.G.S. Red Cliff, Colo. 1970
      7.5 minute series
Arapaho National Forest

With the panoramic view of the Tenmile and Gore Ranges and the superb downhill return run, the loop around Shrine Pass Bowl rates as one of the finest ski tours in northern Colorado. Powder snow often fills the bowl, staying light and fluffy at the high 11,500-foot elevation, especially during the mid-winter months. With a steady 9.6 grade through the fall line, the descent down the south fork of West Tenmile Creek is easily managed, giving opportunity for either the fancy stem and parallel christy turns or merely the wide-tracked, locked-leg downhill plunge.

Drive on U.S. 6 to the top of Vail Pass and park in the large plowed area on the west side of the highway. After the new I. 70 highway has been constructed over Vail Pass, park in the Rest Area parking lot (see map photo).

Begin skiing southwest on an easy climb toward the snow-covered Shrine Pass Road, contouring 20 yards above the northerly branch of West Tenmile Creek. Ahead the view extends for many miles and encompasses a splendid panorama of white, alpine peaks. Closer and most impressive, a long, treeless wall and high summit identify Jacque Ridge and Jacque Peak, named after a Captain J. A. Jacque, silver miner in the 1880s. Farther beyond and left, the dome-shaped ridge of 14,265-foot Quandary Peak rises into the skyline, visible through the saddle of Union and Copper Mountains. Continuing left, the sharp Pacific Peak, Crystal Peak with its north-facing snowfield, then Peaks 10 and 9 in the Tenmile Range can easily be picked out, all in a general southeasterly direction.

Climb gradually over the Shrine Pass Road through a switchback north, then southwest and after 0.9 mile begin curving north-northwest on a high traverse toward Shrine Pass. On windy days follow a lower, more sheltered cross-country course as presented in Black Lakes Ridge (No. 47). Cross through an open hillside of stumps and burned, twisted snags; drop in and out of a prominent gully near 1.7 miles and climb several more yards toward the hilltop. Here a vast sea of white peaks suddenly comes into view on the horizon north: the sharp, glacial-carved Gore Range mountains, one of the most rugged and inaccessible ranges in Colorado. Also visible from this hilltop is a conspicuously treeless mountainside near the Vail Ski Area northwest, identified as "Red" on the Redcliff topo but locally called Siberia Peak.

Continue the northwesterly traverse under several outcroppings of red sedimentary rocks, then follow the treeline on a curve left toward the open saddle of Shrine Pass, marked by a half-buried sign. Mountain elevation across this snowfield, a point which brings both the Gore Range northwest and the Tenmile and Mosquito Ranges southwest into view at once, and after 2.5 miles enter scattered clumps of engelmann spruce on a southwest bearing. The cross-country route stays above the steeper side of the bowl left, climbs gradually in and out of thick conifers, and eventually comes to the edge of a long, wind-swept corridor. Bordered by thick trees on one side and a four hundred-foot ridge wall on the other, this opening has the allure of a secret, hidden passageway. However, heavy cornices hang from the ridgetop and avalanche debris often shows farther down the wall, making this corridor route extremely dangerous. *Do not venture beyond treeline!*

Wind south through the dense spruce for several hundred yards, begin to curve left where the ridge wall, visible through the trees right, bends into a large pocket, and drop toward the south fork of West Tenmile Creek. On windy days the forested south side of the creek basin makes a more sheltered route; on fair days the open, powder-filled snowfields on the north side provide unsurpassed downhill skiing conditions. Drop through more than 400 feet of elevation in the next 1.5 miles; cross carefully under the wires of an old power line, close the loop at the Shrine Pass Road, and ski the final few yards back to the parking area.

Powder skiing

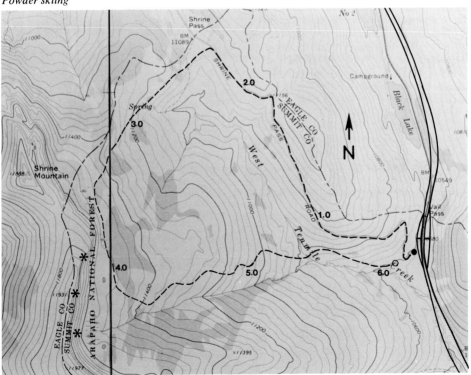

46 SHRINE PASS ROAD

One day trip
Classification: More difficult
Distance: 12.2 miles one way (19.6 KM.)
Skiing time: 6-7 hours one way
Accumulated elevation gain: **560 feet**
Accumulated elevation loss: **2,500 feet**
Maximum elevation: 11,160 feet
Season: Mid-November through mid-April
Topographic maps:
  U.S.G.S. Vail Pass, Colo. 1970
  U.S.G.S. Red Cliff, Colo. 1970
     7.5 minute series
Arapaho and White River National Forests

Shrine Pass and Shrine Pass Road take their names from the large shrine and observatory of the Mount of the Holy Cross that was proposed for construction in 1922 but never built. Today the Shrine Pass Road is perhaps the best known and most traveled ski tour route in northern Colorado. Why so popular? After the first 2.4 miles to Shrine Pass, the tour follows a downhill route, allowing a nice variety of extra-long glides and exciting schusses. Also, the tour offers few problems with orienteering, avalanche, or difficult terrain. Here is the classic tour formula: chauffeur drops off tour group at Vail Pass in morning, chauffeur skis Vail Ski Area compliments tour group, tour group skis Shrine Pass Road to Redcliff, tour group and chauffeur rendezvous in late afternoon and celebrate at the Reno Cafe, Redcliff's famous Mexican restaurant.

Proceed on U.S. 6 to the top of Vail Pass and park in the large plowed area on the west side of the highway. After the new I. 70 highway has been constructed over Vail Pass, park in the Rest Area parking lot (see map photo). Arrange for a pick-up car in Redcliff.

Ski from the top of Vail Pass to Shrine Pass, following either the Shrine Pass Road as described in Shrine Bowl (No. 45) or the cross-country route near West Tenmile Creek as given in Black Lakes Ridge (No. 47). This first 2.4 mile leg maintains a gradual uphill grade and gives vantage to the most beautiful panoramas of the entire tour. From the start the white wall of Jacque Ridge and wind-blown Jacque Peak dominate the foreground south, and then the Tenmile Peaks

pop into view, one by one, on the horizon east. After 1.7 miles this vista expands to include the countless rocky summits of the Gore Range north and the conspicuous, barren face of Siberia Peak near the Vail Ski Area northwest.

Ski past a half-buried sign in the saddle of Shrine Pass which reads "Entering White River National Forest" and begin an easy drop down the wide Turkey Creek valley. Cross a narrower opening in the trees after 3.2 miles, drop quickly into another open snowfield, then stay right of Turkey Creek and follow the roadbed to a famous viewpoint of the Mount of the Holy Cross, marked by a sign. This 14,005-foot spire, highest in the Sawatch Range, appears westsouthwest in a cluster of peaks over twelve miles away, its snowy cross indistinguishable from other snowfields. Drop left after 4.0 miles where the Timber Creek Road, the turnoff to Commando Run (No. 48), holds elevation right. Continue in and out of more clumps of trees, pass a branch drainage right near 4.6 miles, and soon drop steeply toward the creekbed, skiing over an inconspicuous, drifted switchback in the road.

Swing right after 5.4 miles as the creekbed again drops below the road, dip across a conspicuous conifer-filled drainage after several hundred more yards, and eventually descend to the bottom of the drainage. Aspen on the south-facing hillside mark entrance into the Canadian Life Zone as the roadbed proceeds along the right side of the creek, then at the 7.5 mile mark crosses to the left side. Here three log buildings, weathered and dilapidated, rise above snowdrifts on the hillside south, remains from the exciting mining days of the 1880s. Double pole into a long, thrilling schuss from the cabins, bend gradually left on the shaded roadcut, and after 8.0 miles glide on a more level contour from thick trees to open meadows to trees. The road crosses Turkey Creek after 9.2 miles, then soon passes the bridge over Wearyman Creek left, the junction with the Wilder Gulch and Wearyman Creek tour (No. 44).

Continue a steady, rolling drop as the valley narrows and the walls become steeper. Pass the deep Lime Creek drainage right near 10.0 miles, then follow the widening Shrine Pass Road for another mile and come to the yellow-green Redcliff water tank, marked "WT" on the Red Cliff topo. Here the plowed road usually begins: in winter sufficient snow covers the roadbed to allow skiing all the way to Redcliff, in spring these last 1.2 miles, snowbare and sometimes muddy, must be hiked. On this final descent a change in vegetation signals entrance into the Transition Life Zone and gives a different mood to the tour. Cedar trees now begin to compete with the aspen on the south-facing hillside and sagebrush shows through the snowdrifts, both indicative of a milder, drier climate.

"A loaf of bread—a jug of wine . . ."

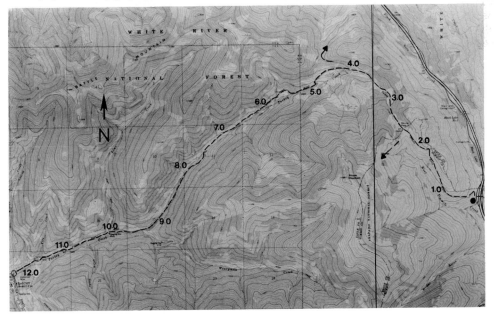

47 BLACK LAKES RIDGE

One day trip
Classification: Easiest
Distance: 4.9 miles *round trip* **(7.9 KM.)**
Skiing time: 3-3½ hours *round trip*
Elevation gain: 730 feet
Maximum elevation: 11,330 feet
Season: Mid-November through late April
Topographic map:
  U.S.G.S. Vail Pass, Colo. 1970
    7.5 minute series
Arapaho and White River National Forests

Top-of-the-world views of the Gore and Tenmile Ranges highlight the loop tour around the high Black Lakes ridge above Vail Pass and create a powerful, almost dizzying feeling of height and distance. The route stays above timberline in the Arctic-Alpine Zone for almost its entire length and protection from the wind simply does not exist. Thus, a day without wind is mandatory for the tour, a rare occurrence during the midwinter months but not too uncommon in March and April. A fire in the early 1900s left Black Lakes ridge and the hillside west filled with snags and stumps. Weather-beaten and colored with shades of browns and golds, these natural sculptures add variety and a macabre beauty to the landscape.

Drive on U.S. 6 to the top of Vail Pass and park in the large plowed area on the west side of the highway. After the new I. 70 highway has been constructed over Vail Pass, park in the Rest Area parking lot (see map photo).

From the top of Vail Pass ski southwest until intersecting the flat, snowy shelf of Shrine Pass Road. On days without wind,

stay on this roadbed all the way to the hilltop (1.7 miles) as described in Shrine Bowl (No. 45), an exposed but very scenic tour route. With less than perfect weather conditions, proceed straight ahead where the Shrine Pass Road switchbacks higher on the hillside and follow a more sheltered cross-country course above the West Tenmile Creek drainage. Twisted, fire-scarred snags mark this hillside as do level-topped stumps, sometimes sticking four or more feet above the snow. The trees from these old stumps obviously were cut in the wintertime when snow covered the bottom of the trunks, a logging method that depended on a hillside of smooth snow to aid in transportation of the logs. The fire probably came after the logging when the hillside was strewn with dead branches.

Wind through a grove of red-barked engelmann spruce near 1.5 miles, soon cross in and out of a shallow, treeless gully, and then turn north and make a switchbacking climb to the hilltop. Ski across the Shrine Pass Road, pass a small saddle farther right, marked as 11,156 feet on the topo, and bear north-northwest on an easy contour toward the tree clumps above Shrine Pass. Red sandstone outcroppings protrude through the snow along this course, dating back to the same geologic period as the formations in Red Rocks Park near Denver and the Garden of the Gods near Colorado Springs. And also along this course, a well-hidden log cabin, roofless and crumbling, can sometimes be spotted near the scattered trees at 2.5 miles, as lofty a site as can be found in these mountains. What a view that mountain man had.

Continue the easy climb north across the barren, wind-packed snowfields to the hilltop, an 11,325-foot elevation mark. With a bird's-eye view of nearly the entire Gore Range north and the Tenmile Range southeast, this high point makes a good spot to orient the topo maps and to identify the distant peaks. The shimmering, 12,000 and 13,000-foot peaks on the skyline north, nearly all without names, comprise the Eagle Nest Primitive Area. In view from the beginning of the tour, Jacque Peak and Jacque Ridge still dominate the foreground south, and behind and left Pacific Peak, Crystal Peak, and Peaks 10 and 9 in the Tenmile Range form an evenly-spaced sawtooth ridge. A long saddle separates Peak 9 from Peak 8,

Peak 7 appears immediately next as a rounded dome, and a regular succession of snowy summits leads to Tenmile Peak east.

Most of these peaks stay in view as the ski route loops south along the Black Lakes ridge. Do not drop east down the steep hillside toward the snowy bowl of Black Lake No. 2 and stay well away from any cornice build-up along the east side of the ridgetop, both potential avalanche sites. Dip through the shallow saddle again after 3.5 miles and continue southeast along the ridgetop, skiing by more pitch snags and twisted, upturned tree roots. Follow the ridgetop until the terrain becomes less steep east and then begin dropping back toward the parking area, an exciting and quite manageable descent when deep powder snow covers the hillside. For an easier return route, contour west around the ridgetop, traverse to the Shrine Pass Road, and ski down the gentle grade of the roadbed to the parking area.

Climbing to Black Lakes Ridge

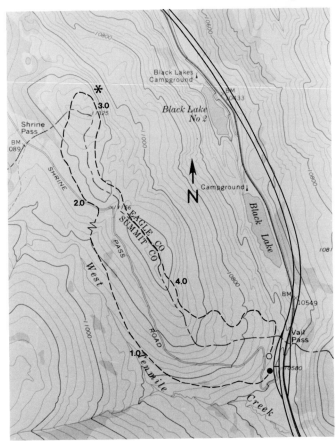

48 COMMANDO RUN

One day trip or overnight
Classification: Most difficult
Distance: 18.7 miles one way (30.1 KM.)
Skiing time: 9-12 hours one way
Accumulated elevation gain: 2,370 feet
Accumulated elevation loss: 4,770 feet
Maximum elevation: 11,760 feet
Season: Mid-November through mid-April
Topographic maps:
   U.S.G.S. Vail Pass, Colo. 1970
   U.S.G.S. Red Cliff, Colo. 1970
   U.S.G.S. Vail East, Colo. 1970
      7.5 minute series
Arapaho and White River National Forests

Brief notes on Commando Run: A Vail Pass to Vail Ski Area route, named by Steve Rieschl's Ski Touring School in Vail, the most challenging tour described in this guidebook. Requirements: A working knowledge of map and compass, route selection, avalanche identification, advanced skiing technique plus a day of clear weather. Take bivouac equipment even if planning a one-day trip. Powder skiing on the north-facing hillsides and in Mushroom Bowl is fantastic, worth all the effort!

Drive on U.S. 6 to the top of Vail Pass and park in the large, plowed area on the west side of the highway. After the new I. 70 highway has been constructed over Vail Pass, park in the Rest Area parking lot (see map). Arrange for a pick-up car at the Vail Ski Area.

Ski from Vail Pass to Shrine Pass, following either the Shrine Pass Road as described in Shrine Bowl (No. 45) or the cross-country route near West Tenmile Creek as given in Black Lakes Ridge (No. 47). Pass a half-buried sign at the top of Shrine Pass which reads "Entering White River National Forest" and then begin an easy drop northwest down the open Turkey Creek valley. Glide through a narrower opening in the conifers after 3.2 miles, proceed on another thrilling drop to a broad snowfield, then stay on the snowy shelf of the Shrine Pass Road and contour northwest above the creek basin. Here two summits over which the ski route

will eventually climb show clearly above the north side of the valley. The first, marked "11611" on the topo map, is mostly forested; the second, marked "11710," is topped with snowfields.

Pass the Mount of the Holy Cross viewpoint near 3.6 miles, wind in and out of scattered conifers for several hundred yards, and then turn right onto the obvious Timber Creek roadcut as the Shrine Pass Road drops gradually left. Follow this shaded Timber Creek Road to a prominent saddle at mile 4.6 but do not drop into the Timber Creek valley north. Climb cross-country west-northwest toward the 11,611-foot summit, begin a half-mile of switchbacks as the mountainside steepens, then maintain elevation about 200 feet below the top and contour around the south-facing side to another saddle west, the 6.1 mile mark. Steep drop-offs north and south make this saddle hard to miss and the thick-trunked spruce here provide a protected place for lunch or overnight camping.

Follow the ridgetop on an easy climb west, begin breaking above timberline after 6.7 miles and continue over wind-crusted snow to the 11,710-foot summit for a top-of-the-world vista. Southeast and south are the dazzling-white peaks in the Tenmile and Mosquito Ranges, east and north are the jagged spires of the Gore Range, now forming an even greater panorama than the one from the top of Shrine Pass. Mount of the Holy Cross, Notch Mountain, Homestake Reservoir all are visible in the white-capped Sawatch Range southwest. Curve north-northeast above the steep-sided Timber Creek bowl right, re-enter a grove of giant engelmann spruce after 7.2 miles, then stay to the left of the ridgetop and drop through deep powder snow to a saddle at 7.6 miles.

Hold a northerly bearing through the thick conifers and continue on a level traverse across the west side of summit "11618." Drop through more rolling powder fields along the north ridge of this summit, break onto the open saddle of Two Elks Pass after 8.8 miles, and begin a final climb up the steep, treeless side of Siberia Peak, marked "Red" on the topo. First however, test the snowpack carefully for stability and *do not proceed if avalanche conditions are present.* Switchback up the east side of the wind-blown peak but stay away from any cornice build-up along the steep drop-off farther right. Soon the moguled sides of Vail's China, Sunup Bowls, and High Noon Ridge show west above the deep Two Elk Creek valley.

Cross Siberia Peak about 50 feet below the summit on the west side, the highest point of the tour. Re-enter the thick canopy of spruce at about 10.3 miles, hold elevation north on an old logging road to the first road switchback, then turn west down the fall line and drop through the fluffy snow pockets of Mushroom Bowl. Intercept the Mill Creek Road north of the creekbed after 12.0 miles, follow the roadbed for 3.3 miles to the Vail Ski Area, and either ski down the maintenance road, shown on the Vail East topo, or climb to the top of Golden Peak and ski down Ruder's Run, a "most difficult" alpine classification.

Ski tour train

49 CHAMONIX TRAIL

One day trip
Classification: Easiest to more difficult
Distance: 2.8 miles one way (4.5 KM.)
Skiing time: 2 hours one way
Elevation gain: 750 feet
Maximum elevation: 8,910 feet
Season: December through March
Topographic maps:
    U.S.G.S. Minturn, Colo. 1970
    U.S.G.S. Vail West, Colo. 1970
        7.5 minute series
Bureau of Land Management

Chamonix! The most beautiful resort town in all of France. Chamonix! Starting point for the stalwart mountain climbers who tackle the Mont Blanc Massif, highest point in Western Europe. Chamonix! A rather short ski touring trail in Eagle Valley, Colorado (U.S.A.) also known as "the road to the Radio Facility mountain." . . . Somewhat of a letdown yes, but in spite of its unfortunate pretensions, the Chamonix Trail does make a delightful ski tour. It begins just outside of the bustling West Vail development and snakes west along the valley wall, passing

by several jutting promontories. These high viewpoints, quiet and serene, provide a relaxing change in tempo from the frantic activity on the valley floor below. One of the best times to tour the Chamonix Trail is in the evening: the myriad of lights in Vail and on Interstate 70, some twinkling, some moving slowly, create an enchanting spectacle.

Drive on I. 70 to the exit ramp into West Vail. Turn north, cross the north frontage road, and pass between the Texaco and Phillips 66 service stations. Proceed on the winding drive through West Vail: turn left onto Chamonix Road, continue to a right turn onto Arosa Drive, and soon bend left. Turn right onto Davos Trail, turn right again onto Cortina Lane, and follow the road to snow closure, a total distance of 0.9 mile from I. 70. Turn around and park along the side of the road.

Rather than ski up the first steep, often snow-bare hill, it is easier to pack the skis to the hilltop, about 70 yards west. Cross through the high game-control fence, pass over the heavy chain across the road, and begin skiing west-northwest over the snowy roadbed, now a very pleasant, gradual descent. The aspen-filled creekbed left rises quickly to road level and eventually the road switchbacks sharply across it. *Be extremely cautious of avalanche danger on this east-facing hillside* (see map photo). Begin a steady climb south-southeast up the other hillside and soon enter the shadows of lodgepole pine, an interesting and abrupt ecological change from the sagebrush and shrubs on the south-facing hillside. Just beyond the 0.5 mile mark bend right and break out onto an open hillside. This high promontory looks down upon the deep Gore Creek valley. The Eagles Nest Restaurant sticks conspicuously above the trees atop the Vail Ski Area east; Meadow Mountain, the former Vail Ski Area site, shows south-southwest, and beyond is a rolling, forested horizon line.

Contour west along the open, sagebrush-covered hillside. The road, often packed and sometimes wind-blown, drops into a small gully, then climbs steadily through a grove of aspen and continues the climb around another knoll. Notice the Rocky Mountain Juniper or "Cedar" that grow in the dry, rocky soil on the hillside here, a tree not common to ski tour routes. Near the 1.0 mile mark cross through an aspen-filled drainage, bend south and soon reach another high viewpoint, an excellent stopping point for a shorter tour. From here more of the steep Eagle Valley opens up, channeling the view to the snow-capped Gore Range mountains beyond. The famous Mount of the Holy Cross, highest and most distant of three sharp peaks south, juts into the horizon line more than 10½ miles away.

Turn north-northwest and proceed on a gradual climb over the snowy roadbed. Look for two magnificent Douglas fir trees on the left side of the road, easily identified by the three-pronged bracts that extend from their cones. The ski route, now quiet and secluded, passes through a grove of twisted, scarred aspen, then begins a slight, winding drop and, near 2.0 miles, dips sharply left across a branch creek. Continue south, gliding easily over the gently-rolling roadbed; soon break onto an open knoll, bend right and follow along the ridgetop. Make several exciting drops and climbs past a small saddle, ski through a band of pine, then a grove of large aspen, and circle around to the top of the "Radio Facility" mountain. This point gives view to both the obliquely-banded Minturn Cliffs south and the sagebrush-covered hills in Eagle Valley west. On a bright day the alpine skiers can be seen in Game Creek Bowl east as faint but moving, black specks. For the return trip, retrace the ski tracks.

Night skiing

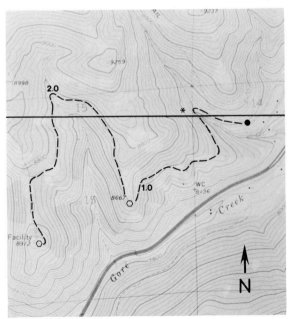

50 TIGIWON ROAD

One day trip
Classification:
  Easiest through most difficult
Distance: 6.1 miles one way (9.8 KM.)
Skiing time: 4-4½ hours one way
Elevation gain: 1,820 feet
Maximum elevation: 9,930 feet
Season: Late November through early April
Topographic map:
  U.S.G.S. Minturn, Colo. 1970
          7.5 minute series
White River National Forest

"There is a mountain in the distant West
That, sun-defying, in its deep ravines
Displays a cross of snow upon its side."

So wrote Henry Wadsworth Longfellow in part of his poem entitled "The Cross of Snow." Photographed by Henry H. Jackson, painted by Thomas Moran, this Mount of the Holy Cross became one of Colorado's most famous mountains during the latter part of the 19th century. Devotional pilgrimages to the mountain began in the 1930s, which led to the construction of a large lodge at the base camp of Tigiwon (the Ute word meaning "friends").

The ski tour, a long, steady climb through deep snow, retraces the old road to the historic Tigiwon Community House. This beautiful lodge can be reserved for $5 per 50 persons at the Holy Cross Ranger District office, Box 0, Minturn, Co. 81645.

Drive on I. 70 to the Minturn Exit 33 and take the down ramp to U.S. 24 South. Proceed through Minturn, pass the Ranger Station at the southeast end of town, and continue another 1.7 miles to the junction with Tigiwon Road, immediately north of the Eagle River bridge. Turn west and follow the road as far as possible—usually a few hundred feet in midwinter—but about one-half mile in April. Turn around and park beside the side of the road.

Begin skiing south-southwest over the flat, fast-gliding Tigiwon Road, a wide, packed path which often bears the assorted tracks of foot travelers, snowshoers, snowmobilers, and dogs as well as ski tourers. Soon swing right and cross under a large aqueduct, elevated by an elaborate steel trestle, then continue through a curve left and glide under the unseen tailings pond of the Empire Zinc Company. After 0.7 mile the road begins to climb steadily, first traversing southeast past a deep ravine, then back northwest up the steep-sided mountain. With each gain in elevation the panorama of the Minturn Cliffs becomes more engrossing. The white snow accents the striations within each sedimentary rock layer and the cliff bands themselves come together to shape a colossal triangular block.

Turn west after 1.2 miles and continue the gentle, rolling climb through shadows of pine and spruce, eventually passing a large ravine which drops away from the road right. Begin curving left through an aspen-lined hairpin turn and ski by signs which mark the Cross Creek trailhead and parking area. This more open area here allows a look straight up the Two Elk Creek valley northeast to the glistening-white range beyond the Sunup, China and Teacup Bowls of the Vail Ski Area. Follow the roadbed on another traverse across the mountainside and as the conifers become taller and full-branched, break into a peaceful, snow-covered clearing at 2.1 miles. An old, weather-beaten log cabin sits on the right side of the road here, a relic of Colorado's pioneer days. The four, mud-chinked walls still stand in spite of heavy snows and fierce winter winds but the roof has collapsed. This meadow makes a scenic lunch spot and a good turning-back point for an easy day's tour.

For the more advanced tour to the Tigiwon Community House, follow the snow-filled roadbed across an aspen-cluttered gully and proceed through two switchbacks on a steady climb up another open, windswept hillside. Re-enter the tall lodgepole pine and continue up the mountainside with long, winding traverses. Loop through two conspicuous branches of Bishop Gulch and after another mile-long switchbacking climb, break into the large clearing which surrounds the Tigiwon Community House. Framed on either side by tall lodgepole pine, a start-lingly new and beautiful panorama comes into view from this snowy island. Long, wavy layers of the Minturn Cliffs appear at the base of the Eagle Valley, cut deeply by the Two Elk Creek drainage, and beyond are the snowy bowls of the Vail Ski Area. The scene is dominated, however, by a spectacu-lar horizon line of sharp, white Gore Range peaks more than 16 miles away.

With an overnight camp the tour may be extended another 2.6 miles to the Half Moon Campground, and then even farther south toward the famed Mount of the Holy Cross. The return trip from the Tigiwon Commu-nity House drops on a near 6 percent grade and after the cool afternoon shade has set up the ski tracks, the trip becomes one long, exhilarating coast, sometimes taking less than an hour.

Near Tigiwon Community House

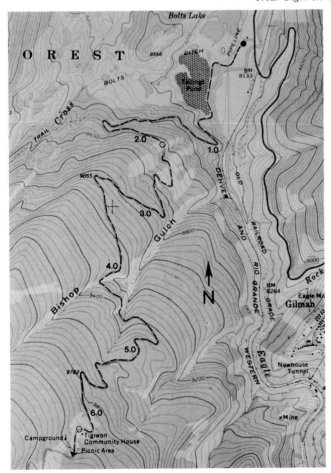

51 LOWER GILMAN ROAD

Half-day trip
Classification: Easiest
Distance: 1.6 miles one way (2.6 KM.)
Skiing time: 1 hour one way
Elevation gain: 430 feet
Maximum elevation: 8,600 feet
Season: Early December through March
Topographic map:
U.S.G.S. Minturn, Colo. 1970
7.5 minute series
White River National Forest

The Lower Gilman Road provides a different setting for a ski tour. Rather than rolling hills or thick forests, the ski route contours along a sheer valley wall, an austere, sometimes bleak, but nevertheless very interesting landscape. In 1879 prospectors, gold and silver seekers who were crowded out of the nearby Leadville district, swarmed this rocky mountainside and discovered the rich Belden and Iron Mask silver mines after digging hundreds of prospect holes. Today the Empire Zinc Company of New Jersey continues the mining operations around Gilman, producing millions of dollars of gold, copper, zinc and silver each year.

Although the U.S. 24 highway parallels the old Gilman roadbed about 200 feet above, the tour is surprisingly isolated and quiet; that is, until a Denver and Rio Grande locomotive blares across the valley floor several hundred feet below. Snow conditions are best for the tour in midwinter; in spring beware of possible wet snowslides and rock slides.

Drive on I. 70 to the Minturn Exit 33 and take the down ramp to U.S. 24 South. Proceed through Minturn, pass the Ranger Station at the southeast end of town, and continue another 1.9 miles on U.S. 24. Turn right and park in the wide pullout area just beyond the second bridge, immediately before the first switchback to Gilman.

Glide south over the narrow, near-level roadcut, immediately crossing under a telephone line. Wind in and out of willow patches on a gradual curve southwest, pass a small cave which extends about 20 feet into the hillside left, perhaps an exploratory bore of some prospector, and continue by several beautiful, full-branched Douglas fir trees. Ski under a rock wall, intriguing with its eroded shapes, and follow the roadcut through a slight curve left. At this point the sun reflects off the rock face and effectively reduces the snow cover. The road, sometimes drifted and hard-packed from wind, bends back right and climbs very gradually along the canyon wall. Soon the buildings of Gilman can be seen on the skyline ahead, and across the Eagle River west the switchbacks of Tigiwon Road (No. 50) are visible.

Come to the edge of a small ravine and begin a sharp bend left. Here the road ends on the U.S.G.S. topo map so follow the route as marked on the map photo on the opposite page. Contour north for about 100 yards, then climb gradually through another switchback and head south toward Gilman again. Curve left into the ravine, skiing by several aspen seedlings that have sprung up on the unused roadcut; cross the creekbed and continue along the opposite hillside, passing 1.0 mile. The snowy road straightens south, crosses under a telephone line, and proceeds on a very gradual climb toward Gilman. On the white valley floor, now about 280 feet below, an old, roofless log cabin can be spotted. Bishop Gulch shows prominently on the opposite mountainside, its south-facing side of snow and rock a sharp contrast to the north-facing side of dark green conifers. And farther south the upper meadow on Tigiwon Road soon appears, eye-catching as it reflects the midday sun.

Only a few scattered aspen or an occasional clump of sagebrush show above the snowdrifts as the road continues south along the valley wall. Curve left into another steep ravine similar to the first, cross a snow-filled creekbed at 1.4 miles, and contour around the protruding hillside. In another hundred yards come to a third drainageway where a rock slide has obliterated the road, thus ending the tour route. Although the roadcut is still visibly intact on the other side of this slide, the instability of both snow and rock make a crossing very dangerous. This stopping point provides a good view of the Gilman buildings, still above on the skyline but now looming much larger. For the return trip, ski back down the road, an easy run which takes only half the time as the trip in. The gentle, constant drop provides ideal conditions to practice the diagonal or double poling techniques.

Train below Minturn Cliffs

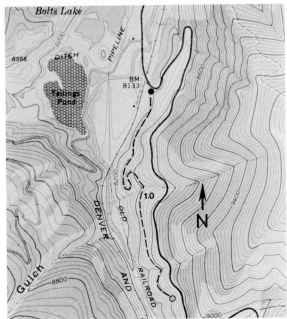

111

52 CAMP HALE

Half-day and one day trips
Classifications:
   Easiest through most difficult
Season: Late November through mid-April
Topographic map:
   U.S.G.S. Pando, Colo. 1970
                7.5 minute series
White River National Forest

Eagle Park, and the old Camp Hale site within, stretches for several miles along the Eagle River, a wide, flat basin immediately south of Pando and several miles north of Tennessee Pass. At its high elevation of more than 9,200 feet, it holds deep snow cover throughout the winter, making a natural playground for skiing. Most probably the first skier to traverse the broad snowfields in Eagle Park was a miner and mountain man who came into the valley with the first rush of gold seekers in 1879. He would have "snow-shoed," as it was known then, not as recreation but as the only practical means of winter transportation, using heavy, nine-foot long boards and a long sapling for a pole.

In 1942 with the opening of Camp Hale, highest Army installation in the United States, Eagle Park was again crossed by skiers, troops of the Tenth Mountain Division who underwent intensive winter training in military operations for World War II combat. The "B slope" at the south end of the park, where in-camp training was held, still shows the cross-posts of the old rope tow. Although the Camp Hale facility has now been completely torn down, skiers are returning to the area. In the spring of 1976 the Holy Cross Ranger district held a ribbon cutting ceremony to mark the official opening of the two superb ski touring trails described below.

From Leadville drive north on U.S. 24 over Tennessee Pass to the Camp Hale site. From Minturn drive south on U.S. 24 past Gilman, the Redcliff turnoff, and several campground areas; cross above the Denver and Rio Grande Western Railroad tracks at the Pando site, and continue 2.5 miles to the East Fork Trailhead at the Camp Hale site, 4.6 miles to the South Fork Trailhead. Park in the large parking area on the east side of the road at either trailhead.

52A. EAST FORK TRAIL
Classification: Easiest
Distance: 3.6 miles one way (5.8 KM.)
Skiing time: 2-2½ hours one way
Elevation gain: 360 feet
Maximum elevation: 9,640 feet

Begin skiing from the trailhead sign on the north side of a snowy pond; drop to the bed of the pond and head south-southeast toward the orange diamond trail markers on the far side. Curve left after 0.6 mile, cross the South Fork Eagle River and continue into the conifers, skiing over a jeep-size roadcut which is not marked on the topo. Pass the South Fork Trail which joins from the right, ski below the open hillside of the old Camp Hale "B slope" right, then re-enter the trees and glide from trail marker to trail marker on a course paralleling the East Fork Eagle River left. The ski route proceeds east through delightful dips and rolls, climbs gradually to a junction with another roadbed above right at the 2.3 mile mark, and soon swings left to a bridge over the East Fork. At this point the alpine cleft of Notch Mountain and the barest tip of Mount of the Holy Cross farther left break above the forested range west-northwest, the first of many beautiful views.

For the trip *up* the East Fork Trail, drop onto the creekbed itself, wind through clusters of vibrant red and orange willows on a 1.2 mile-long trek, and then intersect an old Camp Hale roadbed. As indicated by the trail sign, the tour can be continued farther up the East Fork valley with a steep climb and fast drop ("most difficult" terrain) to views of Sheep Mountain near the Climax Molybdenum Mine east. The return trip down the roadbed north of the East Fork Eagle River is pure delight: the route drops with sufficient grade for long, easy glides and short coasts, and heads directly into a horizon view of the snow-capped jagged summits in the Holy Cross Ridge. To end the tour, re-cross the bridge over the East Fork and continue the gently-dropping trip back down the jeep road.

112

52B. SOUTH FORK TRAIL
Classification: More difficult
Distance: 2.6 miles one way (4.2 KM.)
Skiing time: 1 hour one way
Elevation *loss*: 552 feet
Maximum elevation: 9,640 feet

Ski north from the trailhead sign, dropping on a steady grade over the snow-covered roadbed. Coast through a slight curve right, then bend back left across a tributary drainage at mile 0.4 and enter a stand of full-branched lodgepole pine. Continue the fast, winding contour with a long curve right after 1.3 miles and pass an expansive view of Eagle Park and the Camp Hale site. Leave the roadbed in another few yards with a turn left, as indicated by the trail sign, and begin an exciting cross-country traverse down the open hillside, the old "B slope" on which thousands of ski troopers trained for alpine military operations during World War II. At the hill bottom either turn east onto the East Fork Trail or turn left across the South Fork Eagle River, follow the trail markers across a snowy pond, and end the tour at a second car pick-up in the north parking area.

Kick and glide

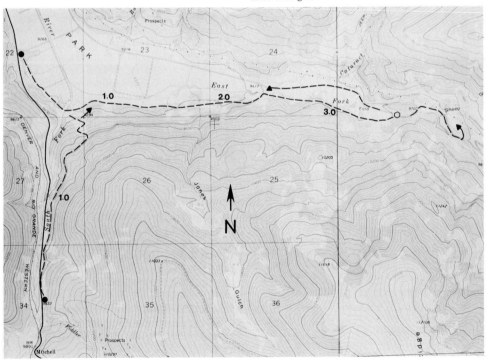

53 CHAPMAN RESERVOIR

One day trip
Classification: More difficult
Distance: 4.2 miles one way (6.8 KM.)
Skiing time: 2½-3 hours one way
Elevation gain: 1,075 feet
Maximum elevation: 9,340 feet
Season: Mid-December through early April
Topographic map:
   U.S.G.S. Sand Point, Colo. 1966
              7.5 minute series
Routt National Forest

Gleaming brilliantly with sunlight, shadowed with deep blue pockets, the Little Flat Tops and Dunckley Flat Tops are seen on the horizon as a high plateau, one of northern Colorado's most prominent and beautiful landmarks. Although the ski touring possibilities in this vast region are immediately exciting, two major problems exist. Access into the heart of the country is limited to long, unplowed roadbeds, often making extended trips of several days necessary to reach a good destination. And, many of the necessary U.S.G.S. topo maps have not yet been published, creating problems with orientation and safe route selection. However, one-color advance proofs of topo maps, complete with contour lines and names (stage 6), are now available for most of the area. For an index of these maps, write U.S.G.S. Geological Survey, Topographic Division, Stop 510, Box 25046, Denver

Federal Center, Denver, Colorado 80225.

The tour to Chapman Reservoir, a very pleasant trip that does not require an overnight stay, begins with an even, 2.5 mile glide over the Rio Blanco County 8 roadbed. It then turns onto a jeep trail which offers more variety in terrain and ends with a delightful run through the smooth snowfields east of the reservoir, the best skiing of the trip. The tour can be extended south for several more miles toward Sand Point and the Little Flat Tops but a climb up the sheer plateau wall is ill-advised due to high avalanche potential. A safer approach would be to ski to Sheriff Reservoir, an excellent tour in itself, and then climb onto the Flat Tops via Sand Creek.

Drive on Colo. 131 to Oak Creek, turn south at the post office, and continue for four blocks on this same street, soon identified as Bell Avenue. Turn right onto Routt Co. 25, curve sharply left after 6.5 miles where a branch road heads west to Trout and Fish Creeks, then join Rio Blanco Co. 8 at the county line and proceed a short distance more to the end of the plowed road, a total distance of 8.5 miles from Oak Creek. Other access routes begin from the nearby towns of Phippsburg and Yampa.

Begin gliding west-southwest over the roadbed on a very gradual climb, contouring above the open snowfields of the Spronks Creek valley left. Throughout the first mile of the tour Sand Point and the spectacularly steep cliffs below can be seen through a basin of aspen and conifers southwest. On the hillside (right) scrub oak and clumps of aromatic sagebrush, characteristic of this lower Transition Life Zone, poke through the snowfields. Curve slightly right after 1.2 miles and then curve back left under a steep cut, passing through a short section which is often snowbare in spring. Follow the wide roadbed onto a north-facing hillside, head west-southwest through a section of aspen, and after 1.5 miles pass a trail which branches left.

Bend west and cross over a small tributary of Oak Creek, then ski into the shadows of more and more spruce and loop through another small tributary near 2.1 miles. A restful panorama of aspen-covered hills, including Pinnacle Peak north, comes into view at this point. Curve left to a southerly bearing, bringing the Sand Point cliff into sight again, and soon come to the Chapman

Reservoir turnoff, marked by a sign and a bulletin board. Turn left onto a smaller, jeep-size roadcut, pass to the left of another bulletin board, and begin a steady climb through a hillside of aspen. The ski route turns left after several hundred yards and maintains the climb to a right turn around a ridge at 3.0 miles.

Follow the roadcut around a knolltop left, curve slightly left and glide through a level section to a saddle area, marked as 9,127 feet on the topo. Turn south again on a climb as an inconspicuous branch road contours east around the other side of the hill. Continue straight near 3.5 miles where another road spur switchbacks left and in several more yards glide under an open snowfield left, shown on the topo as a scrub area. Here the terrain levels and thick clumps of conifers begin to fill the hillside, giving a refreshing change in mood to the tour. With long, easy glides curve around a drainage and continue southwest across a snowy open area. At the 4.0 mile mark pass a sign reading "Little Flat Tops/Chapman Reservoir," take the bottom road fork back into the aspen, and soon break out above the broad reservoir bed, an excellent stopping point for a one day tour. Return over the ski tracks.

Sand Point in the Little Flat Tops

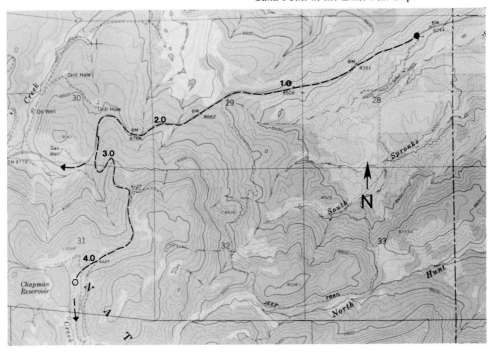

115

54 LYNX PASS

One day trip
Classification: Easiest
Distance: 3.1 miles one way (5.0 KM.)
Skiing time: 2-2½ hours one way
Elevation gain: 310 feet
Maximum elevation: 9,030 feet
Season: Mid-December through early April
Topographic map:
 U.S.G.S. Gore Pass, Colo. 1956
  15 minute series
Routt National Forest

The tour to Lynx Pass can be either a very pleasant and easy one day trip or the first leg on a more adventurous extended trip. With several nights of winter camping, a 40-mile trip from Lynx Pass north to Rabbit Ears Pass via the High Rock Creek, Midway, and Buffalo Park Trails is quite possible. Also, the new Buffalo Park Road, unmarked on the 1956 topos, is not maintained during the winter and provides another trail link between Colo. 134 and U.S. 40 for both snowmobilers and ski tourers. Other options for extended trips are given in the last paragraph of the text. The ski route to Lynx Pass traverses a wide and unprotected snowfield for the first two miles and thus requires a non-windy day for the tour. With the distant goal of Little Rock Creek valley in view from the start, each ski glide seems to produce little progress, creating an appreciation for the vastness of the country.

From Kremmling drive north on U.S. 40 to the junction with Colo. 134. Turn left, follow Colo. 134 over Gore Pass, and continue to the Lynx Pass Road turnoff. From Toponas drive south on Colo. 131, turn left onto Colo. 134 and proceed 8.6 miles to the Lynx Pass Road turnoff. Park along the side of the road.

Begin skiing from the north side of the highway near a sign which reads "Lynx Pass Campground 3." Stay to the right of a shallow basin and break trail north-northwest on a very gradual climb up the open snowfield. Soon the terrain levels and the roadcut near the Porcupine Creek road junction can be seen near treeline ahead, providing a point for orientation. Pass the snow-buried posts of the Rock Creek Range Study Plot at 0.5 mile and continue the northerly cross-country course over smooth snowfields. The ski route climbs over a slight rise which

brings a further extension of the valley into view, and then proceeds past the drifted ruins of a log cabin near the end of the island of trees right.

Climb very gradually to the top of another small rise near 1.5 miles. Contour above the Rock Creek valley which joins from the right and then begin a slight drop past the open Porcupine Creek drainage left. Now in view on the horizon southeast is the beautiful rocky mound of Mt. Powell, a blend of sky-blue and cloud-white colors from this 26-mile distance but in sharp contrast to the forested hills below. Enter the narrowing valley on an obvious roadcut after 2.0 miles, glide through the shadows from a steep cut left, and eventually come to a junction with the Teepee Creek and High Rock Creek trails, both intriguing routes for longer tours. The trail sign reading "Teepee Creek 3/High Rock Creek 6" is on the east side of the creekbed at this junction but often is snow-covered.

Proceed sharply left then right around a branch drainage, ski past a red outhouse and climb another few yards to the top of the knoll. Here the view takes in the snowy basin of Lagunita Lake, named from a Spanish word meaning "little lagoon," and extends to the green buildings of the Guard Station in the trees beyond. Behind, a cluster of rocky tops that comprise the 13,397-foot Eagles Nest now can be seen to the left of Mt. Powell on the hazy horizon. Turn sharply west from the knolltop, follow a conspicuous roadcut into a stand of pine and spruce, and climb on an easy grade to the left of the open park. After another hundred yards break into the end of the park, pass through a picturesque buck fence, then continue back into the trees and soon reach the top of Lynx Pass.

The tour can easily be extended by continuing north on the road down the Morrison Creek drainage, a sheltered route with a rolling downhill grade, usually about two miles to the plowed road. The Morrison Divide Trail, another highly recommended extension, heads southwest from the top of Lynx Pass on a cut immediately across from the Work Center road. The trail begins with a short climb, then levels and continues northwest on a forested ridgetop route, and ends at the Muddy Slides, an interesting geological slide area about eight miles from Lynx Pass. With fast snow in spring this trip can be done in one long day but in mid-winter an overnight stop is usually necessary to make the 11-mile, one-way distance. Shel-tering clumps of spruce along the ridgetop offer excellent camping spots for both tents and snow caves.

*Buck fence near **Lynx Pass***

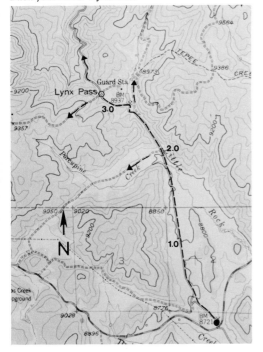

55 RABBIT EARS PEAK

One day trip
Classification:
  Easiest through most difficult
Distance: 4.6 miles one way (7.4 KM.)
Skiing time: 3-3½ hours one way
Elevation gain: 1,214 feet
Maximum elevation: 10,654 feet
Season: Mid-November through early May
Topographic map:
  U.S.G.S. Rabbit Ears Peak, Colo. 1956
        7.5 minute series
Routt National Forest

One of northern Colorado's most distinctive landmarks, Rabbit Ears Peak caught the attention of famed world traveler, Bayard Taylor, who wrote in 1867 about its "two remarkable Alpine horns." Earliest trappers in the region saw the peak as two gigantic rabbit ears and this name was given official status by Col. F. V. Hayden, geologist and map maker of the early west. The 100-foot spires that form the Ears are a crumbly, rose-colored granite, imbedded with many harder pebbles. The tour route from the East Summit stays in thick spruce for the first 1.3 miles and makes an excellent, sheltered tour on breezy midwinter days. However, this first section does follow a designated snowmobile trail and there may be some snowmobile traffic during midwinter.

Drive on U.S. 40 to the Rabbit Ears Pass area and proceed to the large parking lot at the East Summit, marked by a Continental Divide sign. Or drive to the dropoff point for the tours to Long Park (No. 57) and The Divide Trail (No. 58), 1.4 miles west of the East Summit, 1.0 mile east of the Routt/Grand County line (no parking permitted). Note that the 1956 Rabbit Ears Peak topo does not show the new U.S. 40.

From the East Summit parking lot begin skiing north-northwest across a flat, open meadow, following the red-topped stakes which mark the Continental Divide Snowmobile Trail. Enter the trees after 0.4 mile, immediately turn right onto a wide, snow-filled roadbed, then fork left in another 40 yards where the right road branch continues straight. The northerly roadbed tunnels through thick engelmann spruce on a winding, near-level course, and after 1.3 miles leads into a large snowfield around the old East Summit, identified by a conspicuous stone monument. This open area, a nice destination point for an easier tour, provides the first view of the unusual Rabbit Ears Peak, the West Ear a broad slab of granite and the East Ear two distinct pinnacles.

Maintain elevation in and out of the trees on a northerly course along the east-facing hillside; follow the Rabbit Ears Peak roadbed if discernible or merely head toward the Ears on a cross-country route. After nearly 2.0 miles break out of the trees to a panoramic view southeast of Middle Park and the mountain ranges beyond, part of the vista that can be seen from the Ears themselves. Forested, rock-topped Baker Mountain juts into the foreground south-southeast just three miles away, and on the same line of sight beyond is the blue-and-white ribbed Gore Range. An eye-catching cone-shaped mountain spans a gap on the far horizon to the left of the Gore Range—Bald Mountain near Breckenridge about 76 miles away. Farther left are the snow-capped Williams Fork Mountains, then the more jagged Front Range, interrupted by closer, pointed Whitely Peak southeast.

Continue north on a cross-country route back into the trees, climb more noticeably up a short rise, and soon ski out into a long park. Stay to the left of the Grizzly Creek drainage and climb gradually for another mile, now bearing for the steep, treeless range west of the Ears. As the terrain steepens near 3.2 miles, either turn northeast and make several long switchbacks up the hillside to treeline or ski on a more gradual climb toward the top of the white range north-northwest, then loop back southwest. Follow the roadcut west over the hilltop, passing 4.0 miles; drop slightly, then climb another small hill and re-enter the trees. After a very few yards the Ears loom into sight (north).

For the final 200 yards to the base of the Ears, climb very steeply north on short switchbacks, staying well away of the dangerously sharp dropoff east. Be extremely careful if attempting to climb the West Ear: a 21-rung ladder aids in the first pitch but for the next few yards the ancient rock strata crumbles easily and sometimes is icy. The expansive, 360-degree view includes the Mt. Zirkel Wilderness Area north, the Medicine Bow Mountains northeast, and The Flattops southwest, as well as the previously mentioned ranges. Only a few yards away is the sheer blade of the East Ear, covered with rose and rust lichen. On the return trip, cross back over the ski tracks, using a strong pole drag and sidesteps for the first steep descent.

Rabbit Ears Peak

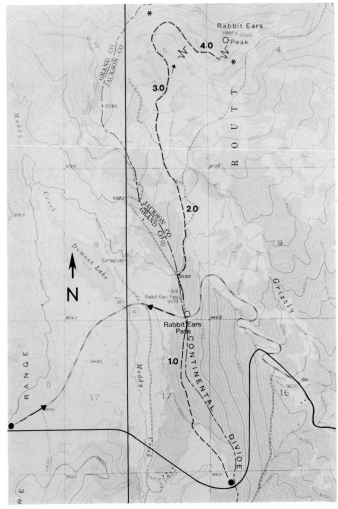

56 FISHHOOK LAKE

One day trip
Classification: Most difficult
Distance: 6.7 miles one way (10.8 KM.)
Skiing time: 4-4½ hours one way
Accumulated elevation gain: 842 feet
Accumulated elevation loss: 405 feet
Maximum elevation: 10,040 feet
Season: Mid-November through early May
Topographic maps:
  U.S.G.S. Rabbit Ears Peak, Colo. 1956
  U.S.G.S. Mount Werner, Colo. 1956
      7.5 minute series
Routt National Forest

Snowfield, forest, valley bottom and lakebed create intriguing variety on the tour to Fishhook Lake. Especially pleasant is the final mile up the Fishhook Creek drainage, an easy path to follow but bordered on either side by tall spruce, producing the allure of a hidden passageway. Except for the fast, exciting plunge to the bottom of the Fishhook Creek drainage, the ski route stays entirely on gentle, rolling terrain, easily managed by beginning skiers. For a closer destination, continue as far as the open snowfield at 4.2 miles. Here a beautiful panoramic vista expands to include the blazing-white Dunkley Flat Tops southwest, the ribbed spires in the Gore Range south-southeast, and the broad west ear of Rabbit Ears Peak east-northeast.

Drive on U.S. 40 to the Rabbit Ears Pass area and proceed to the large parking lot at the East Summit, marked by a Continental Divide sign. Or drive to a dropoff point near the junction with the Dumont Lake road, 1.4 miles west of the East Summit, 1.0 mile east of the Routt/Grand County line (no parking permitted). Note that the 1956 Rabbit Ears Peak topo does not show the new U.S. 40 highway.

With a starting point at the East Summit, ski north on the Continental Divide Snowmobile Trail to the *old* East Summit, following the tour description in the first paragraph of the Rabbit Ears Peak tour (No. 55). Turn west at the old stone monument, drop into the open basin south of Dumont Lake, then contour northwest up the open hillside and intercept the Divide Trail route near the hilltop. This East Summit route, figured for the information capsule, adds about one mile more in distance and one hour more in skiing time than the route from the drop point.

From the dropoff point climb over the snowbank and ski cross-country north for several hundreds yards to the old U.S. 40 roadbed, easily spotted near the poles of an old telephone line. Climb gradually over the roadbed to the crest of a slight hill, a point which brings the Rabbit Ears Peaks back into view, and then turn left on a northerly cross-country contour up the open hillside. Bear slightly left of a half-forested knoll on the horizon and glide over the open, rolling snowfields to the westerly creek drainage that runs into Dumont Lake. With this snowy drainage as a guide, climb west to the top of the hill, curve north into a thick stand of engelmann spruce, and soon join a conspicuous roadcut near the edge of the hill, the Continental Divide Snowmobile Trail.

Follow the roadcut west and northwest on a delightful run through thick conifers, double pole on a slight drop near the 3.2 mile mark, and soon break out into a wide, snow-filled valley which leads west along a branch of Fishhook Creek. Cut straight across this drainageway for a hundred yards, climb the snowfield north near treeline, then rejoin the roadcut and continue to another open, snowy basin at 4.0 miles. Here the ski route begins a climb north up a barren, wind-crusted hillside and continues toward fire-burned snags in a slight saddle on the hilltop. The tall, blackened timbers that dot this entire area remain from a famous forest fire of 1879. Set by renegade Utes "in order that their ponies could travel," the fire destroyed vast acreages of timber in a 40-mile swath along the Continental Divide.

Continue north over rolling snowfields toward the low point on another small rise and bend northwest near 4.5 miles, with the contour of the mountainside right. Drop in and out of a shallow drainage and then pick up the roadbed again, snow-buried but discernible, at the far end of a small park north. From this roadbed look carefully along treeline for the trailcut to the Divide Trail, marked by red flagging and a snow-buried sign, and follow the cut on an adventuresome schuss to the bottom of the Fishhook Creek basin. A longer route into the basin, more obvious and slightly less steep, proceeds along the snowmobile trail markers to the "Bug Road" cut farther west. For the final mile to Fishhook Lake, break trail north up the quiet, secluded corridor of the Fishhook Creek drainage, an invitingly serene ending to the tour. Return over the ski tracks.

Through snow laden trees

57 LONG PARK

One day trip or overnight
Classification: Most difficult
Distance: 17.3 miles one way (27.8 KM.)
Skiing time: 8-9 hours one way
Accumulated elevation gain: **1,505 feet**
Accumulated elevation loss: **4,045 feet**
Maximum elevation: 10,340 feet
Season: Mid-November through early May
Topographic maps:
   U.S.G.S. Rabbit Ears Peak, Colo. 1956
   U.S.G.S. Mount Werner, Colo. 1956
   U.S.G.S. Steamboat Springs, Colo. 1969
       7.5 minute series
Routt National Forest

For those veteran ski tourers who find the Hogan Park Ski Trail (No. 60) a bit too crowded these days, the tour route from Rabbit Ears Pass to the Steamboat Ski Area via Long Park provides an excellent alternative. Few ski tracks ever cross this serene and spacious park in winter because the tour is unmarked and long, often requiring an overnight stop if trail breaking is slow. In April and early May the snowfields form a hard, unbreakable crust and offer the best skiing conditions, mile after mile of long, easy gliding. As with the Hogan Park Ski Trail, the most difficult part of the tour is the descent down the Steamboat Ski Area mountain.

Drive on U.S. 40 to the Rabbit Ears Pass area and proceed to the large parking lot at the East Summit, marked by a Continental Divide sign. Or drive to a dropoff point near the junction with the Dumont Lake road, 1.4 miles west of the East Summit, 1.0 mile east of the Routt/Grand County line (no parking permitted). Arrange for a pick-up car at the Steamboat Ski Area.

Ski from Rabbit Ears Pass to the Fishhook Creek drainage, following either of the two routes described in the Fishhook Lake tour (No. 56). Other excellent access routes are possible from the Hogan Park Ski Trail via the drainages of Fishhook Creek (see No. 60). Intercept the "Bug Road" near treeline beyond the Base Campground site and drop quickly west through beetle-scarred spruce to the bottom of Fishhook Creek, 5.9 miles. In the early 1950s an epidemic attack of engelmann spruce beetles threatened to destroy this entire Park Range forest and left thousands of gray tree skeletons, some of which can still be seen today. Part of the control efforts included a work force to spray diseased trees which worked north through the "Bug Road" access from "Base Campground."

Turn downstream on the snowy Fishhook creekbed, contour several yards along the north hillside until conifers give way to a flat, wide snowfield, and climb gradually northwest through this opening to the Long Park Creek drainage at mile 6.1. Double pole into the drainage bottom and begin a steady, winding climb north along the creekbed, linking the open patches of snow. The drainageway soon widens and becomes lined with more beetle-killed trees, especially on the right side. Continue north under a snowy hillside on the left, curve around a definite protrusion of trees from the left after 7.0 miles, and immediately enter the open snowfields of Long Park proper. This secluded park, covering a vast area of about 1,900 acres, was named after a prospector, Long, who did some placer mining along the creek in the 1870s.

Curve west through the open basin after 7.8 miles, soon pass an extension of the snowfield left, partially ringed with a semicircle of trees, and then swing west-northwest along the park bottom. Only the forested 10,067-foot knoll behind shows above the surrounding wall of trees at this point. Break through a few scattered conifers at mile 8.1, continue west-northwest along the wide park basin, and eventually come to viewpoints of the snowy ridge near Summit 10452 west-southwest, then Mount Werner west, topped with a telephone microwave tower. Bend left at the far west end of Long Park, switchback through thick trees to the saddle between Summits 10432 and 10452, and break out to a beautiful vista of Hogan Park, the deep Walton Creek drainage, and Yampa Valley. On the horizon beyond, the snowy Dunckley and Little Flattops gleam conspicuously amid a panorama of forested hills.

Contour on a slight climb around the south side of Summit 10452, bringing into view the sparsely-forested 10,447-foot summit west. Make an easy drop to the saddle at mile 11.0, maintain a westerly bearing through thick trees around the north side of Summit 10447, then drop quickly to the next saddle at mile 11.5, heading toward the now-visible counterweight on the Summit Ski Lift. *Avoid any possible avalanche paths near the top of Mt. Werner north.* Join the Hogan Park Ski Trail on a final climb west and soon break over the top of the range to the Steamboat Ski Area. For the easiest way down the Ski Area mountain, ski the following runs (4.7 miles): Buddy's Run to the top of Four Points Lift via Four Points Cutoff, Rainbow to Rainbow Saddle, Park Lane to Central Park (or uphill to the Thunderhead Restaurant and gondola terminal), then Why Not Road and Right-O-Way to an end point at the ski area base.

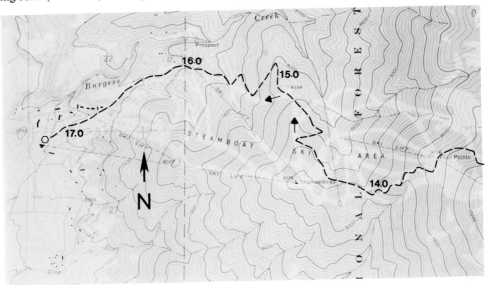

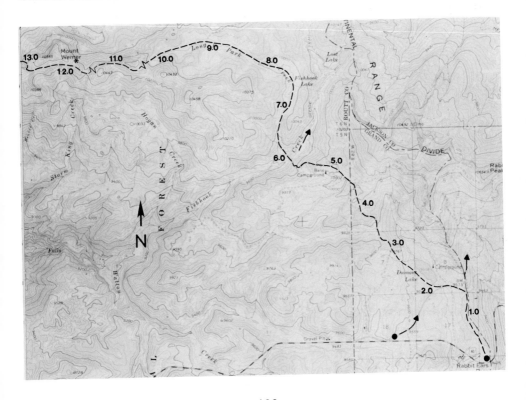

58 THE DIVIDE TRAIL

Overnight
Classification: Most difficult
Distance: 27.2 miles one way (43.8 KM.)
Skiing time: 10-13 hours one way
Accumulated elevation gain: **1,742 feet**
Accumulated elevation loss: **4,102 feet**
Maximum elevation: 10,557 feet
Season: Mid-November through early May
Topographic maps:
    U.S.G.S. Rabbit Ears Peak, Colo. 1956
    U.S.G.S. Mount Werner, Colo. 1956
    U.S.G.S. Buffalo Pass, Colo. 1956
    U.S.G.S. Rocky Peak, Colo. 1962
         7.5 minute series
Routt National Forest

The Divide Trail penetrates the sub-alpine forests of the Park Range on an adventuresome course from Rabbit Ears Pass to Buffalo Pass and then makes a long drop toward Strawberry Park via the Buffalo Park Road. It usually takes two days of skiing with one night of winter camping. The annual Rabbit Ears Citizens Race follows much of this same course and strong skiers ski the entire distance over the prepared track in four and five hours.

Drive on U.S. 40 to the Rabbit Ears Pass area and proceed to the large parking lot at the East Summit, marked by a Continental Divide sign. Or drive to a dropoff point near the junction with the Dumont Lake road, 1.4 miles west of the East Summit, 1.0 mile east of the Routt/Grand County line (no parking permitted). Arrange for a pick-up car at snow closure on the Buffalo Pass Road.

First, ski the 6.7 miles from Rabbit Ears Pass to Fishhook Lake, using the trail description given for the Fishhook Lake tour (No. 56). Proceed north across the snowy lakebed, turn left along the Lake Elmo inlet about 100 yards before treeline north, and climb steadily northwest into the open drainage to Lake Elmo. This natural passageway leads north through thick stands of engelmann spruce, widens slightly near two ponds at mile 7.6, soon passes through a small neck of trees and continues to a slight climb onto Lake Elmo at mile 8.0. From the far end of the lakebed the ski route cuts northwest across a long east-west park, holds a northwest bearing across a forested saddle at mile

8.5, and drops very gradually into the flat snowfields east of Long Lake Reservoir.

Curve west along the tributary toward Long Lake; funnel through a narrower opening after 9.5 miles and soon intercept the old Long Lake roadbed, discernible in the trees northeast of the lakebed. Contour northwest and north on this road through a hillside of conifers, dip through the conspicuous Fish Creek drainage near mile 10.0, then bear northwest again and pick up the roadcut near treeline. The road soon crosses another drainage and climbs gradually northwest to a wide, snowy basin near 10.6 miles. Either continue on the road northwest then north through scattered clumps of trees or cross-country north-northwest along the open basin, reaching the east side of Fish Creek Reservoir after 11.4 miles.

Follow the road on a slight drop across the northeast inlet of the reservoir, pass a sign reading "Fish Creek Reservoir/Long Lake Road," and climb gradually along the left side of the inlet drainage to another wide basin at mile 11.8. Here again the ski route stays in the natural passage, climbing steadily northeast and north for over two miles. Begin a contour around the deep bowl of North Fork Fish Creek after 14.5 miles, soon pass under the high voltage line near a tower right, then continue north-west on the roadcut and ski beneath a Bureau of Reclamation relay station several hundred yards right. In several more yards the roadcut passes a left fork to the Summit Lake Guard Station and makes a thrilling, half-mile drop through the snowdrifts to Buffalo Pass, at 15.8 miles.

Pick up the snowy Buffalo Pass Road on the far north side of the North Fork Fish Creek valley and glide west and southwest on a gradual descent. Although the valley floor left drops below road level on a more inviting grade, it soon penetrates the steep, barren walls of Fish Creek canyon with too high an avalanche potential for safe skiing. Follow the roadbed through short, easy climbs at miles 17.7 and 18.2, break out to a panoramic view of Strawberry Park, Sleeping Giant Mountain, and a blue horizon of rolling mountains at mile 18.7, then stay above the Spring Creek drainage left and make a steep schuss over the open snowfields. The roadbed drops through two winding switchbacks after 20.7 miles, makes a final climb to the saddle near Dry Lake Campground at mile 24.1, and then descends rapidly toward Strawberry Park, usually holding snow cover in spring to a cattle guard at mile 25.9, in winter to a private residence at mile 27.2.

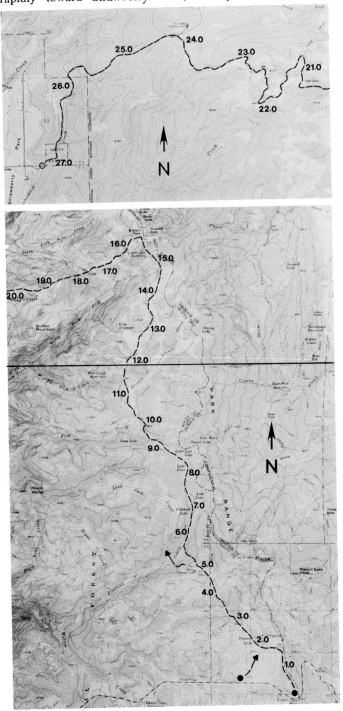

59 WALTON MOUNTAIN

One day trip
Classification: Easiest to more difficult
Distance: 3.0 miles one way (4.8 KM.)
Skiing time: 2½-3 hours one way
Elevation gain: 630 feet
Maximum elevation: 10,140 feet
Season: Mid-November through early May
Topographic maps:
  U.S.G.S. Mount Werner, Colo. 1956
  U.S.G.S. Walton Peak, Colo. 1956
         7.5 minute series
Routt National Forest

Unnamed on the topo map but known locally as Walton *Mountain,* the 10,142-foot summit north of Walton *Peak* is the destination point for one of the most popular tours in the Rabbit Ears Pass area. Pick a clear, non-windy day for the tour so you will be able to stay awhile on the open mountaintop and enjoy the incomparable view—west to Utah, north to Wyoming, and east and southeast to the Continental Divide ranges.

Drive on U.S. 40 to the Rabbit Ears Pass area and proceed to the large Hogan Park Ski Trail parking area, 3.8 miles from the East Summit and 3.7 miles from the West Summit.

Climb the high wall of snow in back of the parking area and ski south for about 20 yards to the ridgetop, a point just beyond the telephone line. Stay off the steep dropoff southeast, especially when avalanche danger is high. Instead, follow a safer course south through the tree clumps along the ridge and make an easy, rolling drop to the Walton Creek basin. Here the ski route crosses the main branch of Walton Creek, then begins climbing very gradually above and right of the easterly creek branch and soon enters a

snowy, secluded park. Continue the easy traverse through open snowfields above the creekbed and after 0.6 mile curve right with the contour of the hillside. As the trail swings south, a vast, treeless snowfield opens on the hillside above, an engaging landscape that is often patterned with ridges of drifted snow.

Ski south on a delightful, winding course through a stand of trees for 50 yards and break out into another snowy park, much larger than the first. The drainage divides at 1.0 mile and the ski route turns left and contours above the left branch, shown as the creek on the topo map. Continue east-south-east under a power line, cross the flat park bottom and intersect a snow-buried roadbed at the far end, usually well-marked with poles. Follow the roadbed on a gradual climb south out of the trees, pass the turnoff point for the tour to Walton Peak, and after 1.7 miles reach a small knolltop which gives vantage to distant landmarks for the first time on the tour. Rabbit Ears Peak comes into view above the forested ranges northeast and the snowy top of Walton Peak shows in the opposite direction.

Bend to the right around the knolltop and proceed west-northwest on a winding contour near treeline, staying above a deep ravine left. Begin curving south after 2.5 miles, cross the ravine just below an isolated clump of spruce and fir, and follow the pole markers on a steeper climb up the open hillside. With each additional gain in elevation on this final climb, you are rewarded with the view of a new range on the horizon. First the snow-capped Rawah Mountains in the Medicine Bow Range appear beyond North Park northeast, then the distant summits of the Front Range come into sight, highest near the Berthoud Pass area east-southeast. And soon after, another cluster of spires spreads across the skyline south-southeast, jagged peaks of the Eagles Nest Primitive Area in the Gore Range.

Ski past the private F.A.A. microwave relay station on top of Walton Mountain and proceed several more yards to a lookout point on the west side. On a clear day look for these distinct landmarks along the horizon line, given here in a clockwise order: the long, level range of the Dunckley Flattops west-southwest, filled with deep blue shadows, the farthest reaches of the Yampa Valley, an eye-catching white patch due west, the faintly visible Vermilion Bluffs west-northwest, about 100 miles away in the northwest corner of the state, the familiar shape of Sleeping Giant Mountain below the horizon northwest, and the gleaming peaks of the Mt. Zirkel Wilderness Area north. An incredible view!

For the longer, advanced tour to Walton Peak, drop into the Walton Creek valley at 1.4 miles and follow the pole markers south and southwest on a fast, near-level course over the open snowfields. Curve right and cross through a band of trees after 2.6 miles, bearing west-southwest on a small trailcut. After breaking out of the trees, the ski route makes a steady climb along the ridge near treeline, then continues through a power line cut to the top of the peak. *Be sure to stay well away from any avalanche danger on the steep west side of Walton Peak throughout the climb.* For the return trip from both Walton Peak and Walton Mountain, retrace the ski tracks to the parking area.

Belly flop

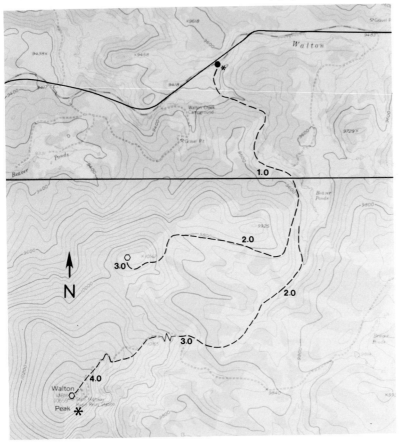

60 HOGAN PARK SKI TRAIL

One day trip or overnight
Classification: Most difficult
Distance: 12.7 miles one way (20.4 KM.)
Skiing time: 6-8 hours one way
Accumulated elevation gain: 1,180 feet
Accumulated elevation loss: 3,740 feet
Maximum elevation: 10,340 feet
Season: Mid-November through April
Topographic maps:
 U.S.G.S. Mount Werner, Colo. 1956
 U.S.G.S. Steamboat Springs, Colo. 1969
  7.5 minute series
Routt National Forest

A classic tour in the Rabbit Ears Pass area, this route from the Pass to the Steamboat Ski Area via Hogan Park has been skied since at least the late 1940s, long before alpine runs were cut on Mt. Werner. More recently the tour has served as the orienteering and endurance test for RMD certification of ski touring instructors. Although now the trail is well-marked and often broken, topo maps provide an essential overview of the terrain: four, flat snowfield crossings, a drop and climb through Fishhook Creek, a long climb through Hogan Park to Mt. Werner, and finally a very challenging drop down the Steamboat Ski Area.

Drive on U.S. 40 to the Rabbit Ears Pass area and proceed to the large Hogan Park Ski Trail parking area, 3.8 miles from the East Summit and 3.7 miles from the West Summit.

Cross to the northwest side of U.S. 40, intercept the old, unplowed roadbed and follow it for about 60 yards to the curve right (east). Note that the 1956 Mount Werner topo does not show the new U.S. 40 but rather the old roadbed, now used for the ski route (see map photo). Stay off of the steep cut to the left of the roadbed, a potential snow slide site. Continue along treeline on a parallel course with the new highway, soon cut north into a grove of tall spruce and after a few more yards break out into the first open snowfield, at 0.4 mile. Orange stakes mark a beeline course northwest over the meadow for a half-mile, then signal a turn north into the trees along a branch of Walton Creek. Another course, marked by occasional flagging, contours along the forested hillside northeast of the

meadow, more protected on windy days.

Cross to the west side of the creekbed, make a short, steep climb up the hillside, and after 1.1 miles enter the second open snowfield, a long north-south basin. Pass more snowfields as trees recede left, contour to a slight saddle at 1.5 miles, here re-enter the shadows of spruce and fir and double-pole northwest down a gentle drop to the third snowfield. For the first time now the view extends ahead for some distance, giving glimpses of the forested hilltops east of Mt. Werner. Follow the trail markers across the open meadow and after 1.9 miles pass the very flat basin of a Fishhook Creek tributary, an excellent passageway northeast and east to the Fishhook Lake and Long Park tours (Nos. 56 and 57).

Continue several yards through a cluster of trees and glide northwest into the fourth snowfield, a vantage point for the forested hilltops seen earlier, Buffalo Pass with its high voltage towers, and the deep, main drainage of Fishhook Creek ahead. Ski back into the trees near 2.3 miles, soon break out on the north side of the meadow, and follow treeline west-northwest over easy, rolling terrain, staying right of the tributary. *With more than five miles to Mt. Werner and nine miles to the Steamboat Ski Area base, do not drop into the Fishhook Creek drainage unless there is sufficient time and good weather to finish the tour.* The ski route loses 160 feet of elevation on a fast, exciting schuss and ends up on the snowy bed of Fishhook Creek, another good link to the Fishhook Lake and Long Park tours.

Climb west-northwest between the 9,595-foot and 9,370-foot summits, then after 3.5 miles drop to a tributary of Hogan Creek

128

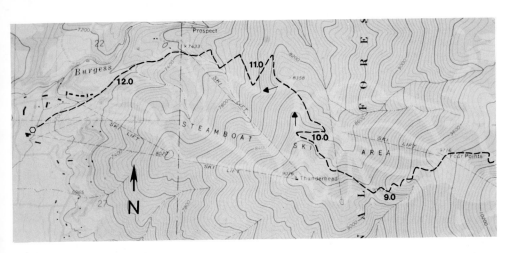

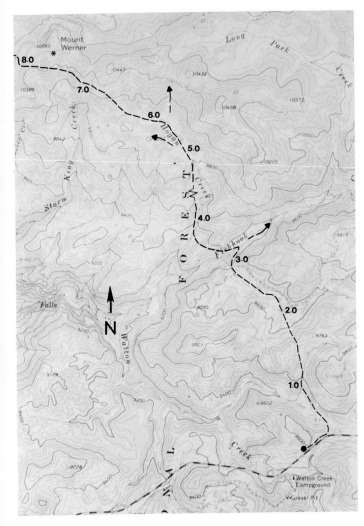

and continue several hundred yards to the main branch of Hogan Creek. Here the ski route turns north and climbs steadily along the basin through scattered spruce. Switchback up an open hillside after 4.3 miles and break into the wide expanse of Hogan Park itself near 5.0 miles. An exposed but very scenic ski route, *not* marked by orange stakes, curves northwest here and follows a ridgetop course along Summits 10033 and 10024, allowing fine views of Walton Creek, Yampa Valley, and a vast sea of blue peaks beyond. Another alternate cross-country route forks right from the marked trail at a snowy "Y" after 5.3 miles and gains elevation earlier on the climb to Mt. Werner.

Contour around the steep Storm Creek bowl after 6.7 miles, then stay low near the basin of Storm Creek or high along the south-facing hillside and make the final strenuous climb to the Mt. Werner saddle, the 8.0 mile mark. *Avoid the possible avalanche sites on the south side of the Mt. Werner summit.* Follow these runs for the easiest course to the Steamboat Ski Area base (4.7 miles): Buddy's Run to the top of Four Points Lift via Four Points Cutoff, Rainbow to Rainbow Saddle, Park Lane to Central Park (or uphill to the Thunderhead Restaurant and gondola terminal), then Why Not Road and finally Right-O-Way.

The first plunge

61 WEST SUMMIT LOOP

Half-day trip
Classification: Easiest
Distance: 3.5 miles *round trip* **(5.6 KM.)**
Skiing time: 2 hours *round trip*
Elevation gain: 280 feet
Maximum elevation: 9,680 feet
Season: Mid-November through April
Topographic maps:
   U.S.G.S. Walton Peak, Colo. 1956
   U.S.G.S. Mount Werner, Colo. 1956
        7.5 minute series
Routt National Forest

The West Summit Loop contains many of the ingredients that make a ski tour so enjoyable. The tour route follows an easy cross-country course, spiced with short drops and gradual climbs, and near mid-loop reaches a definite destination point, an open ridgetop with a beautiful panoramic view of northwestern Colorado. Distant blue mountainsides, flat parks and valley bottoms, clusters of snow-capped summits all blend into the colors of sky and clouds and create a very restful vista. And for a dash of excitement, the loop route ends with a thrilling plunge down another drainage, excellent terrain both for long, easy switchbacks and for the advanced powder turns. With few rocks or trees to get in the way, the beginning skier can hold a slight downhill course in any direction and coast through the snowfields with long, sweeping arcs.

Drive on U.S. 40 to the Rabbit Ears Pass area and proceed to the large parking lot at the West Summit, 3.8 miles west of the Hogan Park Ski Trail parking area, 7.3 miles east from the bottom of the pass.

Begin near the sign reading "Trucks Use Low Gear" and ski north on a wide swath through the trees, intersecting the old U.S. 40 after about 50 yards. Continue north over the wide, snowy roadbed, double pole on an easy coast to the bottom of the road loop, then turn left into the trees and drop on a short, exciting schuss to the meadow ahead. Here the ski route angles away from the new U.S. 40, in view down the valley west, and proceeds northwest across the open snowfield, heading toward a conspicuous island of aspen on the far side. Climb gradually to the left of the aspen grove, at 0.5 mile. Bend left toward a shallow saddle and ski through more aspen and conifers for several hundred yard to an obvious ridge. The jeep road that is marked on the topo does not show clearly through this section but any northwesterly ski route will soon end at the ridgetop.

Turn right as the terrain drops toward the McKinnis Creek drainage west and the Harrison Creek drainage south. Climb gradually along the open ridge, bringing into view a beautiful panorama of mountains and valleys. First, the Dunkley Flat Tops, a distinctive range with blazing-white sides and deep, blue pockets, show above the treetops southwest. Then a vast horizon of mountains can be seen west as the ski route climbs gently toward the 9,618-foot ridgetop, at 1.0 mile. Sleeping Giant Mountain stretches across the Yampa Valley floor northwest, and on the same line of sight beyond, the Bears Ears Peaks jut into the skyline. Farther right, the snowy summit of Sand Mountain and the flat-topped range near Diamond Peak protrude above the horizon line. And to the north, Hahns Peak, an easily identifiable cone, marks the end of the stunning vista.

Glide north-northeast along the open ridgetop for several hundred yards and begin to ski back into the conifers at 1.3 miles. A thick wall of spruce soon screens the view of the mountain range above Walton Creek north as the ski route curves to the right along the edge of the bowl. After 1.5 miles the conifers once again cover the ridgetop and mark a good point to begin the return trip. Bear toward the small strip of U.S. 40, visible at the end of the snowy bowl southeast, and begin a mile-long, switchbacking descent through the open snowfields, a thrilling run that often takes only a few minutes. To close the loop, either turn right along a conspicuous basin and then cut southwest through the trees on an advanced drop. Or follow a longer but easier route to the highway and turn right to an intersection with the old roadbed (see map).

132

Parking lot skier

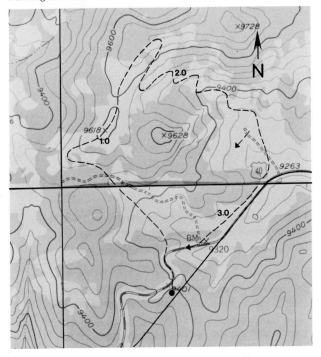

62 STONE QUARRY

Half-day trip
Classification: Easiest to more difficult
Distance: 2.1 miles one way (3.4 KM.)
Skiing time: 1½-2 hours one way
Elevation gain: 960 feet
Maximum elevation: 7,780 feet
Season: December through March
Topographic map:
U.S.G.S. Steamboat Springs, Colo. 1969
7.5 minute series
Routt National Forest

Quarry Mountain, more commonly referred to as Emerald Mountain by local citizens, has long been the site of skiing activities in Steamboat Springs. In the 'teens and 20s of this century the Stone Quarry Road was used many times as a ski route for the traditional community *langlauf*. Each Sunday all the ski enthusiasts, sometimes a crowd of over a hundred, would lace up their calf-length boots, slip their toes under the leather straps on their long, wooden skis, grab their one sturdy pole and shuffle away on a day-long cross-country trek. At the bottom of Quarry Mountain, Howelsen Hill, named in honor of Norwegian-born Carl Howelsen who inspired the early skiing in Steamboat Springs, developed into both an alpine ski area and a nordic jumping hill. Today the tour up the Stone Quarry Road is every bit as much fun as it was 50 years ago, though perhaps a little easier with the lighter skis and more secure pin bindings.

Drive on U.S. 40 to the northwest end of Steamboat Springs. Turn west onto 13th Street, passing the Bud Werner Memorial Library; cross the Yampa River and railroad tracks and curve back west. Turn south at the first intersection, turn east after one long block, and turn south again after one short block. Proceed to the loop at the end of the plowed road and park along the side at the widest point.

Begin skiing south on a fairly steep climb up the Stone Quarry Road, soon gaining sufficient elevation for an over-the-shoulder look at Sleeping Giant Mountain northwest. This colossal personage forever lies on his back, face in plain profile, hands folded over his chest, knees high in the air, and feet tucked up. Climb up a hillside of scattered scrub oak, then after 0.2 mile curve southeast and begin skiing on a more gradual grade. Bend slightly right, contour along the west side of Howelsen Hill, and soon fork south toward Quarry Mountain, leaving the lift maintenance road which circles to the top of the alpine ski hill. The tour route winds through more scrub oak on a steady climb south and, near 0.5 mile, crosses the cut of the old T-bar lift that once carried alpine skiers to the top of Quarry Mountain.

Follow the snow-packed road under a second power line, at which point the small, dun-colored scar of the quarry can be spotted on the hillside directly south. Curve left over the crest of the hill to a view east of the open Yampa Valley and the white runs of the Steamboat Ski Area. Soon turn southwest, bearing toward the top of Quarry Mountain; follow along the old lift line for a short distance, then angle south onto a steeper hillside. The wide roadcut bends southeast at 1.0 mile, maintains a steady climb into thicker scrub oak and aspen, and after about 200 yards turns south again. Prominent features of the Yampa Valley area become progressively more noticeable now: due north is the pointed, granite top of Rocky Peak, east-northeast is the white swath of the transmission line that heads toward Buffalo Pass, and a few more degrees east are the deep, rocky canyons of North Fork Fish Creek and Fish Creek.

Curve west in front of a knolltop, cross a small but obvious drainage, and continue the constant climb through another turn south. For the final 0.8 mile the tour route winds southeast, then southwest through four more switchbacks, eventually stopping where the road narrows considerably and signs read "No Trespassing." From this point the quarry site is only a short scramble east up a branch trail. A 20-foot wall of sandstone protrudes from the mountainside here and immense, snow-buried blocks of stone, discarded from the quarry, lie on the ravine floor 100 feet below. The view from this high lookout encompasses both the town and the ski area as well as a wide panorama of surrounding mountains. Sleeping Giant Mountain, hidden throughout the last half of the tour, reappears northwest, this time far below the horizon. Sand Mountain, often cast with a bluish hue, rises from the valley floor north-northwest. And cone-shaped Hahns Peak sticks out on the hazy horizon north.

Except for possible shortcuts through the scrub oak when the powder snow is deep, the return trip backtracks over the road, an exciting downhill run that often takes less than 15 minutes. The winding, rolling drop provides ideal conditions for double poling techniques and each sharp switchback requires a flurry of quick step turns.

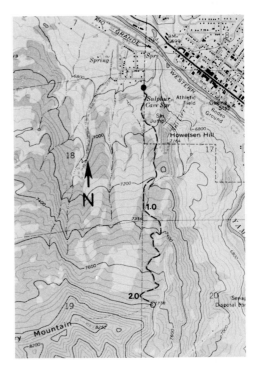

63 ELK PARK

One day trip
Classification: Most difficult
Distance: 3.8 miles one way (6.1 KM.)
Skiing time: 3-3½ hours one way
Elevation gain: 1,340 feet
Maximum elevation: 8,680 feet
Restricted season:
  January, February, and March only
Topographic map:
  U.S.G.S. Rocky Peak, Colo. 1962
          7.5 minute series
Routt National Forest

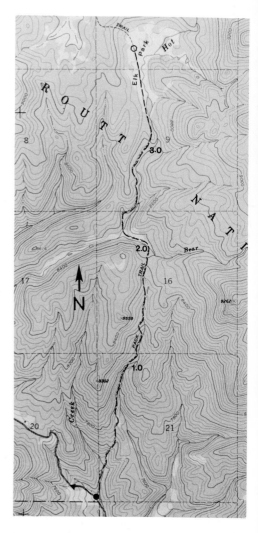

True to its name even today, Elk Park provides a feeding and migration ground for elk as these magnificent animals begin climbing to higher elevations with the spring thaw. Lean from the long winter's fast and soon to start the calving season, the elk can tolerate very little intrusion into their territory by man. For this reason the Forest Service limits the ski touring season in Elk Park to the months of January, February, and March. Please observe this regulation.

Hundreds of squirrel and rabbit prints often crisscross the broad snowfields in Elk Park in midwinter but seldom is there the trace of ski touring tracks. Used much less than the Hot Springs trail (No. 64), this tour route provides a very pleasant escape from the maddening crowd. Although much of the second half of the tour is easy gliding, steep hills near the start eliminate all but advanced skiers. On these climbs the deeply eroded, narrow trailcut makes the herringbone difficult so you will want to use the straight climb technique as much as possible. It helps to put a thick kicker of wax on the skis, a little stickier than usual.

Deep Powder Schuss

Drive on U.S. 40 into Steamboat Springs. Proceed through town on the jagged course to Strawberry Peak: northeast four blocks on 7th Street, east three blocks on Missouri Street, north three more blocks on North Park Drive. Turn east onto the Strawberry Park road, soon curve north and stay on the main road past Stevens/Perry-Mansfield Camp and Whiteman School. Continue to the end of the plowed road, a total of 3.9 miles from Steamboat Springs. Park in the small turn-around area, making sure access is provided to the driveway of the last house.

Below the end of the plowed turn-around, 10 yards above the driveway on the opposite side of the road, an inconspicuous Routt National Forest signpost marks the trailhead. Climb over the high ridge of plowed snow at this point, pass above an old, half-buried car, and begin skiing northeast on the snowy jeep trail toward Gunn Creek drainage. Soon bend left around the hillside and proceed on an easy climb above the creekbed, bearing north toward the rocky ridgetop on the skyline. Stark, crooked branches cast interesting shadows on the snow as aspen crowd close to the trail and then begin to recede toward the hilltop. Continue past a deep ravine which forks northeast and glide into an open snowfield. Here Gunn Creek rises to trail level and soon crosses into another narrow valley northwest.

Follow the jeep trail through a slight bend left and begin a short herringbone climb, bringing into view the flat bottom lands of Yampa Valley and Strawberry Park. Another steep climb increases the vantage to a new creek drainage north with rolling mountaintops on either side. Enter a small, "lone tree" park near the 0.5 mile mark and glide next to the creek on a delightful, aspen-lined course. Cross and re-cross the creekbed, climb steeply to the west side, and, with the midday sun behind, continue up the open, glistening white valley. Just before 2.0 miles re-enter the conifers and aspen, cross a level saddle, and drop into the cool shadows of a forested, north-facing slope. The trail descends gradually to a crossing over Bear Creek and curves northwest into a spacious meadow.

Stay left where a short trail spur forks up the Bear Creek drainage right and ski cross-country through the meadow, bearing toward boulder-strewn Rocky Peak northwest. Turn north across Hot Spring Creek and proceed on a corkscrew climb into the aspen. The jeep trail, now a conspicuous cut, climbs high above the creekbed, then follows a level course through shaded snowfields. Pass a shallow ravine which bends left and after one last climb, break into the south end of Elk Park. Glide north past a stand of dead timber which marks the edge of a snowy pond. Wind through several stumps, often covered with large, mushroom tops of snow and end the tour at the north end of the park. Delicate cream-colored aspen on the mountainside north contrast interestingly with the snow-laden evergreens to the west. The return trip doubles back over the ski tracks and takes only one-third the time as the trip in. And that's coming back as slowly as possible!

137

64 HOT SPRINGS

One day trip
Classification: More difficult
Distance: 2.2 miles one way (3.5 KM.)
Skiing time: 2-2½ hours one way
Accumulated elevation gain: 490 feet
Accumulated elevation loss: 410 feet
Maximum elevation: 7,850 feet
Season: December through early April
Topographic map:
　U.S.G.S. Rocky Peak, Colo. 1962
　　　　7.5 minute series
Routt National Forest

Like the Sulphur, Soda, Lithia, Iron and other mineral springs near the town of Steamboat Springs, the Hot Springs, farther north, have long been a source of fascination to tourists. Bubbling water, too hot (152°F.) to touch until diluted with icy creek water, flows from two main rock fissures, producing a collective output of 400 gallons per minute. The South Hot Spring, 80 feet up the hillside, branches into two rivulets and melts snow from a wide swath of black earth. The North Hot Spring, just above the creekbed, runs through a centuries-old rock channel. On cold, mid-winter days, steam vapor from the springs frosts the nearby pine and spruce, outlining each branch with a delicate filigree of icy crystal.

The Hot Springs are, without a doubt, the most popular ski tour destination in the Steamboat Springs area. On the trip in you may pass several returning tourers, their flushed faces and frozen locks of hair show that they have already spent an hour or two

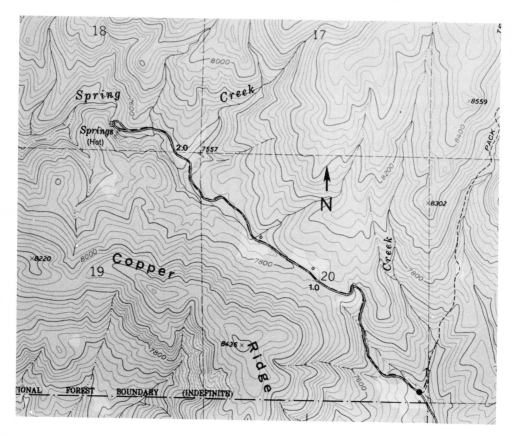

138

soaking in the hot pools. Take a swimming suit and also remember to take a towel for drying off after you get out of the pools.

Drive on U.S. 40 into Steamboat Springs. Proceed through town on the jagged course to Strawberry Park: northeast four blocks on 7th Street, east three blocks on Missouri Street, north three more blocks on North Park Drive. Turn east onto the Strawberry Park road, soon curve north and stay on the main road past Stevens/Perry-Mansfield Camp and Whiteman School. Continue to the end of the plowed road, a total of 3.9 miles from Steamboat Springs. Park in the small turn-around, making sure not to block the driveway.

Begin climbing northwest over the wide, snow-packed road. Angle west through black, briary scrub oak, then turn northwest again, soon gaining about 80 feet of elevation above a branch of Gunn Creek right. Chalky-white aspen, splotched with black gnarls, line the road as it bends gradually north and makes an inconspicuous crossing over the branch creek. Pass to the right of a small clearing and begin a steady spiral climb left. Dip through another small tributary, stay right on a slightly steeper branch where the road forks, and continue the curve left until coming to a lofty vista point. Beyond the forested east side of Copper Ridge, white snowfields in Strawberry Park stretch south toward the much larger expanse of Yampa Valley. Stark ski runs on Mt. Werner, crawling with miniscule alpine skiers, dominate the view south-southeast. And an eye-catching rocky point, interesting with its jumbled assortment of boulders, now pierces the skyline northeast.

Follow the snowy road west-northwest on a more gradual climb; after 50 yards crest over the top of the hillside and glide easily into an open basin. Double pole on a faster and faster drop, bend left and pass below an old cabin, recently renovated, near 1.0 mile. Coast slowly to a stop against a slight incline, then continue through several more small drops and climbs, passing a sign which identifies the rolling hilltops of Copper Ridge south and the three sharp points of Rocky Peak north. Glide past a second old cabin, curve right and begin another exciting downhill run. Control speed with a strong snowplow or pole drag and descend over the winding road to the bottom of the Hot

Spring Creek basin, a drop of more than one-half mile which takes little more than a minute.

Cross a snow-buried bridge and begin a gradual, then steeper climb, passing the Hot Springs sign near 2.0 miles. The road soon levels and plunges down another hillside, providing enough momentum for a long, weaving coast to the Hot Springs turn-around loop. The collecting pools for the Hot Springs themselves, steaming and slightly sulfurous, are a short scramble down the hillside. For the return trip, double back over the road and ski again through as many climbs as drops. From the viewpoint near 0.5 mile, you can shortcut the road loop by dropping southeast onto the steep, open hillside, then telemarking through the scrub oak and aspen—a fantastic run in deep powder snow! The final few hundred yards of the tour become progressively more packed, and surprisingly fast, so speed must be checked with a strong snowplow or pole drag . . . or maybe a "header."

65 HAHNS PEAK

One day trip
Classification: More difficult
Distance: 3.4 miles one way (5.5 KM.)
Skiing time: 2½-3 hours one way
Elevation gain: 1,200 feet
Maximum elevation: 9,380 feet
Season: Late November through early May
Topographic map:
   U.S.G.S. Hahns Peak, Colo. 1962
          7.5 minute series
Routt National Forest

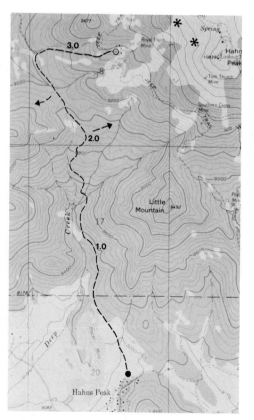

Of all the snow-capped summits in northern Colorado, Hahns Peak is the most easy to identify for it is a high, distinctive cone amid other mountains with rolling contours. A closer view of Hahns Peak, reached in winter by an enchanting ski trek north from the village of Hahns Peak along Deep Creek, reveals the high switchbacks that are carved into its west face, sometimes swept clean by avalanches, and the tiny fire lookout building, now unused, that straddles its 10,839-foot top.

Equally as absorbing as the view of Hahns Peak is the tragic saga behind its name. In late summer 1862 (some sources indicate 1865) Joseph Hahn and two other hardy prospectors crossed the Park Range and penetrated the Yampa Valley, traveling through the vast territory held by the Ute Indians. At a high, cone-shaped summit that would later be named after Hahn, the men found what they were looking for. They swirled gravel and water in their prospecting pans and watched tiny flecks of gold settle to the bottom. In May 1866 Hahn returned to the site of his discovery with 50 more hopeful miners, crossing the four to six-foot snowdrifts on dog sleds and leading pack animals which carried the necessary mining supplies. That summer the men laid out a town, built log cabins, erected rough-sawn sluice boxes, and performed the hard work of placer mining.

Hahn and one of his companions on the first trip, William A. Doyle, decided to spend the winter in their new home. Captain George Way, the other original companion, and others left on October 2 for badly-needed winter supplies. Although Way was expected to return by October 20, he did not return. Hahn and Doyle waited throughout the winter, living off the country, but finally in April with almost no other choice, they decided to snowshoe (ski) to Empire. Caught in a blinding snowstorm on the top of the Gore Range, the men, without any food except for some coffee, wrapped themselves in blankets and spent a long, miserable night of shivering. Hahn was too exhausted to move the next morning and was left in camp where he died. Doyle, snow-blind and "half-crazy" from the ordeal, was found by two ranchers.

Drive on U.S. 40 past the northwest end of Steamboat Springs and turn north onto the Elk River Road (Routt County 129).

Follow this main road through Clark, then stay left after another mile where the Seed House Road turns right and proceed to the village of Hahns Peak, 24.3 miles from U.S. 40. Turn right, continue toward a tour starting point at the north end of the village, and find out-of-the-way parking along the main street.

Begin skiing north from the last cabins in Hahns Peak village, bearing several degrees to the left of the snowy Hahns Peak summit. Follow the roadbed if visible, as marked on the map photo; cross through a willow-filled tributary of Deep Creek and continue past the snowdrifted ruts in the old placer mine several hundred yards farther left. Enter groves of chalky-white aspen and scattered conifers after 0.4 mile, follow the now-conspicuous roadcut on a gradual climb along the east side of Deep Creek, and curve through two prominent drainages miles 0.8 and 0.9. Continue the northerly course on a contour around the steep side of Little Mountain right, then dip through another deep branch drainage, bend left and begin a steeper climb.

Glides become longer near 1.9 miles as the roadbed climbs less steeply, then passes another unmarked road right at mile 2.1 and after several hundred yards reaches the top of a slight saddle. Pass another unmarked road which branches left near the Independence Creek crossing and double pole northnorthwest along the tree-lined road on a slight descent. Break out onto an open hillside after 2.7 miles where Hahns Peak, now suddenly closer and larger, looms into the sky directly east. Turn right where another roadbed drops left; stay on the right (south) side of a snowy branch of Independence Creek and begin another steady climb through scattered groves of aspen. End the tour at any of several good viewpoints of Hahns Peak along this roadbed; *do not continue into avalanche danger beneath the steep, barren west side of Hahns Peak.* Return over the ski tracks or down the snowy bottom of Deep Creek itself, a delightful, rolling run that takes only half the time as the trip in.

Hahns Peak

Editor
  Thomas K. Worcester

Cover Design
  Dean McMullen

Don't let the sport of ski touring go downhill!

You purchased this touring guide because you enjoy the sport of ski touring and want to do it safely. Perhaps the expense and rigidity of alpine skiing drove you away or you just love the solitude of the mountain winter environment. You should be aware that the growing popularity of ski touring has led some to insist that the sport needs to be more closely regulated.

Be a part of the solution

The 18,000 members of the Rocky Mountain Ski Association, a division of the U.S. Ski Association, don't want to see over-regulation destroy the appeal of ski touring. We ask you to join our efforts to resolve the problems caused by increasing numbers of ski tourers without inhibiting the independent spirit of our sport. We're working with the U.S. Forest Service and other concerned groups to make the future of ski touring as enjoyable as the present and the more members we have the more effective we will be.

Stay in touch with the issues

Joining the Rocky Mountain Ski Association will give you a voice in determining the future of ski touring. You will also receive Rocky Mountain SKIING, our monthly newspaper, and stay abreast of important touring issues.

Save on peace of mind

In addition you can purchase low-cost insurance coverage for only $14 in addition to your dues. You'll be covered for up to $5,000 in search and rescue expenses and receive $1,000 in emergency evacuation coverage. The policy also provides $100,000 personal liability insurance and $250 non-deductible ski theft coverage.

Our insurance programs can put money back in your pocket.
We can also save you a lot more than money.
Join today!

- -

RMSA Application

Name _____

Address _____

City _____ State _____ Zip _____

Male _____ Female _____

If this is a family membership, list the full names of all persons included.

_____

_____

Make check payable to:
Rocky Mountain Ski Association
1463 Larimer Square
Denver, Colorado 80202

Check type of membership desired

☐ RMSA Membership . . . . $ 7.00

☐ Family Membership . . . . $_____
   ($14 for first two members and
   $3 for each additional member)

☐ Insurance Package . . . . $ 14.00
   (in addition to dues)

Charge to Mastercharge

Acct. No. _____

Charge to BankAmericard

Acct. No. _____

Signature _____

Total remitted . . . . $_____